THE FISHERMAN'S DAUGHTER

The past held the key to their future...

When Robbie Fraser receives an anonymous note saying 'Your father has disappeared' he is shocked beyond belief. As far as he knows, he has no father. Robbie travels to a small Scottish fishing village to find the man he never knew, but he is met with hostility and the claustrophobic insularity of a small-town community. Only Heather McBain seems to want to befriend him, and from her he learns of the bitter rivalry between their fathers. As she and Robbie start asking questions, buried secrets come to light which could destroy them all.

THE FISHERMAN'S DAUGHTER

The Fisherman's Daughter

by

Molly Jackson

Magna Large Print Books
Long Preston, North Yorkshire,
BD23 4ND, England.

British Library Cataloguing in Publication Data.

Jackson, Molly
The fisherman's daughter.

A catalogue record of this book is
available from the British Library

ISBN   978-0-7505-3188-7

First published in Great Britain in 2009 by Arrow Books

Copyright © Molly Jackson 2007

Cover illustration © Jill Battaglia by arrangement with
Arcangel Images

Published in Large Print 2010 by arrangement with
Random House Group Limited

Magna Large Print is an imprint of Library Magna Books Ltd.

Printed and bound in Great Britain by
T.J. (International) Ltd., Cornwall, PL28 8RW

Prologue

The two divers made their way through the murky water. Their bodies were insulated from the harsh cold of the Scottish sea by their black dry suits and they swam slowly through the darkness, a ray of golden light from their head-mounted torches showing what lay a few feet ahead. The leader carried another torch in one hand, which he swung about from time to time as he searched.

The beam from the torch picked out a large white object in the green darkness, emerging from the sea bed. When he saw it, the diver stopped swimming and signalled to the other, beckoning him over to see what he had spotted.

It was a ship's container standing upright on the sea bottom, one corner sunk into the sand. Although it was a fairly small container, it was still about two metres wide, three metres long and almost as tall as an average man. The sides were of pale ridged metal, one with some painted lettering on it that read 'Field & Company'.

The divers swam towards it, their flippers waving gently through the water. They examined the container carefully, swimming round it a few times, shining their torches up and down it to see if there was anything they had missed. One of the divers unclipped a camera from his belt and started flashing pictures, while the other swam round to the front where the door was. He put out a hand and grasped the door handle and gave it a half-hearted jiggle. To his evident surprise, the handle moved. The container was not locked.

He swam back round to his friend and signalled to him to come with him. The camera would be needed if they were going to open the door. They both returned to the front and the first diver tried the handle again, while the other was ready with the camera. Although the handle moved beneath his grip, the door remained closed. Something had jammed.

They both tried for a few minutes but it did not seem as though the door would give, and they could not exert enough pressure on it underwater. The first diver unclipped a tool from his belt and used it to prise at the lock but after a few minutes he gave up, and signalled to his companion that they should go back. Later, they could return with a boat and a crane so that they could winch the container up. The other nodded. As they were about to go, he put his hand out one last time and tried the handle. This time, something clicked into place and the door swung open.

A muffled shout came from beneath the diver's mask as he jerked back, startled. Floating towards him was a rotting corpse, its eyes gone and its mouth wide open in the grey-green skin. Instinctively, he kicked backwards to prevent the corpse from bumping him. The other diver caught sight of what was inside the container, and recoiled, dropping the camera which fell slowly down onto the sea bed.

This was worse than they had expected.

Behind the first corpse was another and then another. A small army of the dead was floating out to meet them...

Part One

Chapter One

The door closed behind him with a gloomy slam, leaving him in the darkness. Robbie scrabbled for the light switch.

It wasn't pleasant standing there in the blackness, hearing nothing but the hum of the refrigerator coming from the kitchen and smelling the cold dankness all around him. It gave him the shivers. His skin crawled and a vague sense of panic crept into his belly. It wasn't that he was spooked at all – he was far too sensible to believe in all that nonsense; the dead were dead, and that was that – but there was something uncomfortable about being alone in a place that felt so empty.

His fingertips found the smooth plastic of the switch and he flicked it down. Light instantly flooded the hallway, illuminating the worn brown carpet, the paper-lantern light shade and the photographs in their gilt frames hanging on the wall. It was all so familiar he hardly noticed it usually but now his eyes were drawn to the pictures, their colours faded from the years of exposure to the daylight. One was a boy in his school uniform, his little grey tie pulled into a small tight knot at the neck, his two front teeth missing from the wide grin beneath freckles, blue eyes and a pudding-bowl fringe of light brown hair. Another was a graduation portrait: the same blue eyes, the hair brushed upwards in the fashion of fifteen years before and gummed into place with something sticky, the freckles faded a little. The face was still more youthful than adult, with the boyish gawkiness not quite gone despite the suit, black robes and mortar board.

On the opposite wall was a large photograph, almost the size of a poster, hung in pride of place. It was a wedding picture, a formal pose of the happy couple. The bride smiled radiantly beneath her sparkling headdress and foamy veil, her slim figure shown off by the strapless satin dress. The groom, proud and self-possessed in his dark suit with a white rose in the buttonhole, beamed out as if he could not believe his luck.

There isn't a photograph for now, thought Robbie, as he looked at it. They ought to complete the set with one showing him divorced, perhaps with Sinead strutting off in the distance, her nose in the air and her mouth in that nasty, sulky pout she so often had these days. For added artistic interpretation, she could be carrying all his money.

Sinead hadn't even come to his mother's funeral, though the two women had always had a civil relationship. It might not have been love, exactly, but it was affectionate, at least, that was what Robbie had thought. Perhaps he'd been wrong.

The timing had been rotten. Sinead might have turned out to be a mean bitch, but if they'd still been together, she could have helped him through it. As it was, he'd done it all alone: the final illness, death, burial. And the grief. Without any shoulder to cry on, he hadn't got round to crying at all. He felt sad, certainly, and he missed his mother, but

16

something in him hadn't let go yet and mourned her. Perhaps it never would. And it might even be easier that way.

Robbie went through to the kitchen, turning on lights as he went. He hated the dark – he always had. When he'd lived here as a boy with his mother, he'd always shouted at her to remember to leave the door open and the hall light on when she put him to bed. One Christmas she'd given him a special bedside light to have on while he went to sleep. A coloured shade revolved around the bulb so that he could see bright red rockets sailing up through blue space, over the stars towards the moon as it went round. In the morning, it was always off, though he never switched it off himself. His mother must have come in while he lay sleeping.

He opened the fridge and wondered what to have for dinner. Now that he'd been living in the flat for a few days, the fridge had stopped being the bountiful place it had been when his mother was alive. Then, he could always count on something tempting waiting for him. Now it was more like the fridge back home, containing little else but alcohol, a pint of milk and some unappetising leftovers that he felt duty bound to keep for several days before he threw them out. He took out a can of beer and opened it. Perhaps he'd order something to be delivered – curry or a pizza, something from one of those slippery little leaflets that came through the letter box in their dozens. He was exhausted and didn't much feel like cooking. Besides, he was no cook and could only muster something basic, like beans on toast, or something weird that he invented as he went along. A mixture of all the bits and pieces he could find, fried up together in a sauce of ketchup and Lea & Perrins, and served over rice – that was the kind of thing. His messes, Sinead used to call them. They used to laugh about them in the early days – she found them sweet rather than anything else. Later on, she screamed at him and asked why he let himself be so helpless, why he couldn't learn to make anything decent. Did he expect to be waited on all his life? Did he expect *her* to do it? Well, he could piss off ... and she'd stride off, slamming doors behind her.

He could almost hear it now, in the emptiness of his mother's flat. He shook his head slightly. He'd watch television. Bring some light and life into this sorry place.

Taking his beer, he went back towards the sitting room. As he went into the hall, he saw the pile of post by the door that he'd kicked to one side as he'd come in. It would be the usual useless flood of junk mail, no doubt. How long did it take these people to get the names of the dead off their lists? His mother had been buried a fortnight but still she was being invited to take out credit cards and loans, to update her house with a conserva-tory or new blinds or a stair lift, and being urged to donate here or there, or sponsor this or that. He didn't know whom he should contact to tell them all that there was no point – his mother wouldn't be accepting their kind offer of a platinum card with a fifty-thousand-pound limit, or give just £2 a month to ensure world peace. And come to think of it, she wouldn't have while she was alive, either. She just wasn't that sort. She was too afraid of losing everything she had to get into debt. A roof over their head and food in their mouths was all they needed, she told Robbie. All the rest was so much trickery. They didn't need it and what was more, they were poor and they couldn't afford it. It was a message he'd grown up with all his life.

Perhaps that was why he liked to surround himself with things now. There'd never been anything much when he was a boy: one present on his birthday and one at Christmas, that was all – along with some little things like coloured pencils and sweets in his stocking – and it didn't matter how much he begged for something in particular, he got what he got, and that was that. He'd longed for a BMX bike like his friends had, so he could go to the park like them and ride about, doing wheelies and trick jumps. He got a bike but it wasn't right at all; it was a secondhand, old-fashioned thing with big wheels, thin grey tyres and small leather saddle. He'd hated it.

When he'd left school, he'd chosen to study computer science at university, not because he felt any particular affinity for computers, although he liked using them and had saved up from his weekend job to get himself a good one that he could play decent games on, but because he knew that he'd be able to get a well-paid job, and guarantee himself a life away from that all-encompassing, restricting poverty that he'd known as a boy. As a grown-up, he didn't want to be denied, or have to count his pennies like his mother had. He wanted a quality car, good furniture, decent holidays, a top-of-the-range television and plenty of clothes.

'You know how to look after yourself, don't you?' his mother would say, when she came round to his flat and saw the stacks of silver, black and chrome hi-tech equipment.

He would shrug. He worked hard enough for it. He deserved a little something back, with all the hours he put into his job designing Internet software for companies trading over the Web. If twelve-hour days spent staring at a screen under fluorescent lighting didn't entitle him to the odd spending spree, what did? It was something both he and Sinead enjoyed, part of what brought them together, in fact. They loved shopping at the weekends, taking the car out to one of those huge complexes and coming back loaded up with boxes and bags: new gadgets for the kitchen – Sinead adored her limited-edition silver food mixer and set of lavender-coloured French cast-iron cookware – new knick-knacks for the sitting room – how many tealight holders did they buy in the course of their married life, for God's sake? – and of course clothes. Racks and racks of them. Leather jackets, designer jeans, handmade shoes ... even his pants had the name of some gay Italian dressmaker in them. Sinead needed a whole separate room for her lot. The spare room had become like a charity shop, with its piles of high heels separated from their twins, mountains of jumpers and cardigans, rails of skirts and trousers, and more bags bursting with things she really, really needed and definitely had to have...

It was all anathema to his mother. She couldn't

understand it. She would look at everything he owned with something like bewilderment in her face because it just made no sense to her. How many clothes did one person need? She didn't understand what fashion meant, how something that you'd craved desperately one year could mean nothing to you the next year because it was the wrong colour, or length, or fabric or style and was too embarrassing to be seen in and good for nothing but throwing out. She didn't understand that times had changed. Shopping was what people did now. It was relaxation. It was leisure. It was fun.

Robbie switched on the television and sat down on the sofa, an old worn green velvet thing that he'd used to sit on to watch his programmes after school. It smelt the same: dry, musty and in need of a spell in the fresh air. He pointed the remote control at the television and flicked through the channels, still surprised to find himself back at one after only five changes. His mother had never bothered with satellite or even getting the free digital channels. He settled on the news, and took a swig from his can of beer.

I should go home, he thought to himself. What am I still doing here? I'll get this place cleaned up at the weekend and see an agent about selling it, putting it on the market. I need to get on with my life.

But the truth was, he didn't really know what he wanted to get back to. The flat he lived in now was just rented; the one he and Sinead had shared had been sold after the divorce and he'd never got round to buying a new place. He missed the old one and wished now that he'd tried to buy Sinead out, but at the time it had felt so drenched in sadness that he'd not wanted to stay, no matter how much he'd loved their brand-new glossy white kitchen, the mosaic-tiled bathroom and the minimalist sitting room with black lacquered floor and pale modern furnishings.

He looked around at his mother's drab sitting room with its heavy dark furniture, floral patterns and thick damask curtains. Maybe he should just stay here. Get in a decorator to strip it back and tart it up again. There might be good floorboards under the carpet.

He shook his head. No. This place, like his old flat, was too bursting with memories. It would be wrong to stay here. It would remind him too much of the misery in his life and in his mother's. Besides, he hated the neighbourhood, with its high-rise flat blocks and mouldering old streets. The rubbish and the mess everywhere depressed him, and the sight of the cars vandalised and robbed overnight, the feral children flying about in gangs on their bikes, the vomit, condoms and syringes in the gutter made him feel simultaneously angry and powerless. It hadn't been this bad when he was growing up, he knew that. It hadn't exactly been posh, but it had been safer and more welcoming than it was now. There'd been at least a sense of order, of kids doing what they were told, of mums cooking dinner and dads washing cars – the way it was all supposed to be. How his mother had stood it, he didn't know. She must have hated it towards the end. He'd never really thought about it till now, when he came back in the dark feeling uneasy about walking down the street on his own. No wonder she hardly ever went out.

Robbie had always assumed that she was too poor to move, or too worried that she wouldn't find somewhere decent for the same price. That was why it had come as such a shock when he'd gone to the solicitor's office for the reading of the will. He had gone there in all honesty expecting to be told how much was owing. His mother had lived carefully and she'd also worked hard most of her life, teaching music at the local primary school, but he'd known that it was difficult for her to manage on one small salary, with all the bills to pay and him to bring up.

The last thing he was expecting to hear was that his mother was quite nicely off, thank you very much.

'Your mother owned her flat outright, Mr Fraser. I'm sure you knew that.' Mr Ogilvy, the solicitor, had that smooth, unctuous voice you'd expect of a lawyer.

Robbie had blinked in surprise. He hadn't known that. He'd never asked his mother the finer details of her financial position. Occasionally he would say, 'Are you all right, Mum? You would ask me if you needed anything, wouldn't you?' and she'd reply, 'Don't worry yourself about me, Robbie, I'm fine,' and they never said anything more than that. She'd accept the presents he gave her at Christmas, but grudgingly – 'You mustn't spend so much! I don't need it all, I really don't. And what would I be doing with cashmere when a good lambswool is just as warm?' – and that was that.

'She owns it?' he'd asked. 'No mortgage?'

'No. The records show that there was a mortgage originally. But it was paid off some years ago in a lump sum and since then, your mother has owned it. It has increased in value significantly since your mother bought it, I'm sure you'll be pleased about that. Unfortunately, owing to the area, it won't be worth quite as much as it might have been...'

'You mean, since the place has become a drug-infested shithole,' Robbie said. 'Well, I can understand that.'

Mr Ogilvy coughed politely. 'That's one way to put it, I suppose. But you could look at a decent rental income if you didn't want to sell. There are lots of students round there. And you never know when somewhere is going to smarten up and get fashionable. It could be a good investment, if you don't mind being a landlord.'

'I'll bet that it's going to take decades to smarten up round my mother's way. No. I suppose I'll sell. I wasn't expecting anything anyway.'

'There is more. Your mother's will is very straightforward and she's left her entire estate to you. There are no other close relatives, I believe...?'

'None.' Robbie shook his head. 'None that I know of, anyway. My grandparents – her mum and dad – died years back. Perhaps that's how she paid off the bank. They might have left her a bit, though God knows they had little enough as well.'

'And your mother's estate shows the lump sum of fifteen thousand, four hundred and eighty

24

pounds.' Mr Ogilvy pushed a bank statement over the desk towards him.

'Owing?' said Robbie warily. This was what he'd been expecting. Well, the sale of the house should be able to pay that off. That was a relief anyway.

'Oh no,' replied the lawyer, raising his eyebrows. 'In credit. I hope that doesn't make things difficult with you inheritance tax-wise. Lots of my clients are falling into that trap now. What with the cash and the value of the house and the goods...'

'I should think my mother's goods are worth tuppence ha'penny,' said Robbie shortly. 'And I'd be surprised if the house got much more than that. I don't think the tax man is going to be raising a glass to my mum.'

Ogilvy smiled politely. 'Well, that's good. Now, I've got some paperwork here for you to sign...'

Robbie had left the solicitor's office surprised and puzzled. Where had his mother got so much money from? He'd known she was careful, but to have paid off her mortgage and amassed savings – and that was besides some bonds she owned and the pension owing to her from her job. Was she just mean, was that it? Was that why she'd made him suffer all the way through his childhood, denying him things that everyone else had, saying that they could never go away on holiday even though he longed for the seaside and the piers and the donkey rides that his schoolmates told him about? For an instant, he was filled with anger towards her – then he remembered her lying in the hospital bed, wasted and tiny on the white pillows, looking twenty years older than she was, racked with physical pain and the knowledge that she was going to die and leave him, and he could only feel pity for her and something grief-stricken deep inside him, though he didn't know quite what. She'd suffered enough in her life. If she'd had a few quid that she kept for security, so what? She deserved a little comfort, God only knew.

Still, it was strange that she'd never told him.

The news came to an end in a flurry of pounding drums and triumphant music, and then there was a woman on the screen, waving her hand over a grey-green map behind her, explaining the weather.

'And towards the north of England and southern Scotland, there'll be strong winds and rain coming in from the east coast and heading inland...'

He flicked his gaze up at it for a moment, and then back to the pile of letters in his hand. He began to sort them into two piles, one for the rubbish bin and one to be opened. The rubbish pile began to mount up.

Then suddenly he stopped, staring down at the white hand-addressed envelope in his hand. He frowned, lifted it closer to his face and read it again, as though he couldn't quite believe it. It was addressed to him, in neat black capital letters.

Who would write to me? he wondered. Who knows I'm here?

No one knew. He hadn't even told his neighbour where he was going to be – just asked her to keep an eye on the place and he'd be back in a week or so. Yet here was a letter addressed, as plainly as could be, to him. *Mr Robert Fraser*, it read. And underneath was his mother's address.

Open it, he told himself. Find out. Why did he feel so nervous?

He slid a finger under the gummed-down flap and ripped it open. Inside was a single piece of white paper, folded over. He took it out and opened it, surprised to sense a tremor in his fingers. The note was written in more of the same neat black capitals, with no date or address. It simply said:

ROBBIE FRASER
YOUR FATHER IS IN TROUBLE.
HE HAS DISAPPEARED AND MAY
BE IN DANGER. YOU'D BETTER
GET HERE RIGHT AWAY
COME TO KINLOCHVEGAN
AS SOON AS YOU CAN.
A FRIEND.

Robbie felt his heart begin pounding and his breath quicken. He read it again and then again. He let it drop to his lap as he stared unseeing into the distance. He sat there a very long time before he moved.

Chapter Two

The grey road to Glasgow disappeared under the car tyres mile by mile. He had set off early in the morning when it was still dark and had seen the sun rise pinkish and bright on his right-hand side as he drove onwards. The overhead lights had faded and flicked off as daylight revealed the unchanging road.

It was reckless to come like this, on the basis of the note he had received, he knew that. It was madness. But how could he ignore it?

Your father. How often had he heard those words? 'Father', 'Dad', 'Daddy' – those were words his friends used, tossing them about carelessly with no sense of how lucky they were to be able to use them. Robbie had longed to be able to say 'my dad' but he couldn't. Instead, he was always having to admit that there was a void in his life. 'Where's your father, Robbie?' or 'What does your dad say?' or 'Now tell us what your father does for his job, Robbie,' – well-meaning people or uninformed teachers would ask him the same questions and he'd be forced to mumble the truth: 'I don't have a dad.'

He wasn't the only one. There were other kids whose dads didn't live with them, and one whose dad was dead. But there weren't that many like him, who knew nothing about their fathers and never saw them.

He'd stopped asking his mother about it very early on, scared by the mixture of pain and anger he saw on her face whenever he mentioned his father. He was frightened of making her upset or furious with him. He was frightened that if she got cross enough, she might get up and leave him as well, and that thought was too appalling to entertain. She was all he had, there were just the two of them together, to look after each other.

'We don't need your dad,' she would say briefly, and change the subject, ask him where his sports kit was or why he hadn't put out his shoes for cleaning like she had told him.

But then there was the time when he was eight years old and had been allowed to go to a friend's birthday party. The friend's dad had taken five of them to the local swimming baths, then to a burger restaurant and then to play football in the park before they all went home. It had been magical and Robbie had felt alive in a way he hadn't known before.

At first he'd circled carefully round the father like a wary animal – what kind of creatures were these dads? Were they friendly? Did they mean any harm? In the swimming baths, the dad had seemed like an alien life form, with his broad shoulders, huge arms and hands and hairy chest. He'd plunged into the water and risen up laughing and dripping, before chasing the boys round the pool, pretending to be some kind of sea monster. At one point, he'd grabbed Robbie and tossed him up lightly into the air with a playful growl before setting him back in the water to swim away. Robbie had laughed and laughed, and

29

later the dad had spent twenty minutes just with him, teaching him how to dive off the side. He was enraptured and found it hard to tear himself away from the man for long. At the burger restaurant he quietly made sure he was sitting on one side of him, with his little tray of burger, chips and fizzy drink in front of him, happy to be close to him. At football, he ran as fast as he could to keep up with the dad's long strides, until his chest was burning with the effort and he hardly had the strength to kick the ball when it did come his way.

'Come on, Robbie, that's it, my man! Well done!' roared the dad when he saw Robbie tearing up the field after him. He sent the ball towards him and when Robbie saw it coming, he put all his might into it, kicked out and sent it sailing back. 'That's it! You'll be playing for your school soon, I expect.'

Robbie had been light-headed with pride. When his mother came to collect him, he felt a crushing sense of disappointment. He didn't want to go. He wanted to stay here with this dad, who was everything he dreamed a father would be and who made him feel safe in a way he hadn't known before. He was silent all the way home.

That evening as they sat watching television together, he said to his mother, 'Mum, where's my dad?'

His mother looked at him and opened her mouth to reply but said nothing. Instead she gazed at him as if seeing him for the first time in a long while. Her silence began to frighten him, but the experience of being with his friend's dad that day gave him strength. He wanted an answer

– why couldn't he have what that other boy had, what lots of other boys had? Where was his dad?

His mother stared at him, then at last she said softly, 'You want to know about your dad, Robbie?'

He nodded, everything in him straining for her answer. Would she tell him that he lived just up the road, perhaps? Would she say that his dad had been wanting to see him? His stomach tightened with excitement. At last he would get the answer to the mystery that had tormented him for as long as he could remember.

'You don't remember him, do you?'

Robbie shook his head slowly. He didn't remember a man he could call his father, though he had some strange, fuzzy recollections that were more like sensations than memories. He recalled a smell that was warm and comforting. He recalled roughness – the waxy, hairy roughness of thick, weatherproof wool and the tickling, sandpapery surface of stubble. He could remember a sound, a rumble from deep in a chest, like thunder. He had the merest flicker of a vision that sometimes passed through his mind, so hard to make out that it was more like a presence than a picture. Those were the only things he could associate with his father – that and a curious high, mewing noise. That was all. But mostly when he thought of his father, he got only blankness.

His mother pulled him tightly into her, wrapping one arm around him, and said gently, 'He's gone away, Robbie. He went away a long time ago because he didn't want to be with us. You may as well not hanker after him because there's no way

31

on earth he can come back to you. I'm sorry, darling. I know you want a dad so badly and I wish I could give you one. But I can't. It's just the two of us. You understand that, don't you?'

Robbie felt like someone had placed a concrete block in his stomach and a lump of something burning in his throat. Was his dad dead, then? Was it like when the goldfish died and his mother had told him that it had gone away on holiday? He blinked hard. There wouldn't be any dad for him, no one like that big man today who had laughed and played and made him feel so safe.

'You love me, don't you, Robbie?' said his mother, kissing the top of his hair. 'You're happy, aren't you? We're all right as we are, aren't we?'

He nodded slowly. 'Why did he go?' he said in a high, tight voice.

His mother hugged him again. 'Don't think about it, Robbie. It makes no difference how or when. It's you and me together. That's enough for you, isn't it, love? That we have each other?'

He nodded again, fighting as hard as he could against the hot wall of water in his eyes that threatened to spill out and over his face. He didn't want his mother to see his grief. He didn't want her to think that she wasn't enough for him – in case she went away as well.

Robbie thought about all this in the dark hours after he got that letter. All those years, he'd thought and dreamed about his father. For years, he'd pretended that his father was a secret agent or a soldier sent away on a special mission and that he would come just as soon as he was allowed to. Robbie imagined him away on a big adventure, saving up the stories of everything that happened to him to tell when he got back. As he got older, he cast away this childish fantasy. His dad had abandoned him, like so many other feckless bastards. There was nothing special about his situation: his father was just a shithead who couldn't be bothered with a wife and son and pissed off to enjoy himself elsewhere.

So why should he care if his father was in trouble now?

He paced about the empty house with the slip of paper gripped in his hand, thinking. He realised that for ages now, he'd assumed his father was dead. There was no hint anywhere that there might be a father living. He'd been through all his mother's papers and there was nothing, anywhere, about his father. Not a shred. Not a marriage certificate, not a divorce certificate, not a single letter. Nothing. All he knew of his father was his name – Hamish. And that was only because he'd overheard his grandmother say once, 'Doesn't the boy look like Hamish?' and had guessed that must be his father.

Why should he believe this scrap of paper? Perhaps it was just some cruel joke. And even if it were true, what could he do about it? And why should he? He had to think of his mother, who'd loved him and brought him up all those years. She wouldn't have wanted him to go after his father, he felt that instinctively.

But he knew almost at once that he wanted to believe in it. He needed to believe that there was a father there somewhere, and that there was still a chance to find him and ask him all the things he'd longed to know all his life. And yet this note said that, even after all this, his father might be in danger, whatever that meant. Was he sick? Dying? The letter was offering a ray of hope and then snuffing it out almost at once, taking his father away for a second time.

And where the bloody hell was Kinlochvegan?

He'd found it in an old road map, though it had taken some time to locate. He'd followed the road up to the western coast with his fingertip until it reached the very edge of Scotland, a way above the Isle of Skye, and there in the tiniest print was the name of a village that looked no more than a handful of houses. Kinlochvegan. On the edge of nowhere, looking out to sea.

He frowned. How was he supposed to get there? What was he supposed to do? Take the word of someone who couldn't even be bothered to supply their own name, or any kind of contact details, and make his way to the back of beyond? That was before he even began to think about the practicalities of the situation, like his job and the flat and all the little things of life that bind us to one particular place.

Robbie poured himself a whisky and sat on the old green sofa, staring at the map. It seemed impossible. But then – he was free, wasn't he? He didn't have a wife, or a permanent home. His flat could sit gathering dust for months before anyone so much as wondered where he'd gone. Now his mother was dead, he had no family to explain anything to. He had nothing to lose. He'd never been so unencumbered. If there was ever a time when he could get up and go, just follow his heart and do whatever he wanted, then that time was now. There was his job, but he was owed time off and even if they sacked him, he had enough financial security to see him through a few months at least, especially now that he owned his mother's flat and had half the value of his old one sitting in the bank.

I'll bloody well go, he thought, and something like triumph flowed through him. No one can just chuck this at me and expect me to do nothing about it. I'm bloody going.

Packing took hardly any time. Most of his clothes were at his other place.

Whatever I don't have, I'll buy, he thought. What's the weather in Scotland like at this time of year? Cold, I expect. It's always cold there, isn't it?

Robbie knew nothing about Scotland and had never been there. He and Sinead had preferred to take their holidays somewhere warm and a bit exotic: the Maldives or Seychelles or Fiji. A holiday wasn't a holiday unless you boarded a plane and came back with a tan, in Sinead's book, and it was all about doing as little as possible. Scotland sounded like there would be long walks and grey skies. It wasn't somewhere you associated with bikinis and Long Island iced teas by the pool.

'Robbie Fraser's a Scottish name, isn't it?' one of his workmates asked him once.

'Is it?' Robbie replied blankly. 'I don't know. We're English, I think.' His mother was, anyway.

His grandparents lived in Wiltshire.

'Oh, yes,' said his work colleague. 'You must be Scottish somewhere along the line, with a name like Fraser. I'm a Lindsay. Yellow and black tartan. You should look yours up.'

'Right,' said Robbie, and thought no more about it.

Now he thought about it for the first time. He was heading to Scotland to find his father, so he must have been Scottish, or at least partly all the time. Another question he'd never asked his mother and now never could.

Fraser. Scotland. Kinlochvegan. His father. It felt as though a part of his brain had been closed off his entire life. Why had he accepted his mother's silence? Why hadn't he insisted on answers?

He'd shut up the flat around dawn and marched down to the car, parked in the nasty little road behind the apartment block where hoodies hung around offering drugs. He tossed his canvas holdall in the back, tucked his laptop under the front seat and set off. The roads out of London were clear for the first half an hour, but by the time he reached the outskirts there was already a steady flow of buses and cars beginning the daily round of getting a vast population of workers into the city. It was liberating to be heading in the opposite direction, out of the metropolis and away towards something entirely different. With every mile, he felt as if a burden had been taken off his shoulders. He was lighter, somehow.

I've been feeling trapped, maybe, he thought to himself. Was that it? Had he been too long in one place? There hadn't seemed to be any alternative. And once Sinead had left and then he'd sold the flat, he'd felt simultaneously imprisoned and completely unanchored. He'd been going on in that odd limbo for ages now. Then his mother had died.

He stopped at a motorway service station not long after nine thirty and had some breakfast. Then he walked about the edge of the car park and phoned his boss. He explained that there was a family emergency and he needed to take some time off. He said that he'd take it as holiday, not as compassionate leave or anything, bearing in mind he'd just had two weeks off for his mother's last illness and then her funeral.

His boss didn't sound pleased and Robbie could hear the cynicism in his voice. Another family tragedy so quickly? What was Robbie up to? But for once, he, Robbie, had the power – suddenly and amazingly, he didn't care if his boss said, 'You're fired.' In fact, he almost wished he would. The sense of being freed was becoming so strong that he had begun to start dreaming of a completely clean break. Maybe of never coming back.

Come on, you're being ridiculous, he told himself as he got back into the car. You'll wake up to-morrow being bloody glad you've still got a home and job to go to, when all this nonsense is sorted out. It's some kind of practical joke, I expect.

All the same, he veered into the fast lane as soon as he could and sped smoothly northwards as though something irresistible were calling him there.

Chapter Three

It was motorways all the way to Glasgow and then, once he'd negotiated the ring road round the city, everything abruptly changed. All at once he was driving through what he could only describe as scenery: huge hills with craggy tops stretched away on one side, and then stretches of dark green forest beneath a powder-blue sky. It was startling and he blinked once or twice as he drove, finding it hard to reconcile the drab, concrete cityscape he was used to with this imposing natural beauty. The light was clear and lucid, and the trees that edged the road were turning a russet colour as they took on their autumn hues. Then, just as he was becoming accustomed to the view, and the road curving through the landscape, a beautiful loch appeared on his right, glassy and calm. The signs said it was Loch Lomond. Well, he'd heard of that one. So this was a famous loch. He looked out over it as he drove, admiring the transparent grey-blue water.

Robbie stopped the car at a small hotel on the edge of the loch, and had lunch while he gazed out at the view. The water looked so tranquil as it curved away between outcrops of land. Brightly coloured boats were moored down at the jetties, bobbing softly in the afternoon breeze. He thought of the way this vast inland lake had been formed thousands of years ago by the movement of glaciers cutting their way through mountains. The water was melted glacier, probably, a remnant of the Ice Age. Without knowing why, Robbie found it fascinating and almost moving. He never usually bothered to think about land formation or the age of the ground he trod on, but here it was inescapable: the place seemed to echo with the great rumblings and shakings that had occurred millions of years ago to push up these craggy ridges of hill and mountain, and the long slow erosions, the grinding of rock and ice, that had formed the dips and bowls that were now lakes and valleys. He was filled with a strange excitement to be in this place. It was so different to what he knew.

He stretched his legs, walking down to the water's edge and then gazing northwards up to the far end of the loch. He breathed in the clean fresh air and thought again of the note. He pulled the scrunch of paper out of his pocket and reread it. YOUR FATHER IS IN TROUBLE. What could that mean? Money trouble, probably.

He snorted to himself. Yes, that was probably it. His father had somehow heard that his ex-wife was dead and had assumed she'd left something to their son. This note was probably written by him, pretending to be a concerned 'friend', to prick Robbie's conscience and make him come and find him. Then, no doubt, the emotional blackmail would be applied and his father would be hoping to get a nice little legacy.

Well, he could think again. Robbie would take great pleasure in telling him exactly what he thought of him, before explaining that he could take a running jump.

He loitered by the water, trying to imagine what it would be like to meet his father. He practised a few choice sentences, relishing the feeling of drama that surged through him.

I'm doing this for Mum, he thought. I'm going to enjoy telling the bastard exactly what I think of him, and what he did to her and to me.

Then he hurried back to the car, suddenly impelled to be on his way. He was filled now with a sense of urgency and the idea that at the end of his journey something important was waiting for him.

As he drove up through Scotland, the day began to darken. It was late afternoon and he'd been driving since before first light. He'd hoped to reach the west coast by teatime, but the roads were narrow and twisting and he couldn't speed along at the kind of rate he had on the smooth, flat motorway. The light dimmed and lost its clarity and dark masses of grey cloud began to build up in the distance. He tried to increase his speed but somehow the road carried on disappearing at the same rate, as mile after mile went under his wheels. He was startled and a little frightened by the majesty of Glencoe as he passed through the bleak landscape: jagged granite hills covered in a fuzz of brown grass and bracken that couldn't soften the sharp, inhospitable edges.

Robbie vaguely remembered that there had been a massacre here centuries ago. It looked a suitable kind of place, he thought. Harsh and untameable, where human life doesn't seem to count for much.

He passed the turn-off to the Isle of Skye bridge as the light was fading and the wind was building up. He could feel the car buffeted as he drove, and then a light pattering announced the rain was starting. The remaining daylight vanished immediately and he switched on his headlights as the patter grew to a pounding. His spirits seemed to mirror the weather: the excitement and pitch of urgency that he had felt as he looked out over the blue-grey water of Loch Lomond melted away, and instead he was filled with nervousness and apprehension.

'What the hell am I doing here?' he asked himself aloud, as he peered out in the darkness, trying to make out the road through the torrential downpour. 'Where the bloody hell am I?'

The whole thing seemed like a ridiculous wild goose chase. He felt as though he'd fallen for an April Fool, or been the victim of some silly practical joke.

'My dad?' he asked himself. 'I'm looking for my dad? I must be mad. He's been dead for years. I'm a bloody fool and this is the stupidest thing I've ever done.'

What should I do? he wondered. Turn back? He could hardly drive home now – he'd been on the road for over twelve hours. No. He'd find somewhere to stay. Surely he'd pass a pub or a hotel or something where he could find a bed for the night, and go back in the morning. He'd chalk it all down to experience.

Then a sign appeared at the side of the road. His headlights picked it out of the darkness only for a second, but it was long enough for him to catch a glimpse of the word 'Kinlochvegan'. He wasn't able to make out how far it was, but he was within striking distance now.

A remnant of that morning's excitement curled in his stomach.

That's it, then, he thought. I'm nearly there. It's out of my hands.

Chapter Four

The rain eased off a few minutes later but the night was still pitch black. Robbie dropped his speed, worried that he might miss a road sign if he wasn't careful. Soon the car seemed to be crawling through the darkness, which was so intense it was almost solid. They obviously hadn't heard of streetlights up here.

A sign flashed out of the darkness as his lights picked it up. Kinlochvegan was the next turning off to the left. He drove even more slowly in case he missed it, but soon he made out the turning and followed it. The road became even narrower and more winding and he soon gave up all hope of retaining a sense of direction. The sign had said that Kinlochvegan was only eight miles away but before long he felt as though he'd travelled at least twice that, pressing forward into the black night with no sense at all of where he was heading.

Then he caught the first glimpse of yellow light,

and, as the road curled round and downwards, he saw dozens of little bright squares. The lighted windows of a village. This was it, then. He'd arrived. Relief washed through him. It was a comfort just to see signs of life and human habitation – he'd begun to feel utterly alone and completely isolated. Now there was the real prospect of an evening meal, a warm room and a soft bed where he could rest and start to get a grip on what he'd done. He could find somewhere to fill up the car – the petrol gauge was worryingly near empty again, even though he'd filled up twice on the way – maybe have a drink somewhere.

The road took him along what was clearly the main village street. He saw only blackness off to his left, so assumed that the sea lay that way, while on his right the lighted windows carried on upwards. There must be a hill, with winding roads and streets stretching away from the heart of Kinlochvegan. The rain started up again. Robbie began to look out for somewhere to stop – he could see that the road pressed on in the distance, beyond the village, and he had a sudden horror of being back in that unlit blackness again, without the comfort of these streets and houses. Then he saw a sign swinging in the wind above a long low building with light coming from the leaded windows. A pub, surely. He signalled right, and pulled up in front of it.

The driving rain flung itself into his face as he pushed the car door open, heaving it against the strength of the wind. The moment he climbed out, he was freezing cold and soaked almost through.

'Christ!' he shouted but he could barely hear his own voice against the howling of the wind and rain. This wasn't like London weather, which, even at its roughest, still seemed contained and somehow safe. Here the elements had a different kind of power altogether. They had been battened down in the cities. In this wild country, they retained the upper hand.

The car's lights winked orange at him to show that it had obediently locked itself, but he couldn't hear the usual mechanical chirp it gave because of the roar of the wind. Then he turned and ran for the lighted windows of the pub.

He stepped inside to a haven of warmth and light. As the latch on the old wooden door fell into place behind him, the rioting weather outside was silenced. Here, there was a low, beamed ceiling, a vigorous fire crackling in a stone fireplace, dim lamps glowing above each wooden settle and the buzz of voices. A few heads turned to look at him as he entered, but no one seemed much interested in the newcomer.

Robbie shook himself and rubbed a hand over his face. He felt as though someone had thrown a bucket of water over him. He pulled his hand through his wet hair, trying to brush away some of the rain, as he looked around. The bar was not crammed but there were a good number of people in it, men mostly. A group were playing darts in one corner, and the others were sitting at various tables, pints of beer in front of them.

Robbie stamped on the mat, shaking off the last drops of water that clung to him, and then walked towards the bar. A man stood behind it, polishing glasses with a towel. He looked up as Robbie approached.

'Cannae help ye?' he said.

His voice startled Robbie. It was soft and mellifluous and strangely familiar.

'Um, yes...' he stuttered, thinking, *it must be the Scottish accent. It must remind me of someone.* He tried to think of someone he knew with that soft Highland accent, but he couldn't bring anyone to mind. 'Um, let's see...' He scanned the beers. 'A pint of that one please,' he said, pointing to an unfamiliar brand that he thought might be local.

The barman reached for a pint glass and started filling it from the beer tap.

'Terrible weather outside, isn't it?' Robbie said brightly. His voice had never sounded so tight and English to his own ears.

'Aye,' said the barman.

There it was again – Robbie felt the same strange response to the man's voice: almost a shiver going down his spine, mixed with an emotion that wasn't unpleasant but was definitely sad. A kind of nostalgia, perhaps. He felt as though he'd just heard his grandmother calling him in for tea and fruitcake in the way she used to, when he'd been out playing in her garden.

The barman put the glass down in front of him.

'Thanks very much,' said Robbie, handing him a fiver. When the barman handed him his change, he said, 'By the way, do you do rooms here? Bed and breakfast or anything? I couldn't see a sign outside but it was so dark and wet, I didn't stick around to look for one.'

'Aye, we do, but ye'll need to talk to the wife

about that.' The barman looked back over his shoulder to the room behind the bar. 'Rachel! There's a fella here wants to know about the B & B!'

There was a distant answering call.

'She'll be right here,' said the barman. A tall, pale young man had come up to the bar, one hand full of change. 'Be right with ye, Tom.' He turned back to Robbie. 'OK?'

'Yeah, thanks.' Robbie grinned in what he hoped was a friendly way and took a sip of his beer. It was rich and yeasty, and slid down easily, quenching his thirst with its bitterness. He hadn't realised how much he'd been wanting a drink or how tired he was after a day's driving. He began to relax as the alcohol entered his blood and the warmth of the pub eased his muscles.

The tall young man ordered his drinks. Robbie watched him and then quickly looked away as their eyes met. But even though he'd caught his gaze for only a second, there was still time to notice the eerie effect of the other man's eyes. They were grey, but so pale that they seemed almost white, with just black pinpricks at their centre. The rest of the man was very ordinary: he wore a scruffy navy jumper, jeans and trainers and his hair was dark and greasy.

A woman burst through to the area behind the bar. 'How can I help?' she asked Robbie. 'Was it you askin' about the rooms?'

'Yes. I'm looking for somewhere to stay.' Robbie was as polite as he could possibly be, hyper aware of his Englishness and suddenly recalling stories he had heard of how much the Scots disliked the English.

'We've got four rooms, two doubles, a twin and a single. They're all empty as it happens. Nothing fancy – bed, telly, a kettle and some tea bags. There's an en suite as well but only with a shower. There's a shared bath down the hall if that's what you like. We had to put in the toilets and showers for the Americans. They're very fussy.'

'Americans!' said Robbie, rolling his eyes, hoping that she might dislike them more than she disliked the English, so that he could deflect any antagonism away from himself.

She looked him in the eye for the first time and shrugged. 'Whatever, as long as they pay.'

'Do you do breakfast?'

'Eight till ten, in the lounge bar. There's no one else here at the moment, so tell me when you want it and I can rustle it up whenever. Do ye want a room then?'

'Yes, please.'

'Which one? They're all free.'

'Oh – I'll take a double, thanks.'

She nodded. 'Aye. Good. Well, I'll need you to sign the book and give me your card number. Then you can have the key.' She disappeared back to where she'd come from.

Robbie took another furtive glance around the room. No one seemed very interested in his presence. They must all be locals, he thought. They looked alike, with their stocky frames and pale faces, most dressed in rough clothes: denim and coarse wool jumpers or leather jackets. A game of cards was going on in one corner. He looked over, trying to make out what it was, but one of the players returned his glance with a hard stare, so he dropped his gaze and pretended to be interested in the beer mat on the counter instead.

Does someone here know my father? he wondered. He had the sudden, strange feeling that his father might be right here, at this very moment, sipping on a pint and looking over his hand to see what cards he had. What would he look like? Like that man over there – pale-faced and balding, with a smattering of red veins over his cheeks lending him a look of jollity that his cold blue eyes gave the lie to? Or like that old fellow in the corner, slumped down on his own, poring over a newspaper, one hand clutched round his tumbler of whisky. His hair was a mess of white and his face was mazed with wrinkles.

Is that him? thought Robbie, with a sudden surge of excitement. Is that my dad? But when he looked again at the old man as he lifted the tumbler to his mouth, his hand shaking as he did so, he couldn't believe that this was his father. And then he couldn't believe in any of it. It was so much easier to accept what his mother had told him, and to cling onto that distant, dreamy idea of a father, one who had gone away on an adventure and never come back.

'Here's the book, if you want to sign here please.' The woman had come back and was standing behind the bar with the register. She looked at him expressionlessly. Her face was plain and she wore no make-up. Her fair hair hung around her face and she'd made no attempt to style it in any way.

Robbie took the pen she offered and wrote his name and address in the space she indicated.

Then he took his credit card out of his pocket and handed it to her.

'All the way from London,' he said, as he saw her look at his address.

She grunted as if to show how little she thought of that, and he felt foolish, as though he'd been caught out boasting. He spoke quickly and without thinking to cover his embarrassment.

'By the way, I was wondering ... do you know who Hamish Fraser is? I was told he lives here. I've come to find him.'

Her head jerked up and she stared at him. 'What?' she snapped. Then he saw her look down at his card and read the name there: Robert Fraser. She stared back at him again, this time searching his face with her eyes, as though looking for something.

'Do ... do you know him?' asked Robbie.

She didn't reply. Instead, she looked out into the bar and said loudly, 'Greg, this fella's come lookin' for Hamish.'

This time, a silence fell over the bar, and all eyes turned to look at Robbie. One of the men playing cards, the one who had returned Robbie's glance with a hard stare, stood up slowly. He was a tall man, with a dark blue tattoo snaking up his neck from somewhere below his jumper. 'Ye lookin' for Hamish? Why?' he asked. His voice was a thick deep burr. 'Who are you?'

Robbie opened his mouth to speak but the landlady cut in before he could answer.

'His name's Fraser as well,' she said quickly. 'Robert Fraser. From London.'

'All right, Rachel,' said the man, flicking a stern

glance at her. 'Let the man speak for hissaelf. Is she right? Are you a Fraser?'

'Yes,' said Robbie boldly. The quietened atmosphere and the pairs of eyes staring at him were intimidating but he tried to buoy himself up with confidence. Come on, he told himself, you've got nothing to be frightened of. You're not doing anything wrong. He suppressed the small anxious voice that was telling him to be careful what he gave away to this roomful of strangers. Besides, it wasn't going to take a genius to work out that young Robert Fraser looking for old Hamish Fraser was going to be a relative of some kind. 'That's right. I've come up from London to find him. I'm his son.'

There was a gasp from someone, though he didn't see who, and the young man with the eerie grey eyes slammed his glass down on the table, spilling beer over the side. The beefy man called Greg stiffened and something in his stance became more challenging and aggressive.

'His son,' he echoed and looked briefly at the man sitting next to him.

The landlady muttered under her breath, 'I didnae think we'd ever lay eyes on *you*.'

Then the old man looked up from his newspaper and his whisky and said in a shaky, alcohol-drenched voice, 'You've taken your time, haven't you, lad? Where have you been all this time?'

Before Robbie could answer or begin to defend himself, Greg spoke again.

'We don't know where Hamish is,' he said gruffly. 'None of us have seen him for days, maybe weeks.'

'Is he...' Robbie swallowed and then forced himself to say the words. 'Is he dead?'

'Hamish, dead?' exclaimed the landlady. 'How could he be dead?'

The barman stepped up from where he'd been standing and said loudly, 'Now, now. Hamish isnae dead, leastways not as far as we know, and this is a small place, Mr Fraser. We haven't seen him for a wee while, but that's nothing new. If he's dead, he's probably just dead drunk. He usually gets like that when the weather turns bad.'

'So where will I find him?' asked Robbie slowly. He couldn't believe he might be about to hear the answer to the question that had tormented him his whole life, just like that.

'At home, of course.'

'Where does he live?'

The barman raised his eyebrows as if questioning what kind of son didn't know where his father lived. 'He's in Lachlan Cottage. Up the hill. Go out of here and at the side of the car park you'll see a steep path going upwards, follow it up until you come to a terrace of houses. It's last in a row of eight. It's got a blue door. That's Lachlan Cottage.'

'Thank you,' said Robbie and put his pint back down on the bar. He felt oddly calm. He was about to go and find his father. Now it seemed as though he had all the time in the world. He picked up his credit card from the bar. 'Can I let you know later about that room?' he asked.

The landlady shrugged. 'As you like. I doubt anyone else will come through now. If you want to come back, the doors are locked at midnight.'

'It's cold and dark for going up that hill. Especially if you don't know your way.' It was that man Greg again. He was still standing, staring at Robbie. 'Knowing Hamish, he'll be out cold. Why don't I come by and take you up there in the morning?'

'That's kind but no thanks,' said Robbie politely. 'I'm going now. Thank you,' he said to the barman and the landlady. 'I might see you later.'

He walked casually to the door, aware of all eyes on him, and opened it. A gust of cold air hit him and then he went out into the darkness.

A few minutes later, after a quick whispered conference with Greg, the young man with the pale eyes got up quietly and slipped out of the pub after him.

Chapter Five

At first the contrast between the warm dry pub and the storm outside was startling: Robbie was instantly cold and wet again. Then excitement and anticipation surged through him, making him forget the buffeting wind and the freezing air. He was on his way to find his father; a bit of nasty weather was not going to stand in his way.

It was almost pitch dark outside but he stopped by the car and took out the torch that he always kept in the boot, glad of his foresight. The yellow beam made very little difference to the darkness, illuminating the rain for the most part. Robbie held the light downwards and followed the edge of the pavement until he reached a wall. Next to that, he could make out a path heading upwards into blackness. He followed it and soon began to climb. Wet, leafy branches whipped his face as he went and his shoes were soon soaked from the torrent of rainwater pouring down the path, but he kept climbing steadfastly even though he was soon out of breath. The exertion at least made him a little warmer but he had no idea if he was going in the right direction or not.

The path twisted and turned. Sometimes he caught a glimpse of lighted windows somewhere above him, or a flash of light from behind the stone walls that bordered each side of the path. Sometimes he guessed he was now facing briefly out over the steep slope, looking down on the main road where his car was parked. The deep velvety blackness ahead, he guessed, was the sea. Then the path turned back on itself and he was sure that he was facing the cliff itself and put a hand out in case he suddenly hit solid rock, but it never happened. Instead, he climbed onwards and upwards until at last the path widened out and he was no longer being hit in the face by switches of hedge. Now he was walking alongside a row of cottages: an outside light illuminated the grey, granite front and the shuttered windows that allowed just a ribbon of light to escape at the top.

What had he said? Last of a row of eight.

Robbie blinked hard against the rain driving into his eyes and counted the first front door, and then the second. He stopped in front of the eighth and last in the row. Was the door blue? He couldn't tell – it could be anything, any dark colour. Then, under the weak beam of his torch, he made out a sign next to the front door. White letters were painted on a piece of slate, curling and rather feminine. *Lachlan Cottage*, it read. So. This was it then.

He stood for a moment, staring at it. Was this really his father's house? Last night he'd had no idea that twenty-four hours later he'd be standing in the middle of a storm on the Scottish coast, wondering if his father was about to open the door to him or not.

Knock, he told himself. Come on. Knock.

But he seemed frozen to the spot. He was simultaneously elated and terrified. What lay behind the door? The realisation of his dreams – a long-lost father who took him in his arms, hugged him and told him he'd always loved and missed him – or something he'd rather live without. Some curmudgeonly old bastard who told him never to darken the door again, and then slammed it in his face, maybe. And what about him, what about Robbie? What was he going to say? *Where have you been all my life, you piece of shit? Huh?* Or *Oh, hi, Dad. Just thought I'd drop in! Incidentally, someone seems to think you're in trouble. Can I help?*

That reminded him of the note. He'd been carried away with his own fantasies and forgotten it – now he saw it again in his mind's eye. The black foreboding lettering and the sinister message: HE HAS DISAPPEARED AND MAY BE IN DANGER. A sudden chill convulsed him.

Knock, damn you! he ordered himself. He battered the handle of the torch on the door, hoping it was loud enough to be heard over the noise of the storm. After a few moments, he rapped again, and then again. Then he knew for certain – no one was going to come and answer the door.

What now? he asked himself. Go back to the pub?

He thought about a warm dry room, a tot of whisky and a soft bed. It was alluring but... he also pictured that bar, those men drinking there, watching him walk back in, thinking ... what? That man, Greg – there was something menacing about him that made Robbie's skin prickle. He didn't know what it was but something told him it wasn't good; that he should keep his business to himself for now.

Leaning forward, he grasped the door handle and turned it. To his astonishment, it rotated easily under his hand and the next moment the door swung open, revealing a small dark hallway. Without thinking, Robbie stepped forward and went inside, shutting the door behind him.

He stood in the cold hallway for a moment and then stamped his feet and shook his head, sending showers of droplets over the stone floor.

'Hello?' he called. 'Anyone here?' The place felt empty but he remembered the words of the barman in the pub – that Hamish could be dead drunk. Perhaps he was somewhere in the house, passed out, sleeping through the storm.

Straight ahead of him a flight of stairs led upwards into darkness. To his left was a closed door, an old-fashioned rough wooden door with an iron latch. He opened it and went into the room beyond, flicking down the light switch on the inner wall. A bulb flickered into life.

He was standing in a bare, plain sitting room. Its stone walls were roughly whitewashed and he could see how thick they were from the recess of the window, where the low sill was almost two feet deep and formed a seat. A couple of battered old armchairs sat on a rag rug before a large granite fireplace which was dusty, blackened and very cold. A basket next to it was filled with odds and ends of newspaper and kindling wood and a box of matches, and the coal scuttle was half full.

Robbie looked around the room, trying to glean something about the person who lived there. Is this my dad's house? he thought. Is this where he lives? Then he thought, I bloody hope so. Otherwise I'm trespassing. This must be a traditional fisherman's cottage, a couple of hundred years old at least. He noticed the chill in the air. Nothing fancy here. Very basic indeed.

The strange thing was, it reminded him of somewhere. Was it somewhere they had been on holiday? It was the kind of place you might rent for a week or two, to soak up some old-world charm before going back to the delights of central heating and fitted carpets. He tried to remember where he might have been before that was like this place, but he could only recall holidays at his grandparents' house in Wiltshire, and that was nothing like this.

The floor was stone and the walls were decorated only with a couple of old prints. There was no carpet, just two or three rugs made of braided rags. An old dresser was the largest piece of furniture and it held a motley collection of mugs and plates. The only modern note was a small television sitting on a stool in the corner, its aerial draped up high over the edge of a picture frame, and a radio on the mantel above the fireplace. At the back of the room was another door. Robbie went over and opened it. He looked through into a small kitchen, as basic and bare as the sitting room. It was shabby but clean and tidy; the Formica table was neat, the gas stove wiped down and spotless, and washed dishes sat in the plastic drainer. He could see another door in the far wall, which he guessed must lead into a bathroom, no doubt tacked onto the original cottage at some point in the past.

He went back into the sitting room. The whole place felt empty. It wasn't just that there was no one there. It felt as though, even when its occupant was in residence, it was still a shell of a home. Nothing gave away the personality of the man who lived here. It was bleak.

Perhaps upstairs is different, he thought. He went back out to the small hallway and looked up the stairs. There was only silence and darkness above.

Could he be up there? he wondered. Perhaps he's lying in the bedroom, pissed. He tried to imagine what he might say to his father, tried to picture him. But it was impossible.

He started to climb the stairs slowly, realising that the flutter in his stomach was nervousness. At the top, a small landing turned back on itself, leading towards the front of the cottage. He saw three doors. The one at the front must be that of the main bedroom, he thought. It was over the sitting room, so had to be the largest. That was where his father was most likely to be.

Robbie began to walk down the landing towards it and then stopped. On impulse, he opened the door before it first. Behind it was only a large cupboard, full of bits of old linen and towels and some boxes. Then he went back to the first door, the one that led into a room over the kitchen. Something was pulling him back to this room, though he didn't know what it was. Something wanted him to open the door and step inside.

He put his hand on the door handle and paused for an instant, as if he might receive some kind of message from it, and then turned it and went in.

It was a small bedroom. He switched on the light and a naked bulb glowed dully, showing a sloping ceiling with a skylight in it, a wooden floor with a plain navy wool rug, a chest of drawers, a bookcase and a small iron bed. On the blanket lay an ancient teddy bear, its black eyes staring glassily upwards.

Robbie began to shake and his breath came fast and noisy in the silence. Something seemed to have hold of him and he was caught up in a whirl of emotions as he felt himself pulled back through time. He knew this room. He knew that skylight and the bulb and the cracks in the ceiling as thoroughly as you can only know something you have stared at for hours and hours and hours. He knew the feel of that small iron bedstead and felt again the clammy chill of cold sheets on a winter's night. He knew that teddy bear: he had clutched it to his chest on many nights, and whispered his secrets into its furry old ears.

'Oh my God,' said Robbie aloud, his voice cracking. 'This is my room. This is *my* room!'

He leant against the door frame, suddenly weak. As he looked in, he wondered how he had ever forgotten it. It was so familiar to him and yet it was also as though he was seeing it for the first time. Something seemed to be stabbing him in the stomach, and he clutched at it, wincing. What is it? he wondered. Then he realised that the pain of looking into that room was a physical one.

Suddenly energised, he turned and strode back along the landing to the last door. Without pausing for thought, he flung it open and stepped inside. He was ready to confront whoever was in it now. The sight of that small bed and the old teddy had fired him up in some way. He needed answers – *now*.

The main bedroom was as dark and empty as the rest of the house. It contained a double bed, neatly made and covered with a blanket, a wardrobe, a blanket box, a small bedside table, a dressing table on the far wall below a round mirror – nothing extraordinary, everything as shabby and as plain as the rest of the house. No one there. No old man, passed out on the bed and breathing whisky fumes into the room. No one to answer his questions.

Robbie staggered into the room, overcome by the torrent of emotions that had gripped him in the last few minutes. He sat down on the bed and buried his head in his hands. He felt like he wanted to weep but his eyes were hot and dry. His hands were still shaking and his breath came in fast short pants.

A moment later, he got up and went downstairs. In the sitting room, he opened the old dresser cupboard and found what he was looking for almost at once: a bottle of whisky, three quarters full. It was good stuff, too. Talisker, from the Isle of Skye. He took a mug from the shelf and poured a slug into it. He swirled it round, releasing the dark smoky aroma, and then took a mouthful. It burned pleasantly, leaving a peaty trail down his throat.

'Bloody hell,' he said. 'Fucking bloody hell.'

It felt as though he'd just been transported into a different life, in a matter of moments, like Dorothy being swept out of Kansas and into Oz, where everything was different and yet strangely familiar. London, his life there, his job, Sinead – even his mother – suddenly seemed distant and far off and scarcely real. His new reality was this: his father was alive – or had been until very recently – and still living in a place where he, Robbie, had lived as a small boy. He knew that absolutely. He knew this place. He was picking up memories that this house was releasing like tiny transmissions.

Now he could remember the sound of the wooden stairs as small shoes clattered down them, bounding down in a particular way every time. Now he recalled stretching upwards to reach the iron latches on the doors; the smell of the kitchen and the feel of the Formica table. And he recalled something else – his father. And it was bittersweet.

There had to be answers here, he thought, looking round the room. Something here had to give him a clue about all of this. Well, he would drink some more of this fine whisky and then he would damn well find them, even if it took all night.

Robbie forgot the time and he forgot his exhaustion. The whisky soon soaked into his blood, simultaneously relaxing him and firing him up. He began a thorough search of the cottage, starting with the dresser. He emptied the drawers of any papers and letters he could find, making a pile in the centre of the sitting room. Then he looked into every cupboard, even pushing his way to the back of the cupboard under the stairs, although he found only dust and cobwebs and old light bulbs behind the elderly Hoover.

Anything that looked interesting he gathered together and took upstairs, along with the bottle of Talisker. He threw the whole lot on his father's bed before starting on the top floor. In the linen cupboard, he found three boxes of what looked like scrap paper and hauled them through to the bedroom. In the bedside table, he found a photograph album and he put this to one side carefully, saving it up. In the bottom of the wardrobe were shoeboxes full of what looked like letters; Robbie slid them out and added them to the haul on the bed.

Then he replenished his mug and sat down, ready to take a journey into his own, long-forgotten past.

Picking up the photograph album, he turned the pages, staring at each photograph. The black and white prints were carefully gummed onto the thick black paper and captions were written underneath in white ink. There was his father – he would have known that, even without the caption, because he could see himself in the young man's face. He shared that unruly brown hair and the sprinkling of freckles across the nose. *Hamish, May 65* said one, showing his father in jeans and a leather jacket, standing like he was Steve McQueen. He was a handsome man by the looks of things. The photos showed him outside mostly, standing by a stone wall, or sitting looking out to sea. In one he was on board a small fishing boat, grinning proudly into the camera, one arm outstretched as if to show off the magnificence of his vessel.

Then Robbie's mother appeared in the photos, but a version of her he'd never seen before. She was young, lithe and smooth-faced. Blonde hair floated round her face in long tendrils, her eyes were wide and almost heartbreakingly innocent. Her mouth was open with silent laughter. She sat on the stone wall by the bay, her long legs in flared jeans, her shoulders hunched over in a shy pose, her large luminous eyes looking up from under the blonde hair. It was obvious that she was in love with whoever was taking the photograph.

Louise, said the caption simply. *Wedding day* said the next. Hamish and Louise – my God, how old are they? thought Robbie. They look like kids! – he in a pale suit with a dark tie, and she in a long white floating dress with a smocked front, a wreath of flowers on her head. They were smiling broadly at each other, Louise laughing again, her face alight with joy.

Robbie stared at the picture for a long time, taking in every detail of his parents' young faces, full of such happiness and hope. What on earth had gone so wrong? What had turned so sour in their lives that his mother had been able to take him away from here when he was just a tiny boy and lie to him, for the whole of the rest of her life?

He turned the next page, and there he was: a tiny, bald-headed baby with his eyes squeezed shut, wrapped in a blanket and held tightly in his mother's arms. *Robbie*. Over the next few pages he aged quickly, turning from a scrawny newborn to a plump, wide-eyed, fuzzy-headed baby. He grinned and chortled at the camera, held his teddy under one arm and a rattle in one fat fist. There he was, squirming in the bath, splashing his pudgy legs; holding himself up against a table, his bottom heavily padded with nappies; then toddling precariously down the hallway towards the camera. The two last photographs in the album faced each other on opposite pages. One was the fishing boat Robbie had seen earlier in the album: it was moored in the docks, a bright, clean vessel with the name *Bella Maria* painted across the side. The other was the photograph of a beaming three-year-old boy, with a mop of fair hair and big sparkling eyes. His arms were wrapped tightly around his father, who held him up, and both were grinning broadly. Next to it the caption read: *The last picture of Robbie*.

His hands were shaking again and his eyes prickled. What the hell did all this mean? In the past twenty-four hours, he'd had to question his own history. Up until now, he'd believed that his feckless father had abandoned him, not giving a damn what happened to his wife and son. Was that still the case? It seemed that everything he had believed was no longer true – but he didn't have the answers he needed to write the new version.

He shut the album and saw the corner of another photograph slip out from between the pages. Pulling it out, he found himself looking into the face of a young and beautiful woman. It was not his mother. This woman was dark, with large, light eyes – the black and white print made it hard to tell the exact colouring – a soft, full mouth and fine features. There was no clue who it might be, but the photograph looked well cared for and treasured. He turned it over but the back was blank. He slid it back into the album and then picked up the shoebox he'd found in the bottom of the wardrobe. Inside was a stack of old envelopes, each one with the address scribbled out and the words 'Return to Sender' written across the face of the envelope. Each one was addressed to Robbie Fraser. To him.

He rifled through the box. There were about sixty envelopes, each one scrawled on in the same way, and each one unopened. He knew who had written the order to send the letters back. It was his mother's handwriting.

Pulling out an envelope at random, he opened it and took out the letter.

Hello son, it began. *Do you remember how much you liked seeing the boats coming home from fishing? You'd have liked it this morning – what a fine sight.*

64

The sky was the purest blue I've ever seen and the boats came back in a kind of formation, like a fleet of warships... At the end of the letter, his father wrote, *I hope your mother lets you get this letter. I know you've not had any of the others, but you must always believe that I think about you all the time and miss you more than you can ever know. I hope you're well and happy, Robbie. I hope you're liking your school and doing well. What are your favourite lessons? Do you like playing football? I wish I could see you, son. There's so much to say to each other, isn't there? Perhaps we'll see each other soon. With all my love, your dad. xxxx*

'Shit!' said Robbie. His voice was thick and choked with emotion. The letter shook in his hands. 'What ... what the ... *shit!*'

He put his head in his hands and wept.

Chapter Six

He woke not knowing where he was. It was a feeling he hadn't had in a long time – the blinking disorientation, the blankness and bewilderment, followed by a flood of realisation.

For Christ's sake, I'm lying on my father's bed! he thought.

So it was all true, then. It wasn't some long, hugely complicated, vividly real dream. He really had come to Scotland, found his father's house and then...

Robbie glanced down at the floor. The almost

65

empty Talisker bottle explained his dry mouth and heavy head – though a good whisky like that didn't submit his brain to the kind of pounding his London hangovers inflicted – and the detritus of letters and envelopes on the floor told him why his eyes ached. He remembered now: he'd read seventeen years' worth of lost letters from a father to a beloved son. They were full of love and yearning and a desperate need for some kind of contact, even if they would simply be returned unopened. The last one had been written ten years before. It acknowledged that Robbie was a man now and in it, Hamish said that he would stop writing and wait for Robbie to come and find him, if he ever wanted to.

Robbie remembered getting drunker and drunker, and then sobbing his heart out as the dawn came up over the sea, as he mourned all the lost years. He remembered cursing his mother. A cold feeling crept into his stomach as he thought of it. I don't want to have to hate one of my parents, he thought. Why can't I love them both? Why does it have to be a choice?

But something had happened between them, long ago. Something that made his mother take him away and cut off all contact with his father, even though she must have guessed what agony that would cause both Hamish and their son. What could it have been? He could pull theories out of the air, but there was no way he could know if he'd guessed the truth. And who was left to tell him? His mother was dead. His father too, perhaps. But that was the great mystery – where was his father? Why did everyone in the pub seem to think he was sleeping off a booze session when his cottage had obviously not been lived in for a couple of days at least? And it had been left neat and tidy – not in the kind of condition that a drunken spree might result in.

Robbie shook his head. He couldn't begin to confront any of this until he'd had some coffee. He got up and padded downstairs, shivering in the cold air. Was there any heating in this place? He'd have to light the fire and try to warm it up a bit.

He went through the kitchen to the old, ramshackle bathroom and used the toilet. Having used the one in the pub, he hadn't needed to go again until this morning. This was the only room he hadn't been in the night before, and like the others it was plain and old-fashioned. A gas boiler was mounted on the wall above the bath, its pilot light flickering away. So Hamish hadn't planned on being gone long, then, or he would surely have turned it out.

In the kitchen, Robbie boiled the kettle on top of the gas stove – no such thing as a cordless electric jug here – and looked for some coffee. He found a dusty old jar of instant at the back of one of the cupboards. His father's tastes were plain, he thought, surveying the food stores. He might like a good whisky but he was content with the economy lines of everything else. And it was all very simple and unadorned: tins of beans, sweet corn, some other vegetables, soup and tomatoes. Boxes of rice. Corned beef. Tinned ham.

Robbie thought of his own kitchen. It overflowed with gadgets, some never used: pasta makers, bread machine, mixers, whisks, even electric pepper grinders, for God's sake. The contrast with this simplicity was striking. Being in his father's house was like stepping back in time.

I used to live here, he thought, still astonished at the thought. This used to be my home.

He made a cup of coffee thinking, God, how long is it since I had an instant coffee? I'm such a London metropolitan type now. I like my lattes and my americanos, all the freshly ground stuff. But the instant had a familiar, comforting taste that made him think of being a teenager when he made his coffees milky and sweet but still felt like a grown-up when he drank them.

The bread bin was empty and, apart from a pint of milk in the fridge that looked on the turn, there was no fresh food in the house at all.

I'll have to go shopping, get some supplies in, he thought. Then he caught himself up. So he was planning to stay here, was he? The minute that idea occurred to him, he realised it was inevitable. He wasn't going anywhere, not now. He'd come this far and discovered this much. Now he had to know the answers to the mystery of where his father was, and what had happened all those years ago. If there was the faintest chance that he might find his father, there was no way on earth he would let it go. And here he was, with a place to stay, nothing to call him home. He would make Lachlan Cottage his base. If his father rolled up, demanding to know who the hell was staying in his house, so much the better.

Robbie took his coffee through to the sitting room and set about making up a fire in the grate.

Never having lit fires on a regular basis, he was a bit vague as to how to go about it, but recalled reading somewhere that it was best to build a pyramid with the kindling, so he rolled up some newspaper shreds and then started carefully placing the wood around it to form a cone shape. He'd just finished and was wondering whether to light it when he heard a knock at the door.

He sat back on his heels and looked warily in the direction of the hall. Who could that be? Various candidates presented themselves: it was unlikely to be his father – who knocked on their own front door, after all? – so it could only be someone from the pub – that Greg man perhaps – or else a nosy neighbour wondering who had taken up residence in the cottage.

The knock came again: short, sharp and light with a note of urgency.

Robbie got up and went to the front door, drew back the bolt and opened it. On the step stood a young woman, dressed in a puffy jacket, knitted hat, jeans and walking boots. A canvas bag hung over one shoulder. She looked at him with a serious expression. 'You'd better let me in. Come on, now, quickly.'

Her voice was smooth and low, as musical as all the other Scottish voices he had heard. Something in her tone made him obey her, and he stood aside and let her step past him into the hall. He shut the door behind her.

She put her bag down, took off her knitted hat and let a ponytail of soft brown hair escape. 'Come on, then,' she said, leading the way into the sitting room. 'Now, Robbie Fraser–' she stopped and turned, giving him a hard glance – 'you *are* Robbie Fraser, aren't you?'

He nodded.

'Good.' She walked towards the fireplace. She was medium height and slender, though her jeans showed that she had healthy curves where Robbie expected to find them. He didn't much care for the beanpole look that seemed to be everywhere. Sinead had aspired to it, he remembered suddenly. She'd become obsessed with being some minuscule size. It had been very boring, and not very sexy.

The woman turned to him, her eyes amused. 'What are you making here? Building a wigwam, or something?' She gestured at the fireplace and Robbie's carefully constructed pyramid.

'I'm laying a fire,' he said a little stiffly. He was proud of his effort.

'Oh, is that what it is? You must have a short attention span then. That will burn for about four minutes. It looks more like a bed for a hamster.' She indicated the small ball of shredded newspaper in the middle of his wooden palisade and laughed. 'Look, let me. I'll do it.'

'I suppose you know some Scottish secret for how to make a decent fire,' he said grumpily.

'Aye, I do. It's called firelighters.' She got down on her knees and started dismantling Robbie's effort and rebuilding it. Robbie tried not to look at the pleasing roundness of her denimed bottom.

He opened his mouth to ask her exactly why she needed to see him, but she beat him to it.

'I suppose you're wondering who I am,' she

said, without turning round.

'It had crossed my mind. You don't seem at all surprised to find me here.'

'Is that coffee you're drinking?' she asked suddenly, seeing his mug next to the fireplace.

'Yeah. Would you like one?'

'I certainly would.' He liked the way she almost rolled her 'r's. *I cerrr-tainly would.* 'It's pretty cold out there. The air comes off the sea with quite a bite to it.'

He went through to the kitchen to reboil the kettle. Who was she? She knew who he was. Had she been in the pub last night, and he just hadn't seen her? Or perhaps she was the landlady's sister or something, sent up here to make sure he was all right.

The kettle boiled quickly and he poured the water into the mug and took it through with the milk bottle. As he went back, she was striking a match and setting fire to the edges of the paper she'd arranged under a platform of kindling and some pieces of coal and firelighters.

'There,' she said, sitting back on her haunches. 'That should go a treat. Oh, thanks, you're a love,' she said, taking the mug from him. 'Black's fine, thanks.'

'So,' he said, bemused, sitting down himself in one of the armchairs. 'You were about to tell me who you are.'

'Oh, yes, so I was.'

'And you were in a bit of rush to get in here, I noticed.'

She nodded. Her large blue eyes gazed at him guilelessly over the top of the mug. 'Aye. You're sharp. That's true, I didn't much want to linger outside.'

'So...' he said slowly.

'So...' She put the mug down. 'I'm Heather McBain. And I'm the one who wrote you the letter that brought you here.'

Robbie's mouth dropped open. He had never felt his mouth literally drop before and always thought it was just a turn of speech, but now he realised it was entirely possible as he gaped at the young woman in front of him, unable to think of a single thing to say. There were too many questions to know where to start.

'I'll put you out of your misery,' she said. 'I expect there's a lot you'll want to know.'

Robbie regained some control but only enough to open and shut his mouth as he grasped for words. Heather stood up and brushed off her knees where they had picked up wood and coal dust from the floor. Then she stared at him intently for a moment.

'Are you hungry?'

At last Robbie found his voice. 'Hungry? Well, I...' As soon as she said it, he realised he was starving. He'd had almost nothing to eat since lunchtime the day before and his stomach was crying out for food. The onslaught of alcohol had not helped. The gurgling and swishing in his belly would only be quelled by a hearty meal. 'Yes, I am now you mention it. There's nothing in the house here.'

'I didn't think so.' She strode through to the hall and returned with her canvas bag. 'I brought some food with me. You can eat while I talk.'

With some plates from the kitchen, she laid out a picnic for him. It was simple stuff – ham sandwiches, sausage rolls, a banana and an apple – but Robbie fell on it with enthusiasm. The moment he'd swallowed the first mouthful he felt his blood sugar rise and his strength begin to return and with it, his power of speech.

'This is good, thanks.'

Heather had curled herself up on the sofa and was watching him eat while she sipped at her cup of coffee. 'You're welcome.'

'Now,' he said, as he picked up another sandwich – he'd never realised how delicious a ham sandwich could be until now – 'you'd better explain yourself. Why did you write that letter? What did you mean about my father? Do you know him?'

'Oh yes.' She nodded slowly. 'I know him. I've known him all my life.'

Robbie looked at her curiously. The extraordinary emotional journey of the night before had almost wrung him out. He was numbed. It was, he supposed, one of the ways that people coped with intense pain – they just stopped feeling for a while until they could begin to process it. Nevertheless, there was a tiny stab of something that hurt as he looked at the young woman in front of him who had had something he could never have: the opportunity to know his father over all those lost years. 'But ... how ... what I mean is...' He stumbled over his words, still trying to find a way to begin.

'Don't you worry,' Heather said. She smiled at him. 'I know what you want to ask. I'm going to tell you everything. That's why I brought you here. And you need to know it as soon as possible because I don't know how much time we have left. So here's the truth. I don't know if your father is dead or not. I last saw him three days ago, here in this room. He was going out to do something dangerous – to investigate a situation he believed existed here in the village. I've heard nothing since and the phone he has is switched off. I've no idea where he is but I'm worried, to say the least.'

'Then... Why did you send for me? How did you know where to find me?'

Heather held up a hand. 'I'll come to that. First, I'm going to tell you a story. I don't know how much of it you're going to believe, but hear me out before you say anything. Agreed?' She narrowed her eyes at him until he nodded. Then she sat back.

'I know some things about you, Robbie Fraser. I know you and your mum went away from here years ago, to live down south in England, but I've no idea what you know about what you left behind–'

'Nothing,' said Robbie quickly. 'I didn't know anything at all. My mother never told me about my dad–'

A look from Heather silenced him. 'We agreed no interruptions,' she said curtly. She paused for a moment to find her train of thought and continued. 'I've only ever known your dad as a broken man. From as young as I can remember, he's been the loneliest person I've ever met. If you mention Hamish to me, I see an old man,

74

always on his own, sitting on the deck of his boat or on the quayside next to it. Sometimes he'd be mending it, or checking his nets or cleaning up some equipment; often he'd be sitting whittling away at pieces of wood or knotting bits of twine, but he always moved like a man who had nothing to get up for, nothing to work for. Like someone who didn't much care if he earned enough to live on or not. He scraped by, I think. He took that raggedy boat of his out when the weather was good or the fishing was plentiful and managed to sell enough of what he caught to feed himself – and buy whisky. And I hardly ever saw him talking to another soul. Not properly.

'That was what I didn't understand. Hamish was born here. He'd always lived here. He'd been here his entire life. Why did he have no friends? Why did no one in the village pass the time of day with him the way they did with other people? They'd say hello when they passed, sometimes swap a pleasantry or two, but no one stopped for long. It was as though they were afraid of him or something, or as though he'd done something so unspeakable that no one wanted to know him. It was like he was an exile in his own place.

'I was the only person he talked to and that started by accident. I was about seven years old and I was running along the quayside, hurrying home for tea. I always speeded up when I came near Hamish's boat so that I could get past it quickly before he came out or saw me or tried to talk to me. I'd always been afraid of him because my father had told me never to have anything to do with him. He'd said that old Hamish was

75

crazy and that was why no one wanted to know him, that he'd done bad things in the past and he was a wicked man. I ran so fast to avoid him that I fell over a bit of mooring rope just by his boat and scraped my knees badly. I was more shocked than hurt but I was bleeding and I'd grazed my hands as well. I remember him coming out of the *Bella Maria* when he heard me crying. Just the sight of him made me howl even more because I was so scared of him, but he came over anyway. He knelt down beside me and turned my hands over so he could see them, told me not to cry. He was so gentle with me and so comforting. I very soon stopped being afraid of him and when he suggested I go on board with him so he could wash my cuts and put plasters on my knees, I was quite happy to. He was nothing but good to me. When I got home, my mother saw the plasters and asked me what had happened and who had bandaged me up. When I told her that it was the old man on the boat, she looked frightened and told me not to tell my father, whatever happened. So I kept quiet about it. That was the first time I had any clue that there was something that existed between my father and Hamish, but I had no idea what it was. All I knew was that he was a kind man and a lonely one, so I went back to the boat to see him and before long, we were friends. And he was never anything but a good friend to me. I think he liked my companionship and my childish conversation – perhaps I made him think of you, the son he had lost. He told me about you, you know. Not a lot but enough. I was only little but I knew enough not to press him on it –

I could see it was painful for him even then. I spent many afternoons on the deck of the *Bella Maria* or in the hold, helping Hamish while we talked and he made me cups of cocoa or gave me mugs of strong, sweet tea. We invented a game called When Robbie Comes Back, fantasising about all the things we would do together when you came home. "Robbie will be ten years old now," he'd say. "What shall we do to celebrate his birthday when he comes home?" and then we'd make up a day of exciting events – you know the kind of thing, a child's idea of bliss. Funfairs, candy floss, hot dogs, the movies, a trip to the town. When I asked why you had had to go away, he would say, "Robbie's mother had to go and a wee one has to be with his mother, doesn't he? But it's not for ever."'

Heather looked at him solemnly with her wide blue eyes. 'For me, seeing you is a bit like meeting a character from a book. I feel as though I know you somehow, but you have no idea of who I am. I used to talk and think about you all the way through my childhood. And now here you are.'

Robbie stared back. He was lost in the picture of his father and this woman as a little girl, doing the things he should have done with his father. Heather McBain had experienced the closest thing to his childhood that anyone else could have known.

Heather went on, 'One day I asked my mother why I must never mention the man on the boat to my father. The same frightened look crossed her face that I had seen the first time I'd ever

77

mentioned him to her. She told me that there had been a quarrel between them and that it had never been forgiven. She said that everyone in the village knew about it and that they had all known my father was in the right. That was why no one spoke to Hamish Fraser any more and why he was so alone. Everyone had taken my father's side. "And you're to do the same," my mother said to me. "You're not to be friends with that man, Heather, do you hear me? Your father would kill you if he ever found out."

'I hated that. I couldn't understand what Hamish had done. When I asked him, his face darkened but only for a second. He didn't want me to see his feelings, I could tell, and he wasn't going to say anything bad about my father. I never said that I wasn't allowed to see him, and he never asked, perhaps because he guessed I would have been forbidden to visit him and neither of us wanted to admit that out loud. Hamish is a good man – he wouldn't have let me disobey my parents like that. It was easiest for us just to go along as we were, with no one knowing and with us just living for the day, never discussing the future except for the make-believe day when you, Robbie, would return.

'The thing is...' Heather paused. She dropped her eyes to her hands, where her fingers were twisting around each other. Then she looked up at Robbie and stared him straight in the eye with a candid blue gaze that he felt he already knew intimately. 'The thing is, I hate my father. I always have done. Between them, he and my brute of a brother have got this place sewn up and they swagger about like they own it. They're both thugs and bullies. My father's money and his power keep everyone in line in this village and they all pretend that he's some fine, upstanding man. Perhaps some of them believe it. But I know the truth. He's not even half the man your father is. That's why I'm not going to let him get away with it.'

Heather came to an abrupt halt. Now her hands were balled into tight fists, her expression determined, as though her long speech had been designed to provoke her own courage and keep the momentum going of whatever it was she planned to do.

'Let him get away with what?' asked Robbie.

Heather paused. Then she said firmly, 'I'm not going to let him get away with what's going on here.'

'I still don't understand how this involves me and my father.'

'Robbie, I promise you, this does involve you. There are things going back years that you have no idea about. And as for your father... God, I hope I'm wrong, I really do. But there's a possibility he's already dead. I'm so sorry.'

The silence in the room that followed her statement was heavy with Robbie's astonishment and confusion. 'What are you talking about?'

A moment ago Hamish Fraser had been living vividly in his son's imagination. As Heather talked, he had been able to see his father so clearly it hurt. Now, suddenly, they were discussing his death.

Robbie stuttered, 'W-w-why would he be dead?

Has there been an accident? Or is your father involved, is that what you're saying?'

Heather jumped to her feet and began to pace about the room. 'I don't know! That's the trouble. I don't know and I haven't got any proof. But something is very wrong, I'm absolutely certain of it. My father is mixed up in something very big and very dangerous. Hamish went out because he believed he knew what it was and now he's disappeared. It's too much of a coincidence. And I know what my father's like. He's utterly ruthless. He already hates your father from the pit of his soul and with the slightest excuse, he'd be pleased to do his worst. It's just a question of how far he would go.'

'Heather,' interrupted Robbie. The young woman stopped walking about and looked at him. 'Wait a second. Our fathers quarrelled long ago, and you think that all these years later, it's still enough for your father to want to murder my father?'

'I absolutely believe it,' she said simply. 'And if you knew what I know about my father, you'd believe it too. Especially if Hamish witnessed them up to no good.'

'What is this dark activity you keep hinting at?'

Heather gave him a sideways look. 'I don't know if I should tell you yet.'

Robbie was exasperated. 'For God's sake, you've brought me all this way, you can't start making dark hints and not telling me what the hell is going on. And you still haven't answered the question of how you came to know where I lived.'

'All in good time. I want you here because I

can't trust anyone else to help me. I don't want to go to the police because I've got no evidence – not a shred – and no proof even that Hamish has disappeared. I don't even know if your father is dead yet. He may still be alive. But if he is, I think time is running out. The longer he is away, the more likely it is that they have killed him. That's what you and I have to find out.'

'They?'

Heather shrugged. 'My father. My brother. Their cronies. The whole village is in his pay, virtually.'

Robbie ran a hand through his hair. 'And there I was, thinking I'd left all that gun crime and misery and violence behind me on the streets of London. Nothing much disturbs the peace here except rain and wind, I thought. How wrong could I be?'

'We may live a long way from Oxford Street and a branch of Ikea but we're still people, you know.' Heather gave him a cold look. 'The difference is that we all live in each other's pockets. Everyone knows everyone's business here. Secrets and feuds and hatreds can live and thrive for generations.'

Robbie thought for a moment. He had the feeling that Heather was holding something back from him. 'OK, what are we going to do? Where are we going to start?'

Heather stood in front of the fireplace, staring into the flames, and was very still for a moment. Robbie was wondering if she had heard him at all and was about to ask her again, when she said softly, 'I've got to be honest with you, Robbie. I don't know where we're going to start. I have some ideas. But there's something I want to tell you first.'

'Yes?'

'It's about why your mother left your father. Are you ready for this?'

Part Two

Chapter Seven

1958

Magnus McBain was walking back from school slowly. He was alone as usual. None of the other children wanted to walk with him, even if they had been going in the same direction, which wasn't likely. Most of them were village kids. A few came in on the rackety old school bus that picked them up from the most distant farms and brought them in every day. The others that lived outside the village came in on their bikes, or walked in gaggles, big brothers and sisters leading the way, the younger ones trotting along behind.

No one lived out McBain's way. The crumbling old bothy where the family lived was on the edge of some gorsed, forested land, right on the borders of an estate that stretched for hundreds of acres. There were no other families for miles. Sometimes McBain wondered if that was what had lured his father out here. Perhaps it was the silence and isolation that had drawn him to the old place; perhaps it suited him that way. When they'd been in the city, there had been plenty of people to hear his mother's screams and the howls of terrified children, and maybe his father hadn't liked the way the neighbours looked at him the morning after one of his rages. Not that there wasn't plenty of it about. McBain knew that lots of other families suffered the way his did. It wasn't rare for fathers to drink themselves stupid almost every night, keeping food out of the mouths of their children and condemning the family to poverty. Some gambled away the measly wages they earned but most drank them, locking themselves ever more tightly into the vicious circle of misery where the only escape was yet more booze.

Out here, there wasn't anyone to hear the shouts and the quarrels, or to eavesdrop on the punches and the whippings. No one noticed the black eyes and bruises, or felt the fear that shimmered in the air around the house.

She'd said it would be different now, McBain thought grimly as he trudged along the road leading out of the village. That was what his mother had told him before they'd moved. He hadn't wanted to leave the city. He had friends there, it was familiar to him. To most, it might have looked like a terrible place to live – a slum. But McBain and his friends had treated it like an adventure playground and there were always endlessly interesting things going on as they dashed about, causing havoc. There was always some poor stray cat to torment, or some decrepit tramp to bait. One of their favourite games was to trap rats and put them in a milk churn. Then they would drop Billy Jennings's ferret in, and watch with fascinated enjoyment as the rats froze in terror and the ferret snaked his way between them, nipping each one swiftly on the back of the neck until all the rats were dead.

'Why de they nevair try t' get awa'?' piped up

86

Charlie Ferguson. 'They just let the ferret kill 'em.'

'Too scared,' McBain replied. 'When you're that scared, there's nothin' ye can do about it.' He knew what it felt like to freeze in terror, wishing the inevitable danger would somehow go away, knowing it would not, waiting powerlessly for the blow to come.

Yes, it was never dull around the streets where the boys roamed. Drama of some kind or another was always unfolding, amusing the kids between their games of football and their endless mischief. They'd see some woman throwing her husband out, or a father catching his runaway son in the street and giving him a good hiding. They'd seen dead bodies coming out of the houses – often just tiny, sheet-wrapped bundles, sometimes followed by the mother who'd died trying to birth them. They'd seen fires, demolitions, sickness and misery, drunkenness and debauchery, thievery and violence. They'd witnessed parties and jollity, dancing and singing and a kind of mad happiness that proclaimed that you had to seize the moment when it came, for tomorrow would be a return to the daily desperation. There was never a dull moment in the city, whatever else you might say about it. McBain hadn't wanted to leave it, nor had his older brother Jamie. Jamie was eighteen. There'd been another baby between the two boys but that one had died, as babies so often did, so although McBain was only fourteen, he felt close to his big brother and almost like a grown-up himself. Jamie had refused to go. He already had a job working for a builder and had been wanting to leave home anyway. Ending up in some cottage in the middle of nowhere with only his brothers and sister for company was not his idea of a good time, so he had arranged to rent a room in the home of one of his mates and was happier at the prospect than he had been for a long time.

'You wanna go too,' he'd said to his little brother. 'You get yourself some work, boy. Then you can do whatever you like.'

But when McBain had told his mother that he didn't want to move to the other side of the country and was planning to leave school and get a job, she had belted him one and told him not to be stupid.

'I don't want you all to have the kind of life we've had!' she'd hissed, her eyes furious. 'Don't you want some chances? A future? We've got to get out of here if you're going to make anything of yourself.'

'What about Jamie?' McBain said stubbornly. 'He's doing all right. He's earning a living, isn't he?'

His mother turned away, the set of her shoulders stiff. At last she said in a harsh voice, 'Jamie'll turn out like all the rest. He'll learn to love drink just like they all do. He'll get too handy with his fists and get into trouble. Some girl'll catch him and they'll do the same as we have. They'll have too many babies and too little money and he'll never get out of here. But you've still got a chance and so have the others. That's why we're going. And you're coming too, to finish your education and live a different life to this one.'

McBain never found out how his mother had

managed to persuade his father to move out of the city to the coast, or how they'd found this cottage, but a few months ago the family had loaded everything they owned onto an old truck and driven for hours, far from the choking, smoky city and out into the wilderness, where huge mountains loomed over copper, green and black valleys and where the grey road snaked through bare granite and grassy rocks, far away from everything they knew.

With every mile they covered, McBain had felt more desperate and more alone. As the younger ones squealed and squirmed, and his mother turned round with clouts and yells while his father drove implacably north, McBain felt like his heart was breaking. His gang was far behind him now, with their dirty faces and scabby knees and ragged clothes. They'd be racing off on some piece of mischief without him – climbing over the slag heaps, stealing coal, begging for pennies, thieving apples – and in a day or two, they'd forget he'd ever existed. And he missed Jamie already so badly he thought he might die of it.

'I'll write ye,' Jamie had promised. 'An' you come and visit me, d'ye hear? We'll have some fun together.'

But McBain knew his brother would never write. He could barely scrawl his own name, so the idea that he might compose a whole letter was a joke. And as the truck shuddered further and further away, he didn't know how he would ever get back to see him.

McBain's father had already arranged work before they got there, through some shadowy network of friends and contacts. Perhaps that was how they had found the house, as well. On the way up, as they followed the coastline towards it, his mother had had moments of light-hearted cheerfulness, when she'd seemed to realise that they really had left the grotty old slum far behind them.

'It's gonna be so beautiful!' she told them all. 'A house of our own, with no neighbours screaming and yelling day and night. A proper garden you can run about in, all of ye, with flowers and fruit trees. Birds and insects and animals. There'll be a bedroom for every two of you and a big kitchen.'

The children had been wide-eyed with amazement as they listened. They'd hardly seen a blade of grass in their lives, let alone a garden.

'Can we have a dog, Mam?' asked Alec, who was seven.

'A dog, a dog!' chimed in the little ones.

'We'll see what your father says,' said their mother, but he only grunted as he steered the rackety old vehicle around another bend in the road. She said with a smile, 'But don't you be forgetting that there'll be something else, something to keep your minds off whether you've got a dog or not. The sea!'

They all gasped. Even McBain, lost in his misery, pricked his ears up at the magic word. The sea. The mysterious ocean that he had learned covered more of the earth's surface than anything else. At its deepest points, it went down for miles into cold blackness, where strange white boneless creatures lived, things they didn't even have a name for. He was still fascinated at the thought of it. He wanted to breathe in the salty air, watch the waves crashing onto the shore, perhaps even walk to the edge and put his bare toes into the water and feel the sea touching them.

It had been night-time before they arrived and there was no glimpse of the sea to be had. His first impression of the house was of cold and damp darkness. They had not been able to do much more than haul the mattresses off the truck and lay them on the floor of the main room, before they ate some cold stew their mother had brought with them and then covered themselves with blankets as they huddled up fully dressed – the younger ones nestled together like kittens – and went to sleep. Daylight did not show them the idyllic country home of their mother's description, but a broken-down house where there was even less in the way of comforts and modern appliances than there had been in the old terrace they'd had back in Glasgow. The kitchen was little more than a sink and a wooden bench and a rusty old range.

'We'll make it nice,' said their mother bravely as they looked around at their new home. 'It needs a clean and some bits and pieces.'

Their father said nothing but dressed himself for work and was soon gone, rattling away down the overgrown driveway back to the road. He had a place in a garage on the edge of the village, a place that serviced the cars and trucks of the villagers and overhauled the engines of the fishing boats as well. The mechanical skills that he'd learned in the army would serve him well now. When he'd gone, the rest of the family spent the day unpacking the cases and packages that had been hastily unloaded from the truck before their father had left. In the afternoon, they walked into the village so that they could be registered at the school.

McBain walked in front of his brothers and sister. Babies, he thought scornfully, as they chased along behind him, distracted all the time by ditches and sticks and puddles and clumps of grass. Stupid children. I'm the man of the family now that Jamie's not here.

He didn't count his father. He tried to think about his father as little as possible.

Then they rounded a corner and there before them was the twinkling, sparkling blue of the sea. It was a calm day and the soft water seemed to merge with the sky so that it was one great canvas of shaded colour, from baby blue to aquamarine. The waves looked from here like little white-tipped ripples, and above them were smears of white cloud.

'Look, children!' cried his mother. 'There it is! Didn't I say?' She inhaled deeply. 'Ah, smell that! That's ozone. It's good for you. Take it all in.'

Her eyes sparkled in a way McBain had never seen before as she urged them all to breathe deeply.

'Come on yous! Come on, Flora, take in that air deep. You too, Alec. Benjy, smell the freshness. Can you smell it? Can you?'

It was as though she wanted to clean out the black smog and the dirt from her children's lungs and replace it with something good and whole-some and healthy, as though she was asking them to breathe in new life. They all stood there, huffing in air and puffing it out, the children shouting how good it was.

Tentatively, McBain breathed in. The air seemed to sting his nostrils, it was so sharp and cold. But his mother was right, it was unlike the tepid, heavy air he was used to, often ripe with the pungent odours of unwashed humans living too close together. This was quite different. And there it was – the magnificent sea, that lay so close and yet was still so unknowable. It made him think of a big chained bear he had seen at the zoo once: he'd been impressed by its power and scared of what it might be capable of. He'd been frightened of that bear because there was no way of knowing what it might be thinking or what it might do next, and because he knew it could destroy him whenever it chose. He felt the same now, as he looked at the expanse of water before him. He felt the same when his father came home drunk.

They walked on and at last came to Kinloch-vegan. The village seemed like the quietest place he'd ever been in his life, and the school tiny. His mother made them wait in the playground while she went in to register them, and McBain went to the wire fence and looked out. Houses nestled in one and twos and terraces all the way up the hillside. On the main road in the village was a shop or two and a post office and a pub – and that was it. He couldn't understand how a place could be so small. What did people do all day? What jobs could they do in a place like this, if it wasn't working in the shops or at the garage, like his father?

Then his attention was taken by the bay. Dozens of vessels seemed to be bobbing just off the shore, some moored by the quayside, others anchored a little further out. They were pretty, cheerful-looking things: blue ones, red ones and yellow ones, with little white cabins on the top and black funnels. On their decks were winches and machinery that McBain guessed must be for hauling in catches of fish. So that's what they did here, to earn their livings. Of course.

He stared at the little boats almost hungrily. They looked like freedom to him. He imagined running down to the quayside, leaping aboard one and starting the engine and then motoring away out of the bay. Where to? He could go anywhere. He tried to remember his geography lessons. He might go to France. Or Spain. Or Australia. Or was that too far? He couldn't remember. Perhaps even *America*. He felt dazed at the thought. America didn't really exist, he was almost sure. It was too dreamlike, with its movie films and cartoons, beautiful girls and sunshine and music – how he loved that music, the fierce energy of the drums, the twanging guitars and singing of Buddy Holly and Elvis Presley. It took him places he couldn't go in any other way, places like Blueberry Hill and Heartbreak Hotel.

He stared for a long time at the water and the boats. Freedom, he thought, longingly. That's what they are.

'Come on, yous!' scolded his mother as she came out of the school and into the yard. 'Stop dreaming. We'll do some shopping and then we're back home to sort out that unholy mess that's waiting for us. D'ye hear? Plenty of time for dreaming later.'

The children were to start at the school the very next day.

Walking back, scuffing his shoes as he went, McBain thought savagely how much he hated school. Right from the start he'd been an outsider, and no one had seemed to want to get to know him. Of course he was different to all of them. The other children in the class had lived in the village all their lives and had known each other since they were babies. They knew all the same places and spoke the same way. McBain, with his coarse city accent and sharp ways, seemed to put them off. He saw how they looked at him: there was a wariness there and even a kind of fear. He knew he looked different somehow, with his thin, pinched face and sallow skin. His dark hair still seemed to carry the scent of the city on it – smog and grime – and his eyes were still feral and glinting.

He missed his old friends, where he belonged to the gang and where they all understood each other. He missed Jamie.

Kicking at some stones in the road, he wondered whether to go home or not. He knew what waited for him there: his mother, worn out as usual by the strains of looking after the house and somehow conjuring food for the whole family out of the minuscule budget she had left once her husband had drunk his fill; his brothers and sister, squabbling and fighting and never giving anyone a moment's peace. Then later, his father would come back from work and the moment he walked in, everything would change. Something nasty would creep into the atmosphere and all the children would become tense, like small animals poised to flee as soon as they heard the crack of a twig.

No, he didn't want to go back there if he could help it. Perhaps he'd go and sit on the hill and stare at the sea, as he often did when there was nothing else to do. It cheered him up in a melancholy way to watch the water and think about the eternal movement of the waves.

'Hello,' said a voice behind him, making him jump.

He turned round warily and saw a boy walking up the road towards him. The boy grinned.

'I saw you going along this way. I'm going too so I thought we might as well walk together,' he said cheerily. 'I'm Hamish.'

'I know who you are,' said McBain with a growl in his voice. He couldn't help it. Anything he said seemed to come out of his mouth sounding angry even if he hadn't meant it that way. It had earned him the belt for cheek more than once.

'Where are you going?'

'Dunno.'

'Oh. Right, then.'

McBain carried on walking and Hamish sauntered along beside him. He had a long slim stick in his hand and as they walked, he swiped at the grasses at the side of the road, cutting off the seed heads with one sharp blow.

'Are you going to the point?' Hamish asked idly.

'What do you mean?'

'Up there.' Hamish gestured towards the hilltop that overlooked the sea.

'What's that you call it?'

'The point. Macready's Point is its proper name.'

McBain grunted.

'There's hardly anyone ever goes up there. It's a good place for getting away from folks for a bit,' Hamish added, as though he were determined to be friendly despite his taciturn companion.

What does Hamish Fraser want with me? wondered McBain as they walked on in silence. He'd watched the other boy occasionally when they were all in class together and the truth was, he envied him. Hamish always seemed cheerful, and his good humour along with his good looks made him popular with the class and with the teachers. He had brown curly hair, blue eyes and a frank open face. His skin was fair, but being outdoors so much had burnished it. He was rangy and strong-looking, with long legs that could cover the games field in no time at all. Everyone liked Hamish Fraser and sometimes McBain wished he could be this boy, with his easy charm, instead of his clumsy, cross and lonely self. In class, McBain had to sit at the front, which was always the lot of the new pupils. Hamish, on the other hand, held court at the back, sprawling out his long legs into the aisle between the desks and making the others laugh with his jokes and cheeky comments. Any ill-advised word from McBain would bring about the slipper thwacked on his backside in the headmaster's office; Hamish only ever seemed to get reprimands and the occasional detention after school.

The only place McBain could compete with Hamish was on the games field. He could run, as fast as any of them, with his long experience of legging it away from trouble, and was well coordinated, able to kick the football accurately and throw a rugby ball straight. But no one ever wanted him on their team. They'd already seen how losing the ball or coming second in a race could drive him to fury, and how quick he was to use his fists, and foul his opponents. He was always the last when it came to selections. Even Alf, the fat boy, was chosen before he was.

'You've come from Glasgow, haven't you?' enquired Hamish conversationally.

'Aye.'

'What's it like?'

''S all right.'

There was a pause while Hamish considered this. 'Are there lots of people there?'

McBain remembered the thronging streets of the city centre, and the packed houses of the slums. 'Aye. Lots.'

'I want to see the city one day. It must be grand. I've never been there but ma dad has and he said there's enormous buildings, like palaces, everywhere you go. He says those are things like colleges and law courts and museums – places that represent the people, he said. But in the cities, folk live in great houses, too, and there are parks and lakes and things. Beautiful places to sit and look about, he says.'

At this, McBain frowned. Even though he

longed to go back to Glasgow and see his friends and Jamie, he knew that beautiful it was not. Something in him stirred at the sea and the hills and the soft, rain-drenched colours of this place that had never been touched by the bricks and concrete of his home. 'Don't know about that. I've no seen any lakes.'

'Oh.' Hamish seemed disappointed. 'Well, maybe they were in a different part of the city to you. Ma dad said he saw a lake, with rowing boats and ducks and little kiddies throwing bread an' all.' They continued walking for a while before Hamish spoke again. 'You're living out at Fully's Bothy, aren't you?'

McBain didn't reply but stared at his feet as they walked along.

'Funny old place, that. Falling down, wasn't it? Have they fixed it up for you?'

'You ask a lot of questions, don't you?' snapped McBain. 'Why're you so interested in where I live?'

Hamish shrugged. 'Just trying to be friendly, ye know. There's no harm in that, is there? Ye don't know many folk round here yet, so I thought I'd be pally with ye, if ye like.'

He's testing me out, McBain thought. Perhaps he wants to find out if I could lick him or not. He slid a glance over at the bigger boy. I might be small and skinny, he told himself, but I can handle myself in a scrap. Last year I floored Willy Baldwin, and he's two years older'n me and a foot taller. I reckon I could win against this one if I had to. Something told him that Hamish would fight fair and not expect the kind of dirty tactics

99

that McBain had learned on the street. Shall I fight him now? he wondered. He had the vague sense that he would fight the other boy sometime, but that perhaps it was better to accept the offer of friendship for the moment.

'Aye,' said McBain at last. 'They mended the bothy for us.' His father had said someone had fixed the roof before they'd arrived, but it didn't look as though much more than that had been done. His mother was doing her best; there was always a fire burning in the grate and she'd stuffed rags into the holes around the windows and under the door, but it was still freezing cold and draughty there, even now, in the warm weather. He didn't want to tell Hamish Fraser that, though.

'What are you doing now?'

'Nothing. Walking.'

'Want to come out on my boat?' Hamish asked him casually.

His boat? He had a boat? McBain's ears pricked up with interest. Boats he liked. Boats he was interested in. But he had never been closer to one than seeing it from the place Hamish had called Macready's Point. He hadn't yet dared venture down to the docks, though he longed to.

'I was going down there anyway. I've got a mooring on the front. If you're not doing anything, you could come too,' Hamish continued. 'If you want to.'

Did he want to? Of course he wanted to. A trip down to the docks, the chance to get near a real boat, perhaps even to climb inside it and feel what it was like to be afloat – it was exactly what he wanted. McBain frowned. But why was Hamish Fraser being so nice to him? What did he hope to gain from it? Instantly defensive and suspicious, McBain was about to say no, that he didn't want to go and that he was on his way home, but he couldn't bring himself to turn down the opportunity he'd been longing for. He stood there, tongue-tied, unable to say anything.

Hamish pointed to a path back down towards the village that skirted round it and down to the docks. 'Come on,' he said, and sauntered off, his hands in his pockets.

McBain watched him go for a few moments, until the other boy's curly head was about to disappear below the horizon, and then scuttled after him as fast as he could.

Chapter Eight

'That's her,' said Hamish proudly as they approached the docks. 'She belongs to my pa really, but he let me have her as my own for my birthday. He said I was old enough to take care of her now, and to learn how to sail her. Isn't she a bonnie lass?'

They had climbed down the steep path to the village, then walked along the main road to the waterfront where steep stone steps led down into the docks. Fishing vessels were moored all along the four stone jetties, and further out little boats bobbed on the water among the buoys.

101

McBain looked where Hamish was pointing. It was a small boat, painted bright blue with the name *Jolly Jenny* on it in white letters. A slender white mast emerged from her middle section, with sails tightly furled up and roped to it. It wasn't much more than a dinghy, but still McBain felt violently jealous that Hamish should have such a beautiful little thing all of his own.

He followed Hamish down the jetty to where the *Jolly Jenny* was moored. The other boy clambered down the damp, sea-mossed stone steps with the ease of practice, pulled on the mooring rope and brought the boat alongside. Then he stepped aboard, keeping his balance when it swayed below him in the water.

'Come on,' he called, as he set about preparing the boat. 'There's a good breeze up, we should be able to have a fine turn out round the bay.' He looked up to where McBain was still standing at the top of the steps, watching him with an unreadable expression on his face. 'What's the matter? Don't you want to?' He grinned his cheerful grin and teased good-humouredly, 'You're not *scared*, are you?'

'No,' replied McBain quickly and sharply. 'Course I'm not.' He wasn't really scared, either. He was just fascinated by the little boat. Now that he was close up to it, and could see the kit inside it, the ropes and the bits and pieces that obviously all contributed to moving it along the water, he was interested to see how it worked.

'Come on down, then.'

'All right.' He stepped carefully down the slippery stone. When he got to the bottom, Hamish held out his hand to help him aboard. He almost refused it, but seeing how the boat was rocking in the water under Hamish's weight alone, he took it. The other boy grasped him tightly as he jumped forward and into the hull of the *Jolly Jenny*. The change from solid earth to floating wood was sudden and surprising and at once he felt as though he had lost his balance and that he must fall over. One of his arms began to windmill as he fought to stay upright, then Hamish grabbed him by the arm and helped him stabilise himself.

'OK?'

'Yep, fine.'

'Ye'll get used to the movement in no time. It always takes a while to find your balance at first. But ye'll be feeling it tonight when you're lyin' in bed, I guarantee it. You'll feel like you're still on board, swaying all over the place.'

McBain looked around the vessel. It was so pretty, he thought. The inside was painted white and had been well cared for. Across the boat were low benches that formed both seating and storage. The mast rose from the centre bench and below that was a wooden ridge that ran at right angles from it, dividing the boat in two along the middle. McBain watched as Hamish started to make ready.

'It's a good windy day so we won't need much sail,' Hamish explained. At the back of the boat was a locked chest that served as a seat by the rudder. He opened it with a key from his pocket and began taking out what he needed. 'We'll row out until we're clear of the other boats, then I can let her run. She's only a wee thing but there's still a skill to knowing how to sail her right. My pa's been teaching me all about it and he says I'm doing well. But this is just the beginning. As soon as I can sail *Jenny*, I'm going to move up to a bigger boat, with more sails. I'll need a crew. Maybe I can teach you and you could come and be my first mate.'

McBain sat himself down on one of the rough planks that formed the seats and said nothing.

'But that's not my real plan,' Hamish went on, seeming not to mind that his companion was so unresponsive. 'I want a fishing boat – a proper one with an engine and everything. A real beauty, that's what I want. Pa's not so keen. He doesn't mind me sailing and doing some fishing for fun, but he doesn't want me to be a fisherman for my whole life like he's been. He says it's too hard and too dangerous. Ma's got her heart set on me going to college in the town so I can get some qualifications and maybe be something smart – you know, a banker or a lawyer or someone in insurance or something. One of those people in a suit. I've told her that I don't want that but she won't listen. Ever since the headmaster put ideas in her head about me passing exams, she's gone crazy for it.' He shrugged. 'I'll keep her happy, I suppose. And then please myself.'

He sat down, pulled the oars out from where they were stowed and put them into the row-locks. He pushed the boat away from the stone jetty with one oar and once they were far enough away, he dipped both oars in the water and rowed them easily out of the shelter of the dock, skilfully manoeuvring the *Jolly Jenny* among the other boats. Once they were in more open water, Mc-Bain felt the wind spring up to life, buffeting him in the face and riffling through his hair. Hamish chattered on as he stowed the oars and began to make the sails ready, but half his words were lost on the wind. McBain caught some of them.

'...is the centreboard,' Hamish said, taking up a long, slightly curved piece of wood and inserting it into a slot that ran along the central ridge. 'It acts like a keel on a bigger boat...' He turned away and McBain lost the rest. He watched as Hamish pulled down a short stick-like mast that stuck out from the mainmast and attached a line to it that he ran back towards the rudder. 'That's the boom,' he explained. 'You'll need to watch when we gybe. She comes across fast sometimes. Right. I'm going to put up the mainsail now and then we can start.'

As soon as Hamish began to unfurl the mainsail, McBain became aware of the extraordinary power of the wind. It began to nudge and push at the little boat and it seemed suddenly like madness to think that the small flap of a sail that Hamish was carefully tying up could control that great force. Hamish did not seem worried, though, so McBain said nothing and just watched.

They were soon set up, the white sail filling with wind and flapping as the boat juddered on the water. Then Hamish settled himself by the tiller, with the boom line in one hand. He shouted to McBain about the direction of the wind and what this meant about their course, but McBain only heard a few words and what he did hear meant very little to him. Then, suddenly, with a few deft movements from Hamish, the wind appeared to be tamed and they began to move across the water, each smooth forward glide ending with a small bump as they hit a wave, rode over it and continued on their way.

The wind buffeted McBain's face as they flew along. He watched the foamy green sea swirling about the boat as they went and on impulse dipped his fingers into the icy water, feeling a shiver of delight across his shoulders as the cold bit at them and he became aware of the depths below them.

'Sit further up!' called Hamish. 'We need to balance the boat. The sea's stronger than it looked from the shore.'

McBain obediently shuffled up the seat and then turned back to look at the scene in front of him, the pale green sea darkening to grey as it disappeared into the hazy horizon. What lay beyond? If they kept going, where would they end up?

'Watch your head!' cried Hamish. 'We're turning about.'

McBain looked around to see Hamish moving the line that connected the boom to the mast.

'Duck, you great fool. We're gybing and the boom's coming over.'

McBain ducked his head quickly and the boom swung over sharply. Then the sail refilled with wind, the little boat turned and they set off on the opposite zigzag.

'What do you think?' called Hamish. His eyes were bright, his curls blown almost flat by the breeze. 'Do you like it?'

McBain grinned at him for the first time and tried to find the words to explain himself. 'Aye!' he called at last. 'It's grand.'

'Yep,' said Hamish, satisfied.

They sailed for half an hour or so, tacking back and forth with the boom swinging over every time they turned about. McBain watched as Hamish worked his mysterious magic on the little vessel, making it bounce smoothly across the waves and change direction whenever he wanted.

'We've gone far enough,' said Hamish at last. McBain had noticed that the wind was getting sharper and colder and that the far horizon was turning a silvery blue touched with peach. It would be getting dark soon. 'Time to turn back now.'

'No. Not yet,' said McBain beseechingly. The boys had hardly spoken on the trip; the wind was loud and Hamish had been concentrating on sailing the vessel. 'Can't we go on for a bit longer?'

Hamish shook his head. 'Nah. The wind's coming up stronger. We'd better not. Pa says I'm not to stay out when it gets rough. I'm not experienced enough yet.'

McBain felt his spirits sink. He'd be in enough trouble when he got home for being late and not saying where he was going. He could hardly bear to think about another night in that cold bothy, sharing a bed with Alec and feeling his little brother's chilly feet pressed against his shins. As Hamish made ready to turn about again, McBain looked down in the water. It was darkening as the sun went down but suddenly he saw, far below, the shadowy shape of a shoal of fish swooping along.

'Hey!' he cried, leaping up. 'Look at that! I can see fish!'

As he jumped up, his weight shifted and altered the balance of the boat. It swayed jerkily from side to side. McBain was startled by the sudden movement under his feet and began to lose his balance. He hopped from one foot to the other, trying to find it while his arms flailed about.

'Stop that, you bloody idiot!' shouted Hamish. 'You're toppling the boat. Stay still!'

'I can't.' McBain's knees felt like they were buckling under him. The more he thought about trying to get his balance, the more impossible it seemed as he rocked back and forth. His hands scrabbled at nothing as he tried to hold onto something. 'I c-c-c-an't!'

He reached out for whatever he could see and pulled at a line that hung from the mast.

'Don't do that!' Hamish leapt up to his feet and tried to snatch at McBain's hand. The movement set the boat rocking even more violently. Almost in slow motion, McBain felt the instability in his legs reach his torso and, with a sickening inevitability, his whole body began to sway beyond a point where he could regain control. He felt the rim of the hull against his legs as he fell backwards, gently and almost gracefully, and almost had time to think to himself *I'm going into the water and I can't swim* before the savage cold and darkness possessed him.

Under the water he was aware of the great

depth below him and the sudden weight of his clothes and shoes. His woollen jumper was instantly dense and sodden, pulling him down-wards into the darkness. He opened his eyes and saw a whirl of bubbles and green and grey water, and the shadow of the boat on the pale surface above.

What's happening? he wondered for a moment before he thought to himself *I'm drowning*, and the instant that thought formed itself, panic flooded through him. He opened his mouth to yell for help and found it full of ice-cold water. His arms and legs kicked and waved violently as he tried to force himself upwards towards the surface. A tightness gripped his chest and his ears were full of a roaring sound. *I'm going to die!*

A moment later he felt something trying to grab him but fear had made him crazed and he fought at it, imagining it was attempting to pull him further down to his certain death. Then a strong arm wrapped itself around his chest and he felt himself being yanked upwards through the water as he kicked out with his legs, desperate now for a breath. The next minute he broke through onto the surface with a gasp, and began to cough and choke as he spat out the bitter water.

Hamish had an arm round his chest, he realised, and with the other was pulling them through the water towards the boat, which was bobbing unmanned on the waves, bouncing away from them with every second that passed.

'Relax!' shouted the other boy. 'Let me swim, don't fight me!'

McBain tried to do as he was told but he was

still scared out of his wits and hardly aware of what he was doing. They made slow progress as the *Jolly Jenny* seemed to want to slip quietly away from them, but then a current caught her and spun her on the spot for a few minutes and it gave them the time they needed to gain on her. Hamish reached out and grabbed her side, and then pulled McBain up next to him.

'Here, hold onto this.' He put McBain's freezing hand onto the rim of the hull, then pulled himself round to the other side and a moment later he appeared, hoisting himself over the side with all his strength. Once he was in, he went to McBain and heaved him up, rolling him forward into the boat where he lay panting on the deck, sodden and shaking. Hamish fell back onto the seat by the tiller, gasping for breath.

'You bloody fool!' he shouted and then he appeared to be looking for a word bad enough to describe McBain. 'You *fucking* idiot. You nearly bloody killed us both. Lucky for you my pa told me what to do when a man goes overboard. You nearly died! We both nearly died. Christ!' Hamish flopped his head back, his eyes tightly shut and a grimace on his face as he contemplated what had nearly happened. 'God, look at us.'

McBain had been looking at him while he spoke but now he closed his eyes and pulled his knees up as close as he could to his chest. His whole body was shaking violently.

'We should have worn life jackets,' he heard the other boy say. 'Pa will kill me if he finds out. Shit. And you should have told me you can't swim!' The voice seemed to come from a long way away.

'God,' it said. 'Do you know what? I just saved your bloody life! Do you realise that? I saved your life.'

Chapter Nine

McBain scowled. He had a black eye and it hurt to frown but he had forgotten that. He stood alone in the playground, pressing himself up against the wire fence so that he could feel the diamond shapes biting into the skin of his leg below his shorts. Every moment since that awful afternoon had seemed full of misery and fury. When he'd got home that evening, wet and still shocked, he'd taken a walloping from his mother and then, later, a more severe beating from his father, which was why he had this black eye.

And now he was alone as usual over the lunch break but this time it was different. In general he was ignored by his classmates, but today he knew they were talking about him. He saw the sly glances as they walked past and the pointed fingers. He heard the giggles and the muttered taunts and he knew for sure that Hamish Fraser had told them what had happened. That they'd gone sailing and he'd turned gaga over a shoal of fish like a baby and fallen overboard and had to be rescued. It was obvious. Where once he was an outcast, now he was a fool as well, a laughing stock. As the day passed, his classmates got more confident, calling out names and laughing openly.

One boy mimed falling in a dead faint like a girl and then, with his eyes and cheeks goggling, pretended to drown. McBain was filled with a black fury.

He said nothing to Hamish Fraser. They had seen each other in class and Hamish had greeted him with a smile and 'How're ye feeling now? Did you get home all right?' but McBain had ignored him, pushing past to his desk where he sat down and stared intently at its pitted surface. He was too full of shame and wounded pride to utter a word to him, and as it became apparent that Hamish had told everyone what had happened, his embarrassment turned to anger and then to hatred.

How could Hamish do that? How could he make McBain into the class idiot like this? Hadn't he seen how hard it was for him already, how little anyone had wanted to be his friend? When Hamish had asked him sailing, for one sunny moment McBain had thought that he wanted to be his friend, that the popular Hamish Fraser had picked him to be a companion, a comrade. But it turned out that he had only done it so he could jeer and mock him all the better, just like the rest.

Well, he understood now. He wasn't going to be fooled like that again. When Hamish came up to him and said, 'Come on, now, don't be cross. It doesn't matter, you know. It could happen to anybody, everyone'll forget in a day or two. I didn't mean them to find out. I only told my brother when I got home soaked through – I needed his help to get some dry clothes without Ma seeing me. But he's a blabbermouth, the great lump,' McBain turned his back on him, clenched his teeth and muttered, 'Go away.'

'Ah, come on. You don't mean it. Didn't you enjoy it up till then?'

McBain refused to turn round or to answer. In the end, Hamish shrugged his shoulders and went away.

Later, when one of the smaller boys came up, poked his tongue out and called him a stupid name, McBain had turned on him snarling and gone daft with his fists, punching the other boy's face until his nose was a bloody mess and both his eyes were closed and swollen. He was pulled off by a teacher, who sent him to the head-master's office where he got another beating – six burning swipes with the cane. But he didn't care one bit. If he couldn't win this place over with charm, perhaps he could do it with fear instead. Making everyone terrified of him was a kind of power, after all, maybe even more effective than being well liked.

Hamish Fraser soon gave up all his attempts to be friendly to McBain.

A few days after the boating incident, McBain's mother had found a huge salmon wrapped in newspaper on the doorstep, an anonymous gift from some well-wisher.

'I don't usually hold wi' charity,' said his mother, looking at the long silvery body of the fish with delight, 'but I guess this is just a present from a neighbour who didn't have time to stop by.' She was so happy at the thought of being able to feed her children well for a couple of nights that she didn't want to wonder too hard about where it had come from, McBain could tell. But he knew who must have done it, and his heart burned. He didn't need pity or charity, and certainly not from Hamish Fraser.

The next day, he'd found his mother crying into the sink. It turned out his father had found the salmon, taken it to the pub and sold it. Then he had spent all the money on drink and returned home later reeking of alcohol. Worse than that, when McBain had got to school, Hamish had come up to him with a sympathetic look and muttered, 'Sorry to hear that your dad took that fish. My dad told me he sold it.'

'Don't know what you're talking about,' McBain shot back. 'We've got so much fish at home, it doesnae make any difference if we sell some or not. Anyway – I can't stand salmon.'

Every overture from Hamish was met with a cold shoulder. McBain couldn't help himself. He was too proud to accept his friendship now, after what had happened. They could never meet as equals; Hamish would always be the hero who had rescued him, and McBain the sap who had needed it. He'd sooner be on his own all his life than take that kind of bargain.

The school soon forgot that McBain had had his stupid accident, but they did remember his temper. They remembered how poor little Angus Johnson had had his nose broken and flattened by McBain – Mrs Johnson had taken wee Angus out to Fully's Bothy to show Mrs McBain what her son had done to her precious little angel and

114

that had occasioned yet another thorough going-over from McBain's father's fists – and they avoided him carefully. No one wanted to risk that kind of reaction and they were perfectly happy without his company.

Only one person wanted to be his friend. Greggy Macdonald was as unpopular as he was and the two of them eventually gravitated towards each other, drawn by their mutual loneliness rather than any common ground between them. As the time went by, they became a little team, united against the outside world that didn't seem to care whether they lived or died.

McBain was down by the docks when he saw her.

He hadn't been out to sea since that fateful afternoon with Hamish Fraser the previous summer. No one had offered to take him and he was far too proud to ask. But he had not lost his fascination with the sea or the little boats in the harbour. Sometimes he remembered the strange and awful panic that had filled him when the water had engulfed him, but mostly he recalled the exhilaration of being in the *Jolly Jenny* as she flew over the waves, her sail taut with the wind. It had been the most wonderful feeling in his life and he wanted to feel it again.

He was also enraptured by fishing. On summer mornings, he'd get up early when the rest of the family were asleep, and slip out of the bothy and down to the docks to watch the boats coming back with the day's catch. The salty, metallic smell of fresh fish would fill his nostrils as hundreds of slippery silver bodies were poured out of the boats

115

to be taken to the processing plant or off to shops and markets. That was what he wanted to do one day, he thought. But his father wouldn't hear of it, of course. If McBain wanted anything, he could be pretty sure that the rest of the world would do its very best to stand in his way. No, he was destined to be a mechanic, like his father. A good, safe trade that anyone could see would flourish in a world where more and more people owned a car.

He was down at the docks watching the boats being freshened up when he saw the girl. He was sitting on the edge of the stone jetty, kicking his legs over the side and idly dropping stones into the black oily water below, when he looked up. A figure was walking down the jetty towards him – a slim girl wearing a floating flowery dress. She was the most graceful creature he had ever seen and he couldn't take his eyes off her as she approached, one hand shielding her eyes from the sunshine so that she could look out over the water.

As she got closer, she took her hand away and revealed a pretty face surrounded by dark hair and dominated by a pair of large blue eyes. He gawped up at her, intimidated by such loveliness. Then she smiled at him, a bright friendly smile, and his stomach flipped over.

'Excuse me,' she said. Her voice was as soft and gentle as he would have expected from such a vision of sweetness. 'I'm looking for someone. Perhaps you can help me.'

'Um,' stammered McBain, feeling like a clumsy child. 'Sure, I'll do what I can. Who is it?'

'It's Hamish Fraser.'

Course it is, he thought bitterly. Now there's a surprise. 'Oh, well now. Let me see. He's usually on his boat, or near it. The *Jolly Jenny*. It's over there, moored on the jetty nearest the pub.'

'Thank you. Goodbye then.' The girl gave him another ravishing smile, turned on her heel and headed back to the road. As she went, he saw her pass Greggy Macdonald, who was idly kicking an old tin can in front of him as he walked. He stepped back to let the girl by him and then ambled along the jetty towards McBain.

'Who was that?' McBain called as soon as Greggy was in hailing distance.

'Who?' Greggy's lower lip hung down as usual so that his mouth gaped open, giving him a look of idiocy.

'That girl.'

'Girl?'

'Yes, you dunderhead. The girl who just walked by you.'

Greggy looked back over his shoulder and saw the figure in the floral dress making its way to the furthest jetty. 'Oh. Do you mean Mary Burns?'

'I guess I must, mustn't I? Who is she?'

'She's Hamish Fraser's steady. Everyone knows that. They've been going together for a year now.'

'A year?' That was almost as long as McBain had been living in the village. He hadn't noticed Hamish with any girlfriend – but then he tried to ignore him as much as possible.

'Aye. She's a grand girl. She lives along the coast with her father. He's a minister in the kirk along the way. It's a very proper family, they've

117

got a big house and a maid and a gardener an' all that. Everyone was surprised when Mr Burns let his precious daughter go walking out with Hamish Fraser, cos he's only a fisherman's son. She's educated. She goes to a ladies' school. She's not like us.'

'How old is she?' The girl had seemed like a woman to him, from some older, wiser generation.

'No more than Hamish, I'd guess. No more than us. Sixteen?'

McBain stared after her, squinting as hard as he could in the sunlight to spot the red of her dress, but she had vanished. She was the most beautiful thing in the world, he was certain of that. His heart rose at the very thought of her, as he recalled her soft musical voice talking to him. But his lip curled and the scowl that was almost a permanent fixture on his face returned when he remembered what she had asked. She belonged to someone else and of course, it had to be Hamish. The most popular, lively lad in school. And McBain's bitterest enemy.

I've got to see her again, he thought. *But how?*

'Hello there, Hamish.'

Hamish had pulled the *Jolly Jenny* up the beach and mounted her on two wooden planks so that he could sand down her hull. He looked up in surprise when he heard McBain's voice and pulled his arm across his forehead, wiping away the sweat and flattening his brown curls as he did so.

'Oh. Hello,' he said. He scrutinised McBain for a moment and then returned to rubbing at the

118

boat's bright blue hull. 'What can I do for you?'

'Just wondered if you'd like a hand, that's all.'

'Really?' Hamish's voice was cool.

'Aye. I'd like to help you if you don't mind.'

There was a long pause while Hamish considered this. 'I didn't think you were that keen to spend your time with me, if I'm honest. You've not had so much as a word for me for almost a year. I supposed I'd offended you after–'

'Forget about that,' cut in McBain quickly. 'I was ... well, I overreacted. I see that now. I'm sorry. It was stupid of me.'

Hamish frowned. 'You were a bit... Let's say you've not taken it well, have you? But if you want to forget all about it now, I'm willing. I never did see the point of making such a fuss about it anyhow.' He sat back on his heels. 'All right. Grab yourself that wee bit of sandpaper over there and see if you can get to work on the other side.'

'Sure.' McBain picked up the sandpaper eagerly and went round the boat to where Hamish had not yet started. 'Thanks, Hamish.'

'It's nothing,' said the other boy. He frowned again and then returned to his sanding.

Chapter Ten

The two figures were locked in a tight embrace in the shadows for several minutes before one pulled away.

'Don't, Hamish. Not like that,' said Mary softly, putting a hand on his shoulder to show him that he was being too enthusiastic.

'Oh, come on, Mary,' moaned Hamish. 'Don't you like it? Isn't it the best thing there is? Come on, let me kiss you.' He nuzzled into her soft white neck, kissing in the warm shallow at her collarbone and then taking his lips up towards her chin. He settled hungrily on her mouth again and she returned his kiss for a moment before pulling away again.

'No,' she said. 'We mustn't.'

'Don't you like it?' he repeated, hardly able to concentrate on what she was saying, he was so desperate to return to the warm sweetness of her mouth.

'Of course I do but ... it's not right. We shouldn't.'

'Come, on, now. Isn't it the most natural thing in the world? I respect you, Mary, you know that. I'm no rascal trying to have his way with you.' Hamish pulled back and looked earnestly into her iris-blue eyes. 'I love you, Mary.'

'I just...' She looked bewildered, as though she could hardly understand why she wasn't letting herself give in to the pleasure of his embrace. 'I know my parents wouldn't approve.'

'Ah, they've had their turn. How do you think they fell in love? Like this, of course. There's not much lookout for the human race if we're not allowed to do this.'

'We are, of course, but only when we're married.'

'How do we know if we're suited if we can't so much as kiss before we get married? And it's so sweet, Mary, isn't it? Isn't it the loveliest thing you know?' He put his lips on hers again and kissed her until her mouth opened under his and they kissed once more, their arms tightly wrapped about each other. Eventually she pulled away.

'Oh, oh dear,' she said weakly. 'We must stop now, Hamish, we really must. We'll be missed.'

'Five more minutes...?' he begged huskily. He was alight with desire for her but he would only be allowed his kisses, he knew that. He wanted to get as many as he could so he could remember them later when he was alone.

'Five?'

'Two then, two more minutes...'

'Hey there, you two,' said a rough voice.

Mary gasped, trying to get out of Hamish's embrace before they were seen. She blinked as the figure silhouetted against the light came nearer and she was able to make out who it was. 'Oh, it's you, McBain,' she said crossly. 'What do you think you're doing, scaring us like that?'

Hamish sighed. 'What do you want?'

'I've just come to warn you that Mary's mother is looking for her, that's all. She's noticed that she's not there.' McBain stood sulkily in the

121

shadows next to them. 'Just trying to do you a good turn, that's all.'

'All right,' said Hamish shortly. 'Thanks. We'll be in in a minute.' He was in no fit state to go inside. He needed a moment or two to calm down and restore himself to respectability.

'Thanks,' echoed Mary. 'We'll see you inside.'

McBain lingered for a moment before he turned on his heel and headed back into the hall. Mary dropped her head onto Hamish's shoulder. Now that their time was really up, she seemed to want to prolong it.

'Why is that boy always around you?' she asked, her voice slightly muffled by the lapel of Hamish's jacket. 'Wherever we go, he turns up. He's like your little shadow.'

'I know. He's all right, though. He's just a bit intense, that's all.'

'Really?' Mary turned her face up to his, her skin perfectly smooth and pale in the half-light. 'I don't know if I like him. He always has such an angry look in his eyes and sometimes I catch him staring at me in such a funny way, I wonder if he hates me. He's so skinny and small with that thatch of dark hair, he's like an urchin.'

'Don't be too harsh on him. He's pretty miserable at home, I can tell you that. His father's a bit too fond of the bottle and a bit too ready with his fists from what I can make out. McBain doesn't say much about it but you don't have to be too clever to work out what's happening when he turns up with black eyes and bruises and whip marks all over his skin.'

'Does he? Poor boy. I didn't realise. Oh dear, I

feel bad now. If I'd known how he was fixed, I'd have been a bit more charitable towards him.'

Hamish laughed. 'Oh Mary, you're the best girl there is. Always worrying about how you can help other people and whether you've been good enough or not. Your father doesn't have to worry about you, does he?'

'What do you mean?' Mary sounded wounded.

'I only mean that you're a good true Christian who always puts others first, just as your dad would want you to be, that's all.' Mary was silent, so he laughed and said, 'Hey, I'm only teasing, all right? Shall we go back in? I reckon I'm fit for polite society now.'

They held hands and strolled back up towards the entrance of the village hall, where an electric light burned, showing them the way.

'Why's he called McBain?' asked Mary idly as they went. 'That's not his real name, is it? What was he baptised?'

Hamish shrugged. 'I don't know. It's what he calls himself. He said to me once it was his name in the gang he belonged to back in Glasgow. Maybe he's homesick for the city.'

'Who'd want to live in a dreadful great city full of people you don't know? I like it here. It's safe here. We all know each other and watch out for each other. I've got no desire to go to where it's noisy and smoky and dangerous.'

'I don't know. It's exciting too, don't you think? All that bustle and activity, all those opportunities...' They reached the door of the hall and Hamish opened it. A burst of music and talk greeted them. The ceilidh was in full swing now and several sets of dancing couples were pounding up and down the hall. They walked in and McBain appeared beside them almost at once.

'Great, you're back,' he said.

'Where's my mother?' asked Mary, looking about. 'Oh, there she is. She's dancing with Mr McWhirter. I thought you said she was looking for me.'

McBain stared at her, his black eyes impassive. 'She was.'

'She knows you're safe with me,' said Hamish, with a smile. 'Come on, Mary. Do you want a drink or something?'

'Yes, I will have a drink,' she replied, still looking at McBain. 'Thanks, Hamish.'

He pulled her through the crowd, leaving McBain staring after them before he started to elbow his way through in their wake.

'Will he never leave us alone?' asked Mary, exasperated, as she noticed him coming up behind them. 'I tell you, he's obsessed.'

'He's harmless,' soothed Hamish. 'He's jealous, that's all. He hardly ever leaves my side, you know. I think I'm some kind of hero to him, probably because of the time I pulled him out of the water. He wants me all to himself. That or he's got his heart fixed on my boat.' He laughed.

'Maybe,' said Mary, throwing another look over her shoulder.

'Forget about him. We'll have a drink and then a dance. He can't follow us there. They're still only letting two people form a couple, you know.'

Hamish had got used to McBain and though he never exactly warmed to him, he had learned to put up with the constant presence of the smaller boy. Ever since the day he had come up wanting to help freshen the boat, McBain had stuck by him like a little disciple. It was strange because Hamish had long assumed that they wouldn't be friends, since the time when the idiot had toppled overboard. The kid had obviously been so embarrassed that he hadn't been able to bear it, which Hamish thought was something of an overreaction. After all, everybody took an unplanned dip at some point in their lives. It was just that most people had the sense to learn to swim before they went out to sea in a small boat without wearing a life jacket.

Hamish wasn't sure why he'd even bothered with the boy in the first place. Everyone else seemed to have the good sense to leave him well alone and give him a wide berth. But something in Hamish had felt sorry for him. He was aware of his own good fortune: his pa and ma were kind and loved him, provided him with as good a life as they could, and he knew he was happy. Something in McBain's eyes had triggered a response. It was as though he had realised that there, but for the grace of God, he went. If he hadn't been blessed with his family, his charm, his good looks and his ability to win hearts, he could have been like this boy: shut off and frightened and alone. Hamish knew that the marks and bruises McBain wore to school didn't come from rough and tumble the way his did. They weren't from climbing trees or falling off walls. It was all too clear what the real reason for them was. Hamish's father and mother had talked about McBain's father with disapproval – he was often to be seen in the pub, trying to borrow money he could never repay or sell bits and pieces that had come from goodness only knew where. Then the village would hear him singing and swaying on his way back home, drunk as a lord. 'That poor wife of his,' said Hamish's mother. 'How does she manage to bring up a pack of children with a husband like that?'

Hamish pitied McBain. It was hard to imagine his own father inflicting that kind of violence on him. He'd had a whack with a slipper when he was little but hardly enough to hurt him, and now that he was virtually grown up, his father treated him like a man and spoke to him almost like an equal. He valued that, and the trust his father had in him. Not many boys were given their own sailing dinghy to look after, and it was a measure of his father's confidence that Hamish would act sensibly and carefully that he'd allowed the boy to have the *Jolly Jenny*. Hamish never wanted to disappoint him if he could possibly help it. That was why he was so relieved that he had got himself and McBain out of that dreadful scrape that day.

The music ended, and the breathless, flushed dancers came to a halt and then broke up their formations as they made their way to the refreshment tables for a drink. A moment later the fiddle player called up the next dance.

'Come on, Mary. They're making up sets for the Duke of Perth. Do you fancy it?'

Mary smiled at him, her pink lips curving upwards so that the adorable dimples appeared

126

in her cheeks. Sometimes she was so pretty that Hamish could hardly breathe when he looked at her. Her eyes were so incredibly blue, framed with those long, dark swooping lashes, and her skin so soft and white. She was more beautiful than any film star he'd ever seen. He could hardly believe that she wanted to be with him. But she did, and judging by the way she returned his kisses and sighed with such longing when they had to stop, she felt the way he did, the same desperate desire to touch skin and taste the other's mouth.

They took up their positions in their set, the fiddle player struck up the opening notes, the pipes took up the tune and the dance began. Soon the excitement and energy of the movement took over, and they whirled along, enjoying the sensation of being a part of a well-oiled machine as the couples swung, turned and set, one outstretched hand finding another in perfect time. Mary's cheeks were soon flushed and her eyes sparkling and Hamish was breathless as he turned her about, lifting her almost off her feet. This was one of his favourite reels and he whooped as they set to each other.

The music finished with a burst and everybody clapped the band. Hamish laughed with pleasure. 'Ah, thanks, Mary, that was grand.'

'Oh, now, thanks yourself. I enjoyed it.' She curtsied prettily and giggled back. Her soft voice, with its accent just a little more refined than his own, always thrilled him.

'Mary! Come on, we're going now.' Mary's mother appeared as if from nowhere. 'Good evening, Hamish.'

'Hello there, Mrs Burns.' Hamish grinned at her with the full force of his charm. He knew Mrs Burns didn't entirely approve of him. She no doubt wanted better for her precious daughter, whose beauty and demureness could surely take her far. There was even talk that she hoped Mary might go further with her education, perhaps to Edinburgh to the university. A fisherman's son from the local village probably wasn't what she'd dreamed when she'd imagined Mary's future husband, even if he was good-looking and sweet-natured, so Hamish was determined to do his best to make her like him. 'Have you had a nice evening?' he asked politely.

She thawed a little. 'Well, yes, we have. It's always enjoyable to come to the Kinlochvegan ceilidh. I hope you youngsters have had a good time.'

'Oh, yes, thank you, Mrs Burns.' Hamish thought about pulling Mary's soft body close to his in the darkness, and smiled again.

'We'll see you again soon, I'm sure. Come along, Mary.'

'Yes, Mother,' Mary said dutifully and blew a kiss to Hamish behind her mother's back as she followed her.

Hamish watched her go as she vanished into the crowd. Then he felt a tug on his jacket.

'Hamish, Hamish. Come outside.'

It was McBain. Hamish felt a surge of irritation. For a minute he'd managed to forget about his little shadow. 'What?'

'Come outside. I've got some whisky.' McBain's dark eyes shone as he patted his pocket.

'I'm thinking I'll go home now.'

'I'll walk with you. We can have a wee tot on the way back.'

'All right then. Come on. I don't feel much like staying now that Mary's gone.'

A few minutes later, the boys were making their way down the steep road back to the main village street. The nights were light until late at this time of year, and long accustomed to walking in the gloom, they could see quite well. The last strains of the band followed them down the hill.

'I should think you'd be wary of that stuff,' said Hamish as McBain pressed a slim bottle into his hand.

'What do you mean?'

'With your daddy, and everything.'

'What do you mean?'

'Well – everyone knows he likes a drop or two.'

There was silence apart from their shoes slapping on the road. Ah, he's always so touchy, thought Hamish. I've never met someone so proud, who's got so little to be proud about. What is it with this lad? I don't understand it one bit.

'It's true,' said McBain at last, his voice gruff. Hamish was surprised to hear him admit it. 'He does like drink. And it does none of us any good. My ma hates it. That's why she goes to kirk, I guess, and why she's taken the pledge. I don't know why I drink it myself. Helps me forget, I suppose. You know that way it does, when you've had a bit and the burn has gone and it's just getting to feel nice and warm and something in you feels like it doesn't care about anything...'

'Aye. But it does no good in the long run, does

it?' Hamish lifted the bottle and took a strong sip himself. Then he smacked his lips as he passed it back to McBain. 'But it's part of a Scotsman's history, isn't it? It's our heritage. We wouldn't be who we are without it.'

'My ma would hate it if she knew. I saw her once when Jamie came home drunk. She hit him with her fists and then she cried like her heart was breaking. She made me promise not to be a drunk when I was only wee, so I did, of course, because I didn't know what she was asking. Now I do. But do ye know what's funny? Something in me does it just because my ma hates it so much. I can't help feeling angry with her even though she breaks her back lookin' after us all.'

Perhaps it's the darkness, thought Hamish, surprised.

He'd never heard McBain talk like this before and the only reason he could think of was that they couldn't see each other's faces very clearly. Or perhaps it was the whisky itself.

'Do you hate your father, Hamish?' McBain asked abruptly.

'Hate my pa? Of course not. He's a fine man.'

'I hate mine. With all my heart. He's a beast.'

'He's not been good to you, we all know that. But he gives you a home and food on the table.'

'You've not seen our home, have you? Or what gets put on the table in front of my wee brothers and sister. You might not think so much of that if you had. I've seen my little sister crying with hunger, and I've seen my mother give herself nothing so that she can put more on our plates. Being poor stinks, Hamish, and it stinks even more when someone is stealing the money that should go to the family. I'm not going to be poor, I can promise you that. I don't care how I do it but there's no way I'm going to live like my parents, scraping every penny and feeding muck to my bairns. No way.'

There was a pause. Hamish said, 'You've decided you don't want to live like your dad. That's a fine thing.'

'I can make something of myself here. When we first got here, I hated this place. But now I know I can do things here I couldn't have dreamed of in Glasgow. I'd be just like my brother Jamie if I'd stayed. But here... This is the right place for me, I can feel it.'

'This old place?' Hamish gave a low laugh.

'Aye.' McBain took another swig of whisky and passed the bottle to Hamish. 'What about you? Are you gonna stay here?'

Hamish lifted it to his mouth and looked up to the vast, dark blue sky that stretched away above them, and the peppering of bright stars within it. He swallowed the whisky and said, 'There's got to be a bigger life than the one we live here. It's not that I don't love the place. And I want to get married, have a family. Get that boat I've always wanted. Be a fisherman, like my pa. He's never had to answer to anyone but himself and he might not be a rich man but he's a straight-backed one.' He pressed the whisky bottle back into McBain's hands. 'But before that happens, I want to see the world a bit. Look at that sky. Imagine, it's the same sky over the deserts of Africa and the grasslands and plains, and all the cities on the planet. I want to see Paris and Cairo and Rome and New York, and I don't know where else. I think the same every time I take the boat out and wonder if the water that's under me has come down from the Arctic, melted off a glacier or something. I've got an itch to get away from here for a while and taste a bit of what's on offer. After that, I'll be happy to come back and settle down.'

'And marry Mary?'

Hamish laughed softly. 'Well, would you blame me?'

There was a pause before McBain replied. 'No. She's a grand girl.'

'I know. We'll be happy, Mary and me. Do you want to come to our wedding, McBain? You can if you like. It'll be a happy day. I'll let you dance with the bride.'

They walked on in the darkness for a while until their ways came to part. They stood for a moment at the fork in the road. Hamish could see the bright light of the gas lanterns illuminating the windows of his cottage. His parents were waiting up for him. Suddenly he was eager to be in the warmth of home, where his mother would have something hot for him and his father would be smoking his pipe and reading the newspapers, as he liked to do before going to bed.

'Good night then. I don't envy you your walk. It's a way to Fully's Bothy from here.'

McBain shrugged. 'I'm used to it.' He took another swig from his bottle. 'I tell you what, Hamish. I'll dance at your wedding – and you dance at mine. All right?'

'Sure.'

'Promise me, now.'

'All right. I promise.'

'Good. Shake on it?' He held out his hand and Hamish took it. They shook vigorously.

'Night, Hamish.' McBain turned on his heel and soon vanished into the blackness. Hamish headed for the welcome lights of home.

Chapter Eleven

'What qualifications have you got, young man?' asked the registrar. He was wearing a dark blue uniform and his pen was poised. 'Have you taken your Highers? How old are you?'

'I'm fifteen,' replied Hamish. He felt stiff and strange in his best clothes, and his curls had been wetted and then brushed until they lay flat against his head. 'I've not sat my Highers. I can read and write though, and do mathematics. I've got a certificate from my school and the head-master has written me a recommendation.'

He put the envelope containing his reference on the table between them. The registrar looked at it with a frown and ignored it.

'What nautical experience have you got?'

'I can sail a boat. I've got my own little sailing dinghy. I know about knots and sails, wind directions and a bit of navigation.'

The registrar snorted. 'I don't think that will be much good, Mr...' he consulted the paper in front of him '...Fraser. I think you'll find that some fisherman's knots and wet-finger-in-the-wind methods of navigating and judging speeds are all a bit below the standards we require here. If you were to join the Leith Nautical College, you'd have to start from the very beginning, like everyone else, unlearning the scraps you know and commencing afresh. Do you know what the curriculum here is?'

'Well–' Hamish grinned the charming smile that always won people over. 'You'd teach me how to be an officer in the Merchant Navy, wouldn't you?'

The smile didn't seem to be working very well today. The registrar's shoulders stiffened even further, if that was possible.

'Yes, we would. And that privileged position requires work and dedication such as, I can assure you, you've never known before.' The registrar's tight Edinburgh accent became even more pronounced. He clearly did not think much of cocky young lads from fishing villages on the coast who had dreams of parading on the great steamers of the Merchant Navy in an officer's uniform. 'We have three courses here. One is for boys between fifteen and seventeen who want to become cadets, with a view to being officers. The other courses are for catering and deck boys. I take it you'd be interested in the first one.'

Hamish nodded.

'Very well. If you were offered a place, you first would join our training ship, the TS *Dolphin*. You'd live on board her, experiencing the kind of life you'd have in the navy, and learning everything there is to know about how to manage her.

Rope splicing, knots, weather, cleaning, maintenance ... you name it, you will know it like the back of your hand by the end of your sixteen weeks on board. Then you'd progress to the college itself, where you would study mathematics – that is to say, geometry, trigonometry, algebra including quadratic equations, surds and graphs, and mathematical theory and the use of logarithms.'

Hamish's grin began to fade.

'Then there's navigation and nautical astronomy, including chartwork, the correction of courses, methods of fixing position and allowance for tide. The solar system, the celestial sphere and problems in longitude, latitude, azimuth and amplitude.' The registrar was beginning to enjoy himself now, as Hamish's face dropped further. 'General science, including study of modern navigational aids, elementary meteorology and use of instruments. Then there is study of the ship itself: construction and stability, engines, boilers, coal consumption and speed. Marine regulations, the rules of the road, signals and communication by lights. Manual skills including ropes, boating – you might know a little about that already, I grant you – life-saving and swimming. Morse code and semaphore, of course. And we also require that you master good English and the ability to write an essay.' The registrar smiled a tight, unfriendly little smile. 'Is that enough for you?'

'How long would I be doing all that?' asked Hamish, his spirits plummeting.

'The course, including your stint on the TS *Dolphin*, would last forty-four weeks. After that, assuming you passed the course – and you would have to take exams in all the subjects I've mentioned and pass them with not less than sixty per cent in each one, as well as have at least seventy-five per cent attendance – you would then be a cadet, and you could begin your next stint of training on board a steamer belonging to one of the great companies here in Leith. The Ben Line is very popular.'

'All that and I would still only be at the start of it all? It sounds like I'd know enough to be a captain!' exclaimed Hamish. This wasn't what he had dreamed of at all. He'd wanted to leave school and start living his dreams of seeing the world and travelling, but from what he'd heard, he was looking at spending over a year at the college, once he took into account the holidays, before he so much as left the docks.

'Perhaps you've underestimated what it means to take to the sea as your career. It's not for the faint-hearted, but only for those who have the dedication, courage and spirit to see it through.'

'Oh, I've got all that, don't you worry. But I need to think about it. When do I have to let you know?'

'Application forms must be in within a fortnight,' replied the registrar. 'Any more questions?'

'No. No thank you.' Hamish stood up. 'I'll take a form, and be on my way.'

Suddenly the registrar seemed to soften. 'Listen, lad. You've got all the impetuousness of youth, that's plain. I see it all the time. You want it all to happen now, at once, and a year and a half or so training seems like a long time. But it'd go in a flash and you'd have skills that would last all your life, that could provide a good career for you. What else have you got, after all? A job as a fisherman? Is that all you want? Get yourself a place at the college, knuckle down and a bright future awaits you: a good job with prospects to go far, a good wage and a pension. What more do you want?'

A pension, thought Hamish, scornfully. What would I be needing with one of those? He could hardly imagine being twenty-five, let alone old enough to need a pension. That future was so hazy and far away it didn't merit thinking about.

'That's very kind of you. I do appreciate it. I'll go and think about it.' He picked up his cap, made a little bow, and headed for the door.

He wandered about Leith while he decided what to do. His father had brought him up to Edinburgh that morning. They'd set off at the crack of dawn and got to the city when the day was well under way. He'd only been to Edinburgh once before, and it seemed like a momentous journey to make. The city stirred him, with its stark and beautiful castle sitting high on the hill, the tall houses, winding, climbing alleyways and cobbled streets. His mother had brought him just before Christmas last year, and he had seen the shops dressed in their finery and the sparkle of lights everywhere, the bustle of Princes Street as people did their shopping. The city had ever since been touched with a special magic for him, even if the wind that came cutting down the hills brought tears to his eyes and numbed his fingers.

He'd caught his bus to Leith alone, which had

felt like quite an adventure even if it wasn't so far from the city centre. It had taken him to Commercial Street, where the college was to be found on the edge of the Old Docks. He'd been in too much of a hurry to notice much as he arrived, but now he stopped and looked about him.

He gazed out to sea but blocking his view, for as far as he could see, were huge docks. The harbour at home in Kinlochvegan suddenly seemed to him to be little more than a toy dock, where laughably small fishing boats wobbled in the water as they were unloaded. Here, everything was on a much more magnificent scale. Even though Leith itself had the broken-down and seedy air of a place past its best and now on the decline, there was something about those huge hulks that he could see in their berths, row upon row of them: enormous metal ships, their hulls marked with long smears of rust, mould and the passage of the waters they'd steamed through. Above them towered the machinery that winched the loads on and off the great sea beasts, cranes and hoists that stretched into the air above the long lines of warehouses that bordered the docks.

Hamish wandered along Commercial Street and then followed the dock wall round until he came to a large gate, obviously an entrance to the docks, manned by two policemen. He stopped a little way off for a moment and wondered what to do. Then, drawn by the sounds of the docks and shipyards beyond, he walked down towards them.

'What do you want?' asked one of the policemen as he approached. He looked at Hamish suspiciously. 'How old are you?'

It was the usual thing. No one knew if he was a child or a man. It was frustrating. Couldn't they see that he was almost grown up? His mother had made him wear long trousers today and he felt like a real man.

'No unaccompanied children,' said the policeman severely. 'This is not a playground, you know.'

'I'm from the Nautical College,' said Hamish in the most adult voice he could summon. 'I've been sent with a message for the *Dolphin*.'

The policemen looked at each other and then at Hamish. They appeared to think that he was not really worth their trouble. One of them cocked his head over his shoulder. 'Go on then,' he said. 'You'll know where it is.'

Hamish walked past them sedately, nodding politely as he went even though he had an inbuilt distrust of the police, like all the boys he knew. The moment he was past, he grinned to himself, breathed in the salty air and set off to see what he could see.

The docks seemed to stretch on for ever, big square enclosures of water providing berths for ships of all shapes and types, the water level controlled by lock gates. Alongside them on the wharves were long wooden buildings – the warehouses and workshops – and beyond them the shipping yards. Hamish knew that steamboats and freight carriers were built around here, and that great merchant shipping lines had headquarters in Leith. The place felt in a bustle of activity as he made his way along the wharves and around the moorings, finding his way down small roads and over the little footways that spanned the lock gates. He headed towards the largest docks. Everywhere he could see men working – unloading the massive ships, swarming over them as they went about the endless routines of scrubbing down, checking, reassembling and repairing every part of them. He could see sailors in their white uniforms, and a line of cadets practising their whistle commands. Another line of boys in uniforms of dark blue trousers, short jackets and white shirts and ties came marching past – perhaps boys who were even now doing their stint on the TS *Dolphin* and learning how to go to sea.

What shall I do? wondered Hamish. He strolled along the side of one of the docks, looking into the dirty, oily water that rippled gently around the hulls of the steamers. Should I go to the college? Learn to be an officer?

Gazing about at the docks, he tried to imagine living here, first on board the *Dolphin* and then at the college, for almost two years. That wasn't what he'd dreamed of when he lay in bed. In his mind, he'd seen warm seas and strange lands. He hadn't foreseen spending his days and nights around here, without even the beauty of the Kinlochvegan harbour to brighten his days. And that curriculum! It sounded like the worst of his days at school – all that arithmetic and science. Though I'd like to learn Morse and about the boilers and how to read the skies, he conceded to himself. He thought of what that registrar had said – he would have to study the celestial spheres. Didn't that sound romantic? Didn't that have the flavour of his dreams?

140

But he knew what it would be like in practice: books and writing and tests and long hours spent in stuffy classrooms where he could hardly breathe.

'No,' he said out loud. 'It's not for me. I'll just forget about seeing the world and go home. Be a fisherman, which is what I want to do anyway.'

'Hey! Chase yerself!' A rough voice from behind him made him jump. 'Are ye crazy, jabbering away to yerself? Come on, now, move it!'

Hamish turned to see a bulky man with a large sack on his shoulder. He hopped quickly out of the way and the man staggered past him to a pallet at the side of the dock and slapped the sack down on top of it. Then he wiped his brow, turned and started to head back in the direction he'd come from. He disappeared into a shed and a few minutes later emerged loaded down with an identical sack. Hamish stood quietly by and watched him go about his routine another couple of times. As the man passed him again on his way back to the shed, he frowned at Hamish.

'What ye doin' here, kid? Where are ye supposed to be? Are ye awa wit' the fairies or something?'

'I'm visiting. I've just been to the Nautical College.'

'Oh aye? Vairy fancy. You gonna be an officer, are ye?' The man did not appear to be much impressed.

'Dunno.' Hamish took off his cap and ran his hand through his hair, fluffing up the curls that had stuck to his scalp and made him hot. 'I wanna go to sea. I don't want to be studying in

141

the college for years on end.'

'Nancy boys!' said the man dismissively and unconsciously flexed his muscles. 'Nevair done a hard day's work in their lives, that's for sure. Ye want to go to sea, do ye?'

'Aye.'

'Then ye should talk to my head man. He's always lookin' for good strong boys to join our company.' He motioned to the shed behind him. Hamish saw that it was connected to a larger warehouse that had a painted board outside it. It read: *Brewster's Shipping. Cargo and Dry Goods. Far East, Continent, America.* 'Come on, I'll take you in.'

Why not? thought Hamish as he followed the big man towards the warehouse. In the musty darkness inside it he could see stacks of chests and containers, all stamped and stickered with their origin, contents and place of destination. Piles of sacks lay on wooden pallets. Men were moving about inside, shifting the great mounds of goods all over the shed, with seemingly no rhyme nor reason to their actions.

'Come on,' said his guide. 'Yer man's upstairs.' He led Hamish up a flight of rickety steps to an office that had been built into the rafters of the warehouse. It was a small, dusty room, piled high with papers and folders. A woman sat in one corner at a desk and she was typing away as fast as she could, peering over the top of her glasses at a folder on her desk as she did so. Behind another desk, shuffling papers and frowning, sat a small man with a great dome of a bald head and thick black brows. He seemed very caught up in

142

whatever it was he was doing.

'Boss...' said Hamish's new friend hesitantly.

'What is it? Can't you see I'm busy?' The small man didn't even look up.

'I've found a boy outside...'

'Trespasser?' asked the boss sharply, glaring up at Hamish. 'Troublemaker, eh? Do you know what I do with troublemakers? With anyone who dares waste my money by damaging our goods? Because believe me, you'll regret it if you ever do find out.'

'Oh no, boss, it was nothing like that. He wants to be a sailor. Wants to work in shipping.'

'Does he now?' The little man's dark eyes glimmered at this and he got up. He stood at around five feet tall, Hamish guessed, but there was the strength and power about him of a man much bigger. 'Want to go to sea, huh?'

'Aye.' Hamish nodded. He fingered his cap nervously and wondered how he'd got into this situation.

'Want to work for me, do you?'

'Well ... I...'

'What experience have you got?'

'I can sail a small boat. And navigate a bit. I'm from a fishing village on the west coast and I've grown up round the water. My pa's taught me a lot. He's a grand fisherman and there's nothing he doesn't know about the sea.'

'I'm sure. Hmm. A bit of sea-going, eh? Then you'd have to sign up with us for at least three years. Four probably.' The little man stared at him thoughtfully for a moment. 'It's not an easy life, you know that, don't you? But I'll give you an education of the kind you won't get anywhere else. And you'll see the world, boy. That's what you want, isn't it?' He stepped out from behind his desk and dropped his voice so that he was talking almost hypnotically. 'You want to see all the cities and lands there are – the exotic markets, the bazaars, the beautiful women. I know – I was just like you once, and look at me. I run this place now. This is my company. Oh, I grant you, we're not as big as the other lines – the Ben Line, and some of the others. We've got a fleet of only half a dozen ships. But we move treasure across the world, and we see it all, from the blistering heat of the equator to the icebergs of the north Atlantic. We stop at every major port known to man. That's what you want, isn't it?'

Hamish's imagination was alight. He saw himself on the deck of a ship as it steamed into a harbour. Exotic birds flew overhead, the sun blazed down from a perfect blue sky and shimmered on the water while smiling brown-skinned men and women in bright clothes greeted them as they drew near, offering gifts of coconuts and strange fruits. He'd seen it in the films and newsreels, he was sure.

'Oh, yes,' he breathed. 'That's what I want.'

'Good. I like your spirit, boy. I like to see a young fella with independence of mind and a yearning for adventure. You could join us, you know. We need boys like you. Become a deck boy with Brewster's and we'll take you with us. Pay you a good wage and train you up with anything you need to know. You'll learn it all quicker and better than you ever would in some bloody college. That was what you were thinking of, weren't you?' He made a scornful face, sneering at the very thought. 'Forget it, lad. Come wi' us. You'll see it all right away and the chance is there to make something of yerself if you can. It's not a soft life, don't think that. Going to sea is bloody hard and sometimes you'll sweat blood and wish you'd never been born. But it's a good life. Have you got it? Have you got what it takes?'

'Aye,' breathed Hamish, his eyes wide. 'It's what I've dreamed of.'

'Good.' The man smiled. 'Then welcome to Brewster's. We can sign you up right away.'

'You did *what?*' asked his father, his expression torn between astonishment and horror.

'I signed up to Brewster's Shipping Company,' said Hamish proudly. He'd waited until they got back home to Kinlochvegan before he told his parents about his rash decision. 'I'm going to be a deck boy. I start next month.'

His parents looked at each other as the announcement began to sink in.

'How long will you be gone?' asked his mother.

'Four years.' It hadn't seemed that much when Old Man Brewster had explained to him how long he was committing himself to the company. Now, as the realisation of how long he'd be gone spread over his mother's face, it seemed like a different proposition altogether. Four years? Why, he'd be nearly twenty. A sudden pang of doubt assailed him. He'd been so sure as he'd stood in that dirty, messy office that this was what he wanted for his future. He'd felt so clever that he'd outwitted the registrar at the college and got himself a life at sea without having to sit those exams.

But I can't have made a mistake! I haven't made a mistake. It's what I want. And that's that.

Chapter Twelve

'Hamish...' Mary's eyes had filled with tears, their blue taking on a greenish hue, like the sea after rain. 'I just can't believe it.'

'Ah, come on, Mary. You didn't think I could stay here my whole life, did you? I always said I'd have to go away. I need to see more than this little place, and I've been offered my big chance. You understand that, don't you?' He interlaced his fingers with hers. She looked away, out over the hillside and far off into the distance. The breeze lifted her soft black hair and he resisted the urge to put his hand out and smooth it down. 'It won't be for ever. I'll come back, you know I will.'

'I thought you loved me,' she whispered, still looking far out to sea. 'How can you leave me like this if you love me?'

'But that's just the thing!' He was eager to explain. 'Don't you understand? I'm doing this so we can be together our whole lives! If I don't travel a bit, then I'm only going to have the itch, and who knows but when I'm an old man – thirty-five, or something – I'll have to pack up and go on out of here. If I do it now, while I'm

146

young, I'll come back to you, Mary, and set up my fishing boat and we'll get married and have our babies.' His heart felt so full as he watched her beautiful mouth tremble and her face cloud with grief. He had never loved her so much, or felt so racked with desire for her as he did now, sitting with her on this hillside in the fresh summer wind.

'Four years!' A tear now escaped the great pools welling in her eyes and slid down her face. 'It might as well be for ever.'

'Ah, it will go in a flash. And you could maybe go to the college, like you were thinking, and get an education. I think it would be a fine thing for you, Mary, and then you could teach our babies later. You do still want to have babies with me, don't you?'

She turned to look him full in the face, her eyes hurt. 'How can you ask me that? You know how much I love you. That's why it's so hard for me to accept that you want to go away and leave me.'

'I don't *want* to...' He struggled to explain. 'I *have* to.'

'Come on, Hamish. Of course you want to. I'm not stupid. And I do understand. But it's such a long time! And what if something happens to you? What if you meet some other woman and decide you love her best?'

'That will never happen,' Hamish said adamantly. 'You're the only one for me, Mary. What we have is special. No one has ever felt like us, I know it. That's why I can go, don't you see? Because I know we'll be all right. Don't bother your head about other women. That'll never happen, I can promise you that. I could never love anyone like I love you.'

He leaned over and put his lips on hers. Their softness and warmth fired him up immediately and he felt almost wild for her. She opened her mouth to him and he pushed her back gently onto the grassy hillside until they were lying side by side, kissing passionately. He tried to push himself against her, and ran his hand along the length of her thigh, into the dip of her waist and up along her side. He longed to pull open her dress and put his hand inside it. He'd dreamt of what her breasts would feel like and he yearned to touch them. Perhaps, now he was going, she would let him...

He pushed against her again, ramming his groin against her hip, trying to soothe the extraordinary itch he felt for her, but it was useless. There was something else he needed, he knew that, but there was no way she would let him do anything more than kiss her. Once, when they had been kissing in the back of his father's truck, he had pulled her hand towards the unbearable heat, the one he could easily relieve himself when he needed to, but she had snatched it away. Now she wasn't being so stand-offish, and he wondered for a moment if this time she would do what he needed. Just the thought of it fired him up even more.

'Oh, Mary,' he grunted. 'You're so beautiful, ah, God, I love you...' His fingers sought the buttons of her dress and fumbled them apart. In a moment he'd found the soft mound of her chest and ran his fingertips over it, trying to slide them under the tight brassiere she was wearing.

Suddenly reckless, he shoved his other hand up her skirt and started pulling at her underwear, hoping to get access somehow to the most mysterious part of her. As soon as she felt this Mary pulled away, making sounds of protest, though she could not speak with the force of Hamish's kissing. She put her hand against his chest and tried to push him away. Breaking free, she cried, 'Hamish, what are you doing?'

He was panting and his eyes were wild, he knew that. 'Mary,' he said hoarsely. 'Come on, don't tease me so.'

'Tease you?'

'I didn't mean that,' he said quickly, seeing he'd offended her. His only thought was to return as quickly as he could to the sweet warmth of her mouth and the delight of feeling her soft body. 'But ... I love you so much!' It was the only way he could think of to express his desire for her.

'If you loved me, you wouldn't try and do those things to me,' she said, pulling her dress back together. She sat up.

'But don't you like it?'

She looked pained, clearly trying to reconcile the physical longing that possessed her as strongly as it did Hamish with the mode of behaviour, the standards of conduct, that she'd been taught. 'It doesn't matter if I like it or not, Hamish, you know it's wrong.'

Hamish fought with his disappointment. 'All right then.'

They sat in silence for a few minutes, then Mary broke it, saying quietly, 'You're the one who's going away. You're the one who's leaving. And you want to take advantage of me before you go.'

'You make it sound ... all harsh and cold. It's not like that. I'll come back to you, you know I will.' He reached out for her and she let him put his arm around her, but their previous intimacy was gone.

'Four years,' she said softly. 'Imagine what can happen in four years.'

'I won't change.'

'Perhaps not. But what about me?'

Hamish was aghast. 'What do you mean? Are you saying you could forget me? Don't you love me?'

She turned her gaze on him again, pulled her knees up under her chin and rested her head on them. 'You know I do. And I'd never stop. But you seem so sure that you'll come back and that everything will be all right. Sometimes I worry about what will happen, about the future and how we don't know anything about it. You might get lost at sea, or I might get sick. We might never see each other again.'

'But we could spend our whole lives afraid of the future, and what then? Do we hide away here and never see anything of the world, or dare to have adventures? We've got to take risks sometimes.'

'Why? Why can't we stay where we're safe and enjoy what we've got?'

Hamish laughed. 'Oh, you're being silly. I've told you already, if I don't go, I'll never be happy. I don't understand what you're worried about. We're young and healthy and we've got years ahead of us. That's why I can go away now, don't you see?'

'I wish I could be as sure as you,' said Mary wistfully. 'But I'm afraid, even though I don't know why.'

Chapter Thirteen

McBain tried hard not to show his jealousy, but it was difficult. He bent his head lower, scrubbing at the *Jolly Jenny*'s side, so that Hamish couldn't see his face. They had pulled the little boat all the way up the stony beach and put her up on props so that they could tend to her hull. Small white clouds scudded across the blue sky and a strong wind blew smartly off the sea.

'So you told the college where to stick it?' he said, scraping off some sea moss with his penknife.

'Aye,' said Hamish carelessly. 'They were begging me to join them but I said I didn't have time for all that. I want to get on in the world and all the maths lessons on the planet aren't gonna help me.'

'When are you leaving?'

'In a fortnight or so. That's when I've signed up to.'

'And do they pay you?'

'Aye, of course they do! I'm gonna be a member of the crew, aren't I? I'm gonna be a deck boy,' he said proudly. 'And Mr Brewster said that if I'm good, I'll be promoted in no time.

151

I'll have to do my stint at the bottom, of course, but quick learners climb the ladder fast. And in the meantime, there's adventures to be had. Think of all the places I'm gonna see! The Far East – that's Arabia and places like that, I think. And the Continent. France and Spain and Italy, where everyone grows oranges in their gardens cos it's so hot. Can ye imagine...?' He chattered on as they worked.

McBain said nothing while he absorbed Hamish's boasting. He didn't want to show how much the news affected him, but his mind was in a whirl. Hamish, leaving! On the one hand, he was appalled at the news. He couldn't imagine life without Hamish now. He'd spent all those months shutting him out in furious silence and had made a solemn vow never to forgive him, but he couldn't help feeling that being Hamish's friend made life more pleasant than being so alone, with only wee Greggy for company, for all that counted. Even though he'd become friends with Hamish only as a strategy, to get close to that angel, Mary Burns, he knew that he would miss him and he envied the other boy all the excitement and prospects that were opening up before him. Should he, McBain, do the same? Could he?

But then ... another voice was telling him that this was the opportunity he had been waiting for. With Hamish gone, there would be room in the village for a new top dog, and was there any reason why McBain shouldn't fill the spot? Of course, there was the little matter of his unpopularity. Although he wasn't the outcast he used to be, no one seemed able to warm to him the way they did to Hamish. They tolerated him politely but no one sought him out or asked his opinion, or suggested a walk up to the point or a boating trip. When the other kids bought cones, played puddocks or built guiders – those boxes on wheels that they rode at full tilt down the hills – they never wanted to include McBain.

'Hey, Hamish,' he said, interrupting the flow of Hamish's chatter. 'What about that bint of yours? How's she taking the news, eh?'

Hamish stopped and stood up straight. He shrugged. 'Oh. All right. She doesn't want me to go, of course. But she knows my mind and she's gonna wait for me.'

'You've got yourself a smasher there, ye know.'

'Aye, I know.' Hamish grinned at McBain. 'But she's only a lassie, isn't she? Plenty more of those in the world.'

McBain grinned back. 'Surely are, pal.' He felt a secret triumph rising inside. 'And you'd be doing yourself wrong not to take your pick, wouldn't you?'

'Aye.' Hamish's expression was nonchalant. 'Mary'll wait for me, all right, I'm not worried about that.'

'Yeah, she'll wait. And don't worry, I'll make sure no one steals her from ye.' McBain bent his head again, so that Hamish wouldn't see his glee.

'For Christ's sake, woman, you have the brazen front to put this before me, do you?'

The children cowered down, their eyes wide. They knew what this meant.

Their father thrust away the plate of food their

153

mother had placed before him, so that it skittered across the table, spilling potato as it went. His face was already twisted with fury. That's how it went. One moment all was well and the next he'd flown into a terrible temper. But you never knew how or why it happened.

McBain hadn't been sure what the situation was when his father had come home. It wasn't so long ago that his dad had started his own mechanics workshop and for a while, things had been better. He had been fired up by starting his own venture and hopeful for the future.

'This is our guarantee, lad!' he'd proclaimed to his son. 'Now we can really make a go of things and get on in the world. See?'

He'd even said that Jamie would most likely come from Glasgow to join them, now that there was work for him. There'd been a loan from the bank to set up the workshop, but McBain's father had said it was worth it for the independence of being your own boss. For several weeks after the garage had opened – just a small shed with a pit for putting the cars over while they were being worked on and some workspace at the back, with a glossy new sign over the front saying 'McBain's Mechanics' – his father had barely touched the booze. He would come home walking straight, smile at the children and ask them what they'd done that day. The tension in the house melted away and, rather than running off when their father came home, the little ones vied with each other to sit on his lap and show him what they'd found in the garden or on the roadside that day. Their mother seemed to lose several years and

154

some of the deep lines on her forehead, and she was heard laughing for the first time in months. It had felt like a fresh start.

But it hadn't lasted. The business was all right but it was competing with the larger garage already established in the village, and McBain's father took every lost customer as a personal insult. Then there were the repayments for his bank loan, which he resented bitterly, even though he'd needed the money and accepted the terms at the time. Then Jamie had sent a card to say that he wasn't coming to live with them after all as he had taken an apprenticeship as a butcher and was happy in his lodging house, spending his evenings out on the town with the other boys and his days lugging carcasses into a cold room for butchering.

Everybody's mood had sunk after that. And then McBain's father had come home late one night, with the familiar stagger, the reek of stale alcohol on his breath and the fury that poured out on the whole family indiscriminately and for no cause that they could understand. His mother had regained the stooped look she carried in her shoulders, and her habit of flinching at any sudden noise. The children stopped wanting to sit on their father's knee and relearned the knack of fading into invisibility when he came home.

His face was red now. He'd come in, wheezing and swaying, and flung his toolbag down on the floor. Instantly there was a sense of danger.

They had all been sitting round the table eating their supper, a mix of mashed potato and onions with tiny pieces of fried bacon to give it flavour. As he entered, everyone had frozen almost as they were, forks halfway to mouths.

He's off his head, thought McBain, taking his father in with a sideways glance. His head was wobbling on his neck as though the joints had been loosened, and he was breathing thickly through his nose. McBain knew what this was – it was whisky-drinking. Beer-drinking wasn't so bad, somehow – it made his father good-humoured and lively at first, then drooling and drowsy and finally asleep so deeply that even the Second Coming wouldn't waken him. The spirits were different: they set some devil loose inside him that seemed to goad him like a matador pricking a bull until it was maddened and out of control.

The only person to move was his mother, who got to her feet and fetched her husband's supper from the kitchen. The children had all been eating voraciously, filling their hungry stomachs, but something about the food had not pleased their father. He'd taken one mouthful and spat it back onto the plate.

'This–' he held one trembling finger out towards the food he'd sent flying across the table – 'what kind of sorry meal do you call this?'

'It's all we have, Finn,' said his wife gently, trying to defuse his rage. 'We thought it was fine enough.'

'Did you?' he sneered. 'Well, I don't call it enough for a man who's been out at work all day, slaving to keep his family! And you're insulting me with this – it's bluddy cold, woman.'

'It's all we can afford. And you're late back, that's why it's cold. I didn't know you were going to be stopping on your way home.'

'All we can afford? What do you do with the money I give you?'

McBain saw his mother's jaw tighten. This was unfair, he knew that. His father drank most of the money he earned and his mother had to be canny and clever to get the family fed at all. She grew as much as she could in the garden, eked out every scrap of food, conjured meals out of leftovers when there were any, and cadged from the butchers and grocers, persuading them to give her cheap bits and pieces or damaged stock that they might otherwise throw away. All the family's clothes were home-made, or castoffs got for free or very cheap. She sewed and mended, repaired and restored and handed down everything she could, and hadn't bought herself anything new in years. Even when the children were at their naughtiest, they knew better than to damage their precious shoes or tear up their clothes. There would be nothing new to replace them.

The idea that she was responsible for their wretched poverty was ridiculous. McBain knew it, and his soul filled with hatred for his father, who could blame so unjustly the one person who kept the household together.

'Come on, Finn. Eat your supper,' said his wife. She would not answer him back, McBain knew that. She was not so stupid as to provoke him unnecessarily.

'Eat that shite?' he jeered. 'Not on your fuckin' life.'

'Mind your language – the children are here.'

He looked about him. 'Oh, aye. Here they all are.'

A shimmer of fear ran over the children and they turned their eyes down to their plates, each one hoping to escape their father's notice.

'Here's my parcel of bairns – and what's the point of 'em? Eating me out of house and home – little vultures, that's all they are.' He caught McBain's eye, the only one of his children who was looking at him. McBain didn't mean to look defiant but he knew there would be something accusatory in his stare. He wasn't going to drop his gaze though; he wasn't going to show that brute he was afraid of him, even though he was.

'What are you looking at?' asked his father, his voice ominously quiet. 'Huh?' There was a long pause while the two of them stared at each other.

His mother, standing by the table, reached out a hand and put it on her son's shoulder. 'Don't, lad. Don't.'

'Why not, Ma?' asked McBain. 'Why do we always let him get away with it? He's been like this for long enough. It's time someone stood up to him.'

'What?' His father pounced on his words, almost hungrily, as though this was giving him the excuse he longed for. His eyes seemed to glitter with anticipation. 'What did you say?'

'I said it's time someone stood up to yer. You make our lives a misery. I'm surprised Ma has put up wi' you this long. She must be awfuy frightened of ye.'

'Is it a skelp you're looking for, boy? I'll tan your bluddy backside for you if you cheek me.'

McBain said nothing. A tanned backside was nothing new to him and he knew he could survive it if he had to, but he didn't particularly want one.

His father pointed a finger at him and shouted, 'This one's a nasty piece of work! You're a big heid and nothin' else. My best boy's the one back haime in Glasgie, an' here I am, left with the dregs. I know what you're like, you little louse. You're the one that slinks about with that sour look on your face like you could turn cream soon as look at it. You'll never amount to anything, that's for certain.'

McBain shrugged. His father's insults meant nothing to him. 'There's nothing you can say to me,' he retorted, even though he knew that he would now be in for a real hiding. 'At least I'll never be like you – a plastered old geezer who hits the wee people that can't hit him back.'

At this, his father put back his head and roared almost like a lion, making the little ones jump and Flora start crying silently into her plate.

'Ah'll git you!' he shouted, and staggered round the table towards McBain. 'I'll teach you some manners, you little gobshite! I'll make you sorry you ever talked to me like that.'

The children slid off their chairs and ran to the corners of the room to hide themselves as much as they could. McBain stood up. He was prepared to take what was coming, he knew that. His father pounded towards him, his blood clearly up, and as he got close he swiped his great fist through the air, aiming at McBain's face. McBain ducked easily. His father's reactions were always dulled when he'd been drinking, and half the time it wasn't too hard to miss the flailing blows. But when they did land, you usually knew about it.

His father swung out with the other hand but McBain saw it coming and moved aside again without much trouble. Yelping in frustration, his father knocked two chairs out of the way and kicked at them before turning back to his son. His black eyes, eyes like McBain's own, were full of anger but also a kind of excitement that showed how much he wanted to hit out at anything and anyone if only he could. His fury seemed to increase and McBain began to feel scared. He backed away but his father came after him, tottering like the unsteady monster in the Frankenstein films. Soon, he realised, he would be in the corner with no escape from his father, whose bulk and height gave him an advantage. He would be trapped, and he would only be able to duck the blows for so long...

Suddenly, he wondered what he had done, firing his old man up like this. He was in for the beating of his life, he was sure of that. I must be crazy, he told himself. He guessed that his fear showed in his eyes, because his father looked suddenly triumphant and McBain felt himself wilt. All his defiance melted away, to be replaced by fright as he anticipated the pain he was about to feel. What would it be this time? Another black and blue eye? Perhaps a huge handprint over his cheek, as he had had once. Or a violent punch to the stomach, a place where no one would see the bruises.

His father had him in a tight spot now. He had been backed right up against the fireplace alcove.

The coal bucket, which rarely had more than a few pieces of coal and some dust in it, cut coldly into the backs of his legs, and he caught the reek of his father's breath, which smelled like rotting meat that had been soaked in meths.

What will he do? wondered McBain. Everything seemed to be moving in slow motion while he waited for that blow to come. His whole body was alert to it, waiting for it to land. Then the hand came up but instead of hitting him, it grabbed him by the throat.

'I'm gonna make you sorry,' hissed his father. His eyes were red and bloodshot, and purple veins showed all over his face, squiggling away into his stubbly skin. 'I'm gonna make you wish you'd never been born! Hell, *I* wish you'd never been born. Everyone wishes you'd never been born! You're one of your ma's lesser bits of work, aren't you? The runt of my litter. An' you know what they do to runts, don't you?'

The hand at McBain's throat started to tighten, squeezing and pressing so that no air could pass. Strangely it didn't hurt him, but the panic that began to well up inside him was almost physical.

Aw, shite, thought McBain. The bastard really wants to kill me this time... He tried to breathe but the hand round his throat was implacable in its grip, and his father's meaty fingers were pressing down as hard as they could. He could not quite believe what was happening and expected, every second, that he would be released so that he could gulp in the air he craved, but the pressure continued. The desire for air overcame him so that he could think of nothing else. His eyes felt as though they were bulging from his head. Then a high-pitched sound began, like a distant siren, and gradually he became aware that it was his mother screaming.

'Get off him, you great brute! Can't you see you're killing him?'

Through the buzzing in his head that seemed to be getting louder the longer air was denied him, he realised that she was dancing furiously about his father, beating him with one fist and yanking at his arm with her other hand. 'Let go!' she cried. 'For God's sake, Finn, look at him! Give him air!'

Abruptly, his father let go and as McBain sucked in a breath with relief, his lungs and throat burning, his father turned and with one mighty swipe from his muscled arm, he sent his wife flying. The blow itself was silent but the awful crunch as her head hit the corner of the hearth where she fell was horrible to hear.

'Pish off, woman!' he shouted. 'I'll do whatever I choose in my own damn house, do you hear me?'

There was no reply.

McBain, still fighting to regain his breath, was only dimly aware that the crumpled form lying in front of the fire was not moving. It was only when little Flora began to wail, 'Mammy, Mammy!' that he realised what his father had done.

He looked at his father and saw for an instant something in his eyes that he had never seen before. His father was frightened.

Chapter Fourteen

The most almighty racket was coming up from somewhere below decks. Hamish stood nervously, wondering what it meant. He'd been ragged all week about this ceremony and what it would entail, and he'd heard more and more outlandish stories until he had no idea what to expect.

The rest of the crew stood about, grinning in anticipation.

'Hey, come on, don't look so scared!' said Jimmy, the young cadet who had taken a shine to him since they had left port. 'You're no gonna be killed, you know. It's good fun. And everybody gets it. There's usually more than one but not this time, eh?'

'I'm not scared,' bluffed Hamish, pushing back his shoulders to try and look tougher. It wasn't much good on board this ship. He was a scrawny weakling in comparison to most of the others, even if he'd grown muscles he never knew he had since joining the *Arran* and learning the true nature of hard work. All about him were sailors who boasted arms of iron, with huge bulging biceps and stomachs rippled with muscle.

The noise – a strange attempt at music by the sounds of it, a discordant mixture of bangs and rattles – grew louder, and then an extraordinary procession came into view. At the front was a man

163

with a long white beard made of cotton wool. He was bare-chested, but wore over his shoulders a trailing red cloak that looked suspiciously like a bedspread, and on his head was a crown cut out of gold paper. Outlandish as he looked, it was really the person next to him who drew the eye, along with applause and whistles of appreciation from the crew. It was a pouting, simpering, hip-swinging beauty, her face well made up with red paint and her long blonde hair – which looked suspiciously like unpicked rope – falling over her shoulders. She wore a green tunic that fell to her feet and covered her hairy, knobbly legs. It was the second mate, dressed up to the nines and doing his very best impression of a real cutie.

Behind this odd couple came a procession of followers, all in the most bizarre dress they could invent from their deck clothes and uniforms. Some had borrowed bits and pieces from the Chinese crew, others had made extraordinary moustaches and beards from the ship's ropes or things they had bought in ports. They all came skipping behind King Neptune and his lady, Mrs Neptune, making as much noise as they could with their musical instruments – pot lids, sticks and any other implements they could get their hands on.

Aw, they look harmless enough, thought Hamish, laughing with the rest at the ungodly sight. But he still felt the fluttering of butterflies in his stomach.

The long, winding procession made its way round the decks and everyone stopped to watch it, even the Chinese who were on painting duty and never usually could be distracted from their endless task of recoating the entire ship in fresh paint. When it reached Hamish again it came to a halt and the music stopped, leaving a strange ringing silence in the air.

'Ho!' declaimed Neptune, whom Hamish now recognised as one of the electricians. 'Who is the foul pollywog brought before me?'

One of the crew pushed him forward and up onto an upturned crate that was to serve as a kind of dock for the weird trial he had to undergo. 'Here he is, o King of the Sea.'

'Isn't he revolting!' sneered the lovely Mrs Neptune, who in real life was always kind and friendly towards Hamish. 'And I hear he's committed the most truly terrible sins we've yet had the misfortune to bring to trial.'

'I have a list of his sins here.' Neptune held up a scroll in one hand. 'I shall read them.'

Hamish tried to smile but could not. His heart was pounding. They can't really hurt me, he thought, with a small panic rolling in his stomach. They can't do anything really bad – can they?

His pal Kenzie had told him that on some ships the ceremony of crossing the Line was so violent and cruel that it resulted in serious injury. 'But don't you worry,' he'd said, seeing Hamish's face, 'the captain won't have any of that on board the *Arran*. He doesn't mind some high jinks but he'd never let anything serious happen. There's rules for what can happen and how far they're all allowed to go.'

Hamish had been reassured but now he was beginning to wonder exactly what the limits were. There was a sense of expectation and relish in the air that gave him the collywobbles. They'd been at sea for weeks now and the weather had been calm and serene, with hardly a puff of wind or the sight of a cloud. At first the endless blue skies and the hot sunshine had been an extraordinary and very pleasant change from the grey, cloudy Scottish weather, but now it was getting somewhat wearisome and they were all suffering from boredom. There was a little craziness in the air that Hamish could tell came from a crew of grown men being locked up together with no expectation of seeing land for another two weeks. There had already been a couple of raucous parties with much drinking and singing which were needed to let off some of the pent-up energy that they were all suffering from, but everybody had been looking forward to Hamish's baptism.

'You're the only pollywog on board, which is all the worse for you, I'm afraid. You'll get all the attention from the rest of us shellbacks.' Kenzie laughed.

'Pollywog?'

'You know – virgin sailor. One who hasn't crossed the equator. Everyone who's crossed the Line and been initiated is a shellback – and that's all of us.'

Now King Neptune unrolled his scroll and began to declaim Hamish's sins. Hamish had been warned to look submissive and accept everything without complaint, so he bent his head and listened as the list of his misdeeds was pronounced. It seemed that just about everything he had ever done on board was some kind of crime

166

or other. He had failed to empty buckets quickly enough, or scrub the decks adequately; his knot tying and rope splicing were messy and pathetic; he'd slipped going down one of the ladders and fallen on the lower deck. Hamish was indignant at some of the charges, which he regarded as simply trumped up, but he damped it down and continued to listen meekly. Then the sins began to become more personal.

'He is guilty of eating like a hog at dinner!' shouted Neptune, to roars of agreement and approval.

That's rich! thought Hamish, who had often been glad his mother had not had to witness some of the revolting eating that went on in the messes.

'But worst of all, the most heinous of all his crimes, is the terrible smell of his disgusting feet!'

Hamish was surprised. He'd never been aware that his feet smelt – no more than anyone else's anyway – but before he had time even to think about protesting his innocence he was wrenched forward off his crate and flung to the deck.

'He must be examined and his fault must be corrected,' proclaimed Neptune.

The next minute Hamish was being roughly tied down and his shoes yanked from his feet. Everybody made a great show of what a terrible stench was now loose in the air, although Hamish couldn't smell a thing.

Don't worry, relax, he told himself, even though the sensation of being at the mercy of the entire crew was not a nice one. He tried not to show he was frightened. A moment later, the world went black as a blindfold was wrapped round his eyes.

This was very nasty indeed, he decided. Now that he could not see, the panic was worse, and he needed all his self-control to master it.

'First, we must clean his feet.'

Someone began to scrub violently at his feet with something hard and rough, like a giant pumice stone. It was painful and ticklish at the same time and Hamish couldn't help yelping and squirming to escape the very unpleasant sensation, but he was held down at once and the scrubbing went on and on until he thought it would never stop. It was a horrible torturous feeling that became almost unbearable.

'There,' said Neptune as the scrubbing stopped at last. 'That's a little nicer, isn't it? Or does he need a bit more of a clean?'

Hamish was yanked up and put on a chair. Then his feet were plunged into a bucket of icy water, which made them sting and hurt like mad. Next was a bucket of something foul and slimy which he couldn't begin to guess the contents of, then something that smelled chemical and felt slippery, then finally hot, hot water that he thought must be taking the skin off. With each new sensation he couldn't help yelping and shouting aloud, each cry earning him a mild whip across the back with what felt like a hose and a command to be quiet and take his punishment like a man.

'But these feet are still awfully smelly!' shouted Neptune. 'Perhaps we're going about this the wrong way. Maybe we could clean 'em all day and those stinky things would never get any better. I wonder if it's something in his insides?'

The other men chorused their agreement with whoops and shrieks.

'Perhaps he needs a clearing out? Maybe that would get rid of the horrible smell, huh? What do we think? Does he need some medicine?'

The answering shouts were even louder and more raucous. Hamish felt himself lifted up and thrown onto the deck once again. King Neptune ordered him to be bound and he felt ropes being tightened round his wrists and ankles.

'Now – the medicine!'

His mouth was forced open and a funnel jammed in. Before he had time to wonder what they were doing, the most appalling mixture hit his open mouth and slithered over his tongue. There was an instant before the terrible taste of it registered but when it did, he began to heave and retch immediately. He couldn't help swallowing some of the hideous stuff as he struggled for breath between violently gagging and coughing.

Whatever this brew was, it was unimaginably horrible, a slimy, foul-smelling liquid containing blobs of solid matter – Hamish did not dare even wonder what they might be. He couldn't help himself but vomited up everything in his stomach, thrashing his head to try and escape the funnel in his mouth, but it was held firmly in place. Just as he thought he was going to drown, or choke to death in a mixture of poison and his own sick, the funnel was yanked away, he was allowed to turn his head and everything poured from his mouth onto the deck.

'What a messy, disgusting boy!' cried Neptune, to the accompaniment of shouts of laughter and cries of 'uugh!' 'How ungrateful. He doesn't like his medicine. I've been preparing that for days! As you can all probably tell.'

Hamish lay dazed and panting, the indescribable taste still searing his mouth, trying to stop himself from throwing up again. When will it all be over? he wondered helplessly. Great God, it's much worse than I thought...

There was a pouring sound and then a splatter. It seemed that rather than waste the rest of his lovely medicine, which had the grim odour of rotting fish somewhere in its fetid smell, it would be poured all over Hamish. Now he was coated from head to foot in the revolting mixture.

The court of the King began their rowdy music again, this time bellowing pirate sea shanties. As they roared and sang, Hamish felt himself lifted up and carried roughly over the deck.

Oh, Christ, they're going to throw me overboard! he thought in sudden terror. He knew that he would be baptised at some point. Would they go that far? They were riding high in the water as they were lightly loaded, and the drop over the side must be immense. And he was tied up. How could he survive? He felt fear curdling him all over.

Then he was on solid ground again and hands were untying his bonds.

'Now I pronounce that you shall be baptised,' said Neptune, and a moment later Hamish was underwater. He knew where he was now – the ship had an old swimming pool where the crew cooled off on the hottest days. He was under its surface, held down by two strong crew members, and his lungs were burning with the need for air.

Just as he was reaching the limit of his endurance, he was popped to the surface. Gasping and choking, he breathed in the welcome air. His blindfold was removed, and he blinked in the sudden blazing sunlight.

'Here,' cried Mrs Neptune in her high falsetto. 'You are now officially a member of Neptune's court and a shellback. You must drink a toast to his high honour and your safety in his kingdom.' She thrust a bottle of beer into Hamish's hand and made him lift it to his mouth. He was so grateful for the cleansing liquid that he gulped it down. It was the best beer he'd ever tasted in his life.

'But I don't think he's quite baptised,' said Neptune. 'Do you?'

And he was plunged back under the water. As before, just when he felt he could not stay another minute below the surface without passing out, he was yanked up and forced to drink a bottle of beer. Then he went back under again, and over and over it was repeated until he'd downed six bottles and was giddy with lack of air and drunkenness, to the great amusement of everybody watching.

At last it was decreed that he was well and truly baptised. Neptune presented him with a certificate made from a cut-up chart, on which was typed a command to all to recognise that Hamish was now his liege subject and had the freedom of his kingdom on the occasion of being questioned and lawfully initiated in the prescribed manner, and that all dwellers in the sea – sharks, dolphins, mermaids and the rest – were to treat him well should he fall overboard. It was signed 'Neptune Rex'.

Hamish tried to read it but he was too drunk and felt too ill to be able to focus on it. The others were still jubilant however, and they continued to sing and dance noisily, drinking beer while they did so. Each one warmly congratulated Hamish on his membership of their brotherhood.

For the first time since they had left port all those weeks ago, he felt like he belonged.

Chapter Fifteen

'Hey, Dad, I'm off home now, all right?'

McBain wiped his oily hands on a rag. His father came to the edge of the pit where he was working on the undercarriage of an old truck and looked up.

'Aye, son.'

'Are ye staying later?' McBain asked.

'Thought I would try and get this finished tonight. McAlistair says he needs it back to-morrow.'

McBain nodded. 'All right then. Well – make sure it's all safe and locked up 'fore you come home. I'll tell 'em to keep your supper for you.'

'Thanks lad.' His father disappeared from view again, going back to his work beneath the chassis.

McBain let himself out of the workshop and stopped on his way to look at the newly painted sign that now hung over the garage doors. It read 'McBain & Son' in fresh red letters on a white background. He gazed up at it, his hands thrust into the pockets of his blue overalls. Now that was something. It felt as though life were about to begin properly for him. This was something for him, at last.

He'd always planned to leave school as soon as he could and go back to Glasgow as fast as he could, find Jamie and live with him, perhaps take up an apprenticeship. He'd wanted to go the minute he turned fourteen but his mother begged him to stay on at school for longer.

'Get yerself an education, son,' she pleaded. 'You only get one crack at it, I'm tellin' you, and it'll stand you in good stead for the rest of yer life.' It had been her dearest ambition for McBain to sit his Highers and get a proper qualification, and then an office job. McBain knew that her secret wish was for him to be teacher or an accountant or someone like that, a man who commanded respect and who didn't have to work with his hands and dirty his clothes to earn a living. But if one of her children was ever going to do that, it wasn't going to be him, he knew. He had no talent for schoolwork. He hated it. He couldn't see it as achieving anything, and little ticks on pieces of paper meant nothing at all to him. Now – show him a boat that went out empty and came back full of fish. That was an achievement. Show him a car that wouldn't start and then after a bit of tinkering and mending on its engine, would purr like a cat and run as smooth as you like. That was an achievement you could see and understand.

That was the kind of thing he valued.

Now, of course, there was no one to care whether he stayed on at school or not, so he had left as soon as he could. By then his dream of returning to Glasgow no longer had the power over him it had once possessed. Now he wanted to stay in Kinlochvegan and make something of himself, so he had joined his father in the workshop. They were in business together now, and business was going well. While the sign might read 'McBain & Son', as though he was the lesser of the partners, it could just as well read 'McBain & Father', for the real state of affairs was that he was taking over more and more. He was hungry to learn something practical after so many years of reading and writing, and after only six months or so, he was already an accomplished mechanic. Not only that, but despite his hatred of book learning, he was proving that he had a talent for managing the business. Book reading he might not like, but balancing the books was something else altogether, and he had a flair for it. It made sense to him. He understood that as long as more was coming in than was going out, things were good, and the higher the ratio, the better. He wanted more and more business and he was finding ways to bring it in, ways that might be called sneaky if anyone got to know about them, but he took great care to make sure that they didn't.

McBain got his bicycle and set off on the road home. His father used the truck and while he could have used that, he preferred the bike. It was hard to hear yourself think, sitting in that

174

roaring machine, while on the bike you could listen to the sounds all about – the birds, the breeze, the goings-on in the village. No, this way was better and just as fast, he suspected, for the truck had to clamber dead slow over the potholes in the road on the way to the bothy.

He passed the other garage on his way through the village and was pleased to note that it was already shut for the night. If he had anything to do with it, they wouldn't be in business much longer at all. And he had plans that would further remove custom from them and send it his way. He was thinking about a petrol pump at the side of the workshop. At the moment Andersons had the one and only pump in the village, and everybody filled up there. But if McBain could get two pumps, charge just a little less and offer car cleaning and tyre pumping as well ... surely he'd win all the business in the village hands down. The trouble was, he'd need money from somewhere, and a supplier...

He pondered these problems as he cycled. Even though they seemed insurmountable, he enjoyed thinking about them.

I don't know why I feel so different, he thought to himself. When you think about all the bad that's happened, I ought to be miserable – but I'm not.

He was beginning to realise that the unaccustomed lightness he felt was what being happy must feel like. What was making him happy? The business? Yes, that was part of it. Home? There was no denying that things were easier there now, even if it was still hard to think about what had

175

happened and what it had meant for them all. But he suspected that a huge part of it was that Hamish was gone.

Almost as soon as Hamish had left the village, he had walked about the place with a lighter step. It was as though he had taken McBain's worst feelings about himself with him and left him unburdened by all the self-hatred. It felt almost as if other people looked at him differently too. Without Hamish to judge him by, they seemed to think more kindly of him. Hamish was always so popular, so good-looking, so charming, that he put everyone in the shade and made them seem wanting by comparison. Finally, now that he was gone, McBain had a chance to shine and he was enjoying it immensely. He no longer felt like he had to skulk around the edges of the room at the ceilidh, or that everyone was jeering at him behind his back. And now that he was working at the garage, he seemed quite respectable. He'd even had a dance or two with girls and one had offered to kiss him, if he wanted, though he hadn't taken her up on it.

The strange thing was that the more people began to like and accept him, the more he felt contemptuous of them, though he tried to hide it. They were so easy to sway after all, and he couldn't forget all those years he'd been made to feel like an outcast. He'd never forget. But his revenge would be his success. If it was in his power, he would become the most influential man in the place. No one would be able to so much as sweep his front path without getting McBain's permission first.

He'd received several postcards from Hamish since he'd left, though it had all gone quiet for a while now, and he'd imagined that these cards would make him sick with jealousy as he learned of all the exotic places and foreign lands the other boy was seeing. Instead, he felt a rush of joy with each one he received, for every new card came from somewhere further away.

The further he's gone, the more I like it! he thought to himself. His life was better without Hamish in it. He felt like a bigger man without him around. If McBain had his way, Hamish would never come back.

He put his bike into the little shed that stood at the side of the bothy and went in. Summer had long vanished and winter was going that way too. The mornings and nights were brighter now. There was no denying that it had been a hard winter for all of them. Christmas had never been much fun in their house, but this year it had been particularly sorrowful. It was a time he was glad to see the back of, and he longed for summer to come and wipe away the memories of the cold and darkness, the shivering, lonely, mournful children and the father locked in some hellish place that they could only guess at.

Inside, the lamp was lit and the fire was burning. McBain was only just beginning to realise how much his mother had sacrificed by making him stay at school. He could have left two years ago and been earning money. Seeing how much difference his extra wage made to the family made him sad that she hadn't let him do his bit earlier, when she could have appreciated it. Now they could have the fire burning whenever they wanted it, which in the cold little bothy was almost every day, even when it was blazing outside. There was more food on the table and fresh milk in the cold store; the children were fattening up and their cheeks were pinker and their eyes brighter. McBain was sure they were not catching so many colds – at least, he'd noticed that the youngest ones no longer had the constant streams of snot they'd had before.

His mother would be happy, he thought. Perhaps she'd even think it was worth it, what had happened to her. Things probably wouldn't have changed without that.

'You're home,' said Flora. She was at the stove, stirring a pot of something that smelled delicious.

'Aye. What's that?'

'Rabbit stew. Alec's catching 'em by the dozen.'

'Fine!' said McBain with satisfaction. Free food was always a good result, even if Alec should not be helping himself to rabbits from the estate land. But they were pests, weren't they? And who would miss them when there were so many? He watched Flora stirring for a moment. She had become the little woman of the house, even though she was not ten years old yet, and cooked nearly all their meals.

'It's almost ready,' she said. 'Is Pa coming home with you?'

'He's staying late. Best to eat without him and we'll leave his in the pot for him.'

'I was getting it ready early anyway so I could feed her before we sit down.'

'Aye. Good idea. How is she today?' He looked over at the small figure swathed in blankets in the chair by the fire.

Flora shrugged. 'Oh, she's the same as ever an' I don't suppose she'll ever change.'

The woman by the fire moved slightly and murmured.

'She can smell the food, I s'pose,' said Flora matter-of-factly. 'She always makes that noise when she's hungry and knows it's nearly time for her supper. I'll feed her and get her into bed 'fore we all sit down.'

McBain grunted. It was curious, he thought, how the tables had been turned. It wasn't so long ago that his mother was the one feeding Flora and making sure she got to bed. Now it was little Flora taking the burden on herself of caring for the woman who had given birth to her, and there could be years of nurturing ahead of her. Apart from the damage to her brain that had robbed her of all her faculties, their mother was healthy. Although she had little exercise and her muscles were wasting, she appeared to be fit. It was, he supposed, the natural order of things that the girl of the family should take on their mother's mantle. It was Flora who cleaned the bothy, struggled with the great mangle to wash their clothes, cooked the meals and cared for the ones who were smaller than she was, as well as her sick mother.

He watched as Flora spooned some stew into a bowl and took it over to the woman in the chair. She looked quite normal except for the dead light in her eyes, and the way her head rolled to the left and her mouth drooped at the right, letting the

179

occasional spool of dribble fall out. Flora talked gently and comfortingly to her mother as she ladled the food into her mouth, crooning occasionally just as a woman would to her baby.

Nothing had been the same since the night McBain's father had sent his wife flying to the ground. After she had hit her head, they had all thought she was dead. She'd looked dead: completely pale and motionless with her eyes rolled back in her head. But McBain had put his head on her chest and heard the tiniest sigh from her, even though the children were crying so hard it was difficult to hear anything at all. His father had been like a man who'd seen the Devil himself, almost gibbering with fear.

'I've killed her! I've killed her!' he whispered to himself over and over. All the anger and violence had gone out of him in an instant, to be replaced by horror as he was shocked into sobriety by the realisation that if he had done a murder, it was prison for him for the rest of his life. And there was no shortage of witnesses to speak of what he'd done: his terrorised children, so long a victim of his rages, now had his fate in their hands. If they chose to tell, then he was condemned, and why would they not choose, if he had really killed their mother, the only person who had ever shown them a scrap of love and kindness?

It was McBain, cool and calm in the crisis despite his own near escape from his father's murderous rage, who saved the situation. Realising their mother was still alive, he sent Alec off on the bicycle to fetch the doctor with all haste, and to tell him that it was a life-and-death emergency.

'Hey there, stop your greetin',' he ordered the wailing children. 'Can't you see she's alive? Eh now, she's not dead, she'll be fine. And you–' he turned to his father – 'you come with me.'

His father followed him obediently into the bedroom and they stood there together in the darkness. In the twenty minutes that followed, McBain told his father exactly how it would be and what would happen if he didn't go along with it. They emerged not long before the doctor's car came bumping up the track towards the bothy, and the man who came out of the bedroom was a very different one to the man who had gone in.

When McBain had explained that his mother had tripped and fallen by accident, the doctor gave him a disbelieving look. It was no secret that the poor woman was beaten on a regular basis, and something like this had had to happen eventually. But everyone, even the bairns, went along with the story and there was nothing for it but to accept it.

After that, the power in the house had changed hands. The violent drunken bully had disappeared as if by magic, to be replaced by a meek old man whose punishment was to live daily with the results of his actions in the form of his wife. She had been put to bed unconscious by the doctor, who had said that in cases like this there was nothing to be done but to wait and see. Some people made full recoveries and some never woke, but lived on in the strange land between life and death. For six weeks their mother lay asleep in bed, her limbs curiously tight, her hands curled up and her mouth twisted into a grimace that never changed. Then, to their great delight, she woke up.

'Mammy, Mammy!' screamed Flora. 'You've come back!'

And the youngest chuckled with delight to see his mother's eyes open again. But the joy was short-lived when it became apparent that she did not know any of her children, and neither could she speak or understand or control her limbs. The doctor visited again, and said that all hope was not yet lost, that some cases like this eventually regained more of themselves, and for a while there seemed to be some improvement. Her limbs straightened out, partly through Flora gently massaging them over and over until they relaxed open, and she got back some of her bodily control. But her personality and her spirit had vanished, and they all knew now that those things would never come back. Something in her head had been damaged beyond repair and it had taken with it the woman they'd all known and loved, leaving just this shell behind.

McBain was the head of the family now.

Chapter Sixteen

The excitement as they approached land was almost tangible. The whole ship vibrated with it as everyone prepared to reach their destination. The captain had decreed that the *Arran* had to be sparkling before she pulled into Bangkok harbour, and Hamish worked all hours almost to the limit of his strength as he washed and scrubbed the decks until they shone.

Life as a deck boy was, he'd found, nothing short of the hardest labour he could ever have imagined. Once he'd said to the second mate, 'Why do I have to do these horrible jobs, sir?' and the second mate had looked at him pityingly and said, 'Because no one else will do them, of course. Why do you think?'

And if there was anything foul, gut-churning, mind-numbingly boring or endlessly long to be done, it was the deck boy who was called on to do it. He was the bottom of the heap, even below the Chinese crew, although he managed to escape the beatings and almost sadistic violence that the Chinese bosun inflicted on his fellow Chinese. The captain turned a blind eye to the terrible state some of them were in, but he was unlikely to have been so understanding about a Scottish-born lad, so Hamish was lucky. Whenever the bosun was asked about the latest crew member to appear battered and bruised, he simply said, 'Muchee trouble. Fell over.' And it seemed that this transparent lie was accepted.

In fact, Captain Harding had taken a shine to Hamish and showed him marked favour.

'You're a lucky one,' an English junior officer had said a little bitterly. He himself was not a favourite with the Scottish captain. 'Deck boys don't usually get so much of an easy ride.'

If this was an easy ride, Hamish thought, he'd hate to see a difficult one. Life in Kinlochvegan now seemed like some far-off dream of unimaginable luxury. What did I do with all my time? he

183

wondered. It seemed now that he had had limitless hours to think and dream. Now he was on his feet all day and sometimes all night, scurrying about the enormous ship, cleaning, fetching, carrying, sitting on watch and obeying the endless orders he received from just about everyone he met during the course of the day. When he slept in the tiny cramped bunk in the heat far below decks, it was the dead sleep of exhaustion in which the only dreams he remembered were ones of racing to carry out yet more impossible commands.

But he did love it, far more than he had ever expected. There was a magic to the deep sea that he had never found on his little dinghy, and watching the sun sink behind an unbroken horizon of glittering sea as the *Arran* steamed on over the great waters was an experience that stirred him to the depths of his soul. He had already known moments of fear, when storms blew up and mountainous waves broke over the ship's stern so that she groaned and moaned as if she wanted to give up the ghost. But she never did. She always fought her way through, taking them safely out of the tempests and back into the calm again. He had learned about the astonishing camaraderie that bound crew members together after they had endured the extreme weather and the fear for their lives, as well as the long hours of boredom, and the ceaseless repetitive work that kept the ship alive and running. Hamish wondered if half the work they were given was simply to keep them all busy so that they were less able to feel disgruntled as they sailed on through the immense and lonely ocean.

The captain had noticed him from the start and had liked it when Hamish said he was from the west coast. 'I'm from the Western Isles myself,' he'd said. He always seemed to look a little more kindly on those who'd come from his homeland – at least, that was what the English officers said. He'd once taken Hamish aside and told him that if he worked hard and well, he would personally see to it that he rose more quickly from deck boy than most. There were usually years of slaving away as a general skivvy before there was any hope of promotion – or so Hamish had been told, mostly by the cadets and junior officers who were proud of the training they'd completed and considered themselves far above him by virtue of their certificates.

The captain had had a friendly word with the youngest member of the crew when they'd finally approached port. 'Watch yourself there, Hamish. There's temptations in port. Any sailor will tell you. There'll be girls, there'll be drink, there'll be blaggers, rogues and thieves. Just mind yourself.'

Sure enough, their first port of call in the Philippines, where they had unloaded some of the stuffs they'd brought from Leith, was an extraordinary experience of which Hamish could now remember very little. He'd been in many bars and drunk vile liquids that had sent his head spinning after just a few sips, and seen beautiful girls with skins of the softest brown dancing and talking. He'd been far too shy to speak to any of them, though he'd seen other crew members disappear off with them for anything up to an hour and return looking a great deal happier. He knew what they were up to, but didn't consider any of that for himself. These exotic beauties were all very well, but there was Mary to think about. She was the only girl for him, the one he dreamed of whenever he had a moment to himself, or when the long hours needed whiling away with a daydream as he worked. Her beauty was so far beyond any of these foreign ladies. The others might need to find their relief with them, but they didn't have Mary waiting for them at home. Hamish wrote her long letters whenever he could find the time, but they were rarely posted. They could send letters when they got to port, but by then most of them seemed hopelessly out of date so he didn't bother and ended up sending a hastily written scrawl that ended: 'Don't forget me because I'm not forgetting you. Your Hamish.'

Now they were approaching the place he really wanted to see: Bangkok. All the sailors seemed to think of this port as the most exciting and vibrant, the very best place to be. Here the ship would be loaded to the lines with cargo. Hamish had already seen the first mate with his elaborate model of the hold and his little scales, working out how to stow everything so that it would fit on board and balance the ship.

He clambered up on deck as they approached the coast of Thailand and made their stately way up the river towards the harbour. The ship was spotless and gleaming as the captain had commanded, and all her flags were fluttering in the breeze. For a few precious hours, work was over. Tomorrow they would start unloading, most with very sore heads, but for now excitement and adventure beckoned.

A sound began to drift over the decks. It raised goosebumps on Hamish's skin as he recognised it. It was the wail of the bagpipes and they were playing 'Scotland the Brave'. The captain had ordered that the pipes always play as they entered a port, to announce their safe arrival and to create the sense of occasion that this huge old ship merited.

He rushed to the side and looked at the land on either side of the river, a dense mixture of lush greenery and wooden huts. The banks were thickly lined with boats and junks and a bustle of activity seemed to be going on everywhere. The heat as they steamed slowly further inland grew stronger, and the pressure of the atmosphere increased until Hamish felt as though it was actually weighing him down. Then the harbour opened up in front of them, with the city stretching off into the distance behind it.

'Hey, Hamish.' He'd been joined by Tam Ferguson, a junior officer, decked out in his uniform of white shorts, shirt and peaked cap. 'You comin' ashore with us later? Once we've had dinner, we'll be allowed to go wild.'

'Count me in,' said Hamish quickly. He was keen to see all he could of the strange city unfolding in front of him.

'We'll take you and show you some of the crazy places. But if anyone asks, you're eighteen, OK? Some of the bar owners are fussy about things like that. Not that you'd notice once you're inside. And try to look a bit smartish, if you can.'

Hamish nodded, excitement rising in him. This was one of the experiences he'd been promised, one of the reasons he endured all the hours of back-breaking work. The crew all talked of Khlong Toey and its markets and nightlife with relish, and it was evidently one of the favourite stop-offs.

'You gotta see these girls,' said Kenzie to Hamish one night, when he was describing the delights that awaited them. 'Beautiful, they are! And you'll see more of a woman than you've ever dreamed of, right close and next to you! I'm tellin' you, it's incredible. And you won't believe how cheap it is. Your money'll never go farther than it does here, and that's the truth.'

Hamish was expecting to have the time of his life.

'Look at those girls,' whispered Tam, nudging Hamish hard as they walked past a group of women standing on a street corner. Hamish glanced over. Out of the five or six girls, two had real beauty; they were exquisitely made up and wearing white summery dresses and high-heeled sandals. They were petite and demure, incredibly slim but with soft curves, brown skin like milky coffee and almond-shaped dark eyes. Kenzie had been right; these creatures were gorgeous. Not a patch on Mary, of course, but he could still hardly take his eyes off them.

He whistled softly through his teeth.

'Better watch yourself, though.' Kenzie giggled. 'Neil Buchanan got a little close with a girl like that not so long ago and guess what ... she only turned out to be a boy.'

'What!' exclaimed Hamish, astonished. He'd never heard of such a thing. 'Aw, come on now. Don't take me for a monkey. He must have made a mistake.'

'Well, I know you're just an innocent from the west coast, Hamish, but even you must know the difference between a boy and a girl. And Neil certainly does now.'

'How can a boy look so like a girl that he fools a man close up? It's just not possible.'

'Oh yes, it is. Look at those girls again. Can you see that the taller ones are fellas? Look at their Adam's apples and their big hands.'

Hamish's mouth fell open. 'No – I don't believe it! Those pretty wee lasses are *lads*?'

'Most likely. And not as sweet as you might think from lookin' at them. Watch your pockets when they're about is all I'm saying.'

Hamish shook his head at the craziness of this foreign land. He couldn't imagine for a moment why a lad would want to look like a female anyway. Who would choose being a lassie over the obvious superiority of being a man? There were lots of other questions that puzzled him but he didn't have time to ponder them now – there was too much to see and do. They had docked a few hours before and once dinner was over, they were free to go ashore and see what they could find in the slum area of Khlong Toey, one of the most deprived areas of Bangkok. As well as the heat, the noise and the dirt, Hamish was aware of the huge numbers of people everywhere. Wherever he looked he saw hundreds and hundreds of Thais – girls, boys, men, women, and children. Even though night was falling, the place still seemed as busy as during the daytime, with bicycles and rickshaws cramming the streets, fighting their way through the streams of people. Stalls lined the road selling drinks and food, the aroma drifting up deliciously to mix with the more acrid smell of the harbour and the pungency of the slums.

'Come on. Let's get on,' said Tam, pushing a path forward through the crowd. 'I want to get to the bar.'

'Where are we going?'

'It's an old favourite of the seamen who come here. You'll see all sorts – lots of Dutch and Germans. It's called the Blue Elephant.'

Soon they were on a street that was lined by bars. Outside each one stood a Thai man in a neat black suit and bow tie.

'The doorman,' explained Tam. 'It's his job to get the customers in. Don't know why they think a little fella like that is going to get us interested. It's the girls we want to see.'

They wove their way through the morass of people until Tam stopped suddenly. 'Here we are.'

The building was a two-storey wooden shack, like all the others that lined the street, with a low sloped roof and a veranda at the front. Outside stood one of the ubiquitous doormen, smiling and urging passers-by to come inside. A sign propped up by the door read in English, 'Blue Elephant – 20 Baht entrance fee. Over 18 only.' Below that was lots of writing in a foreign script so pretty that Hamish thought it looked more like decoration than writing. Above the door was a faded, peeling blue wooden elephant, rearing up on his hind legs, raising his trunk above his jewelled headdress, dowdy now from age.

'This is our boy,' said Tam. He led Hamish up to the doorman. 'Two please.'

The doorman looked briefly at them both and said, 'Eighteen?'

Hamish nodded, trying to look older. Well, it wasn't that much of a lie. He was almost seventeen after all. And he was not the green young thing who had first boarded the *Arran*. He could drink like the rest of them now – maybe not quite as much, but he was getting there.

Tam pressed some money into the man's hand, an amount that Hamish guessed was their entrance fee plus a bit more to sweeten their path. With a short bow, the little man opened the door and let them in.

At first, Hamish was disappointed. He'd expected more – his imagination had painted pictures of something like a maharaja's palace: silken cushions on the floor, musicians strumming away in the corner, punkah-wallahs with feathery fans keeping the customers cool, gorgeous women drifting serenely about. It was not a bit like that. For one thing, it was as crowded as the streets outside but three times as noisy, and the heat was mixed now with the smell of beer and sweat. The whole place was filthy: the floor was sticky and the walls, no more than painted boards with the occasional poster tacked up, were running with condensation.

'Isn't it grand?' asked Tam with satisfaction.

'Oh – aye,' said Hamish, trying to pretend that

this was the kind of place he'd always wanted to visit – the reason for his voyage halfway across the world and all the hours of labour he'd been forced to do.

'And look at that!' murmured Tam. 'Now that's what I'm talkin' about.'

Hamish followed his gaze and as he looked, he realised for the first time that a jukebox was playing hits from America at full volume. He could make out the blaring of guitars and the beat of drums and the roar of someone singing. On a raised dais, against a curtain of shimmering silver, he could see a beautiful girl dancing and shaking her body in time to the beat. She was wearing only a red sequinned bikini with tassels that trembled and sparkled as she gyrated. Her breasts rose, round and smooth, from the bikini top and her hips curved up into a tiny waist. She spun round on her heels, shaking her bottom as she turned, tossing her long dark hair.

Hamish gasped. He'd seen some pictures of girls in bathing suits in a magazine once, but never thought such gorgeous things could exist in reality.

'Now *that's* a girl,' said Tam with evident appreciation. 'I reckon even Neil Buchanan would take a bet on that one.'

A few hours later and Hamish was beginning to understand the hold that the Blue Elephant had over its customers. The dirty, noisy shack had a curiously seductive atmosphere and, full as it was of foreign sailors drinking themselves stupid and looking for girls, was somehow friendly and familiar.

Hamish didn't know how many drinks he had sucked down now, only that the racket in the bar was curiously fuzzy, his head felt loose on his neck and his fingers were numb. He was happy, though, he knew that, even happier now that more boys from the *Arran* had joined them. All his pals were here now, talking and laughing, their faces red and their shirts sweaty. A thick cloud of cigarette smoke hovered in the air just above their heads and Hamish found he was holding a cigarette between his fingers. When had that happened? Did he smoke? He supposed he must now, and took a drag on it that set him coughing and choking until tears ran down his face. No one noticed: the noise of dozens of languages being shouted above the sound of the raging jukebox drowned it all out. He picked up a cold beer, sucked on it and regained his equilibrium.

Then he noticed a soft female voice whispering in his ear in a language he guessed must be Thai. He looked up to see two exquisite brown eyes full of concern set in a beautiful smooth brown face. She must have seen him choking, though he couldn't make a damn bit of sense from her words.

'No, no, I'm all right. I'm fine,' he said loudly. It was obvious from her blank look that she did not understand him.

He'd been watching the girls all night. There seemed to be dozens of them in the bar, most dressed in skintight summer dresses and high-heeled shoes, their faces made up and their hair curled into elaborate styles. They looked like movie stars, with their gorgeous bodies, flawless faces and American-style clothes and hair. Some of the girls were dancing, waiting for men to come and join them. Others sat at the bar or at the many tables crammed into the room, smiling and nodding at the men they were drinking with. Language barriers were not a problem, it seemed. There was nothing that couldn't be said with a smile and a nod and a flutter of dark eyelashes.

This girl put her head on one side and looked at him. Hamish's heart did a flip and then began to melt. She was so pretty he couldn't stop looking at her, and realised that he was simply staring with his mouth hanging open. There were already four or five girls with their group, but they were talking to the older sailors, the ones who knew what they were doing and had the confidence to pick up the girls who came and offered themselves. Hamish had been content just to watch.

Once the others saw that he was with a girl, the shout went up.

'Hey, look at that! Wee Hamish has a lassie!'

'Oh, now, this is your chance, Hamish. She can make a man of ye, you know.'

He'd never found any of the shore women attractive before. He found the knowledge of the way they earned their living off-putting. But this girl – she looked so innocent, he couldn't believe that she was like all the rest. No. She was different, he could tell.

Tam bent down and murmured something in the girl's ear, and pressed some money into her hand. She nodded, took Hamish's hand and pulled him down off his stool.

She can't be much older than me, thought

Hamish. Her hand was smooth and cool in his. The chorus of laughs, jeers and shouts grew louder as she led him quickly through the crowd, away from his friends. He didn't know where they were going but suddenly he knew he would rather be with her than anyone else in the world.

Chapter Seventeen

'Mary! Come downstairs! There's someone here to see you.'

Mary was curled up on her bed, reading a book, but when she heard her mother shouting she put the book down and got up. Sliding her feet into her shoes, she wondered for a moment who it was visiting her – Arabella Seaton, maybe? She was back from her fancy boarding school and often wanted some company. Or Caroline Johnson from the church, who had said she might come by with some piano music that Mary wanted to borrow.

She looked into the mirror and inspected her face. She tidied her hair, tucking away a few loose strands and smoothing it down neatly, and pinched lightly at her cheeks to bring some colour into them. She looked fine, she knew that. The very picture of a healthy, radiant seventeen-year-old girl on the brink of life beginning.

Except that it wasn't beginning. She had no idea of what she wanted to do. All she cared about was that Hamish was far, far away over the seas. When he'd gone, it was as if he'd taken all her energy and vigour with him, leaving her desperate for him. She wrote screeds of letters to him, posted nearly all of them but seldom heard anything back, beyond a line or two scrawled on a card. She worried that he had forgotten about her and that his new life was taking him somewhere she would never be able to follow, so she spent hours in her bedroom, dreaming and reading, wishing her life away.

She knew who was downstairs, though. At first it was a bore and an annoyance, but now she was becoming accustomed to it and almost beginning to look forward to the visits. The first time that she'd gone downstairs and found that it was Mc-Bain waiting for her in the drawing room, with his shabby clothes, oil-stained hands and stubby workman's fingers, she'd been very displeased. She'd never given him reason to think that he had the kind of friendship with her that meant he could call on her at home. In fact, she'd always tried to ignore him as much as possible. He was Hamish's pal, after all. What on earth did they have to say to each other? And the look on her mother's face showed that she was just as horrified as Mary at her caller.

But she had been pleasantly surprised. McBain had irritated and annoyed her when Hamish was around but now that he was gone, the younger boy was not quite the burden she remembered. And he always seemed to have some news of Hamish to pass on to her, which was irresistible in itself.

She ran lightly downstairs to the front room.

The manse was a grey stone Victorian place, with great high rooms and arched windows. Mary's mother had made it homely and beautiful, and very comfortable. Mary was the only child in the house, and she was naturally tidy, so the place always looked in perfect order.

She stood in the doorway for a moment and watched McBain. It was obvious that he always made an effort when he came calling, changing out of his mechanic's clothes and scrubbing his face and hands, but there was still the aura of the workshop around him, the bitter reek of oil and the grease under his nails that he could never get rid of. Now, as she watched, he moved slowly about the room, as delicately as he could manage, as though aware how out of place he was among the china ornaments, embroidered cushions and silver picture frames.

'Hello,' she said.

He jumped and turned to look at her. His face was such a strange one, she thought. It was by no means handsome – thin and sunken, with sallow skin, and dominated by those heavy black brows. His nose was fleshy and broad and his lips thin. He had nothing of the fineness of feature that Hamish had. But something in those dark black eyes was intriguing. Was it because it was so difficult to know what he was thinking?

'Oh, hello, Mary. I hope you don't mind me coming by.'

'Of course not. Would you like some tea? I can ring for some.'

'Um – well, I...'

'Or to go for a walk, perhaps?' That was what

they usually did. McBain did not seem at ease sitting in a drawing room sipping tea served to him in a fine china cup by the housemaid. Once they were outside, everything was easier.

'Aye, a walk.' McBain was evidently relieved. 'It's a lovely fair day.'

They went outside. The manse was set far back from the road in large grounds and they often wandered around it when McBain came to call. There was a stone seat at the back, by a small summer house, where they usually ended up sitting as they chatted.

'So have you had any news from Hamish?' she asked eagerly, almost before they were out of the front door. McBain was right – it was a lovely day, with blue skies and a fresh breeze blowing.

'I've brought a card,' said McBain. 'I'll show you in a bit.'

'Another one?' asked Mary plaintively. 'How come he writes so much to you and hardly to me at all? I don't understand.'

McBain shrugged. 'Perhaps he's just busy and thinks a card wouldn't be any good for you. You deserve better, maybe.'

'I deserve *something* at least. He may be busy but I'd rather have a postcard than nothing at all. After all the letters I've written to him!'

'He doesn't know how lucky he is. Lots of girls wouldn't write at all, I think.'

'You're right.' Mary sighed. 'Oh dear. It feels as though he's been gone for ever. I can't imagine what it will be like to have him home.'

They walked slowly round the house and into the rhododendron garden.

'Where's the card? May I see it?'

McBain pulled a black-and-white postcard out of his pocket. The top bore several brightly coloured foreign stamps and the writing was the sloping copperplate they had all been taught at the village school. 'Here you are,' he said, handing it to her.

Mary read it as they walked.

Dear pal

How are you? I am having lots of adventures here at sea as you can imagine. We have seen dolphins and flying fish, did you ever? They were quite a sight. It's warm weather and you will not recognise me when you see me, I'm almost black. Lots of great stories to tell you one day about my time at sea and in the ports. Take care old friend and give my best to Mary. Yours sincerely, Hamish.

'Is that all?' she cried, when she had finished. It was a bitter disappointment to see how little Hamish appeared to think of her. Who cared about stupid dolphins and flying fish – what about the love he had sworn to her? Why did he have no time to write when he could send McBain postcards almost every week, telling him to take care and promising to relate all the wonderful stories of what had happened when next they met? What about the intimacy she and Hamish had shared, the kisses and the embraces, the declarations of love and the promises to wait for each other? Had they all just been forgotten? It hurt her so much – but there was nothing she could do about it. All she could do was write, and that seemed to make no difference at all.

McBain shrugged his shoulders. 'I don't think he's being cruel on purpose, Mary. Probably he's just not thinking.'

Cruel? Yes, that was it. He was being cruel. And not thinking was the worst thing it could possibly be, when she was thinking of him constantly, day and night, dreaming of when they would be reunited.

'Don't be sad, Mary. Think of what you've got here. You've got plans, haven't you?'

Mary blinked hard, trying to hold back the tears that were pricking her eyes. 'My mother wants me to go to college in Edinburgh after I've taken my Highers. But I won't do it – not while I'm still waiting for Hamish. Going to college is like saying it's all over for us and I just can't do it yet. It can wait a year.'

'What will you do instead?'

'I don't know. Sit at home, I suppose. Help my mother. There's lots of work to be found, you know. She does so much for charity. Perhaps I'll help her with that.' There was a tone of resignation in Mary's voice, as though she was prepared to embrace a life of philanthropy and serving others if she could not have the man she loved. 'What about you?'

'Me?' McBain seemed surprised she should be interested in him.

'Yes. You said last time you were here that you were thinking of expanding the business.'

'Oh – yes. That's right.' They came up to the stone seat and sat down on it. 'I was gonna think about getting a petrol pump for our garage. But

I've changed my mind about that now. I'm gonna get a boat instead.'

'A boat?' Mary blinked. 'For a garage?'

'I know. It doesn't seem what you'd expect. But I don't want to work with cars and trucks – not really. My real love is the sea. And I'm gonna get a small fishing boat and see if I can make a go of catching fish. My pa's plenty all right looking after the garage and it will go on supporting itself. But I've never wanted to get under a car the same way I want to get out to sea.'

'You boys! You're all mad! I can't understand it. What is your passion to be out there on the water, where it's so dangerous? And fishermen spend their lives getting up in the middle of the night and sleeping through the day, risking all of it when the storms come! Hamish is the same – goodness only knows where he is at the moment and if he ever manages to get back alive, what do you think he wants to do then? He wants to go out to sea as a fisherman himself. Perhaps you two could work together – then you could keep an eye on him for me, keep him safe.'

'Perhaps,' said McBain in his gruff voice.

Mary persisted. 'But what is it? You could have a perfectly good job on the dry land, earning what you need. Why go to sea?'

McBain stared out over the manicured lawn and bushes of rhododendrons, away towards the house. 'I don't know,' he said at last. 'All this is all very well, you know. But – it's *soft*. I can't really explain it better than that. Once you've been on a boat and felt the power of the sea ... well, you don't ever really feel satisfied with anything else.'

'Do you wish you were at sea, like Hamish?'

McBain's black brows knitted into a frown. 'Yes and no. There are things he's got that I can't have. But it's also the other way round.'

Mary stared at him for a moment, trying to understand his meaning. Then she looked down at the card in his hand. 'Can I have this?' she asked.

'No,' he said quickly and snatched it deftly from her hand. 'Better give it back to me. I've promised the stamps to my little brother, see.'

'Can I borrow it? When you've taken the stamps off?' She so longed to have something of Hamish to look at, to kiss.

'Oh, yes, I'll bring it back.' He put it carefully away in his pocket. 'I'll bring it back another time.'

'Why do you have that boy over here, Mary?' Her mother looked at her sternly across the supper table. 'It's bad enough that you associate with the Fraser boy without this one too.'

'I don't have him over. He just comes. He's not doing any harm, is he? And anyway, what's wrong with him?' Mary forgot that it was not so long ago she was begging Hamish to get rid of the troublesome and irritating McBain. Now she felt quite defensive of him. It was no surprise that her mother disapproved of McBain. She was from a good Edinburgh family and never forgot it, and as a result, there were few people around here she considered her equals.

'The McBain family are not respectable,' Mrs Burns said, delicately loading her fork with fish. 'They're from Glasgow – working people. And they say that Mr McBain has reduced his wife to idiocy in a drunken rage, poor woman.'

'That's not true,' said Mary hotly. 'McBain told me all about it. His poor mother had an accident and hurt her head, and the grief has reformed his father. They've had their misfortunes but I think we may say that they're now respectable.'

'I'll be the judge of that, Mary. I don't like having the boy here and I'd appreciate it if you told him that he's not to visit.'

'I like having him here. He's my friend.'

'Is he really that bad, Jean?' asked her father mildly. He was always attempting to keep the peace. 'He seemed harmless to me when I met him.'

'James, please leave these matters to me. I hope you're not implying that I don't know best when it comes to the people Mary should be associating with.'

'Of course not...'

'I shall have him here if I like,' declared Mary, who was just as stubborn as her mother when she wanted to be. 'If you must know, I like him. I know he looks odd, with that funny face and all that black hair, but he's gentle underneath, I know he is. And I won't ban him from here just because he works hard for his living. After all, isn't it the rich who won't be going to heaven? Don't forget that Jesus Christ ate with tax collectors and sinners and the poor. I think that Our Lord would want me to befriend him and be kind to him.'

'Don't make that kind of flippant remark, or

invoke the Saviour when you do it, young lady!' cried her mother, scandalised. It seemed that the idea that the McBain family might get to heaven before her was unthinkable.

Mary stared at her plate sulkily. She had been feeling miserable all afternoon whenever she thought about Hamish and she was glad of an excuse to vent some of her frustration. Her mother was quite wrong, she was sure of that. The more she knew of McBain, the more she could see that he was a fine young man. And besides, she would see whomever she wanted, whenever she wanted. Just let her mother try and stop her.

Chapter Eighteen

Hamish spread the silver jewellery out on the blanket of his bunk. It was so pretty – intricate and finely worked. A necklace and some bracelets. Mary would love them, he was sure of that.

Kenzie had taken him down to the markets before they'd left Bangkok and shown him where to buy it. All the seamen bought presents here, trinkets for their mothers, sisters and sweethearts. It was cheap but solid and decorative. Siamese silver, they called it.

But it would be months before he saw Mary again. He had signed up to a double tour without realising it. Before he could go back home they'd be making another circuit of all the ports and cities they'd already been to, on the endless round of loading and unloading the ship, taking goods from one place to another.

He wrapped the silver up again in the handkerchief where he kept it. For some reason, he felt a little ill when he looked at it. It reminded him of why he had bought it in the first place. They'd been in Bangkok three nights and every night they went back to the Blue Elephant. Each time he found her there, waiting for him, the beautiful Sri with her lovely eyes, her soft mouth and her gentle embraces. The first time they'd been together he had hardly known what was happening, he was so drunk. She had led him upstairs to a small dark room, and inside had pulled him down onto the bed beside her. He had wanted to sleep instantly, but she kept him on the right side of consciousness with her caresses until he became aware of a power building in him. He came to full alertness to find her beneath him, opening her mouth to his kisses and guiding him inside her, into the sublime warmth and pleasure to be found between her legs. It was a feeling like nothing he had ever known before and he had climaxed almost at once, with a shout.

Afterwards she had taken him back downstairs to where the others made knowing remarks and jokes at his expense, but he hadn't cared a bit. He was still off, floating somewhere, overcome by the extraordinary experience he had just had.

The next night he found her again, and this time he was not drunk. She took him by the hand again and they went upstairs. He was eager to retaste the pleasure of the night before but he wanted to touch her all over, feel her small firm breasts and run his hands all over her smooth skin. He needed to discover her, as though she had all the answers to the questions he'd been longing to ask. She was a woman, that mysterious desirable creature with the body that lured and tempted him in so many different ways. Now she let him touch her, understanding that tonight, this was what he wanted. But when he had kissed and stroked and explored her all over, she reached out and took him in her hand. He groaned and twitched and then surrendered to her. This time she used her mouth to give him a delight that left him shaken and breathless.

On the third night, he'd wanted to enter her immediately and he took his time, thrusting until he was on the point of climax and then stopping until he could start again. He finally allowed himself to finish with a shudder but only after he could bear the sensations no longer.

'Oh, Sri. Oh my God,' he panted. 'You're so gorgeous, you're so beautiful.'

'Yes,' Sri said, 'beautiful, very beautiful.'

But he didn't think she had really understood him. He saw her only one more time before they had to leave.

Now he was consumed with guilt. The bliss of what he had experienced was wearing off, to be replaced by a sense that he had done something truly terrible. The others had mocked him about it, telling him that they all did it, even the married boys, and he wasn't even engaged. But he knew that he had done something worse than them because for a while he had loved Sri, and he had loved her more at that moment than he loved Mary.

But he realised that he had been in the grip of some kind of enchantment, because now he longed for Mary with his heart. Now she was the real person and Sri, still working in her noisy bar, taking men upstairs into those tiny bedrooms, was just a dream. It was stupid to feel anything for a little Thai prostitute. It was stupid to have had anything to do with her. And he had heard enough stories of sailors with the clap to know he had taken a silly risk and if he got away unscathed, he was lucky.

Hamish locked the bundle of jewellery safely in his locker and then threw himself down on his bunk, groaning. It wouldn't be so bad if he didn't relive his experiences with Sri every night in his imagination, still feeling the force of his climaxes with her. He tried to stop himself – but he simply couldn't and now the guilt was almost too much to bear. He'd wanted to confide in Tam or Kenzie, but there was no way that they would understand what he was going through. They'd never met Mary, for one thing, and how could anyone who didn't know her appreciate her purity, her uniqueness? They wouldn't be able to. They'd think she was just another ordinary girl, like their sweethearts.

The urge to confess was a powerful one. He got up, went to his locker and took out some paper and a pen. Then, slowly and carefully, he began to write and once he'd started, it flowed freely and he wrote faster and faster until he'd covered two sheets.

He stuck it into an envelope without even reading it through and slid it under his pillow. He would post it in the next port, though God only knew when they'd be on dry land again, and perhaps he'd get some form of relief now that his conscience was no longer so heavy.

'Hey, have you heard about the captain?'

Hamish shook his head. As deck boy, he usually found out about everything last of all. 'What about him?'

Tam leaned against the rail and watched as Hamish cleaned the brasses. 'He was taken ill in the night. The doc had to give him an emergency operation they say. Very gory and bloody. His appendix had burst and his insides were all gangrenous. Nasty.'

'Will he be all right?' Hamish was concerned. He was fond of the captain.

Tam shrugged. 'He's made it through the night anyway. But the rumour is that he'll be invalided off at the next port and we'll have a new captain meet us.'

'Really?' Hamish could not imagine any other captain than Captain Harding. How would they all function without him?

'Oh, don't worry, they're all much the same you know. Once you've got used to the little oddities of one and forgotten about the oddities of the other ... well, it's much of a muchness, you'll see. Don't worry about it.'

The captain, it transpired, had been very ill indeed

and he was far too weak after his operation to run the boat, but it all went so smoothly that it virtually ran itself. When they pulled into their next port, he left the ship to be taken back to Scotland on the next homebound boat. The *Arran* still had far too long a tour of duty for him to be able to stay aboard.

They piped him off and there was a sense of gloom about the whole occasion as the usually hale captain was wheeled away in a chair, with his blanket over his knees. A few hours later the new captain came aboard and life on the *Arran* changed for ever.

Chapter Nineteen

McBain could hardly believe what he was reading. What on earth was Hamish thinking of? Was he mad? Had he gone crazy?

The letter was dated weeks ago and it had spent a long time winging its way to Kinlochvegan and into McBain's hands. But he could not understand for the life of him why Hamish would write such a thing, making such a confession – placing his friend in such a position of power.

McBain looked at the flimsy sheets of paper in his hand, and laughed. This was all he needed. He didn't even have to try and forge anything, the way he had with the postcards he'd been showing to Mary over the months. It had taken hours and hours of practice before he had been sure that he could make a good approximation of Hamish's handwriting. It helped that they had both been trained in the same rigorous style by their teacher at school, but he had still needed to work at getting the swoops and curves as Hamish would make them. Then he had had to steam off the stamps as carefully as possible, reusing them over and over and hoping that Mary wouldn't notice that the postcards he was receiving from Hamish always came from the same country.

The truth was, Hamish had sent him barely a line in months. He was quite sure that his old friend had forgotten all about him, all about Kinlochvegan and probably all about Mary too. And why wouldn't he? He was seeing all the most exotic sights that the world had to offer. No doubt home seemed tiny and unimportant to him now. McBain could understand that up to a point – though how anyone could forget about Mary, he had no idea. She was his absolute ideal of womanhood, and he lived for the afternoons when he would put his latest creation carefully in his pocket and walk the six miles to the manse to call on her.

He was sure she didn't guess how he felt about her. She wouldn't realise that the amazement he had felt when he had first laid eyes on her had grown and deepened into an obsessional love that verged on worship. For him, she was the most perfect woman in the world, and he knew that some day he would have her as his very own. It was ordained, he had absolute faith in that, but he realised that it would take a while until Mary saw it from his point of view and understood that they were meant to be together into eternity, and until then, he would move gently, not frightening her by showing her the force of his love. He would show her that when she had forgotten about Hamish Fraser and returned his affections instead, as he was certain she would in the end. For the moment, she assumed he was being kind, bringing Hamish's cards to her even though the messages – brief, careless and passed on through him – cut her to the quick, he could see that.

His only worry was that Hamish would suddenly start writing to Mary himself and undo all his work, perhaps even reveal the truth about the postcards. But he was banking on the fact that Hamish had already shown himself to be a terrible correspondent, and that if he did get round to writing to Mary, he would be unlikely to mention a few postcards he'd sent to McBain. Or hadn't sent, as it turned out.

The excuse to see Mary was one he couldn't do without now. And the gentle chip-chip-chipping at Mary's love for Hamish was a work that he was now committed to, whatever happened.

That was why he wanted to sing and laugh and dance a jig when this letter had arrived. In it, Hamish wrote every detail of an affair he had had with a prostitute in Thailand. It was almost too good to be true! McBain read it three times before the real implications began to sink in. Hamish had given in to temptation and was now, from the sound of the letter, very very sorry indeed. Tortured by his guilt, he had needed to confess and had thought his friend would hear

211

him out without judgement or condemnation.

Well, he couldn't have been more wrong. As far as McBain was concerned, Hamish had condemned himself out of his own mouth. Sure, there were bound to be temptations abroad, and foreign women with loose morals willing to teach a young sailor the facts of life. But if you had Mary waiting for you at home... McBain was amazed that Hamish could ever have considered sullying himself with some little foreign whore. Well, he would pay the price.

He turned the paper over, reading the story again and looking at the practical nature of what he held in his hand. Then he began to plan how he would use this marvellous new opportunity.

He was so eager to get to the manse that this time he took a car from the garage and drove it the six miles to Mary's house. He was there so quickly that he was much earlier than he'd expected and he had to wait for almost an hour in the car, parked at the side of the road looking out to sea.

His heart was beating fast and his hands were clammy and trembling. This is it, he thought. This is the moment! Even though he couldn't express it to himself – for he'd never had the gift of the gab – he knew that the time had come when fate had shown him the turn in the road. His future was waiting for him from this day forward. He got slowly out of the car, crossed the road, and began to walk up the long gravel driveway to the front door of the manse.

Mary looked up at him, her eyes wild and her face deathly pale. 'But I don't understand!' she cried. 'He wrote this to you?' She held out the sheet of writing paper imploringly towards McBain. 'Why? Why?'

McBain gazed back at her. It had worked much better than he could ever have planned it. He'd pulled out a postcard, supposedly sent from Hamish, and as he'd done so the flimsy sheets of Hamish's letter had come with it, floating to the floor.

'What's that?' Mary had asked quickly.

'Nothing, nothing,' McBain replied, scrabbling down for the letter. Mary had darted forward first and picked up the top sheet. McBain snatched up the second.

'This is Hamish's writing! Has he sent you a letter?'

'Mary, no, give it back! Come on, that's not for you, it's private...'

'Why? What could he write to you that he wouldn't want me to know?' She laughed nervously. 'I'm going to read it.'

'No, Mary, please, please don't read it.' He put out a hand as though to take it from her but she moved it away out of his grasp. 'Please – it's private. Hamish wouldn't want you to see it, I'm begging you...'

Her eyes were frightened but she spoke with a careful casualness. 'Now, now, you're overreacting, I'm sure. There's nothing Hamish could say to you that he couldn't say to me, even if he is swearing like a sailor now. After all, he is one.' And she'd read it. He had hated watching her face change as she read the pages, but he had also known that it was a necessary suffering. She had to go through this trial so that she could come to a better life. Without this, she would never know how worthless and stupid Hamish Fraser really was, or how much happier life would be for her once she accepted that he, McBain, was her rightful partner. Still, seeing the blood drain from her cheeks and the tears in her eyes, and hearing her gasps of horror as she read had been painful for him – it wasn't hard for him to seem upset and emotional himself.

'I'm sorry you've had to read this. I didn't want you to – I feel like an idiot.'

She shook her head as she gazed again at the treacherous page, speechless.

'I can't believe he would do this to you, Mary,' he said tersely.

She whispered, 'I've never heard of such things, never thought that *anyone* would do them ... and then to write them down! How could he even find the words, the guile, to write them down...! And ... *Hamish*. My Hamish.' A tear coursed down her cheek, and then another. 'I thought he loved me,' she said softly.

'He does.'

'He doesn't! How can he? How could he have done such a thing if he loved me?' Mary looked up at him, her eyes full of tears. Then she saw that McBain was holding the second page of Hamish's letter. 'Give me the rest of the letter,' she demanded, holding out her hand. 'I need to know everything.'

'No, Mary, I can't...' He shook his head.

214

'Come on! You must! I have to know everything now.'

She went to try and snatch it from him, but he stepped away and put the sheet behind his back.

'I can't do it. You can't see it. It's worse...'

'Worse than that?' she cried, going pale again. 'How can it be worse? Let me see it!'

McBain held the second half of the letter tightly. The first had told in detail what Hamish had done with that little tart. After that, he had written of his guilt and regret and desperate desire to see Mary again and cleanse the muck he felt on his soul. He asked McBain if Mary could ever forgive him and said that he would confess it all to her when he saw her again and beg her to believe in his true love for her.

'I can't let you see it,' he said slowly, and in front of her eyes, he ripped it into tiny shreds.

She screamed with anguish. 'What did it say? Tell me, tell me!' She started to cry in earnest now, covering her face with her hands and rocking backwards and forwards. 'Please, you must tell me.'

McBain pushed the torn scraps of paper down into his pocket and took a deep breath. 'He said he'd fallen in love with this girl, because she's beautiful and because he wants to rescue her from her life. He wants to marry her and settle down somewhere where they can raise a family together. Australia or Africa, he said.'

She stopped crying and said in a low, despairing voice, 'Didn't he mention me at all?'

'Aye.'

She looked up at him with a spark of hope.

'He said to tell you he was sorry and that he hoped you'd understand and forgive him, and that you'd find someone better than him.'

This seemed scant substitute for the anguished devotion for Mary that Hamish had poured out, but she wasn't to know that, of course. Perhaps the very terse brutality of it made it more convincing.

Mary stared at the sheet she still held in her hand, as though it might read differently if she looked at it again. McBain watched, his triumph matched by pity for her suffering.

'It seems like he's serious about this other lass, then,' he said slowly.

Mary threw the paper to the floor and put her head in her hands, sobbing hard. 'I can't believe it!' she said, muffled by sobs and her hands. 'I just can't believe it.'

But McBain could tell that she did believe it. Surely it was what she had counted on. Right from the start, her great fear had been that Hamish would find someone else, a woman with the allure of the exotic and with a knowledge of the world. McBain had seen that and that was why he had staked everything on this deception. It was almost bound to succeed, because Hamish had destroyed himself out of his own mouth and because, even though she didn't know it, Mary wanted to believe that he was going to marry someone else.

She looked up at McBain. Her face was tear-stained and twisted with grief. But she was still beautiful to him. 'It's all over,' she said in a broken voice. 'Even if he came and begged me to take him back, I never would now. I could never forgive him for this. Never.'

As she wept again, McBain allowed himself one small, dark smile of triumph.

Part Three

Chapter Twenty

Life on the ocean wave had changed Hamish. When he had set out as a deck boy all those months ago, he had been a scrawny lad with a white face and a whiter backside. Now he was twenty-one years old, broad in the shoulder and muscled all over his body from the hours of hard labour he'd put in almost every day for all that time. And he wasn't the deck boy any more, either. There was some other poor lad far from home, missing his mammy, learning what hard work meant while he vomited from exhaustion and unaccustomed physical exertion.

Now Hamish Fraser was brown all over – even his bum was sun-kissed from days sunbathing naked, or diving and swimming in the warm blue seas off the islands. His thighs were like iron, his stomach rippled like a washboard and his arms were thick with muscles. He knew he was strong, but so was every other man aboard except, perhaps, the doctor. It was what was expected.

He went above deck and shivered in the unaccustomed cold. They were most definitely in the northern hemisphere now. He remembered his crossing the Line ceremony when he'd been well and truly given the treatment. Well, he was a doughty old shellback now, who'd handed out the same kind of stuff to green youngsters on their first crossing, though he'd never forgotten the real fear he had felt that day and tried to tone down what he put others through.

The skies were grey already. A stiff salty breeze blew in across the bows, ruffling his short hair. The curls were long gone, cut off as soon as the kink in them first showed through. Scotland, he remembered, was bloody cold, and he'd maybe spent too long in balmier climates. Am I mad? he wondered suddenly. Should I just have stayed away?

But it was impossible to remain away from home any longer. Much as he had enjoyed the warmth of the southern sun, he yearned for the bracing chill of an autumn morning in Kinloch-vegan. He wanted to see frost sparkling along the hedgerows and on the branches of trees. He craved a wintry Scottish night, when he was by the fire in his pyjamas and dressing gown, warm and toasty with a cup of something hot, while the wind buffeted and blew about outside like a thing possessed, and rain lashed the cottage.

He needed to see his parents again as well. He'd begun to miss them badly of late. Every old person he'd passed in the streets, even wizened old men in the streets of Hong Kong, with their sunken faces, coolie hats and little black clothes, had made him think of his mother and father. He'd begun to be terrified that he would hear that they had died before he could see them again, and dreams of their passing woke him in the night, leaving him shaken and tearful even though he laughed off his superstitious nonsense in the day-time. Once, overcome by sentiment and feeling a bit homesick, he had sent a telegram to his mother on her birthday. The Sparks had told him that he could send a radio message and arrange for a bunch of flowers to be delivered at the same time, so he had decided to do it, even though the cost was quite considerable and made a dent in his savings. There was a set list of messages so he had chosen the one that seemed most appropriate, which was 'Not only now but always do I think lovingly of you, Mother dear'. He'd thought his mother would be pretty pleased with that, and she was, it turned out. His father wrote to say how much his mother had loved the gesture but – *it's probably best if you don't do that again, son,* the letter continued. *Your dear mother could not pass that bunch of flowers without crying her poor eyes out and it stayed on our kitchen table until it had almost rotted away to nothing.*

Hamish laughed when he thought of it but it did nothing to quell the desire he felt to see his parents again. They had understood when he had abruptly left the Brewster Shipping Company – at least, that was what they had written to him, but perhaps they were simply accepting the inevitable. He had tried to make it plain how impossible it had become to stay on board the *Arran* after Captain Harding had left. His successor, Captain Bailey, had been a foul man with a streak of wickedness in his soul and the moment he boarded the poor old ship, the whole atmosphere had changed. Morale plummeted and misery reigned. It was as if the canker in the captain was infectious and it began to spread through the rest of the crew, from the top downwards. Within a couple of months, cruelty and bullying had become commonplace and it seemed as though all the camaraderie and laughter had vanished. Hamish suddenly understood how an unhappy ship could be a dangerous place to live at sea, and more than once he had felt fear rolling in his stomach as drink and anger and violence brewed in the dark nights, and there was the scent of murder in the air.

It had never come to that, thank God. A few nasty incidents but nothing really serious, unless you counted the destruction of the spirit of a happy ship. Quite soon Hamish realised that he couldn't live with it much longer. They had left the Philippines and he was longing for some leave and eager to find out when he would be going home, when the captain summoned him to his cabin.

'I've been looking over your contract, lad,' he said, showing Hamish the scrappy old bit of paper he had signed that day in Leith, so long ago now. 'I don't know if you realise it but you've signed yourself up to five years on board, without home leave. You're only entitled to shore leave.'

'What?' said Hamish, open-mouthed. The captain gave him a hard look and he hastily corrected himself. He knew that the man had nasty, old-fashioned punishments that he enjoyed inflicting on deck boys, who would never find anyone to fight their cause for them. 'Sorry. Excuse me, Captain, sir. What do you mean?'

'Brewster's a wily fella, I've always known that, and he must have seen you coming. You've willingly given up all your rights to go home, according to this.'

'There must be some mistake, sir. I'd never

have agreed to that.'

'Well, you did. Look.' The captain tossed the paper in front of him. Hamish read it and saw at once that he'd been had – he really had put his name to such outrageous terms, even though he had blatantly been hoodwinked.

'But of course I'm not going to hold you to this,' said the captain, his tone kinder.

Hamish looked up at him in relief. 'Thank you, sir. That's very good of you. For a terrible moment there, I thought I wasn't going to get home for five years.'

The captain chuckled. 'Now, what kind of monsters do you think we are?'

Hamish laughed as well. 'And I've already done one double tour of duty. Captain Harding held me to that one. All my old pals have been back home already for a month.'

'You'll get home, but it won't be for a while, so don't get your hopes too high.'

'When?' asked Hamish anxiously.

The captain shook his head, saying, 'Let's not talk about that now. Just so's you know what you've signed up to and that I'm not so harsh that I'd keep you to it. I know what the crew all think of me. It's a question of discipline – you can't let it slip for a moment or there'd be sheer anarchy. Believe me, I know what I'm talking about. So you can tell 'em I'm not so bad as they say, all right?'

'Yes, sir. Thank you, sir,' said Hamish, relieved that he was out of a sticky spot.

The captain had been lying, he knew that now. It took months and months before he realised

225

that, though. He had been led on by the eternally dangling carrot of his promised home leave, watching other crews come and go and come back again, until he had finally had enough. After a skinful of rum, he'd gone to the captain and shouted and yelled until the captain had said he'd have him dumped at the next port, he didn't give a shite if it was against regulations or not. Then he'd said that, on second thoughts, Fraser could get the fuck off his boat now and never come the hell back, and forget the wages owing him.

Thank God they'd been in port at the time, or Hamish could have found himself overboard – the captain had been so furious he had been foaming at the mouth like an animal. As it was, he had minutes to gather his stuff and skip off the *Arran*, leaving everyone behind. Now he realised that the captain had taken a decision to milk him of every drop of hard work until he could take no more, and then sack him. A lawyer could have told him in an instant that the contract he signed as a fifteen-year-old could not possibly have been enforced and that he was due his leave like anyone else, but Hamish did not guess that. Instead he put his faith in Captain Bailey, and he'd been made a fool of.

He'd found himself stranded in a foreign port with his bag over his shoulder containing all his savings, and his most pressing fear was that he would be robbed and lose the lot. But luck was on his side for once, and he fell in with some Dutch merchant seamen in a bar, the kindest and most cheerful group of people he'd ever met.

They spoke excellent English too, even though Hamish's Scottish accent caused a few problems at first. He was welcomed aboard their ship and given a berth for as long as they were in the harbour, which was only a few days. But by the end of that time he'd got himself a place on another boat, an Australian one this time, and now he was a junior seaman and no longer a deck boy.

The long voyages with that boat took him even further south, to the great continent itself. He had always longed to see Australia and it was his dream come true to visit it. Scotland and home became ever further away, remote and unimaginable, until his old life almost felt like a dream. When he wandered in the blazing sunshine around the city of Perth, it was almost impossible to bring to mind little Kinlochvegan and everyone there. He got extended shore leave when they'd arrived in Australia, a whole month off, and he'd had a whale of a time, renting himself a room in a boarding house and living it up with his new mates.

And then there'd been the girls. When he thought back to his first experience with Sri, and the way he'd behaved afterwards, he felt rather foolish. He must have been some kind of idealistic boy to think that he was going to keep himself pure for Mary, and then to write the whole thing down and send it back home to McBain ... how many kinds of idiot was he to do that? He could only hope that McBain had done the right thing and torn that stupid letter up. It hadn't taken too long before he'd grown accustomed to his guilt and then stopped feeling it altogether, and when temptation was placed in his way again, it was all too easy to give in to it.

By the time he reached Australia, he couldn't remember how many girls he'd been to bed with. He'd even had to visit the ship's doctor a couple of times with the malady that often affected young sailors. It wasn't until he was in Perth, though, that he slept with a girl without having to pay her for it afterwards. She was a bright, pretty thing that he met at a dance. They rock and rolled together, her yellow netted skirts swirling round his legs, until she let him take her outside for a breath of fresh air and a walk in the moonlight that turned into a fine bit of hanky-panky up against a tree in the park. He saw her again a few times after that and they enjoyed a sweet, romantic time together. He was sad when he had to reboard his ship and say goodbye to her for ever.

'Maybe I'll come back one day,' he said to her. 'I like Australia. I could live here. There's something in the air that makes a man feel positive.'

'You won't forget me, will you?' she whispered plaintively, and he said that of course he wouldn't, how could he?

Afterwards, when they'd said goodbye, he felt a sadness that had nothing to do with things ending with that young girl. It was because his thoughts turned to Mary, and how much he had loved her and how he had made the same promise that he would never forget her and then ... well, he hadn't forgotten her exactly. But he was a different person now, and who was to say that she wasn't as well? He remembered the passion he'd felt for her and how much it had hurt to leave her, but it was all very dim now, faded by the months at sea. He had one small photograph of her which he took out and stared at, all the time at first and then less and less as the corporeal reality of the person in the picture became ever harder to summon up.

Now, as he got closer and closer to home, he was beginning to think of her more and more, and she began to grow more vivid in his mind, like a photograph developing. Things that he had long forgotten started to come back to him: the sound of her voice suddenly rang in his mind. He saw flashes of her face in front of his mind's eye, and recalled the velvet blue of her eyes and the cushion of her lower lip. Excitement at the thought of seeing her again grew inside him.

It was the thought of Mary that had finally decided him that the time had now come to go home. At first it was his parents that drew him back, and a sense that he had at last quenched his thirst for adventure and sightseeing – at least for a while. Then, on the voyage out from Australia during a storm, a monster wave had passed over the ship. They had emerged soaked through and carrying water, but safe, and the experience had left him shaken. For once, he'd considered the possibility that he could die on his travels and never see his home again. He'd thought of Mary that time, and was filled with a longing to see her again. It had been strange and intense and hadn't lasted long, but the echo of it, along with his other feelings, had been enough to set him on the path home. His contract with the Australians had come to an end and he decided not to sign up again, though they had tried to persuade him to stay. He was popular amongst them.

'Ah, come on, Jock, mate. One more tour, eh? One last drink in Manila?'

But Hamish had made up his mind. He had a healthy pot of savings and he was determined to go home at last, and see what happened when he got there.

Chapter Twenty-one

He felt as though he were almost home when he arrived in Inverness. He spent a couple of days there doing some business before he finally took the bus that rattled along the road to the coast.

It was spring and the evenings were just becoming lighter but even so, it was pitch black before he was deposited on the main street, with his sackful of belongings at his feet. He was disappointed. He'd been hoping for a view of that petrol-grey water of the harbour, sometimes so clear that you could see the stones on the bottom. He'd wanted to glimpse the little village from afar, the white, brown and grey cottages nestled into the hillside above the main streets, which were lined with close-built terraces painted in pinks and blues. These houses seemed as if they were trying to bring some candy brightness to the soft dull colours of nature, the greens and rusty browns of the hillsides, the blacks and greys of the slate and granite, and the infinite palette of blues and charcoals that made up the sea and the sky.

He'd yearned to see the little harbour, with the stone-built jetties, and boats moored in the bay, and the coils of ropes on the quayside. He'd even hoped to see the school and the hard-lined plain kirk that both stood above the village on the small winding roads that led away from the main street. Perhaps, he'd thought, there might be a welcome of some kind. But as he shivered in the night air, realising again how accustomed he now was to the balmy evenings of the tropics, the reality was very different. And why shouldn't it be? Who knew he was coming home, after all? He'd sent a telegram saying what time his bus would be arriving, but most likely it hadn't come in time. The Kinlochvegan post office was not known for its speed or efficiency – in fact, he remembered now, everything moved at a snail's pace in this sleepy little village, so far from the bustle and activity and swarms of people that he'd seen in all those different places across the world.

He picked up his rucksack and turned for home. The disappointment began to seep out of him, to be replaced by a rising excitement. If no one had come to meet him, then they didn't know he was on his way at this very moment...

The Fraser house was on a small road off the main street, facing out over the harbour. It was a long low building, older than most of the village houses and unusual in not being a terraced cottage like so many of the others. It was stone built, and its lumps and bumps and deep-set low windows were unlike the more recent smooth-surfaced brick cottages. It was painted in a thick coating of whitewash to give it an extra protection against the weather and the salty water that came off the sea and ate into everything. Now it gleamed in the darkness as he approached, and the lights in the windows showed that his parents were still up.

He rapped on the door. There was a pause followed by the sound of one of the kitchen chairs scraping across the flagstone floor and then, a moment later, the door opened and his father stood in front of him, a questioning look on his face and his glasses in his hand. His expression transformed as he gazed at Hamish and took in the fact that his son was standing there in the doorway. Hamish laughed at the sight.

'Hello, Pa.'

'Oh – well! Hamish! What a surprise, lad, we didnae expect ... we didnae know!'

'What, what? What's that you say?' came the sound of his mother's voice, high-pitched with excitement, and then she appeared at his father's side. 'My wee boy! Oh! Oh!'

And he was engulfed in a huge hug that seemed to last for ever, though he didn't mind. He laughed even more, delighted at their surprise and joy, happy to breathe in the scent of his mother: warm, sweet and comforting. After many questions that he barely had time to answer, he was at last brought to the armchair in front of the fire, with his shoes off his tired feet and a cup of tea in front of him.

'Where's Ian?' Hamish asked, looking round. He had hoped his brother would be at home too.

'In Fort William. He's training to be a surveyor now, you know,' said his mother. 'We don't see him much at the moment.'

'Wee Ian, a surveyor!' exclaimed Hamish, surprised.

'Not so wee now,' said his father. 'He's eighteen and all grown up. Things have changed a bit while you've been away, Hamish.'

'I suppose they must have. It's hard to imagine, though.'

'You'll see tomorrow when you have a look around.'

'*You* haven't changed, though.' He grinned at his parents, happy to be with them again in all their familiarity.

'No, not us.' His father smiled. 'But you're a man now, Hamish.'

'I wouldn't have recognised you!' chimed in his mother. 'Look at you, so tall and broad. Did they feed you well then, on the ships? You've got so brawny. You've been gone so long and you've come back a man. I don't know where my little lad has gone.' Her eyes welled up with tears.

'Ah, Mam. Don't cry. I'm here, you know, all I've done is grown up and seen a bit of the world, got myself a bit of experience. But underneath I'm still the same. Still your boy.' Hamish grinned. 'And I've got a bit of surprise for the both of you as well.'

'Oh aye, what's that?' asked his father.

'I spent a day or two in Inverness before I set

off on my way back here. I wanted to stay long enough to get some business done.'

'What kind of business?'

'Well – I've put down a deposit on a cottage here in the village. Lachlan Cottage up the hill above the pub – do you know it?'

'You've bought a house?' gasped his mother. 'How much did that cost you?'

'It's three hundred pounds. I found it in an agent's in Inverness. I only went in to see what things cost and what the likelihood was of getting myself somewhere of my own to live. And what do you think – they had that place on their books.'

'Aye, it's been for sale for months, standing empty since old Rab Buckler died in it. You remember that miserable old miser who never had a kind word for anyone – not that I should speak ill of the dead. He left it to his great-niece and she put it up to sell, but no one round here wanted it.' His mother sniffed. 'We all remember nasty old Mr Buckler too well to want to live there.'

'Aye, well, I dinnae care what he was like. I said I would take it sight unseen if they knocked a hundred off the price. I've got almost five years' worth of wages which I've barely spent. I didn't earn a fortune, though I got a deal more once I'd stopped being a stupid sap and left the *Arran*. The Australians gave me some nice little bonuses too. I've got enough to try and realise a few dreams, though. My own little place, and a boat.'

'That's a lot of money, Hamish,' said his father solemnly. 'Can you really afford it? Have you gone into debt?'

'I've got a mortgage on it, aye. I went into the bank as well and got myself a loan approved. But I put down a half-payment, see, so it was easier to get the money.'

His father frowned. Any kind of debt was a shameful matter in his eyes, but then, he'd inherited this house from his father and he in his turn had inherited from his father – so there hadn't been the need to pay for a house to live in. Of course it was impossible without a mortgage. Hamish was just lucky that the bank seemed to accept that he could support the loan, perhaps because of the distinct impression he had given that he was returning as a senior officer to the Merchant Navy, thanks to the Australian contract he'd flashed at them.

'And now you've spent all your money,' said his mother, looking worried.

'Oh, no. I've got a bit left over, enough to get started with.'

Both his parents seemed surprised.

'I'm telling you, you don't need to worry about me. I'm well set up and if I ever need to go back to sea, I've got a job waiting for me. And if things ever got too desperate, I'd go to Australia. Honestly, you've got to see it to believe it. Forget America – Australia is the land of opportunity. If you could just see Perth...'

But they were looking at him as if he were making it all up. A life away from Kinlochvegan and Scotland was not something they could imagine – and how could any place be better than here?

'Well, there's plenty of time to tell you all about

it. And I've got some photographs in my rucksack too. I can show you some of the boys I sailed with and the ships I've been on...' He took a sip of the hot tea. 'Ah, that's nice. I've been all over the world, Ma, but no one makes a cup of tea like you do.'

She smiled, pleased at his flattery. 'And what are you going to do tomorrow?' she asked. 'You'll be surprised at how it's all changed, I promise you that.'

But Hamish didn't really believe her. How much could a sleepy little place like this change, after all? He'd seen sights that would have turned his mother's hair white, if it wasn't snowy already. Both his parents looked older now, he had seen that at once. Perhaps, if he'd stayed in the village, he would have thought that they looked no different from when he was fifteen, but the long absence meant he saw quite clearly that they were marked by time. His father was more stooped and the lines on his face were deeper, though he looked fit and well and no doubt was still taking his fishing boat out at the crack of dawn for the morning catch. His mother looked more fragile and vulnerable, her eyes a softer, more watery blue and her frame more tired. He felt a rush of fondness for them and a deep sense of happiness that he had come back.

'Tomorrow I'm going to see Mary, of course! How is she?' He saw his parents exchange a glance and his mother look worried. A sudden fear gripped him. 'She's still here, isn't she? She hasn't left the village, has she? Only she did talk once of leaving and going to Edinburgh...'

'Oh, no, no, she's still here,' said his mother quickly.

'Well – is she sick?'

'No, she's quite well I believe. I've not seen much of her lately, to be quite frank. Did you not write to her yourself?'

'Um, yes, of course,' said Hamish, a little guiltily. 'Well, I did at first, you know ... then it got harder and harder to find the time. You've no idea how busy they kept us, I scarcely had a moment to myself.' As he said it, he remembered the hours he had spent scrubbing and cleaning and polishing, and almost believed that he had truly had barely an instant in which to write a letter. The long hours of lying in his bunk, or reading a book, or drinking 'singing syrup', as some of the sailors dubbed the nasty liquor they all poured down their throats, in a broken-down bar in some fetid harbour somewhere, were completely forgotten.

'Do you mean that you didnae really keep in touch with her?' His mother looked at him reproachfully. 'That sweet girl! She probably thought you'd abandoned her. That's probably why she–'

'Tssst.' His father broke her off with a hiss. 'Best to talk to her tomorrow yourself, son.'

'Come on, tell me. What's happened?' He had a sick feeling that he knew what it was. 'Is there another fella? Is that it?'

But his parents refused to answer him. 'See her yerself tomorrow, lad,' was all they would say.

Chapter Twenty-two

He rang the old brass bell outside the manse and waited impatiently. He hadn't rung ahead, even though his parents now had a telephone in the house, because he had enjoyed surprising them so much the night before that he wanted to do it again. Even though his mother had warned him against taking Mary unawares – 'No lass likes to be visited by a sweetheart without a little bit of warning' – he had decided to ignore it. It wasn't as though Mary needed frills and make-up and fancy hairstyles to look beautiful. In fact, he had always preferred her when she was entirely natural to when she had got herself ready for one of the local dances.

Hamish sighed impatiently. How long had he been waiting now? At least five minutes, surely? He pulled at the bell again, and its deep clang rang out. The front door opened at last, revealing a housemaid in a black dress and white apron.

'Yessair?' she said curtly. 'What do you want?'

'You're new here, aren't you? So you won't know who I am. Well, listen, I'm an old friend of Mary's, see? Tell her to come to the door, will you?'

'Miss Mary is resting.'

'I'm sure she is, but she won't want to rest any more when she knows I'm here.'

'What is your name, sair?'

'No, no... I'm not going to give my name,' said Hamish, impatient that she was so dense. 'Don't you understand? It's a surprise. Now go and wake her up.' The housemaid did not move. 'Can't you understand plain English? I'm an old friend of hers!'

A voice came from inside the house. 'Who is it, Annie?'

The little housemaid stepped back into the darkness beyond the door and Hamish heard her say, 'There's a man here who wants to see you, miss, but he won't give his name.'

'I'll deal with it.' The door opened further and revealed Mary standing there in the hallway. Hamish gasped as their eyes met. Mary turned pale.

She was, he thought, far more beautiful than he remembered. But she wasn't a girl any more. Her hair, still as cloudily dark, like the hair of a film star he'd seen in a movie once, was shorter and carefully styled with a wave in it. She was wearing make-up too – her dark lashes were thick and her lips were red – a silk blouse and a lavender-coloured straight woollen skirt and high-heeled shoes. She wasn't just a woman now – she was also a lady. He felt suddenly rough and crude. He had only put on his usual shore clothes – canvas trousers, a shirt and a navy jumper – and they seemed inadequate now. His tanned skin looked like the skin of a peasant, a toiler in the sun, and he was aware of his shaggy hair, just growing out of its sailor's crew cut.

'Hello there, Mary,' he said hoarsely.

She gaped at him. Colour was rising in her face

now, taking away the ghastly pallor he had seen there a moment ago. She tried to speak but didn't seem able to find the words until at last she said, 'Hamish! But... I don't understand...'

'Mary, you're looking so well. You look beautiful.' He tried to find his manners, to be less clumsy. 'I'm sorry, I should have telephoned you first, warned you I was coming, but I was so eager to see you I couldn't wait. You don't mind, do you?'

She shook her head slowly, her blue eyes still wide with astonishment. 'No, I don't mind. It's just that...'

'Mary, will you come with me? I want to show you something. Will you?'

'Where to?'

'Just to the edge of your driveway, that's all. Come on.' He started to feel better, his optimism began to return. So she looked different – but so did he. A few moments more and they'd be back to their old selves, he was sure of it.

'The edge of our driveway?' she asked, confused.

'Yes.' He grasped her hand and pulled her out of the house. She skipped down the step towards him and the next minute they were both walking down the gravel driveway, he marching forward in his enthusiasm and she trotting along beside him, delicate in her heels. 'Oh Mary,' he said as they went. 'I've missed you so much since I've been gone, you can't imagine. It's been so horrible being apart from you.' As he said it, the long months when he had scarcely thought about her melted away and he only remembered the agonised nights of the early months, when he had longed for her so desperately and kissed his little black-and-white photograph of her. 'Have you missed me too?' He didn't wait for an answer as they reached the edge of the velvety green lawn of the manse. 'Look!'

She followed the direction of his finger with her gaze. 'Look where?'

'Over there.'

'At Kinlochvegan?' The village was clear six miles away, its little tiers of houses climbing downwards towards the sea, following the curve of the bay round.

'Yes, at Kinlochvegan, but more precisely at Pike's Row and at the eighth cottage in the row which has a blue front door and is called Lachlan Cottage.'

Mary looked confused. 'I don't think I can see it, Hamish. It's too far away.'

He laughed. 'I know, I know. It is far away but the point is, it's there – and it's mine! I've bought it! At least, I nearly have. All the boring paperwork still has to be done and the contracts signed and so forth, but I've put down a hundred and fifty pounds and it's going to be mine within six weeks. And when I go to Inverness to collect the keys, you could come with me! Or you could meet me when I get back and we could go there together, if you like. What do you think? Would you like to?'

'You've bought your own house...' she said quietly.

'A man can't live with his mother all his life. Especially if he's ... well, any man who wants a

241

wife needs to have a home to take her to, doesn't he?' His voice dropped and he spoke to her softly. 'I'm not going to rush things, Mary. I know I've only been back five minutes and you've hardly had time to realise that I'm truly here, but I've been dreaming about our future for so long now, I can't help wanting it to start right away. I know, I know,' he said as he saw the frozen expression on her face, 'it's all going too fast. I'm sorry. I'll slow down.' He smiled at her. 'I suppose we're going to have to get to know each other all over again, aren't we?'

'Hamish,' she whispered, her expression unchanged.

'Yes?' His smile faltered a little.

She said nothing, but held out her left hand. A ring sparkled on the fourth finger. He looked at it as the significance of it sank in.

'I'm engaged.' She spoke quietly and calmly but there was a tremor in her hand.

'Engaged!' he said, aghast. He stared at her white face. 'What to – I mean, who to?'

She didn't answer. Instead, she pulled her cardigan more tightly about her and said shrilly, 'Why are you acting like this? I don't understand! I waited for you for ages – I waited for you to write me a letter, hoping for more than some stupid little nothing saying you sent me your best, or passing on good wishes through your friend. I got one or two letters to start with and then I waited and waited – and nothing came! Nothing! I wrote to you so many times, desperate to find out how you were feeling and if you still cared for me. I thought of you every day and every night. But there was not a word from you, just those post-cards you sent to McBain. How could you write to him and not to me? How long did you expect me to wait like that? And then ... then...' She faltered. 'You know what happened next!' she said furiously.

'No, I don't, what do you mean?' But he couldn't help a guilty look passing over his face. She was right – he had never really written her love letters, at least not after the first few months. But he had written her reams and reams that he had never sent. Didn't she realise how hard it was to send letters from a ship in the middle of the Indian Ocean? And then, once he had let it go for a while, it seemed too hard to pick it up again. And he'd sent McBain a post-card or two but, as with his letters to her, only in the early months.

'Are you going to play games with me, Hamish? I'm utterly bewildered by all this. You told me it was all over. You didn't have the guts to tell me yourself, I realise that, but I got the message all right, just as you wanted. McBain came here with your letter. All about some girl that you'd met in Bangkok and what you'd done with her. What possessed you to send that *filth?* McBain didn't want to show me but I made him. I've never been so humiliated in my life as I was when I had to read what you'd done with that ... *prostitute* ... when you'd vowed that you'd be faithful to me, that you loved me ... how could you?' Her eyes filled with tears. 'It was four years ago and still I can't help weeping when I think about it. I'd never dreamed you could do something so

243

hurtful. If you didn't love me any more you could have told me, let me down graciously, in a private letter. Sending all the details to McBain, showing off about the *fornications* you'd been getting up to, telling him to pass on the news – you couldn't have done it more hurtfully. So–' the tears were gone and now her eyes blazed with anger – 'I take it you didn't marry her then. Or perhaps you've divorced her? Did you have a parcel of bastards with her and then sail away, like seamen are supposed to? Or did she leave you? Whichever it is, it seems you've decided to forget all about her and pretend she never existed. It seems you've decided to *insult* me by coming here like this and insinuating you might be so kind as to marry me and let me come and live in your pathetic little cottage...'

'Wait!' he said, breaking into her torrent of words at last. He felt sick. So McBain had shown her that stupid letter he had written about Sri all that time ago. He had betrayed him. But what was she talking about – *marriage?* Where had she got hold of that idea? 'Mary, I've no idea what you're going on about. I didn't marry her!'

'Oh.' Her lips were trembling, though whether with grief or with fury, he couldn't tell. 'Poor girl – I feel almost sorry for her. Abandoned her, did you? Like the cad you are. And I suppose that if you didn't marry her, there were plenty of others – common little foreign working girls who slept with you in exchange for a few pennies?'

She stared at him, waiting for him to answer, but he couldn't say anything. He couldn't bring

244

himself to lie to her, and pictures of all those steamy little bedrooms where he'd been entertained by the harbour girls flashed through his mind, along with images of the delightful things they had done to him and the pleasure he had enjoyed with them. He couldn't deny it. But why should he? He was a normal man, wasn't he? Could any woman seriously expect a man to be faithful to her for five whole years, with the kind of temptations on offer that he faced all the time? She was being unfair.

'So there were more,' she said quietly. 'I'm sure you might be able to remember some of them if you tried very hard. As it is, you needn't bother.'

'But Mary, I never forgot you...'

'Well, that is a comfort, I must say. Now, does that make it better or worse, I wonder, to know that you thought of me while you frolicked with those whores?' She spat out the last word with biblical fervour. He almost jumped, to hear the usually mild Mary speak in such a way.

'I don't know where you got the idea that I intended to marry Sri. I never meant to do any such thing. It was nothing, I promise, it was just ... I was drunk, I was young, the others persuaded me into it...'

'Don't give me your ridiculous excuses.' The anger seemed to go out of her suddenly. She looked away into the distance for a moment, frowning. She put her hand up to her hair and then pressed it into her cheek and sighed. 'Oh ... God. It's all too late now, anyway.'

'McBain should never have shown you my letter,' he said. 'It was private – and I never said anything about marrying anyone. All I said was how much I loved you and how much I wished I hadn't done ... that.'

'It's too late for lies now. I saw it written in your own hand. And of course you said you wanted to marry her–' She paused for a moment and frowned, as though remembering something. Then she shook her head. 'How could I forget a thing like that, when the last words you'd said to me were that you wanted to spend your whole life with me?'

'I don't understand,' he said, confused and sickened. 'It doesn't make sense ... I never said those things. I don't know how you could have read them. You saw them, in my own hand?'

Mary nodded her head impatiently. 'Yes, yes. But don't you see, Hamish, it's too late now anyway. And you never wrote to me again, you never said you'd made a mistake. You vanished from my life as though you'd never been there at all. What made you think I would wait for you when you left me so completely alone?'

He was helpless, unable to answer her. He couldn't begin to put into words how remote she had seemed to him when he was thousands of miles away from her, how difficult it had been to imagine life going on in Kinlochvegan without him. For him, they had all been frozen in time – the village, the people, his family and Mary herself – as if in a fairy tale, waiting only for his return to come back to life and resume where they had left off.

She said softly, 'You can hardly blame me if I gave up on you. Even without that frightful letter,

I would have done so eventually. It's been five years.'

He knew she was right. There was no answer to be made to that. The sunlight caught the diamond in her ring, making it sparkle and glint as though it had tiny electric lights burning inside it.

'Mary ... who is it? Who are you engaged to?'

She stared him straight in the eye and said, 'To McBain, of course.'

Chapter Twenty-three

'He's in a sorry state. This is no way for him to go on.' The sound of his father's voice floated up from the sitting room below.

Hamish lay on his bed in the darkness, still as a statue, letting the conversation below settle into his mind. He was somewhere else, very far away, at the same time.

'He was never like this before.' So Ian was downstairs too. 'Perhaps it was that time at sea that changed him.'

'Mebbe. But I can tell you, lad, I've never expected to have Alfie Tucker call me from his pub and tell me to come and bring my boy home because he's unconscious on the floor with drink. That's why your mother and I thought you might be able to help.'

'I don't know what I could do. When has Hamish ever listened to me?'

'He might now. I wish you'd seen him the day he came back. So full of excitement and optimism, looking forward to his future. And then, almost the next moment, it was as though he'd collapsed. There was the first blow of learning that he'd lost that lovely girl of his. It was a shock. Perhaps we should have prepared him – his mother and I blame ourselves for that, for not telling him, but we didn't like to interfere in the lives of the young people and their romances. Not our business, we thought. But he seemed at first to put a brave face on it. He didn't seem to care much to start with. Then he got lower and lower. I think he found that the village had changed much more than he was expecting. He didn't know his little pal had done so well here – and it seemed to bring him down greatly. And then...'

Hamish waited to hear what his father was going to say, feeling indifferent to whatever it was. He was floating somewhere far away, untouched by all this concern on his behalf. Couldn't anyone understand that there was no hope now?

'Then there was the wedding day.'

Oh yes, Hamish remembered that. Well, not the end of it, if he was honest. And he'd turned up at the kirk half cut to start with. His mother had tried to persuade him not to go.

'Why do you want to put yourself through that? She's marryin' another feller, now let her go,' she urged him.

'But you don't understand, Ma,' he'd said. 'I made a promise, you see. I said I'd dance at his wedding. So I will.'

Everyone had looked anxious when he'd arrived at the kirk, as though he was going to cause a fuss, perhaps announce an impediment to the marriage at the vital moment, but he hadn't. He'd wondered if he might but at the last minute he'd kept silent. Because what could he offer her instead? Himself? He was sullied beyond repair, he could see that now. He'd infected himself with an incurable, vile sickness when he'd slept with those poor slum girls and he'd never be good enough for her again.

She'd come into the church, so beautiful in her white gown and flowers, like some princess in a story. There was a kind of exquisite agony in watching her walk down on her uncle's arm, to be married by her father, and to see McBain waiting for her at the top, in the place where he should have stood if he hadn't failed her so completely, so utterly and so shamefully. I deserve this, he'd thought grimly. I deserve every tortured moment.

Then, later, he had kept his promise and danced at McBain's wedding, just as he'd said he would. But throughout it, he was in a daze at the reality of what that wedding meant. Mary, his Mary, his sweet girl, was going to be possessed by ... that.

He knew he had done wrong. But he also knew that he had been betrayed.

He hadn't made a scene, though. He had simply drunk himself insensible. Someone had taken him home to his parents' house, as they always did when he was drunk, even though he now had a place for himself, ever since the sale of Lachlan Cottage had gone through. The drinking had helped, he'd found. Being unaware of what was going on around him seemed to numb the pain, and he liked not having to be so unhappy all the time, so he'd got used to sinking as many drinks as he could as often as he could.

Now he was a regular at the pub, sitting on a stool at the bar, downing drink after drink. Then waking up here in his old bed, getting himself together before he went back to the cold loneliness of Lachlan Cottage again.

The door to his bedroom opened and a figure came quietly into the darkness and sat down next to the bed.

'Hamish?' it said softly. It was his brother. His parents must be at their wits' end, sending for him. But they'd wasted Ian's time. There was nothing he could do, unless, along with all the surveying, he'd also learnt how to undo the past.

Hamish grunted.

'Are ye all right?' Ian waited but when Hamish didn't reply, he went on. 'This is a sad, sad business, Hamish. I'm sorry to hear you're so low. Pa has told me all about it and I do understand how you must be feeling, I really do. To lose Mary like that...'

Ha, thought Hamish. You understand bugger all, mate.

'But can't you see that this isn't helping? You've got so much else. Think about it – there's your little cottage. And you're going to have to keep up the payments on that. You need to work again. Earn a living.'

Aye, very practical, thought Hamish. God, I'd love a drink. A bit of rum.

'And then there's that boat you bought. She's sitting on her mooring going mouldy. You haven't touched her since she arrived.'

When Hamish had been carefully planning his future in Inverness, before he'd returned to Kinlochvegan, he'd also ordered his own boat. She was a beautiful little vessel with a white hull and a blue cabin with a red roof. Along her side was painted the name he'd chosen for her: *Bella Maria*. Beautiful Mary. Six weeks later she had arrived on the back of a truck, ready to start her work as a small fishing boat, but then, to Hamish, she was just another bad joke, another reminder of how rotten it had all become.

Ian waited for Hamish to say something, but when there was no reply from the figure on the bed he said, 'Listen, I've got an idea. What are you doing, letting your life fall to pieces like this? You've got too much going for you. Ma and Pa told me what you said to them when you arrived, about Australia and how you could always start a new life there. Why don't you? Why not join a ship again, and sail over there and make a new start? It's obvious that this place doesn't have anything to offer you any more...'

'No,' said Hamish quietly. Ian paused, waiting to hear what else he would say.

'No, I'm not going anywhere.'

'But you're drinking yourself to death here. One day you'll fall off the pier or smash your head open on the road or get yourself knocked down... Go somewhere you don't have to remember her, or see her about. I know you loved her, but you just have to forget about her now and get on.

There are plenty of other girls in the world, you know. You're sure to meet someone you like even better than her.'

Hamish turned over and stared into the darkness. No one could possibly understand that not only was there no other girl in the world for him, but that seeing Mary was going to be his own special self-inflicted punishment. He wouldn't be going anywhere now.

The village had changed a great deal from the small sleepy place he had left almost five years ago, just as his mother had said. It felt larger and there was more bustle and activity now. The docks were certainly busier, crammed with fishing boats that were bigger and more modern than the little vessels he had been accustomed to. A long low wooden building had been erected at the far side of the harbour, painted a pale yellow.

'What's that place?' Hamish had said to his father not long after he arrived. They were walking down by the sea, crunching along the stony shore.

'It's a warehouse, built by your friend McBain.'

Hamish frowned. 'What? What for?' He couldn't understand what his father meant, and for a minute he assumed that McBain had built it himself for someone else. 'Is he a builder then? He always said his daddy was going to make him be a mechanic.'

'Oh aye, and he's done very well. Have you seen the McBain garage? It's up the hill, you'll remember it was no more than a rusty old shed when his dad started it up. It's quite the smart thing now. The boy was hard to warm to, I'll give you that, but he seems to have a good business head on his shoulders. That place is humming now – he gets custom from all the village. Some of the folk even come from the town, he's got such a reputation for efficiency. And he's taken in some of the village lads and trained them up too, given them a trade and a way to earn their living while they stay around here. He's done well...' His father's voice trailed off as he remembered who he was singing McBain's praises to. He gave his son an apologetic look. 'Sorry, lad. I know he's done badly by you, but he's brought something to this place, I can't deny it.'

'What does he need a warehouse for?' Hamish looked back at the yellow building. 'Keeping spares there, or something?'

'No – that's the odd thing, really. He doesn't seem content with the cars and trucks. He wants to fish. Those big boats over there–' his father gestured back to the large fishing vessels moored by the docks – 'those are his. He started out with one a couple of years back, and before long he had four of 'em. Seems to have a bent for the sea as well, and he's taken on some of the other lads to work on the boats for him. Remember Gerry Connelly and Stevie Bruce? They've given up their own wee boats now and captain his instead. They said what was the point of toiling on their own for a scant reward and all the costs, when they could take a regular wage off the boy and still do what they loved. Then a while back, he got permission to build that warehouse. You can't

253

see from here, but behind it there's several trucks he uses to take the catch to the processing plants. And the rumour is, he wants to turn that warehouse into his own processing plant in due course, keep more of the profit for himself. He's bound to get permission for it now he's got the smaller place up and running. And it would be a fine thing for Kinlochvegan if he did. It would really put this place on the map.'

There was a silence as they walked along together. Hamish's shoulders were hunched and his hands were thrust deep in his pockets as he absorbed his father's words.

'What about you, Dad?' he asked abruptly. 'Did he ever ask you to work for him?'

His father paused, and cleared his throat before answering. 'Well, son, he's asked a lot of the old fishermen. He knows we know this sea and the fish like our own homes. He wants to use our canniness and our experience. But you know – I prefer being on my own. I like the solitude out at sea. I don't know if I'm made for a life on a big boat, with lots of lads alongside me and the constant clatter of machinery and winches and freezing units and whatever else. So ... I turned down his kind offer.'

They continued to walk, Hamish's shoulders hunched lower than ever.

He had not seen or spoken to McBain when he'd first got back. After his visit to Mary, he had become quite reclusive, unwilling to venture out first from his parents' house and then from Lachlan Cottage. There had been no overtures from

McBain himself, though of course he would have heard immediately that Hamish had returned. Mary would have told him at once. He made no effort to see or speak to his old friend and this, in Hamish's eyes, confirmed that McBain had betrayed him.

Thinking it over, as he did time and again, Hamish knew that McBain must have been playing a very long game indeed. When had that letter telling him all about Sri been written? Years ago. And if he planned then to show it to Mary and somehow start courting her himself, well ... he must have had his eye on her for months before that. Looking back, Hamish thought he could see now why the younger boy was always hanging around him and Mary. He had always assumed it was himself the boy wanted to be close to – God, what an arrogant fool he was! Now it was clear as day that it had been Mary he wanted. And Hamish had been stupid enough to hand him the very thing he needed to shatter the pair of them apart and let him win the prize.

What will I say to him when I see him? he wondered. Will I hit him? Perhaps I should. He deserves to be hit ... after all, I never wrote that I wanted to marry that girl, Sri. He must have put something on the letter himself, changed it somehow so it read differently. Mary was talking about something I'd never written...

But he had no idea how he would react to McBain when he saw him again. He couldn't shake the feeling that he deserved to be treated in this way, that his own actions had brought all this punishment justly upon him. And as he learned how his rival was flourishing and prospering, it seemed that fate was on McBain's side. He had Mary, he had a business, he had the respect and admiration of the village. His future was bright. He had everything Hamish himself had hoped for, and there didn't seem to be anything left over for him.

In the event, the confrontation came unexpectedly. Hamish was taking a walk up and out of the village to the old point, where he used to sit and look out over the sea. As he came to the top of the path, he almost bumped into McBain, who was coming down.

'Sorry,' he mumbled, before he realised who it was. Then the two men stood and stared at each other for a long while before either of them spoke. Hamish noticed that McBain had not grown much, not upwards anyway, but he had put flesh on his frame and that thin face had got a little rounder. Now his thick black hair was cut short and his brows were heavier. He seemed to have more confidence, by the way he held himself. He looked older – like a man, rather than a boy – and it suited him.

'Hamish,' he said at last, in the same gruff voice he remembered. 'Well, well.'

Hamish nodded at him. He had expected to feel rage when he finally came face to face with McBain, but instead he felt only a sense of utter distance from the other man. He might as well be a total stranger.

'I saw you at my wedding. I saw you dancing. You were pretty sotted, weren't you? S'pose I can understand that, though. It can't be easy when you've let a woman like Mary slip through your fingers.'

'You know what you did,' Hamish said simply. 'You stole her.'

'I just let her know the truth about you and what you were really like. Do you think I could have stood by and let her marry you, knowing what you'd been up to? Was it fair on her to let that happen? God knows what filthy diseases you've picked up in those godforsaken places. I was never going to let you touch Mary with those hands.'

'You betrayed my confidence. I trusted you.'

'Did you want me to *lie* for you?' spat McBain. 'Cover up for you?'

'But you did lie. You told her I was going to marry that girl, that I didn't want her any more.'

'No. She came to that conclusion on her own. And you never did anything to change that, did you? You left her far behind.' McBain grinned coldly. 'Listen, Hamish. Let me tell you a truth or two. You were cock of the walk here once, weren't you? Leading your charmed life, making everyone else feel small. You can forget about that now. You're finished here. Why don't you go back to sea? We don't need you any more. Have you seen what I've done? I've come from nothing and now I've got money. I've got money, and I own things, and I run things and I give the old fellas and the young fellas jobs that feed their families. People look up to me. I've done it all on my own and I've only just started. I intend to run things around here from now on, do you see? So why don't you piss off?'

'Why do you hate me so much?' asked Hamish.

He could see it burning in the other man's eyes, as though providing the fuel for the mission he was on.

'Oh, don't flatter yourself! I don't hate you. I wouldn't even piss on you, I wouldn't waste my water. I hate what you did to Mary – you should have seen her crying over you before she saw sense. It almost broke my heart. And I hate your stupid pride and arrogance and I can't pretend I'm not taking a great delight in making people see you for what you really are. And by the way,' he sneered, 'would you like to know what married life with Mary is like, eh?'

Hamish brushed past him and tried to walk on towards the point, but McBain shouted after him, his words carried on the wind.

'She takes me to heaven, Hamish. Every night! Straight to heaven...'

Hamish walked away as fast as he could, trying to block the sound from his ears.

Chapter Twenty-four

1965

The little green camper van bounced along some of the rougher roads, used all its might to climb the steep mountain trails until the poor engine wailed in torment, and trundled merrily along the level parts of the journey. They all took turns to drive it, except for Shirley, who hadn't learnt to drive and anyway preferred to sit in the back tuning the little transistor radio and trying to pick up some music. When the signal was lost, as it mostly was, they amused themselves singing as they went along.

'This scenery is something else,' said Johnny, as they wound their way round the purple and grey snow-capped mountains of the Highlands.

'It's amazing, isn't it?' said Louise, awe in her voice. 'I've never seen anything like it. It's so fierce-looking. It makes Wiltshire seem like the tamest place in the world. Isn't it romantic?'

'It's nice and all that,' said Peter. He had adopted an American twang in homage to his favourite movie star, Paul Newman. 'And, like, these mountains are crazy, man. I didn't think we were going to make that last one!'

The little van had climbed and climbed until they had thought it wasn't possible to go any higher without entering the snowy regions of the very top. Then the road had levelled out, the views before them spectacular, before they began the twisting trail downwards on the other side.

'Imagine what it's like here in the winter,' remarked Johnny, who was driving. He shook his head to get his long fringe out of his eyes so he could see the road. 'I wouldn't want to be stuck in the place when the weather turns bad and you get snowed in for weeks on end. There's just nothing going on, you know what I mean? Nice for a visit and all, but give me Birmingham every time.'

Johnny was a town boy, there was no doubt about that. He liked to spend his evenings down at the Plaza ballroom in Birmingham, dancing to all the hits with the prettiest girls and drinking the vodka he'd smuggled in past the bouncers.

'Oh no, I think it's beautiful. I don't think I could ever get bored of this,' said Louise. 'I read Sir Walter Scott and Robert Louis Stevenson when I was growing up, and Scotland is everything I dreamed it might be.'

'Yeah, but did you dream that it might knacker Trevor's engine? Cos that's the way it's going at the moment.'

Louise sighed and stared out of the window. Johnny did not have a romantic soul. He was good-looking and a snappy dresser, and always very practical, but he didn't see the world the way she did. Outside, she saw magnificence and beauty on a vast and almost overwhelming scale. It was as though the whole of Scotland were a great, natural cathedral built to honour the beauty of the earth.

'Hey, did you see that?' asked Peter. He squinted through his square black-rimmed glasses. 'There was a sign there for a village.'

'Well, that's a bloody relief,' said Johnny. 'I thought we might have to go another fifty miles before we found somewhere – somewhere bigger than four houses and a boat, anyway. We'll turn off and see if we can find a garage. There must be someone who can look at a car engine.'

'No!' exclaimed Louise. 'I thought we were going to push on down to Skye! I thought we were going to try and get there today.'

'Listen, honey, we won't get there any day if we don't get this little baby a bit of loving care and a

260

drink, OK?' said Peter.

Louise bristled. I hate that stupid affected voice of his, she thought. He's never even been to America. I don't know how Shirley puts up with it.

'We'll get to Skye tomorrow,' Johnny consoled her, seeing how disappointed she was. 'We wouldn't get there before dark anyway, and you wouldn't see much then. Besides, we don't know when the ferries go and the chances are we'd have missed the last one in any case. It makes sense to have a stop now.'

'And I'm starving,' added Shirley from the back. 'I want some grub.'

At the next sign, they turned off and followed the road as it twisted its way towards the coast. At last, just as Louise was beginning to doubt that the village actually existed, it opened out in front of them and they found themselves trundling along the main street. Johnny stopped the van in front of the shop and went in. He came out with some chocolate bars and the news that there was a very good local garage and they would find it if they carried on along the main street and up the other side of the village, heading on their way back to the big road south. There was also a pub.

'Looks like we've found our place for the night anyway. I wonder if the pub do grub?' said Johnny. 'I could really do with a decent meal.'

'Oh, I hope so,' said Shirley longingly, as she unwrapped the chocolate bar Johnny had handed her. She was always hungry.

There are worse places to stay, I suppose,

thought Louise, gazing out of the window. The village seemed quaint enough, with its little terraced houses and the horseshoe-shaped bay that provided some shelter from the great sea she could see beyond it. She had wanted so badly to get to Skye, which she imagined as the most beautiful and romantic place in the world – the place where Bonnie Prince Charlie had fled to in his little boat all those years ago – but it wasn't so long to wait until tomorrow.

'I wonder if they do rooms,' she said. 'I'd love to sleep in a bed. The van's all very well, but...'

'You mean Trevor,' said Peter, who had given the van its name. 'Don't hurt his feelings, baby.'

'Trevor, then,' she said impatiently. 'The point is, if we're not going to Skye, then I want a bath and a bed tonight and I don't care how much it costs.'

They puttered on through the village until they found the garage. It was a large, well-kept workshop with a sign over the front that read 'McBain & Son'. The man who looked over Trevor for them was old – at least fifty – with grey hair, though in places you could still see the black it used to be. He said the engine needed tuning and a few small replacements.

'Can you do it for us by tomorrow?' asked Johnny. 'Only we're on a bit of a schedule, see. We have to press on cos we've got to be back home in five days.'

'Oh aye.' The older man nodded slowly. 'We pride ourselves on our service here, ye know. Come back at eleven tomorrow and it'll be ready for ye.'

'Thanks. That's great.'

'Yeah, like, far out. Thanks!' added Peter. 'Now come on, guys and gals. Let's go and find that pub.'

The foursome got their belongings from the van and wandered back into the village. Louise was glad they'd decided to stop now. The evening was drifting in and she too was feeling hungry. The idea of treating herself to a bed was a good one, she thought. In fact, now that the van was going to be in the workshop overnight, they'd all have to book beds. At least it would stop any arguments about the budget being too small for such luxury.

The lady behind the counter in the pub seemed very stern, even while she was agreeing that they could have two of her rooms. She looked at them suspiciously and eyed the girls' fingers, searching for evidence of wedding rings. When she didn't see any, she put the girls in one room and the boys in another without asking, but Louise didn't mind that. Peter and Shirley were shagging away like there was no tomorrow – she'd often had to lie in her sleeping bag pretending she was asleep and that she couldn't hear all the rustling and moaning and sighing going on just a few feet away – but she and Johnny weren't at that stage yet. He'd asked her along on this trip so he could get a little further with her, she knew that, but she wasn't sure whether she wanted to or not. She'd let him kiss her after they'd made a campfire a few nights ago and sat round it. Peter played his guitar and sang, while Johnny made one of his little paper cigarettes with the black stuff crumbled into it, and they'd all smoked it a bit. It made Louise feel dizzy and slightly sick, but she'd still let Johnny kiss her. She'd been in the mood somehow. She'd liked it, sort of, once she got used to the odd sensation of his tongue thrashing about in her mouth, but she wasn't sure she wanted to do it again.

'Are you and Johnny going out, then?' asked Shirley when the girls were settling into their bare little room.

'I don't know. No. Not really.' Louise was brushing out her hair and putting on a fresh cardigan for the evening. 'We're not like you and Peter, anyway.'

'Oooh, isn't he just dreamy?' said Shirley. She had a beehive hairdo which she covered thickly in hair lacquer and, as far as Louise could see, it never moved or changed, just got another coating of sticky hairspray. She also favoured panstick make-up, kohled eyes and mascara she applied by spitting on a little black cake of goo, turning it into a paste and brushing it through her lashes until they looked like black matchsticks.

'Not really my type,' said Louise, then added quickly, 'but he's really nice. I can see why you like him.' She looked at her reflection in the mirror. She wasn't into beehives like Shirley but preferred a French look, with Capri pants, a white shirt and ballet pumps. She'd even considered cutting off her blonde hair to a gamine crop like Jean Seberg, but she liked it long. She ran her hand quickly over it now. 'Let's go and get some dinner. I'm starving.'

The pub had some tables on one side of the

room, decorated with pink paper tablecloths and paper napkins. The boys were already waiting for them when they came down.

'Good solid food,' said Johnny with satisfaction, looking at the menu. 'No offence, Louise, but I'm looking forward to this.'

They'd been cooking on the little camping stove in the van, but there was a limit to what they could produce.

'They don't do haggis,' said Peter in a disappointed voice.

'Just because we're in Scotland, it doesn't mean people exist only on haggis,' commented Louise. 'I'm having fish and chips.'

'Ham, egg and chips for me,' said Shirley. 'I might even have it twice, I'm that hungry.'

When they had all ordered their food and had their drinks – beer for the boys and lager shandy for the girls – they chatted quietly and Louise had a good look about her. It wasn't so different from English pubs, really, with the big polished wood bar and the old fireplace. There were a few people sitting over by the fire who looked as though they might be locals, and a pair of old men playing dominoes. Just a quiet evening. No tourists other than themselves. Well, it was a bit isolated, this place. No wonder it wasn't much of a destination in itself – just somewhere you would find as you passed through on your way to somewhere else. There was a sense of self-containment here, though, she thought. As if the village doesn't really need anywhere else – as though it could get on perfectly well on its own.

They were tucking into their meals with relish

when the door opened and a man walked in. She saw him immediately and was drawn to him at once, though she couldn't understand why. He went to the bar, ordered a pint and then took it over to a table and sat down. He pulled out a newspaper and proceeded to read it. All the time he was doing this she couldn't resist flicking glances up at him, in fact, she couldn't help it.

He's very nice-looking, she thought to herself. He was a handsome fellow: tall and well built, with an open face and regular features. His hair was dark brown and curly, and looked as though it hadn't seen a comb for ages – or maybe the wind had mussed it. His hands were large and strong-looking, and he'd stretched his long legs out into the room while he read. Yes, she thought again, he *is* good-looking. There's something natural about him. Not like Johnny with all that hair combing and grease he puts on it and the hours he spends staring in the mirror.

She had an urge to get up, walk over to him and touch him. Something about him made her long to stroke him, because he looked like he would be an incredible mixture of textures: the softness of his hair, the smoothness of his skin turning into sandpapery stubble, the rough woollen jumper he was wearing and the tough calloused hands that showed how he earned his living. He's so ... *real*, she thought. Then she laughed at herself inside, because it was funny that she was so attracted to a big hunky Scottish fisherman rather than the pale and slightly weedy student from Birmingham. Maybe it's my romantic soul, she thought. Or my primitive instincts.

All the way through the meal, Louise was aware of the man sitting by himself. While they ate, he downed two more pints. When Shirley had finally finished her second plate of ham and eggs – 'Best I ever ate!' she said wonderingly. 'Where do they get their stuff from?' – Louise said casually, 'Why don't we take our drinks over there to the fire? Looks cosy over there, doesn't it?'

'Trust us to take our holiday in a country that has to keep its fires burning even in the height of summer,' said Peter as they all went over with their drinks. Louise made sure to get the table next to the man she had been watching.

'I like it,' she said stoutly. 'I hate the heat. I'm never happier than when bundled up against the cold. And you know what I love about this country? The light! It's so clear and transparent and the summer evenings are so long that I don't find them depressing, even if they are a bit chilly.'

'Did you think we were going somewhere hot?' Johnny asked Peter pityingly. 'Did you get it confused with Africa? Easy mistake, mate.'

'OK, man, cool it,' said Peter. 'Yeah, like, very funny.'

'I wish we had of gone somewhere hot. I like Spain,' said Shirley. 'I've not been there but my aunt has and she says it's lovely. Not like France, which is very dirty apparently.'

'Good wine, though,' said Johnny.

'I don't like wine. Not unless it's very sweet. But in Spain they do this lovely fruity punch called sangria which is supposed to be delicious.

I wish I could try that. I love Spain.'

She's a bit of a nitwit, thought Louise. How can you love somewhere you've never been? She turned her head to look at the man on the next table and to her surprise found herself staring straight into his bright blue eyes. He was smiling at her, and her stomach seemed to cave in and she felt her hands shake.

'You like Spain, do you?' he said suddenly to Shirley. 'Aye, it's not bad. But you want to get further away than that if you're gonna travel. Go to the East and see something really special. Look at temples and markets and bazaars and see how different life can be all over this world. You'll be amazed at how people exist, what they eat, how they speak, the way their lives work. I've seen a family of ten living in one small wooden hut, cooking over an open fire, doing their business in a pit behind their house. Might seem like hell on earth to you – fine for them. It's what they're used to.'

Louise looked over to Shirley and thought with disappointment that of course he'd like her best. She's got that bright peroxide beehive and all that make-up. Of course she'd attract him.

'Oooh, the East?' said Shirley in her little-girl voice. Then she wrinkled her nose. 'But it's full of little yellow men and nasty insects – and snakes! I don't like snakes. No. My auntie stayed in a very nice resort in Spain where they gave you proper English food and drink all included, like at Butlins, and you could stay by the pool all day.'

The Scotsman laughed out loud, a booming,

rumbling noise that Louise felt down to the tips of her toes. 'Well, if that's what you like!' He leaned towards Louise. 'Not very adventurous, your friend, is she? Where are you from?'

'England,' she said, her voice coming out in a small, strangled croak. She coughed. 'England.'

'I'd guessed that much. What are you doing in this place? We don't attract many English youngsters.'

'We're students, travelling for our holidays. Scotland was my choice, really. I've always wanted to see it. We're off to Skye tomorrow.'

'Skye? Aye, that's lovely. You'll like it. You're a student, are you? What are you studying?'

'Music.' The soft burr of his voice seemed to set something off inside her, fizzing and burning.

'Sounds like you've travelled a bit yourself, though,' said Johnny, butting in, pressing himself forward as though to indicate his presence next to Louise. She was irritated by him and wanted the focus of the man's attention back on her.

'That's right. I was a sailor for five years, travelling all over the world...' He went on talking in that beautiful soft voice and she felt as though she could not hear enough of it. She was absorbing his words and listening to what he had to say, but also floating along the top of them on the deep buzz of his voice.

The boys were absorbed by the older man's story, asking him questions about the East, about Thailand and the Philippines, Hong Kong and China, and the long voyage to Australia.

'Did you see any sharks, man?' asked Peter, owl-eyed behind his glasses.

'Aye. Lots. They're beautiful-lookin', too. Nasty and beautiful at the same time.'

'And tidal waves?'

'We were hit by the biggest waves you've ever seen. One was so huge it made our second mate piss his pants. He was on watch and saw it coming, big as that mountain outside, roaring towards us at a hundred miles an hour...'

They bought him pints to keep him talking, and he told story after story of his time at sea. Eventually Shirley said she was tired and went up to bed. Peter followed her not long afterwards, probably to take advantage of his girlfriend being on her own for a bit.

'Come on, folks, it's drinkin'-up time!' called the landlord.

Louise was startled. She had been unaware that the time had gone so fast, mesmerised as she was by the man beside her. She was fuzzy-headed too with the unaccustomed drinking, but happy.

'Do ye want to come up to my place?' he asked idly. 'It's only just up the hill. I've got some drink up there if you want to make a night of it.'

Johnny shifted unhappily. 'It's a kind invitation, Hamish–' such a lovely name, thought Louise, when he'd introduced himself – 'but we've had a long day and shouldn't get too high tonight, you know?'

'I'll come,' said Louise suddenly. She couldn't bear to think he was going to leave in a moment and she would never see him again.

There was silence. Hamish raised his eyebrows questioningly and looked at Johnny. Johnny said, 'I don't think … really, Lou... it's not...'

'I want to go,' she said loudly. 'Why shouldn't I? It's up to you if you don't want to go, you know, but I'm perfectly able to make my own decisions.'

'I don't mind,' said Hamish easily. 'She won't come to any harm with me, you don't have to worry about that. Alfie!' he called suddenly to the landlord. 'Leave the back door unlocked, will you? I'm taking our friends up the hill for a wee while. They'll be back later.'

'All right, Hamish,' answered the landlord, and carried on collecting glasses.

'I'd better come,' said Johnny reluctantly.

'Ye don't have to worry. I'll look after her.'

There was a long pause before, looking defeated, Johnny said, 'All right then. If it's what you want, Lou.'

They went up the hill together, the man walking easily and confidently in the darkness, the girl following behind, trying to follow in his footsteps and hurrying to keep up. At the cottage, he poured them both a tumbler of whisky, and they sat down facing each other by the empty grate.

'Is this your own place?' asked Louise, suddenly wondering what on earth she was doing here. The walk had sobered her up and now she realised that she was alone with a strange man, even if he was the most attractive man she had ever seen.

'Aye. I've not done much to it though.'

'No, I can see that.' She sipped nervously at her drink, trying not to screw up her nose at the bitter taste.

271

'Now, you were pretty keen to come home with me, weren't you?'

She didn't answer, feeling suddenly embarrassed.

'You were staring at me with those big grey eyes of yours all night, like I'd just saved your little doggie from drowning or something. But I've got to tell you – I'm no hero, if that's the impression you've got.' He smiled at her. 'I'm not the man for you, is what I'm saying, and if you've come here thinking you've found yourself a little romance … well, you're wrong. I'm not in the market for that.'

'Do you … have a girlfriend?' she asked in a small voice.

'No. I don't. But that doesn't mean I'm looking for one, do you understand? I'm happy to talk to you and to share a drink. And there's no pretending you're not a pretty wee thing, with that long fair hair and those big eyes – it's a pleasure to be here looking at you. But there'll be no more than that. How old are you?'

'I'm nineteen. Nearly twenty.'

'And you're studying music?'

'That's right. I'm going to be a music teacher, I hope.'

He nodded. 'I can tell you're a good girl. That boy down in the pub – he's not your boyfriend?'

'No, no,' she said quickly. 'He's just a friend.'

'I see. So – where have you been? What have you seen?'

She started to tell him about their motor tour in the little van and the sights they had seen since they'd arrived in Scotland. The first tumblers of whisky slipped away and he poured more. He gave her his jumper when she shivered – it smelt warm and smoky and male, and she breathed it in with pleasure.

At last he stood up and said, 'It's late. I'll take you back to the pub.'

'No...' She stood up, swayed and realised that she was drunk. 'Don't make me go.' She leaned against him, savouring the strength she could feel in his body.

He looked at her hard for a moment before he said, 'Aye. You're in no state to walk back down that hill. I'd have to carry you down. Come on then. You can stay here. You'd better take my bed and I'll take the sofa.'

He led her up the little rickety flight of stairs and into his bedroom. He helped her under the covers of his bed. 'Sleep well now. It's late. I'll take you down in the morning before your friends get worried.'

'Don't go,' she said pleadingly, clutching at his hand.

'Now, what did I say, wee lass...'

'Please don't go.' She pulled him down and he sat on the bed, looking at her, a curious bemused expression in his eyes. 'Stay with me.'

'You don't want to give up, do you?'

'Kiss me ... kiss me, Hamish.' She got onto her knees on the mattress and wrapped her arms round his neck, dropping soft kisses over his face.

He muttered something, trying to pull her arms off him, but without much force. Then she moved her lips to his, and began to kiss his mouth, pressing harder and harder against it as she felt his resistance weaken. She became more insistent until he finally opened his mouth and kissed her back. All her senses soared – this was nothing like being kissed by Johnny, with that wet, thrashing tongue. This was all softness and warmth and sweetness that made every part of her tingle.

He pulled away for a moment. 'Ah God, girl, what are you doing to me?' he groaned. 'Christ – I'm only human, you know. I'm just a man...'

But she wouldn't let him say any more, muffling him with kisses as she gently brought him down onto the bed with her, until they were locked in a powerful embrace, both yielding to the desire that had possessed them.

Chapter Twenty-five

It was like waking up with a little ray of sunshine in the house. She was as eager as a puppy, waking him with a cup of tea and a smile and loving energy – if she had had a tail, it would have been wagging ten to the dozen.

'Lassie – where're you getting all this buzz from? You drank a skinful last night and you've only been asleep for four hours.' He rubbed his eyes. She had drawn the curtains and let the fresh morning sunlight come pouring into the little bedroom.

'Isn't it a gorgeous day?' She turned with a dazzling smile, and then jumped onto the bed next to him, throwing her arms around him and nuzzling her head into his chest. 'Mmmm – you're so delicious.'

He laughed. 'You're not so bad yourself.' It was true. She was the prettiest girl he'd seen for a long time, not just in her features but with the vigour of youth and the light that shone in her eyes.

'So you don't regret last night?' she asked winsomely.

'No, you little vixen, I don't regret it even if you did disobey me and use all your womanly charms on me.' But now that it was done, he realised how much he had craved the release she offered him. Not many of the women he had slept with had wanted him as badly as she had. Most were being paid for their trouble, and the young girl in Australia hadn't been fired up with the kind of passion that gripped this woman. He was surprised and flattered and, now, glad that he had met her the night before. And she would be leaving today, so no recriminations or difficulties later ... and he'd used one of the condoms he'd brought back from his travels to prevent any nasty surprises.

As if she could read his mind, she said, 'Oh! We're leaving today. I can't bear it! We've just met and now we have to say goodbye.'

'Aye. It's very sad.'

She looked pensive. 'Maybe I can persuade the others to stay another day or two. But we have to be back in five days and it will take a while to drive back down.'

'And you want to see Skye.'

275

'Oh – that. Yes. Well, I did want to see Skye, but now I'd much rather be here with you. Perhaps we can stay another day, though. Shall I ask them? Wouldn't that be lovely? Don't you want me to stay?'

'I've loved the time we've been together,' he replied evasively.

She sighed happily. 'So have I. I've never felt so wonderful.' She hugged him again and kissed him. 'Just in case I have to go – shall we say a special goodbye now?'

As it was, the girl's friends were keen to leave Kinlochvegan and go on their way.

Their morning passion was more intense than the night before, as though the sunlight that glowed on both their faces made them more aware of the pleasure they were giving each other. She sighed and cried out, her eyes clenching shut and then opening wide with the sensations she was enjoying. The golden hair spread over his pillow and milky shoulders and soft, rose-tipped breasts excited him more than he could understand, and the entrancing warmth inside her forced him on and on, until he couldn't stop himself exploding with a fierce climax. When he came to himself, he saw that she was crying.

'What's the matter?' he asked breathlessly. 'Did I hurt you?'

'No, oh no... It was just so beautiful. I've never known anything like it!' She sobbed gently, tears glinting on the ends of her lashes. 'Oh Hamish. It was so beautiful.'

They washed and dressed and he took her back

down the hill to the pub.

'Goodbye, goodbye,' she whispered as she hugged him. 'Just in case we don't meet again.'

'Take care of yourself, lassie.' He dropped a kiss on the top of her head. 'And thank you. You've made me very happy.' He left her there, thrusting his hands in his pockets and walking back up the hill with long strides, his spirits high for the first time in many months.

The happy glow stayed with him for days, and in a fit of optimism he cleaned the *Bella Maria* from bow to stern and freshened all the nets. He'd got into the habit of taking her out three or four times a week and was keeping himself going with the money he made from his catch. He also tidied the cottage and sorted it out a little.

His mother was pleased to see his change of mood and that he didn't feel the need to spend his evenings at the pub for several nights at least, and she ran up some curtains for the cottage that she'd been meaning to make for ages.

'I'm so glad to see you a wee bit happier, Hamish,' she said. 'This place needs to be a bit brighter, you know.'

He felt as though the encounter with the English girl had revitalised him. Over the past few years he had been sapped of so much of his energy, partly because he had taken to drinking so heavily; when he wasn't actually drunk, he felt bleary and depressed, and so drank again to get himself out of feeling so low. When he did go back to the pub, he had to endure a lot of good-natured ribbing about his conquest. Alfie Tucker

277

had not kept his mouth shut and the news had spread quickly through the village, a tasty little morsel of scandal to chew over. He didn't mind – in fact, he laughed along with them.

'Well, you all do know how irresistible I am!' he said. 'Poor wee lassie is only human, after all.'

He was walking back home early one morning a week after the girl had left, when he saw Mary coming towards him down the steep path that led from the kirk. She must have been to the early service, he thought. He hardly ever saw her. He had even made a point of avoiding the places where he might meet her at the times she could be there, staying away from the village shop and the post office and keeping far away from the side of the harbour with the McBain warehouse and processing plant on it. Above it, on the hillside that faced back towards the village, a large house was being built for McBain and his wife. Until it was completed, they were living in a rented cottage not far away.

McBain and Mary had been married for three years and, at occasions and village gatherings when she and Hamish had been thrown together, they had managed to avoid speaking to each other. She did not even look at him, though he stole the odd glance at her when he could. He could not tell whether married life suited her or not: outwardly, she seemed the same; her beauty, as she aged, seemed to be even greater. She didn't smile or seem particularly happy, but Hamish didn't know whether to put that down to her dislike of seeing him.

He lived in dread that soon he would hear

Mary was expecting a child. That would mean he could no longer pretend that McBain never slept with his wife, or even touched her. But the news had never come.

As she walked towards him in the early morning light, he felt his innards clutched by the sick, violent, somersaulting sensation that he always had when he saw her. It was excitement but a nervous, unpleasant kind that had no thrill in it.

She was wearing a blue dress almost the same colour as her eyes, and her dark hair was loose. She had grown it longer, he noticed. As she came towards him, he saw that she was pale and her lips were tight.

'Good morning, Hamish,' she said as soon as she was within earshot.

The first words she had spoken to him since that day just after he had returned. Her voice was not the warm, intimate thing of his recollection, though – it was frosty and edged with anger.

'Mary,' he said, bowing his head respectfully. 'Or should I say Mrs McBain?'

'Say what you like,' she replied. 'It makes no difference to me. Not a scrap. You know, Hamish, I've felt sorry for you over the last few years. But not any longer. I've heard about how you disgraced yourself, picking up some poor child in front of the whole pub. I thought you'd changed, but you clearly haven't. How can you embarrass yourself – and everybody – like that? It's as though you've sullied the whole village. I'm ashamed to talk to you.'

Humiliation swirled through him, but anger

grew alongside it. How could she speak to him like this? Why should she show him disgust and revulsion, when he tortured himself every day over her and had to live each one knowing she belonged to someone else and that she had deserted him?

'Mary,' he said hoarsely. 'Would you deny me any comfort at all? Don't you know how lonely I've been?'

She seemed startled, and the cold distaste on her face was replaced for a moment by confusion. It looked for an instant as though his question had reached her and touched her somehow. But then her expression hardened again. 'Don't you understand? It's not acceptable to take some strange girl to your cottage and use her – it's animal. It's bestial. It ... disgusts me!'

Hamish thought of the pretty English girl, her blonde hair and her long slim legs; he thought of her rolling about on his bed, giggling and singing and begging him to kiss her. Was that truly disgusting? Was it so wrong? Was he to be denied any natural human contact at all? 'I'm sorry you feel that way, Mary,' he said slowly, 'but you gave up every right to care about me and my behaviour when you married that man.'

'Not when you shame Kinlochvegan! Those people were our visitors.'

'You never used to be like this. Is this what living with *him* has done to you?'

'How dare you? How dare you comment on my husband, on my life ... after what happened?'

'How dare you comment on mine?'

She looked furious now and her voice was shrill as she said, 'Then I will never speak to you again, Hamish, as long as I live.'

'Fine. Do whatever makes you happy.'

Mary stood staring at him for a moment, quivering with indignation, then she marched past him and away towards the harbour without another word. Hamish turned and watched her go. The flame of cautious optimism that had burned in him for the last week was well and truly doused. He felt the habitual misery well up again in him as he turned back to resume his homeward climb.

A fortnight later, Hamish was at home in Lachlan Cottage with only his whisky bottle for company. He had resumed his old habit of drinking away the evenings, but now he avoided the pub and sat in front of the fire instead. Outside, rain was falling steadily and everything was sodden. There was a loud rap on the front door.

Hamish went to the door and opened it, expecting to see Mrs Campbell from next door wanting to borrow something. To his astonishment, the young English girl was standing on his doorstep, an umbrella sheltering her from the downpour and a huge bright smile on her face.

'Hello,' she said. 'Surprise!'

'What the hell are you doing here?'

'I've come to see you, of course. Can I come in?'

He just stared at her, stupefied, until she said, 'Are you going to let me in or not? It's fairly wet out here, you know.'

'Yes ... yes ... come in.' He stood back and she came in, dripping and shaking herself.

'It's jolly wet, isn't it? I had quite a climb up from the main road. It's like a small river is pouring down the pathway and I was rather worried that I would slip over and be washed all the way back to the bottom. The bus had quite a time getting here from Inverness as well. What a long ride that was!'

On and on she chatted as she took off her wet coat and put the umbrella in the stand to dry. He remembered her name suddenly.

'Louise,' he said, breaking into her tide of chat, 'what are you doing here? Why did you come?'

'To see you, of course!' Her eyes were bright and shining.

'But–' He stopped, baffled.

'Aren't you glad to see me? You must have missed me – didn't you?' She gazed up at him with those wide grey eyes, a vulnerability in them that he couldn't help being touched by. 'I know it's mad coming here like this, but I couldn't resist it. I haven't been able to think about anything else but you since our night together. You're not angry, are you? Please say you're not.'

'I'm not angry but ... what are you doing here?'

'I've come to stay! If you'll have me.'

He couldn't understand her for a moment. 'Stay here? How long for? Are your friends with you?'

'No. I came alone. And I want to stay for as long as I can.'

'All right, let's sit down and talk about this. What do you mean, stay here? And do what?'

Hamish led her into the sitting room and sat her down on the sofa. He still couldn't believe that she was really here in his cottage again.

'We got home after our holiday but I couldn't stop thinking about you. I've nothing to do until I go back to university in a month. My mum wants me to work at the vet's like I usually do in the holidays – I help out in the reception for a bit of extra money. But all the time I was thinking about what happened between us, how amazing it was – and I suddenly thought – why not come to you? I know it's madness but I couldn't help feeling that I'd been offered a chance and that I had to seize it, and act on it. Do you know what I mean? So I'm here, if you want me.'

'Louise – this is very sweet, I'm so touched, but we hardly know each other. Don't you think you might be being a little rash?'

She leaned forward and grasped his hands. 'Oh, please don't say that. Give it a chance! Let me stay here tonight at least. You can't send me away, I've nowhere else to go. And then decide in the morning. Please?'

He started to laugh. 'You're an impulsive wee lass, aren't you? Well, you're right, I can't send you away. There's no bus now till Wednesday so you'll have to stay.'

Louise laughed as well, a joyous sound. It lifted something in him and he smiled at her.

'See? You're glad I came! I knew you would be.'

'You know ... perhaps I am.'

In the end, she did not go back home to England. Hamish, released by Mary's pronouncement, felt free of guilt and able to enjoy the deliciousness of their physical union. Once she was back in his bed, warm and inviting, he felt as though he really had missed her horribly, and in the morning there was that same sense of a light being switched on. Her happiness and optimism were infectious. Her presence lifted him back out of the trough he had been falling into again, and it suddenly seemed as though she were the answer to something.

'Don't your parents mind that you've come here?' he asked, stroking her hair as they lay in bed together.

'They can't stop me. Now that I'm at university, they understand that I'm grown up. I can do whatever I like.'

They spent almost an entire week in bed together, locked away from the world in a cocoon of sex and romance. At the end of the week, Hamish felt that he couldn't afford to let her out of his sight again, and that she possessed his last chance of happiness. When she talked about returning to England and going back to university, he felt panicked. If she left, he was sure he would never see her again. One night, after they'd made love, he asked her to marry him, and she wept with happiness and said yes.

Chapter Twenty-six

'They say she won't come through this time.'

Flora passed a cup of tea to McBain, who sat stiffly in one of the armchairs. He'd never felt at ease with his brothers and sister and now that they had all grown up, he was even less comfortable. Besides, Flora had made no bones about what she thought of his marriage to Mary Burns.

'You're a fool,' she had said plainly. 'Anyone can see you two are different. You shouldn't have married above yourself, we all knew that misery would be the only result.'

He'd been furious with her, though he hadn't said anything but only allowed his attitude to his sister to cool even further. Besides, apart from visiting his mother, he rarely had the time or desire to make the journey to Glasgow, where Flora now lived.

'Did they say how long? When they thought she...' He searched for the right words.

'When she'll die? They don't think she'll last the week.' Flora sighed. 'A blessing, in many ways.'

Their mother had been in a private nursing home for three years now, paid for by McBain. Flora had moved to Glasgow to be near her and had got married herself only recently. Though she was only just eighteen she seemed more like a woman of thirty-five, a legacy of her years of looking after her mother and the young family.

Even now she had the younger ones living with herself and her husband, although it seemed that, at last, the burden of constantly visiting their mother was going to be lifted from her. Mrs Mc-Bain had been steadily declining, becoming more and more frail, and now it was apparent that she was in the last stage of her life. A persistent cold was turning more serious and it was likely to become pneumonia.

'Have you heard about the bothy?' McBain asked suddenly.

'No. Why would I hear anything? I'm too far away from the old place for that.'

'The estate have decided to take it down. It's being demolished. They say it was about to fall down on its own anyway and it's not safe to live there any longer.'

'It wasn't safe to live in at any time.'

'I'm offering to buy the stones from them. I can make use of them in the new house.'

Flora sniffed. 'Oh yes. Your new house. How is that coming along?' She never seemed to approve of anything McBain did. He felt that he had done something for the family by expanding their business, earning some money and getting them out of that miserable little hovel they'd lived in. He'd paid for this private home for his mother, and helped Flora and her husband get their Glasgow terraced house and even provided money for the upkeep of the other McBain children. And yet ... always this ingratitude and disapproval. Why?

'It's well on the way to being finished,' he said. 'We should be in before Christmas.'

'What you'll be needing with six bedrooms, I've no idea. There'll be just the two of you rattling round in that great place. Is that wife of yours showing any sign of producing a bairn for you yet?'

Flora always knew exactly how to touch the sore spot.

'No,' he said shortly.

'Too grand for childbearing, no doubt.'

He put his teacup down, hardly touched. 'Look, I've got to be going.'

'I'll telephone you if there's any change,' said Flora. 'I don't think it will be long now.'

The long drive home gave him time to think. He made this journey once a month to see his mother and it always afforded him a welcome breather, a time of peace and silence unmarred by the constant interruptions he had at home and at work.

The prospect of his mother's death left him curiously unmoved. It felt as though she had died many years ago and this was simply the end of a twilight existence, during which she had been almost forgotten. His father had never even visited her, and certainly never spoke about her. He had aged a great deal over the last few years and now only did a couple of mornings a week at the workshop, spending the rest of his time in the small cottage McBain had bought for him. His spirit had long been broken, and there was hardly anything left of the fearsome drunkard who had presided over the children's early years. But if he appeared to have forgotten the wife whose life he had ruined that terrible night, McBain himself had fond memories of the mother she once was, even though they were gradually being erased and replaced by the speechless, drooling husk she had become.

It wasn't the prospect of his mother dying that had hurt him that day. It was Flora's jibe at Mary, and the childlessness that he knew everyone was beginning to comment on.

This wasn't the way it was supposed to be, he thought, as the granite landscape opened up in front of him. He was over halfway back to Kinlochvegan, and he began to think about everything that waited for him there. The mechanical workshop and garage were running smoothly and he had cornered the local market nicely; the other garage had closed down a year ago and he had promptly gone to the owner who had run it and asked him to become manager of McBain & Son, freeing him to spend more time building up the fishery business. And that was doing very well indeed. His strategy of taking on the older, wiser fishermen in the area and using their expertise to maximise the catch, and therefore his sales, had worked excellently. His expansion into processing had begun promisingly too, though there was a way to go yet before he had achieved what he intended. Nevertheless, the money was coming in at a healthy rate, enabling him to start work building the home he had always dreamed of: a large, new, two-storeyed stone house looking out over the bay, with all the modern comforts he craved. There would be two bathrooms, hot running water, central heating, a telephone, a television, even a washing machine ... and Mary would have everything she wanted too.

Mary. The thought of her stirred the black depression that lived in his depths and which he tried to suppress as much as possible. Whenever he felt it looming up out of its pit, he thought of everything he had achieved and concentrated on all the good things in his life. He'd think of Hamish Fraser and how, as Hamish's life spiralled downwards into misery and failure, he, McBain, was climbing up and up, towards wealth, position, respect and all the things that made life worth living. That always brought a warm glow of satisfaction.

But the most important thing in his life was not making him happy. His marriage to Mary was not what he had hoped it would be. He'd grown up adoring her from afar, dreaming of the magical future that was waiting for them, the boundless happiness they would enjoy – but it wasn't turning out like that at all. Mary was a lady, he knew that: a girl brought up in a comfortable home, surrounded by every luxury, waited on and provided for by the housemaid and the cook. She played the piano and arranged flowers, and went to the theatre wearing a white fur jacket and gloves.

Life with Mary would be far from the miserable cold poverty he had known, instead it would be full of charm and grace and beauty, all illuminated by her radiance. And her style and class would be an asset to him, pulling him up the social scale and making him a gentleman. Perhaps she would teach him about books and music, and how to talk about learned matters and discuss politics and issues of the day. He had had the vague idea that he would be able to do these things by some method of painless absorption, that merely being around her meant that he would become the man he wanted to be.

There was a mental picture McBain always had when he imagined them together in the future. He saw himself with a black moustache, smoking a pipe by the fire – though he'd never smoked a pipe and never wanted to – clad in one of those rough tweed suits that he'd seen the estate manager wear when he came to Fully's Bothy. He was reading the paper, while nearby Mary sat quietly smiling to herself and knitting something – a scarf or a baby's bootee, perhaps. On the floor two small children played happily, though they were merely fuzzy outlines that he hadn't bothered to fill in.

That was what he had expected. He had wooed her slowly and patiently with that in mind, holding fast to his imaginary picture of the future even when it seemed he would never win through. For many months, even years, she mourned Hamish. The blow he had dealt her was a severe one and McBain knew that her heart had been broken. Seeing her pain and desperation had made him love her even more, and hate Hamish with a new and blacker hatred, for he almost came to believe his own lies about Hamish's intention to marry a Thai prostitute.

Mary hadn't loved him at all, not at first, he knew that. But gradually, as it seemed that Hamish would never return from abroad and as his image faded from her heart, Mary grew fonder of

McBain. His devotion and persistence flattered her, he knew that. His business acumen and growing prosperity impressed her, and slowly she began to see the two of them as equals. It became harder and harder for her to imagine a life without him in it, tending to her every need and hanging on her every word. When he asked her to marry him the first time, she'd said no, but in a manner that gave him hope. On the third time of asking, he told her that he would offer her his whole life and make sure she had everything she ever wanted, and she finally said yes.

Thank God he had managed to persuade her when he did. Thank God her parents hadn't managed to talk her out of it, though he was sure that old cow of a mother had done her best. For Hamish returned just a few weeks later, only to discover that his sweetheart was now spoken for. It was one of the happiest moments of McBain's life, hearing how Hamish had turned up to claim his girl and been rebuffed by the ring on her finger that showed that ownership had been transferred to him. It still brought a smile of delight to his face to think about it.

It was a triumph for him when Hamish Fraser danced at his wedding to Mary Burns. He wouldn't forget it. He had won, and everyone in the village knew it. McBain was the better man, for Mary Burns had chosen him over the other fellow. And now, with his business success, he was revered all over the place.

But ... but... Even recalling that victory and how it had made him feel could not help the situation he found himself in. Here he was, driving home to his beautiful wife and almost dreading being alone with her. Why? When she belonged to him now? He'd won her fair and square, and yet all those fantasies he'd had had not come true. It bewildered him and saddened him. If he was honest with himself, it also made him angry.

Why was Mary not happy? That was the thing he fretted about, going over and over it until he worked himself up into a state of frustration. What more could he do for her than he had already done? He'd offered her his heart and a home and the prospect of money coming their way. And even if she tried to pretend she was happy, he knew she was not.

Didn't she understand that he couldn't be happy if she wasn't? Why was she making him miserable like this? And he knew that she didn't like him touching her. At first she had not seemed to mind and had even made an effort to enjoy going to bed with him, but as the weeks went by she had become more and more reluctant, though why he had no idea. Now she stiffened when he touched her and he could feel the resistance in her, even though she said nothing and allowed him to do what he wanted. He couldn't understand it.

One thing he did know. She would have to start being a bit more compliant. He wasn't going to go on like this. She'd have to start being happy and do what normal women did, and have babies. McBain was beginning to wonder if Mary thought she was too good for the kind of life other women had. If that was the case, he would have to show her that she was no better than anyone else, and that she had a duty to fulfil in return for the home and clothes and food he provided.

Mary McBain would have to be tamed.

Chapter Twenty-seven

With a sick feeling, Mary heard the car draw up outside.

She got quickly off the bed and straightened her clothes, smoothing down her skirt and pulling the wrinkles out of her stockings. At the dressing table, she paused and looked in the mirror. She picked up a comb and pulled it through her dark hair. Then, satisfied that she looked decent, she hurried downstairs to the front door to greet her husband.

The time had gone so fast. She'd been looking forward to this day all week, knowing that McBain would be leaving early for Glasgow and returning late, giving her a whole day of peace, and now it was over. Not only that, but it had turned miserable and sour. It had started well – the sun was out and the rain they'd had so much of lately had at last dried up, so she had taken her basket to go into the village and do some shopping. In the line at the butcher's she had stood behind Mrs Tucker, who took great pleasure in telling her the latest gossip – in fact, she could hardly wait to spill it out to Mary, that much was obvious. When she'd got back home she'd gone straight to bed and lain there for the rest of the day, not sleeping but simply staring into space and trying to absorb what she had been told.

'You're back,' she said brightly as her husband came in through the front door.

'Aye. Of course.' He put the car keys in their tray and took off his coat.

'How was your mother?'

'Not good. She's dying. They don't expect her to last more than a week or so.'

'Oh, that's terrible. I'm sorry.'

'Don't be,' he said briefly, almost with a shrug. 'It's not as if you ever knew her.'

'No – but she's your mother.'

McBain walked past her and into the sitting room, where he sat down.

'Shall I get you a drink?' she asked, following him.

'A beer.' When she returned with it, he said, 'Did you not have time today to tidy up?' He gestured at the room. Mary followed his gaze. The sitting room was not particularly untidy, but some newspapers were piled haphazardly on the coffee table and a teacup from earlier was still there.

'Well, I...' she faltered. She had noticed lately that her husband was becoming more pernickety about the way things were at home. He was fastidious himself about things being put away and everything being kept clean – she thought it was probably something to do with the chaos he had grown up in – but he had begun to demand the same of her. 'I'm sorry. I'll tidy it up now.' She got up and began to do so while he observed her, slurping occasionally on his beer. She could sense his bad mood and that he was looking for things to criticise, but, she reminded herself, he must have had a difficult time seeing his mother so close to the end of her life.

He watched her for a while and then said with a sneer, 'You've not got your housemaid now, you know. There's no one else here to tidy up after you.'

'I know, dear,' she said, trying to sound serene and unruffled. 'I'm perfectly happy as I am.'

But she knew there was an element of truth to what he said. She had never had to do housework in the past, and found that it did not come easily. Even though she liked the house clean and neat, getting it and keeping it that way without help was a mysterious process and one she hadn't managed to decipher. Similarly, she struggled with cooking more than very simple things, and even those were not very successful. She often cursed her mother for keeping her out of the kitchen and not teaching her the way to run a household. But her parents had dreamed of great things for her, not a life where she would be a simple housewife. Her mother, always a snob, had once had high hopes that her daughter would marry into academia or perhaps a wealthy landowner – even, in her dreams, an aristocrat. After all, Mary was graceful and beautiful enough to adorn the arm of the highest-born in the land, her mother had been quite certain of that.

It had been irritating for Mrs Burns when her daughter had fallen in love with Hamish Fraser, but not disastrous. After all, she was young and bound to grow out of her infatuation – when she matured and began to understand the ways of the world, she would see that an uneducated fisherman was scarcely the best she could hope for in life. The match a woman made was vital in shaping the whole course of her existence and the status she would enjoy. Mary had been raised a lady and a lady she must stay. When Hamish went away, Mary knew her mother had been delighted. But, in the light of subsequent events, she no doubt now wished she had been happy with the Fraser boy. At least his parents were respectable people and Hamish was good-looking and charming.

If only she hadn't taken against McBain so strongly! Mary thought. It was partly because she detested him so much that I was determined to accept him.

It was something she could hardly admit to herself. But the news she had heard today had shaken her so badly that, for the first time, she had to confront what she had done.

'I heard something today,' she said lightly, unable to prevent herself from talking about it. 'I bumped into Mrs Tucker. She said that Hamish Fraser is getting married.'

McBain frowned and then laughed. 'Married! Who would marry Fraser?'

'The girl who visited here a while back – do you remember? We heard about the English students who came through. He's marrying one of them.'

McBain looked disbelieving. 'That's ridiculous. He can't know the lass well enough to marry her. He's a fool if it's true. But then, it's only a girl who doesn't know what he is who'd be stupid enough to bind herself to him.' His expression changed and he looked at his wife keenly. 'And how do you feel about that, Mary?' he asked.

She tried to appear nonchalant. 'Well ... of course, I'm interested in what happens to Hamish. He and I were once so close, as you know...' Something warned her to stop. McBain's jealousy of Hamish had not diminished with time, or even with his marrying Mary. Instead of being secure in his own achievements, McBain seemed to view Hamish as more of a threat than ever, and Mary's relationship with Hamish was no longer the thing that had brought her and McBain together, but something shameful she had done before he had shown her the light. More and more, McBain began to act as though Mary had dallied with Hamish only to annoy him, her husband, as if she had always known that McBain was the one she loved but she had insisted on playing games with him by pretending she felt something for Hamish.

McBain scowled at her. 'Close! Yes, I suppose you were. And now he's marrying someone else.'

'She arrived here a fortnight ago apparently, and they're engaged. They've applied to be married in the kirk.'

'And your father didn't tell you? Oh no, I forgot. He doesn't speak to you any more, does he? Not since you sullied the family name by marrying me.'

Mary dropped her gaze. It was true that her marriage to McBain had caused a division in her family. Her mother had not been able to speak to her since the wedding day and her father, obedient to his wife's wishes, had gone along with the break. It was painful to Mary, but she had wanted her parents to respect the choice she had made. The problem was, she no longer was sure if she respected her own choice, and that shook her faith in herself and made her ashamed. She had been so proud, so headstrong and stubborn! And now look at her life...

'Well, well. So Hamish is getting married. It's all to the good, in my opinion. Now perhaps you'll put him out of your mind. Perhaps you'll do your duty by me.'

'What do you mean?' Mary was sure she had never given her husband any indication that she was anything less than happy in her marriage to him.

'You know what I mean.' McBain put his beer bottle on the table and stared at her. 'Flora asked me today why we haven't had any babies. She thinks you consider yourself above such things.'

Mary paled. This was what she was most afraid of, this side of her husband. The experience of making love with him was nothing like she had expected, and it had become more and more repellent to her. Nonetheless, she wanted to have a child, so she bore his frequent attentions as best she could. Why she wasn't getting pregnant was a mystery – but she had no idea of what to do about it. Surely allowing him to do *that* to her at least once a week had to result in a baby eventually?

She laughed lightly. 'Flora is a tease, isn't she? That's very silly and I'm sure she must have been joking. You know I'd do anything to have a baby.'

'Anything except take pleasure in our bed,' said

her husband.

She felt that she must tread very carefully. McBain's attitude towards her had been changing over the past few months, and it had left her bewildered. She had married him because she was utterly convinced of his devotion. He was her adoring slave who lived only to serve her, that had been plain, and when she'd imagined a future with him, it had been one in which she would always be certain of his unceasing worship. It would, she felt, make up for the fact that while she was fond of him and loved him too in a way, she didn't feel the kind of overwhelming passion she had felt for Hamish. But she was sure she would never feel like that again about another man, so it was the best she could hope for, to love and respect her husband in a less romantic fashion.

It seemed that she had made a terrible assumption, for almost as soon as they were married the balance of the relationship began to change. Her courtly lover had gone, to be replaced by this unpredictable man who never seemed entirely happy with her, no matter how hard she tried to please him. Her background, her past, even her beauty had all become reasons for resentment. A wife, far from being his goddess, was his possession and he couldn't abide any suggestion of her having a will of her own.

He waited for her to say something.

'You're my husband,' she said at last. 'Of course I take pleasure in our bed.'

'Good. Then show me.'

He rose up from the sofa and came towards

her. Was he going to take her here, in the sitting room? He liked that, she knew. He enjoyed throwing her onto the rug, lifting her skirt and taking her quickly, both of them fully clothed. She steeled herself to endure it: the hard kisses, the bites and grazes from his teeth, the pain as he entered her and the brief, unpleasant experience as he bucked above her and then rolled away, spent.

A few minutes and it will all be over, she told herself. A memory came back to her unbidden of herself and Hamish swept away by the passion and beauty of their embraces. She pushed it away. She had to forget about all that if she was to bear this.

He began to unbutton her blouse and his breathing thickened, filling the room with the sound of it. A shudder ran through her but she hid it as best she could.

'You are beautiful, there's no denying that,' he said as he grasped one of her breasts. 'You're made for pleasure, even if you can't feel it. Well, that's not my fault. I can't be blamed if you're not a normal woman and I'm going to get a child on you if it's the last thing I do.'

Chapter Twenty-eight

McBain was asleep. Mary slipped out of bed and padded downstairs. She was unsure what she was going there for and she drifted aimlessly through the rooms, ending up in the kitchen, where she sat down at the table.

This place doesn't feel like home, she thought, looking around. I can't believe that I live here.

It was a rented house, and perhaps that was why. Their new home was being built across the way, on the hillside overlooking the harbour. Immediately below it was the warehouse and processing plant – apt, really, as the house was built on the proceeds of McBain's small fishing fleet. Would that place feel like home? She hoped so, but she feared that no home she ever lived in would be able to feel like the familiar, comfortable manse where she had grown up. Was it the surroundings or the people in it that made a place a home? If it was the people, then perhaps she was condemned never to have a home again.

Seized by an impulse to go outside, she put on her coat and a pair of boots and let herself out of the front door. She walked down to the road and out over the village and the harbour. The lights of Kinlochvegan twinkled below her. She traced the main road with her gaze, and up the hillside to the small row of terraced cottages where she knew Hamish lived. A light burned somewhere along the row – perhaps it was Lachlan Cottage. She imagined them together, Hamish and his English girlfriend, perhaps sitting by the fire, talking and laughing together as she and Hamish used to do. He loved to laugh and joke, and he was easy to be with.

It was shocking, of course. Mrs Tucker had stretched her eyes and said breathlessly how scandalous it was, for they were living together in Lachlan Cottage, and no sign of the girl's parents, and the wedding was going to be so soon it was almost as though they *had* to get married ... and everyone remembered how the lass had stayed in the cottage and now she was back, perhaps begging for a ring to make her respectable ... on and on it went until Mary had had to flee without the leg of lamb she had intended to buy.

Shocking – but no doubt people would forget in time. And Hamish would not care about such things anyway, not now. She remembered how she had met him on the path and berated him for his behaviour after she'd heard about the way he'd entertained the young student in the cottage overnight. She had probably looked like the worst kind of moralising old harpy but the truth was that she had been deeply, desperately jealous when she had heard about it, just as she was now that she knew he was getting married.

Remembering the scene, as she had told him off in that awful, shrill way, she felt a great judder of embarrassment. And then he said ... he had said how lonely he was. Just the memory of

302

that made her want to weep. What if she had done what she had longed to do, and thrown herself into his arms and told him the truth – that she had made a horrible mistake, that she still loved him and knew he loved her, that she forgave him everything in the past and all the other women, and only longed and longed for them to be together again? What would have happened then?

But it was no good. It was all too late. She had made the most devastating mistake any woman can make. She had married the wrong man, a man she didn't love, and there was no escape. The only way out would be divorce. For a moment, she considered it, but then shut it out of her mind. It was impossible. Divorce was shameful, a terrible stigma. It was not respectable and it was unholy. What was worse, it would finally close the door on any hope of reconciliation with her parents and, as long as she was a married woman, there was the chance that they might finally come round to her marriage.

Besides, she could never let them know what she suffered. It would break their hearts.

Perhaps if she could just give them a grand-child, her parents might thaw towards her, and she longed so much for unconditional love from someone – a baby might give it to her. But there was no sign of one.

She rubbed at her neck and arms, still sore from where her husband had gnawed at her and held her roughly down on the bed. This was something she had never known could happen between a husband and a wife. It must be something she did wrong that made McBain so vicious towards her when he made love to her, for it could not possibly be normal. She could sense the urge in him to frighten her and see her cower in front of him, and she had seen how much it excited him when she became truly afraid. He had begun to grip her and twist her skin when they were in bed together, and once he had slapped her. Only recently she had awoken in the night to find him turning her over roughly onto her stomach. He'd held her face down on the pillow as she struggled, not knowing what was happening, and then parted her legs and entered her without any preamble. It had hurt as he forced himself in; she had not been ready to receive him and the pain had made her whimper, which only spurred him on. It had been over quickly, which was the only mercy, and then he'd gone to sleep without saying another word.

The fear of this night-time secret that lay unspoken between the two of them was increasing. She was afraid that this urge in him could only grow stronger with time and that he would be compelled to go further to find his satisfaction, and she didn't dare envisage what that might mean.

Why didn't I guess? she asked herself. The cold night wind began to bite through her coat and the thin nightdress she was wearing, chilling her. She must go back inside, back to the bed where her husband lay sleeping. She didn't want to think of the consequences if he woke up and found her missing.

She turned on her heel, away from the village that lay sleeping below her and back towards the house.

Any ordinary woman would want to leave a cold night and go back to the warmth of her bed, she thought despairingly. But I can hardly bear to think about it.

Instead, she imagined Hamish curling up with his girlfriend, the woman who would soon be his wife, and pictured their passionate embraces, whispered conversations and jokes, the laughter in the night. It made her feel weak because she could not help putting herself into that other woman's place.

'I didn't realise,' she whispered out loud. 'Oh Hamish, I didn't know. I thought that every man's kisses would be like yours. I thought I would always feel what I felt with you. I was so stupid. I never realised that it was you and I alone who could feel that way.'

Back in the bedroom, she slid quietly under the covers next to her husband's sleeping form. The warmth from his body provided a little comfort, and she lay waiting for sleep, her eyes wide in the darkness.

'Where have you been?' he growled.

'Downstairs for some water. I couldn't sleep.' She tried to sound normal.

'You were gone a long time.'

'Yes. I sat there for a while.'

'I have a cure for sleeplessness,' he said and turned over towards her. He ran a hand down her arm. 'Shall we try it?'

Again? she thought, her heart sinking. She had

already endured enough tonight, hadn't she? But she smiled, even though he couldn't see her, and said, 'Of course, my dear.'

Then she willed herself to relax. It was always worse when she resisted.

Chapter Twenty-nine

For Louise and Hamish, life was bright and full of happiness.

Do I love her? Hamish sometimes wondered when he looked at his wife. She seemed so absurdly young and girlish. Sometimes, when she lay on her stomach in front of the fire, reading a book as one of her legs swayed idly in the air, he thought that she looked no more than a schoolgirl, even though she was twenty.

Do I love her? She makes me happy. Having her around makes me feel good. And I do desire her. How could I not – with that long slim body of hers and those winding arms that can't seem to get enough of me, and all that vigour and vitality... It seemed that nothing could dent her high spirits – days of rain were the same to her as days of sunshine – except when he went away fishing. Then, when he left the warmth of their bed, she would snake her arms around him and beg him to stay with her. When he was adamant that he must go and fish and earn their living, she would say that she was frightened that he would not come back, that she would lose him.

So he laughed and said he knew the sea too well to die there.

But do I love her? he asked himself again. He had begun to think that he had no idea what love was, and what was real and what was not. Nothing he felt for Louise matched the intensity of what he had felt for Mary – but was it love he'd felt for Mary? Or some teenage infatuation experienced with all the intensity of the first time? Who could say that it would have lasted?

No. He wanted to love Louise, he *needed* to love her. And so he damn well would. She deserved it because she had made sacrifices, coming here. She'd left her university course, her home and her friends and family, and come to Kinloch-vegan, where she was a stranger and a foreigner, so she was owed his love because he was all she had.

The villagers did not seem to want to know her, and their attitude to Hamish had cooled as well. He guessed at what it was. Everyone knew she had stayed the night up in the cottage and that they had lived together before they were married. The place was old-fashioned in many ways and pre-marital sex, if it did go on, had to be well hidden, for it could not possibly be condoned. There was the sense that Louise was a modern English girl, with the kinds of ways they'd heard about. Things were going on in London that ordinary people found shocking – drugs, music, free love; hippies and swirling patterns and strange influences from abroad. No doubt she was part of all that, and wanted to bring her louche ways here; the result was that she was often cold-shouldered by the people she met.

Louise didn't appear to notice. She didn't seem to have need of anything apart from his company and the time they spent together in the little cottage. When Hamish wasn't fishing, she would go with him down to the harbour and spend time aboard the *Bella Maria*, helping him with the maintenance and cleaning. He even took her out on her a few times, but the sea didn't capture her imagination as it did his. Nevertheless, she went because wherever he was, she was happy to be there too. From the moment he had put the ring on her finger and they had been declared husband and wife, she was entirely bound up in him. It had been just a normal Friday morning but he'd dressed up and wore the only suit he owned, a pale blue two-piece he'd had made for him in some hot country, he forgot where. Louise's parents had come up for the occasion and brought with them a wedding dress, a long white cotton dress with a smocked front. It was not really much of a wedding dress but then, by the looks on the anxious faces of both sets of parents, it was not considered much of a wedding either. Ian was the best man, there were only a handful of guests – Louise hadn't asked any of her friends to make the long trip north – and the wedding breakfast was a meal in the pub afterwards. The photographs had been posed outside near the sea wall. Louise had brought a camera with her when she came and was always taking pictures, wandering off alone occasionally, or going exploring when Hamish was out at sea or asleep. Her father took the wedding pictures, the two of them posing together, shining with happiness and optimism.

He knew that both his parents and hers thought they were being foolish, rushing into something that they had not considered seriously enough. But, he thought, they had a chance. Louise loved him, he knew that. And he loved being with her, and luxuriating in her welcoming body. Why shouldn't it work out, after all?

He was deeply asleep when she woke him up. The curtains had been opened and daylight flooded the room. It took a while before he came fully to consciousness, blinking in the sunshine. He'd come back to the house not long after nine that morning and headed for bed, instantly falling into the dreamless sleep of exhaustion.

'Hamish,' she was murmuring, stroking his back and arms with her soft hand. 'Wake up, I have something to ask you.'

Then he was staring into her wide grey eyes, noticing the freckles on the pale bridge of her nose. 'What is it?' he mumbled. 'God, I'm tired.'

'I want to ask you something important. Here it is. Are you ready?'

He turned over to face her properly. 'Aye.'

She smiled. 'Do you think you can love anyone as much as you love me?'

He breathed in sharply and hesitated. 'No ... no, of course not, sweetheart. Why do you ask?'

Had someone been talking? he wondered. Given her some idea of what had happened in his past? He'd told her many things, but never about Mary. But she looked too happy to be accusatory.

'Well, you're going to have to!' Her eyes danced

merrily and she giggled. 'We're going to have a baby!'

His mouth dropped open in shock as he absorbed her words, then he laughed as well, hugging her happily. 'That's wonderful news, lassie. Oh, god – a baby!' It was no surprise really, when he thought of how often they made love and with what enthusiasm. She had a body that felt so ripe, it was no wonder she had quickly fallen pregnant.

'Are you happy?' she asked, the vulnerability he had already learned to recognise showing in her eyes. 'Have I done well?'

'Ah, you've done fantastically. I cannae believe it, that's all. I'm gonna be a father! It's splendid news.'

She laughed with glee and they lay in bed together, making plans, choosing names and building castles in the air for their baby to live in.

The pregnancy advanced slowly, or so it seemed. The early weeks went on endlessly and it was months before they thought they could see a bump.

'Look, I'm as flat as a pancake!' she cried, hoisting up her top to show him her golden, peachy stomach. 'When will I start to show?'

'There's a little hummock there, isn't there? I can see it, I'm sure.'

'Where? No, I only look a little fat, that's all. Not pregnant. Oh, I do want to wear my maternity clothes as well.'

Her mother had sent up a parcel of clothes that Hamish thought were quite hideous: great, sack-like smocks and dresses like tents. Why she wanted to wear those, he had no idea. She had no morning sickness either. Her only symptom was that by seven o'clock in the evening she wanted to curl up and sleep, and she could no longer drink anything but plain water. Tea, coffee and anything else repulsed her.

He felt tender and caring towards her and, as the bump finally did begin to show, absurdly protective towards whatever it was that was growing inside her. Something most definitely was growing, for her stomach filled out and her breasts began to swell and occasionally produce drops of milky liquid. But when he tried to imagine the baby inside, he simply couldn't. He knew what babies looked like, all right, but the idea that there was one curled up tight inside this girl, one that was of his making, seemed like a ludicrous idea. He would believe it when he saw it, and until then it remained just an idea.

Then, one evening, she said, 'Put your hand here, quick!'

For a while she had felt the fizzings and flutterings of the baby moving inside her, and they became stronger and stronger until she had begun to say 'Ouch' and 'Oh, little baby, you're kicking me!'

She grasped his hand and put it on her stomach. 'Can you feel it?'

'What?' Then it came, right under his palm. The flesh of her stomach jumped and he felt the jab of a tiny foot. 'Yes, I felt it!'

She giggled and he looked up into her eyes, laughing as well.

'It must be a boy,' he said. 'He has quite a kick on him.'

'Girls kick as well, you know. Otherwise it would be an easy matter to know which kind you were having.'

'Oh, that's a boy's kick, I'm sure of it.'

'I don't mind what kind it is. Do you?'

'Och, no, I've no preference. I'd like a lad to show the sea to, to take fishing, to build a guider with. And a lassie – well, she would be my princess.'

'Wouldn't a lassie like to see the sea too?'

'Would she? I don't know. You're a lassie and you're not very interested.'

'True, I suppose. But I don't know if that's because I'm a girl. I don't feel the magic of the sea the way you do. It's like it enchants you and draws you out there, night after night.'

He stared thoughtfully into the fire that burned away in the grate. She knelt down so that she was sitting at his feet. 'Perhaps you're right,' he said at last. 'I've never been able to imagine a life away from the sea. I've grown up beside it. Whenever I've been in a place where I can't hear it rolling and crashing, or just breaking gently, outside my window, it's felt like something is missing. When I left home, I left it for the sea, and on board I was closer to it than ever. On the ships, I saw it in a way I'd never had to see it safe at home. Even as far out as I went in my little dinghy, I never saw waves like the ones out on the ocean. It was the stuff of nightmares – the great grey towers of water climbing over you until you didn't understand how they could reach so high without falling inwards into themselves. Sometimes, when a great wave came travelling across the ocean, it sucked up the water in front of it to feed itself, leaving a hole hundreds of feet deep. If you were unlucky, your ship would plunge into that hole and the wave would roll over the top of you, sealing you off from the outside world for ever. Ships have disappeared that way. I never saw that, of course. The waves I witnessed – well, we climbed them and then, before we could reach the curl and turn upside down, they'd moved across us. The boat would be drenched – and we'd find sea-water in drawers and cups and in our shoes for weeks afterwards. But every time we'd find something wet and spoiled, we'd say a prayer of thanks to Neptune or Poseidon or one of those old sea gods. Better wet than dead.'

'The sea could kill you so easily,' Louise said softly, running a hand over her belly – it was a habit she had now.

'Oh yes. We humans, we don't go well in the water. Not the deep stuff anyhow. It's not meant for us, and it's a great liberty we take every time we venture forth upon it, believing we can tame it. But you know something?' He put a hand on her head that glowed golden in the firelight, and stroked her hair. 'I don't believe I'm meant to die at sea. My mother told me I was born with a caul so I was in the waters inside her until the very last minute – and that means good luck, and I think it means some spirit of the sea is looking after me.'

'I hope so – oh, I do hope so,' she said, her eyes

wide. 'If I believe that, then I'll be able to sleep easily when you're out fishing.'

'Sleep easy, darling. Remember, you have to mind our bairn.'

The baby was born in the middle of the night.

'They often come in the middle of the night,' said the midwife to Hamish, when he let her in. He had run down to his parents' house to telephone the doctor and ask him to send the midwife and to come himself. 'And very often when it's a full moon. The tides of the sea and the tides of the belly – they're all the same, so it seems.'

He was not able to witness the birth himself. 'Not for fathers to see,' said the midwife firmly, and shut the bedroom door. But he heard the agonised shrieks of his wife as she laboured, and he paced back and forth, just as he had been told his father once paced when his mother was bearing him. The noise was almost intolerable and more than once he was on the point of bursting in to see for himself what was going on. He hated the idea of Louise being in so much pain and felt a terrible guilt that he had brought it upon her. Not being able to see her was, he thought, worse, because he imagined scenes of gore and horror, the baby tearing her open as it was born.

The doctor came, and when he went into the bedroom Hamish caught a glimpse of his wife. She was on the bed, her huge white belly thrust upwards into the air, her legs splayed open towards the midwife. Her face was grey and her hair hung in sweaty tendrils round it, as she opened her mouth for another scream. To his

314

astonishment, he saw her belly rise up and a great tremor seize it as the muscles inside it clenched and pushed. Then the door slammed shut and he saw no more.

Christ! he thought. Can this be right? Is this what nature intended? It's so ... violent, so bestial!

He knew about the pain of childbirth, of course, but now that he understood what it meant, it seemed astonishing that bringing life into the world was so dreadful, so tortured and so dangerous.

After hours and hours, it seemed, the house was quiet at last. The bedroom door opened and the midwife came down, her face calm and smiling.

'All is well,' she said. 'It wasn't too bad for a first time, either. She was quick and fairly easy.'

Quick? thought Hamish, appalled.

'Would you like to see them?'

'Yes – yes,' he said hoarsely, and went up the stairs. What would have happened to Louise? Surely, after all that, she would be fundamentally changed, a different woman. He prepared himself for someone blood-smeared and despairing. He found her pale and blue around the lips, but tranquil, a gentle smile on her face. The great torrents of pain were gone and in their place was a white-wrapped bundle sucking at her breast.

'Do you want to see him, Hamish?' she asked, her voice high but joyful. 'Do you want to see our son?'

Chapter Thirty

The news of the birth of Hamish's son was almost more than Mary could bear.

Then she saw them. They looked very young to her eyes but perhaps that was the way they were dressed: he was in jeans and a shirt open at the neck while she wore a long gypsy skirt and an embroidered blouse. They were walking along the seafront together, pushing their pram, obsessed with the little thing inside to the exclusion of all else. She felt clumsy and old-fashioned in her tight skirt with its matching jacket and she thought of her husband, carefully knotting his tie every morning in front of the bedroom mirror. The two of them looked as though they came from a different generation to this pair.

She was standing not far from them on the main street as they went by, and Hamish never even noticed her. Perhaps that stung the worst. He had always been so alive to her. Whenever she'd been nearby, he'd been unable to function normally. Occasionally she'd felt exasperated by this and wanted to tell him to pull himself together and think of a life without her in it. Now that he had, she was full of despair. It felt as though she were drowning in the middle of the sea, and a lifeboat had gone past her, not hearing her cries for help.

The sight of the young couple out with their

baby made her want to weep. After she got home, she ran up the hill high above the house and finally did weep. Hamish was lost to her now, that much was plain. He was married, he was a father and he never gave her a second thought. He had no idea how she was suffering and how much she needed him. And, to rub salt into the wound, he was a father and knew the joy of holding his baby in his arms. She remembered a history lesson and how, on hearing of Mary Queen of Scots having a baby, Queen Elizabeth I had said despairingly, 'The Queen of Scots is lighter of a fair son, but I am of barren stock.' It ran through her mind over and over – 'I am of barren stock.' Why was she not having a baby? Why was she enduring the things her husband did to her, if she didn't have the comfort of a child? It seemed so cruel.

She thought about Louise. It was the first time she had seen her close by and she was struck by the difference in their looks. While she was dark, pale and curvaceous, the other woman was a slender fair blonde with golden skin and freckles. She could not deny that Hamish's wife was a pretty girl, with a frail look about her that prob-ably appealed to his protective instinct.

He must truly love her, she thought. And she obviously adores him. That look she gave him as they bent over the pram. It was shining out of her eyes. But then – how could she help it?

It hurt so much to imagine them together, but she couldn't stop herself. She couldn't prevent the pictures she conjured up of them together in bed – in her mind, their marriage bed was one of unutterable sweetness, tenderness and love. The opposite of her own.

But there was no choice in things now. She had made her decision and she would simply have to bear it as best she could.

She dried her eyes and stood up. With a heavy sigh, she began to make her way back down the hill to the house.

McBain pushed himself back from the table. Mary jumped up to clear his empty plate and take her own, still almost full, back to the kitchen.

'So the fisherman and his Sassenach wife have got themselves a brat,' he called after her.

She was instantly on her guard. Anything to do with Hamish was dangerous territory and she tried to avoid it as much as possible.

'Yes,' she said lightly. 'A little boy. He's to be called Robert, so I've heard.'

McBain picked at his teeth, his brows knitting as he frowned. 'Who told you?'

'Oh, you know. The gossip always gets around. I hear it in the shop or up at the kirk.' She still went regularly to the kirk, even though it was painful to see her father. He would occasionally speak to her when her mother wasn't present, but only in furtive whispers and with a guilty look that hurt her to see.

'Why didn't you tell me?'

'I didn't think you'd be interested,' she said, coming back to the table. This kind of questioning always made her uneasy. Anything to do with Hamish seemed to fire up that secret, vile side of him.

He blinked at her slowly. Those black eyes, she thought. When did I ever think that I could see love in them? When were they ever soft and gentle and tender? They must have been once, or I would never have married him. I truly believed he loved me and would cherish me all my life.

'Maybe,' he said quietly, 'you didn't want to tell me about how another woman seems able to have a baby as soon as her husband looks at her.' He got up, went over to the drinks cabinet and poured himself a whisky. As soon as he had earned a bit of money, he had insisted that they go to an Edinburgh department store and order furniture. He wanted smart, high-class things like they had at the manse, and he made Mary choose everything.

'This?' he would say, pointing at a table or a console. 'Is this the kind of thing you had?'

She never knew what to reply. She wanted to please him, but nothing in the shop was like the antique furniture they'd had at home. This drinks cabinet, though, with its polished walnut and pink glass, was his own choice. She could tell that he thought this was what a prosperous business-man would have in his sitting room, arrayed with heavy glass bottles of bright liqueurs and coppery spirits, with a cocktail shaker and an ice bucket. That meant he had arrived.

He sipped on his drink. 'Have you been to the doctor?' he asked shortly.

'Yes.' The memory made her wince. The whole thing had been humiliating. She had seen old Dr Lindsay and he had asked her personal questions about how often she made love with her husband

and whether he ejaculated inside her and so on. Then she had had to endure an examination.

'I can see no reason why you can't have babies, Mary,' he'd said kindly, when it was all over. She straightened her skirt and nodded. 'Now, this isn't at all a medical opinion but I've heard one of those old wives' tales that says it helps to bring a babe on if the husband and wife truly love each other, and if the wife finds satisfaction in ... her intimate relationships with her husband. Do you ... well, do you find that is the case with you?'

She had no idea what he meant by satisfaction but she remembered the extraordinary physical sensations that had possessed her when Hamish touched her, and the sense that they were supposed to lead somewhere, to reach some kind of conclusion, and thought he must mean that feeling, of being exquisitely teased.

It didn't matter what he meant really, because she was certain she felt nothing of the sort in bed with her husband. The emotion she felt most often was fear, and the sensation, pain. She wouldn't dream of mentioning it to another soul, though, and certainly not to Dr Lindsay. She was sure that she must be the only woman who had to suffer such indignities and that, somehow, she had brought them on herself.

McBain broke into her thoughts. 'And he thinks you're able to bear children?'

'He sees no reason why not.'

'It must sting, then – that Hamish is a father.' He liked to talk about Hamish, watch her reactions, play on the emotion she had once felt for the other man. It aroused him somehow – at

320

least, it always made him hungry to have her and to inflict his worst punishments on her.

'Of course not.' She busied herself clearing up the table. The meal had been adequate but it was true to say she was no cook. It didn't matter much to her anyway – she had very little appetite these days and was losing weight fast.

He watched her for a while, then seemed to lose interest in her. He turned to his paper and his whisky.

She went back to the kitchen, relieved that the dangerous moment had passed.

Washing up the dishes, she thought, another evening, just the two of us! This can't make him happy, can it? Can he really get pleasure out of this awkwardness? Was this what he wanted me for? It bewildered her completely that their lives had turned out this way. Then she remembered McBain's mother, dead now and little mourned, and the marriage that she had endured, one that finally robbed her of herself and condemned her to a living death. Perhaps it was because McBain had known only his parents' marriage, one of combat and aggression, that he seemed happy with the relationship he had with Mary. He didn't seem to have any comprehension that it could be a partnership of mutual support, a friendship. For him, it was a power struggle that he was determined to win.

There was nothing she could do but submit.

Mary had just posted some letters and come out of the post office with her basket, when she was grabbed by the arm. She was too startled to understand what was going on for a moment, then she realised it was Hamish's wife and that she was talking to her in a fast, urgent manner.

'Excuse me, excuse me, I'm so sorry! You don't know me but you look kind and I need help. Can you help me, please?'

The girl's face was white and strained, her eyes huge and full of panic. With one arm she held a baby, well wrapped up in a woollen blanket, across her chest, and with the other she clutched at Mary.

'Please?'

'What can I do?' asked Mary in a faltering voice. Was something wrong with the baby? Did this girl not know who she was?

'You must help me. It's my husband, he's ill. I've left him up at the cottage in bed, but he's a raging temperature and he can't speak and he's all swollen. I don't know where the doctor is – Hamish has always fetched him before. I've tried his parents' place but no one is answering the door and I don't know what to do. Where can I find the doctor?'

As the other woman's words sank in, Mary herself began to panic. 'Hamish is ill?'

'It looks serious. I'm frightened! And I'm worried that the baby will fall sick as well.'

'I'll take you to the doctor at once,' she said. 'Come with me.'

They hurried together along the street. It was hard to know that one of the terraced cottages along the front was the surgery if no one had told you. It looked just like any other little house. Mary led the girl into the waiting room. Mrs

Connelly was the doctor's receptionist and she looked up as the two women came bursting in.

'Hello, Mary. What's wrong?'

Mary indicated Louise. 'This is Hamish's wife. She says that Hamish is very ill – the doctor has to go at once. It's an emergency!'

'He's with Mr Threlfall at the moment,' said Mrs Connelly slowly. 'I don't know when he'll be free.'

'Oh please, he must come at once!' gasped Louise.

'Mrs Connelly, you must get him immediately. Mr Threlfall can wait, but Hamish could be seriously unwell. He has a high temperature and...'

'And swelling. And he can't speak,' added Louise, her voice high with tension. 'I know something is not right.'

'Very well. I'll let him know.' Mrs Connelly disappeared down the hall and the two women stood together in the waiting room for a moment.

'Thank you for your help,' said Louise. She hugged her sleeping baby tightly, rubbing its back. 'You've been so kind.'

'It's nothing,' Mary replied. 'I want to help. How is the baby?'

'Oh, he's fine. I'm keeping him well away from his daddy, at the moment, though. He's so little!' She pulled the blanket back for a moment and revealed a downy head and peaceful face. The long eyelashes swooped downwards upon plump cheeks and the lips were like a little cherub's.

'He's a pretty boy,' Mary said, her heart aching.

'Oh, do you think so?' The young mother was simultaneously pleased but also in complete agreement. 'He is sweet, isn't he? He's a little angel, no trouble at all – well, except for the crying and he's not very good at sleeping on his own, poor little mite.'

Mary put out a hand and touched a tightly clenched little fist.

This is Hamish's child, she thought as she stroked it. This could have been my son.

The doctor came down the hall and a moment later had his bag in his hand and was following Louise back towards Lachlan Cottage. There was no reason why Mary should accompany them, and she had to watch them go, her stomach fluttering with nerves as she imagined Hamish up there in bed, at the mercy of a high fever and whatever it was that had possessed him.

There was nothing she could do. She went home, trying to shut all her fearful thoughts out of her mind. Somehow she would find out how Hamish was – she always found out in the end.

Chapter Thirty-one

It was a glorious early summer day. The sea was a brilliant blue and the sky above it stretched away in flawless turquoise, unmarked by any clouds. The sun was climbing higher and gaining in strength with every hour. It felt more like high summer than June.

Hamish was hauling nets on board the *Bella Maria* when she went past. He still felt weak from his long illness. He had been in bed for six weeks; the first two he could not remember except as a long, confused dream that sometimes surfaced into reality. The last four had been convalescence. It had been strange for him to feel so incapacitated. He was used to being at peak physical strength and his body had never let him down, at least, not until now. The sensation of being laid low was not one he enjoyed, even if his days had been brightened by little Robbie. Louise brought him every day to play on the bed. The doctor had assured them that Hamish was no longer infectious so it was safe for the little fellow to come and lie on the counterpane, chortling and grinning.

Robbie was the greatest pleasure of his life. He looked at the baby and could not believe that he had had a hand in making him, for the boy was so beautiful, so innocent and so new. He had big, shining blue eyes, a tiny button nose and a gummy smile that melted his parents' hearts. At five months, he was on the verge of learning to roll over, and he liked to kick his fat little legs as hard as he could while waving his arms about and cooing prettily.

'Isn't he lovely?' Louise would say, delighted with her baby. 'Isn't he darling? Do you love him?'

'Of course I love him,' Hamish would say, looking in wonder at the tiny pink fingers clenched so tightly around his big thumb.

'And me? Do you love me too?' she would ask. She could not hear often enough that he loved her and he had told her so often that he had ceased thinking about what it really meant.

'You made this gorgeous son for me, didn't you? Ah, he's a beauty!'

And the baby would trill and crow for them, staring up at his parents with adoration.

In the end, though, even if he was still weaker than he wanted, he had to get up and go fishing. He had to earn money and he needed to get back on the sea. Even though he had enjoyed the weeks at home with the little lad, he was finding himself chafing at Louise's clinging ways and neediness. She was never satisfied, but always required his reassurances; she never knew when to leave him alone and when to allow silence to fall on the cottage. For her, no talk meant they weren't being friendly and so she kept up a ceaseless chatter that almost drove him mad. And while he loved the baby, he didn't need quite such a running commentary on the boy's every breath.

He was mulling it over as he inspected the nets on board the *Bella Maria* when his eye was caught by a flash of blue. He looked up and saw Mary walking along the docks. McBain was building a whole new jetty for his own use, next to his warehouse and processing plant. She must be heading there to see him.

It was a long while since they had laid eyes on each other. As she came closer, he pretended to continue his work but carried on observing her. She was much thinner, he noticed. The blue dress he had seen the previous summer, when it had clung tightly to her curves. Now it was loose and unflattering. She looked paler too, he thought. And there was something dead about her skin and hair, which had always been glowing

326

in the past. Her skin had had a milky translucence with a pearly shine to it, and her hair had had dark glints in it. Now that inner life had quite gone.

He remembered the bright, confident girl he had loved so much. It seemed like another lifetime ago. He recalled the passion he had felt for her, uncompromising and complete, and the way it had been reciprocated.

That's all long gone now, he told himself. Best to forget about it.

As she came level with him, he became absorbed in his work, but he could not help looking up at her. She was staring directly at him, but as their eyes met she swung her head away and speeded up, walking quickly past towards the new jetty.

That's strange, he thought, frowning. There was something odd about her face... As he replayed the moment in his mind, he realised that she had had a shadow down one side of it, and that, as she had walked past, she had lifted a hand to cover her left eye and cheek. Why would that be?

Then suddenly he flung his nets to the deck and leapt onto the dockside, filled with an energy he hadn't known since before his illness. He strode along the dock after her, but she had already reached the warehouse. She wasn't going to it, it seemed, as she skirted the building and soon he saw her climbing the steep path above it that led up towards the new house that McBain had built. It had been finished just a month or so ago and was now the grandest house in the village: brand new, warm and full of modern conveniences. Mary was the envy of every other housewife in Kinlochvegan, especially as it was said that she had a washing machine.

'And no children,' said one of the jealous ones. 'So what on earth use she gets from it, I can't think!'

Hamish watched her progress up the hillside, her blue dress a bright spot against the green.

I'm bloody well going to! he thought, invigorated by his fury. He was sure now of what he had seen and it filled him with rage. He hurried after her up the hill and got to the house not long after she had arrived there.

The front door was painted a thick, sticky-looking black, with brass trimmings. He rapped the knocker sharply and then waited on the doorstep, fiddling with one of the small pieces of twine he kept in his pockets to knot and twist at odd moments, and controlling his breathing with difficulty. He was tired out from the climb – his fitness levels had obviously dropped considerably while he'd been lying in bed – but he was also so furious he could hardly breathe.

The door opened and Mary put her head carefully round it, still concealing the left side of her face. When she saw who was standing on her doorstep, her eyes widened in shock and she gasped.

'Hamish! What are you doing here?'

'Is he here? Is he?'

'No, no, he's not here. He's out to sea this afternoon...'

Hamish pushed the door open and stepped

inside. 'McBain!' he shouted. 'Are you in here?'

'I told you, he's not here.' Mary pushed the door to behind him. 'What are you doing here?'

He turned to look at her as she stood in the shadows behind the door. 'Mary,' he said, 'come forward and look at me.'

'No,' she whispered.

'Yes. I've had enough of this stupidity! We've not looked at each other or spoken to each other in years. We've made a mess of things and it's not just going to go away if we ignore it, is it?'

'*I've* made a mess,' she cried, putting her hands to her face. 'I've done a terrible thing. I should never have married McBain.'

He grabbed one of her arms and pulled her gently into the daylight of the hall. He could see now what he'd suspected. Around her left eye was a huge purple bruise, and over her cheekbone was a red weal where it looked as though she'd been hit hard.

'I ... I fell over,' she whispered, flinching under his gaze. He felt a wave of sorrow wash over him as he looked at her. She was nothing like the proud, spirited Mary he'd once known. He could feel her trembling under his grip and saw the way she cowered almost involuntarily. 'It's not true, is it?'

'Yes – yes it is.'

'Come on, Mary. No one gets these injuries falling over. They're obviously marks of violence. Is this what he does to you?'

'I don't want to talk about it!' she cried and yanked herself away from him, standing against the wall with her back to him.

They stood in silence for a while and he heard her sob. The anger had drained out of him and instead he was filled with pity.

'Hamish, it's all right for you,' she said at last, her voice muffled. 'It's worked out. You've fallen in love, you've got married and had a son. You're happy now.'

He felt so sorry for her. It was true. He *was* happy now. A great deal happier than he had been when he'd returned from the sea and discovered he'd lost her for ever; a great deal happier than when he'd spent months on end drinking himself stupid, thinking he was the loneliest man on the planet, and a great deal happier than when Mary had shouted at him that early morning, berating him for everything he'd done wrong in his life and for daring to find a little comfort where he could. If he could ever have hated her, he hated her then. It was the memory of that encounter that had sent him so willingly into Louise's arms, he could see that now.

'Aye – the little lad makes me very happy, that's true.'

'And her ... your wife?' Her back went very still as she waited for his reply.

'Louise...' He paused. 'Something in me does love her. She came to my rescue, you see, when I didn't know if I could get much lower. She's given me back my self-respect and she's made me feel like a man again. I owe her a lot. And she's a sweet little thing, no mistake. So needy, though – I've never known anyone so desperate to be loved.'

'Then she's lucky she met you,' whispered Mary. 'You love her, don't you?'

Hamish opened his mouth. He wanted to say, 'Yes, I love her. My life is as happy as I could imagine,' but he couldn't. At last he said, 'I'm fond of her. It's impossible not to be. But ... Mary ... I can't feel a millionth for her of what I felt for you. Louise and I are two souls who need each other, but not two halves of the same, like we were.'

He heard a muffled cry escape her. It wrenched at his heart and he went over and gently put his arms round her.

'I was such a fool,' she said, and he could tell she was weeping again. 'I thought you'd done me the worst wrong in the world...'

'I did an awful thing – I betrayed your trust, I see that. But I never wanted to marry that girl. McBain must have done something, doctored my letter somehow, to make you believe I didn't want you any more.'

She carried on as though she had hardly heard him. '...but it wasn't the worst thing, at all! I know McBain would never be unfaithful to me but the way he spends every day grinding me down, wearing me down, trying to defeat me ... the things he does to me when we're alone! The way he ... he ... in bed ... he...'

'Don't say it,' he exclaimed, suddenly agonised. The most terrible possibilities were occurring to him. If McBain did not mind hitting his wife, where would he stop?

She spun round and faced him. 'Yes, it's true. You always wanted to make love to me, Hamish, and I wish I had let you now. I wish I had just one memory of what true, good, kind love feels like so

I can hold it in my mind and take it out and remember it when I need it. I need it often, Hamish. So many times he wants to ... *use* me in the way he likes. It's not love, it's a punishment. At first he was just a little rough but now – he wants to beat me while he has his way with me, he wants to tie me up and hurt me, I can't begin to tell you how, I'm so ashamed!'

A wild mixture of emotions gripped him: he was appalled and disgusted, and filled with fury towards McBain. If that man were here now, he could not answer for what he would do to him. But stronger than that was the overwhelming tenderness he was filled with for his first and – yes, he knew it was true – his only love. Being with her again was intensely sweet, like coming home. It felt unutterably right. But it was cut through with a deep sadness that they had locked themselves away from each other, perhaps now for ever.

'Oh, Mary,' he said, his voice breaking with pity for her. 'Oh, my little love.'

She lifted her face to his and it was impossible to resist the mute invitation she offered him. In an instant, they were kissing, lost to everything but each other.

So many times he had imagined what it would be like to make love to Mary. In his dreams, it had been a wild and erotic experience in which he explored and revelled in every part of her body. In reality, it was something that seemed deeply serious and extraordinarily beautiful.

Their wild abandonment and the first fury of

their kisses calmed down and she led him quite slowly to the spare bedroom – 'Not the other one, not *his* bed,' she whispered – and they lay down together on the bed there.

'Mary,' he said, his voice hoarse. 'Is this what you want?'

'More than anything in the world. I've dreamed of this. I never thought it could happen.' She reached up to pull his mouth back to hers.

It was slow and infinitely tender, each watching the other intently throughout, as though they could not believe that they were there together. When he finally entered her, she put her head back slowly, her eyes closing involuntarily, her chin lifting and her mouth opening with the intensity of the sensation. Her arms tightened round his back and she twined her legs with his as though she wanted the two of them to become part of each other for ever.

They made love slowly and for a long time, neither wanting it to end. It was their first and last time, they were both sure of it, and they wanted to wring every last drop of sweetness from it.

'Mary,' he said as he moved inside her. 'My darling.' Between kisses, he muttered how much he loved her and how she belonged to him. Gradually they began to lose themselves in their physical delight, and their lovemaking grew more passionate until both were possessed by an intense climax. When he looked at her afterwards, she was laughing.

'What is it?' he asked.

'The doctor! Satisfaction, he said – did I feel satisfaction! I had no idea what he meant.' Her

333

laughter was joyful. 'Oh, Hamish. I do now. I know it now.'

He walked home in a daze, hardly able to comprehend what had happened. They had not been able to linger together, though it had been the hardest thing to leave her.

'He could be back any moment,' she'd said sadly. 'You must go.'

So he had gathered himself together and left her, with a tender kiss and very few words. Neither knew what to say. They could not promise to meet again soon, nor could they bear to admit that this was their goodbye. So they parted without saying anything important.

He let himself into Lachlan Cottage. Louise was in the sitting room, dancing Robbie on his feet, holding him by his fat little fists while she sang to him.

'Hello, darling,' she said as he came in. 'Did you finish up with the nets?'

He was confused for a moment, and then remembered what he had been doing that morning. 'Oh, yes. All done. How's the wee lad?'

The baby looked up at him and chortled, which made Louise giggle.

'Oh, he's so happy to see you! Are you happy to see your daddy, darling? Are you? Oh yes you are! Mummy and Daddy are here with you, aren't they?' She looked up at Hamish, her face shining with pleasure. 'That's what he likes best – when we're all together.'

'Yes,' he said. A great pain filled him and he almost bent under its force.

'Are you all right?' she said, concerned.

'Oh, fine – just a little weak still. I think I'd better lie down for a moment.'

He went upstairs, his wife still singing to his baby son. His heart was heavy and he thought, I can't leave them. I could never leave them.

Part Four

Chapter Thirty-two

Heather breathed in the fresh morning air. There was nothing like it, she thought. It was something peculiar to Kinlochvegan, she was sure – this particular salty sweetness.

She began to walk down to the docks, wondering at the stillness of the place. At this time of the morning the city would be rushing with people on their way to work, catching buses and buying coffee, dashing down Princes Street or across the Royal Mile. Here there was nothing to disturb the tranquillity but the occasional faint purr of a trawler engine and the mewing of the seagulls overhead.

It had been over ten years since she'd left, an angry young woman off to a new life in Edinburgh as a student, determined never to come back. She'd been as good as her word. There had been too much keeping her in the city: her lover, her flat, her career. And when there was time for a break, she didn't want to go to some backwater on the coast. There were exciting places to see and explore – there was Paris, Rome, Madrid, or a villa in Greece. She'd made new friends and a proper life for herself, a life where people liked and respected her. That made a bloody nice change, if she was honest.

But now she was back, and there was someone she was desperate to see.

'Hamish! Hamish! Are you in here?' Heather ducked her head into the cabin of the *Bella Maria*. Her eyes took a little while to adjust to the darkness, then she saw that on the table were the oddments that Hamish habitually toyed with: knots of twine, some pieces of driftwood and a penknife he used for whittling. He must be nearby.

'Heather, is that you?' He came out from the shadows near the bulkhead. 'You're back!'

'Aye, it's me!' She came down into the cabin, a big smile all over her face, and gave the old man a welcome hug. 'How are you?'

'I'm the same as ever, sweetheart. Nothing's changed at all but – och, you look bloomin', darling. You've grown prettier than ever. A real woman now. When did you get back?'

'I came home last night. I could have stayed in Edinburgh but the time felt right to make a clean break with everything there. So I decided I would come home, even though it would once have taken wild horses to drag me back. But there's no point in hiding for ever. I need to face things and make some long-term decisions. I had to see my mother. And I wanted to see you again, of course!' She grinned at him.

'Well, I'm touched, young lady. And it's always a pleasure to see you. I've missed you all these years but I hear it's been well worth it. The ladies in the shop are always gossiping about young Heather McBain and her glamorous life. You've done fine things, haven't you? Got yourself that education?'

'Aye,' she said, sitting down at the table, picking up a bit of driftwood and looking at it idly. 'I did all right. I could have done better at university but you know what, I was having too much fun. I got myself a degree, anyway. Then I met a man and we moved in together, then I got a job in this creative media agency, working in public relations. I turned out to be very good at it – though it wasn't difficult if you were prepared to put the time in, to be honest. Then a few months ago, I broke up with my man. He wanted to get serious and I just wasn't ready for all of that – not with him, anyway. We had great fun together but I wasn't sure if he was the man I wanted to have children with and all that stuff.' She waved her hand carelessly to show that it was still far too early to be thinking about settling down. 'So once we'd got rid of our flat and I was homeless, I had a choice. Find another flat and carry on the same as before, or make a change. So I sold almost all my stuff and put the rest into storage, resigned from my job – I know, very reckless – and decided to come home. Strange, really, because I never thought I'd see it again when I left.'

'I remember. You couldn't get away fast enough – but who could blame you? Ah, lass, I'm glad you enjoyed yourself. Well, well!' He chuckled, sitting down opposite her. 'A degree from Edinburgh University. Your parents must be very proud of you.'

'Ha!' she said, turning her eyes upwards. 'For all the notice they took of it. I think Mum was pleased but she couldn't bring herself to show it. And as for my dad ... well ... you know all about

341

that. He'd sooner cut his arm off than be happy about anything I did.'

'They didnae come to your graduation, then?'

'Course not! Don't be an eejit. Dad showed less than no interest in my further education. If it hadn't been for Mum sending me the odd cheque or two in secret, I don't know how I'd have managed. As it was, I had to waitress the whole four years I was at university. Not that I mind, really. It's good to know that I stood on my own two feet and got myself through it. I've seen too many rich English bastards hooraying their way around the place, never knowing what it means to go without a meal or not to have a fiver in your pocket at any given time. I never wanted to be like them, little Daddy's girls and Mummy's boys. I've got my self-respect, you know? It's just...' she looked slightly wistful '...well, I would have liked it if my parents had been a bit proud of me. I know Mum once dreamed of going to Edinburgh – she told me in one of those rare moments when she let her guard down – so I'd hoped it would mean something to her when I got there. But Dad has never let her be proud.' Heather's face darkened. 'I wish she'd learn to stand up to him! How can any woman let herself be trampled all over like that?'

'Now, Heather,' Hamish said gently. 'You don't know what her life is like. It's wrong to judge her. You've no way of knowing what you'd do in her situation.'

'I'd never let myself be treated by any man the way she lets herself be treated by my father!' she said hotly.

342

'Well, that's good. But that's your choice. You know what they say about walking a mile in another man's moccasins.'

'Hmm.' Heather looked away and shrugged. 'Talking about it doesn't change anything, anyway. She's still under his thumb and he still hates me.'

'I can't believe he hates you, lass–'

'Yes, he does! He always has, ever since I was a child. There's something about me he can't stand.'

'It's true you've always had a difficult relationship...'

'Difficult! That's an understatement,' she snorted. 'The only thing that's stopped him from beating me to a pulp has been that he can't be bothered. He's too busy basking in the sunshine he thinks comes from Callum's backside.'

'Oh yes. The prodigal brother. He's certainly making a big noise in the village these days.'

'Is he?' Heather grimaced. 'I can imagine.'

'He's building himself a house further up the hill – quite outlandish, it is. All glass and steel, like something from a science-fiction story. And he races around in that smart red sports car of his, revving up the engine and making it roar.'

'Mum mentioned something about the house. Where does he get all the money?' Heather's face reddened. 'It's very hard for me, Hamish, seeing the way he's treated. He's like a little crown prince or something, he's given everything he wants. I know he's Dad's deputy and does a lot of work for the business but ... for me, after slaving as a waitress for four years to put myself through university without any help at all from my father ... well, it's hard to accept that Callum gets anything he asks for. And how on earth does fishing manage to provide such a great living? That car of his must have cost thousands, and as for the house...'

Hamish stared intently at the piece of driftwood he'd taken up in his hand, and gently whittled off another piece. 'Life isn't fair, sweetheart, that much we know.'

Heather frowned. Now that her eyes were fully adjusted to the gloom inside the little cabin, she could see that Hamish had aged even more in the years she had been away. He had never looked young, at least not as far as she could remember. Her father dyed his hair so that it stayed the same shade of Elvis black, and his extra weight made his face full and kept it freer of wrinkles. It was hard to believe he was the same age as Hamish, or near enough – the other man had white hair and deep, pitted lines running across his forehead and down his cheeks, and his tall frame was skinny. But how old could he be? Surely only in his fifties. He looked about fifteen years older than that, at least.

'You know, in a strange way, it was Mum that brought me back here,' Heather said, watching Hamish's knife scrape away at the wood, revealing the white core within. 'I've just got the feeling she needs me at the moment, I don't know why.'

'How is she?'

'She seems the same – still thin and working like a dog to care for those selfish pigs. But she's even more removed from life than she used to be,

344

as though she's locked away from us all, watching from inside her private room. I don't know why I felt that I had to come back and make sure that she was all right but now I'm here, I'm going to stay for a while. My father hates having me back home, of course, and so does Callum ... but who cares.'

'That's the spirit, darling.'

'I've got a job at the pub, just to keep me busy until I figure out what I'm going to do with myself.'

'Well, then, I'll see you there. I'm there most nights.'

'Hamish, you're not still drinking, are you?'

'If you're still breathing, I'm still drinking. And I hope things carry on the same way, thank you very much.' He grinned at her. 'I can see what you're like, wanting to dash about and make everything all right. You're wanting to rescue your mother and wanting to rescue me. Well, just watch out, Miss Heather McBain – or you might be called upon to do some real rescuing one of these days.'

Chapter Thirty-three

'What do you think then, Dad? Pretty cool, huh?'

Callum came clambering over the building site towards him, his black hair blown about by the wind. His eyes were alight with excitement, his hands thrust deep into his coat pockets against the chill wind.

'Aye, son. It's very nice.'

'Nice! C'mon. It's bloody fantastic!'

McBain looked again at the collection of mud and concrete that formed the basis of Callum's new house. It didn't look much to him, but then Callum was probably seeing it as it was going to be – a brand-new home built exactly as he wanted it, an open-plan, modern, two-storey, glass and steel creation that would make its mark on Kinlochvegan. 'When will they finish?' he asked his son, who was staring at the foundations with obvious glee. There was no sign of anyone at work on the site.

'They say it's a sixteen-week build but I'm not expecting it to be done in less than twenty. There're always hold-ups and unforeseen hitches, aren't there? And this bloody weather is so unreliable. We'll see.' Callum turned and grinned at him. 'In by Christmas, eh, Dad?'

McBain couldn't help smiling back at him. There was something infectious about Callum's moods. He always felt everything so strongly and always had, ever since he was a boy. His happiness was extreme and came in great waves of unalloyed joy – when he was happy, it lifted everyone up, but by the same token, his bad moods were terrible things that plunged anyone nearby into a similar state of dreadful misery. It was impossible to tell what would trigger a very good mood, or a very bad one.

Nonetheless, McBain adored the boy, even with his unpredictable nature. He was so unmistakably *his* son, with those heavy dark brows over the black eyes and his stocky frame. Callum had not been easy, that was true, but it was McBain's greatest pleasure to get him to smile, and his greatest sadness was when his boy was miserable. As a result, he spoiled him, he knew. It was a rather silly indulgence to let him build this house on the hill – it would cost thousands. But, on the other hand, perhaps it was a sound investment. Property, bricks and mortar, land – the only things that really lasted these days. Very likely they'd end up with a nice little profit in a few years. Anyway, Callum deserved a reward, for all the extra business he'd brought the way of McBain & Son. Admittedly, it was not the kind of business he'd envisaged when he'd set out all those years ago, taking over the small garage his father had invested in and turning it into a large and successful concern. But he'd never been one to close his eyes to opportunity – and Callum could be very persuasive when he wanted to be.

'Shall I see you back at the house, son?' he asked.

'Aye, see you there, Dad.' Callum flashed him a bright smile and got into his little red sports car, revving it for a few moments before he roared off down the hill.

McBain stayed at the site a few minutes longer, looking at the foundations that would one day become the house of Callum's dreams. It pleased him that the boy did not seem to want to leave Kinlochvegan, that he saw his future here, though of course he was just like any young man of twenty-one, attracted by the excitement and adventure that a big city could offer. That was why he never asked questions when Callum disappeared off for days at a time. Usually it was the same thing – some friend invited him to a shindig that ended up going on longer than expected, or he was meeting up with pals in Glasgow to drink and dance and chase girls, just as any father would expect.

It was after one of his disappearances that Callum came up with the idea of extending the family business with another arm that he referred to as 'an import operation'.

'I met this guy, Dad. His name is Karl and he's completely straight up, no messing. He's a brilliant bloke and he's very interested in doing some business with us. I told him about our fishing operation and he thinks we could do something on the side that will make us some real cash – but it's completely safe!'

McBain had suspected that his son was taking drugs on his party expeditions, and this confirmed it. There was no way he'd meet characters like this Karl otherwise and one didn't need to be a genius to work out what sort of thing Karl was suggesting. Well, McBain didn't like Callum taking drugs but what could anyone do about it these days? That was what young people did, and there was no point in trying to pretend otherwise or stop them doing it. McBain felt that as long as he didn't try and prevent Callum taking drugs, then Callum would probably be sensible and not get addicted to anything or binge on it or anything stupid like that.

But importing the stuff? McBain had been unsure. Of course, in the first place it was illegal and the penalties for being caught were harsh. In the second place, it was always a bad idea to get involved with the kind of people who moved in the dark and dangerous world of drugs and criminal gangs. But then Callum had told him what they'd be expected to do and what kind of money they'd get, and it was certainly tempting. But still – he'd said no.

Callum had been by turns pleading and demanding but McBain had stood firm. Yes, it was easy money but it couldn't possibly be worth the risk. He'd intended to stay immovable on the matter, until Callum, furious at being thwarted, had said that if his father didn't want to get involved, that was his affair but he, Callum, was going to do it anyway, all on his own if he had to. Didn't his dad understand? This Karl was a golden bloke, a bona fide, who would protect them from all the nasty business that went on at either end of the operation as long as they did this one, simple thing and didn't ask any questions. And he wanted that money – it was *easy* money.

Once McBain realised that Callum was serious and that he intended to go ahead with it whatever, well – there was no choice really, after that. He had to go along with it too, to make sure that his boy was all right. And, on reflection, he was pretty sure that he could handle anyone if he had to, criminal or not. There was no one in his life he had not been able to triumph over eventually.

Callum had been right. It was easy, ridiculously easy. The trawlers went out every day, week after week, month after month, just as they had for years. Who would suspect them?

McBain and Callum had taken one trusted lieutenant with them, Greg McDonald, who had once been McBain's only friend and who had stayed loyal to him over the years. His reward for his unquestioning fidelity was a job for life with his old friend. McBain knew he could be trusted absolutely because his fate was bound up with that of the McBain family; and he was also less than quick on the uptake and not likely to bother anyone with difficult questions about legality, risks and the rights and wrongs of the matter.

At first McBain had been nervous and ill at ease, jumping at the slightest noise and unable to contain his edginess. He expected at any point to hear the voice of the law and see Royal Navy gunships with customs officers aboard, or feel a hand clapped on his shoulder. Despite his fears, it was entirely straightforward. On a starlit night not long before dawn, they rendezvoused with a pleasure craft – God only knew where it had come from and no one was going to ask – and a man who passed over several canvas bags full of wrapped kilo bricks sealed tightly with masking tape. Barely a word was exchanged, and in a matter of minutes they were heading off on their normal course, to do some fishing for the sake of appearances.

Callum had been elated. 'See, Dad?' he said excitedly. 'Didn't I tell you? It's easy money!'

McBain had had to agree. When they'd returned to shore Callum had overdone the nonchalance just a little, carrying the bags off with a casualness that indicated there was something a bit strange about them, but no one was around to notice. That was the great thing about the whole operation. No one was interested. There was no local police station – the nearest was in the next small town, fifteen miles up the coast. McBain doubted that it would cross anyone's mind to suspect that anything out of the ordinary was going on; Kinlochvegan wasn't that kind of place. A bit of spicy gossip about how Mrs Brodie was redecorating her kitchen was about as interesting as it got.

Callum disappeared off to Glasgow with the contents of the bags well hidden in his car. He'd wanted to take one of the flashy ones from the garage – a Merc or a Beamer – but McBain had told him not to be so stupid. 'Take a banger, go slowly and whatever happens, don't draw any attention to yourself! I'm serious, Callum. This isn't a game, you know. You won't be so cheerful if you get caught with that lot in your possession.'

But Callum had laughed and said, 'Yeah, yeah, all right, Dad.'

He'd returned after two days in a brand-new red sports car, grinning all over his face.

'What did I tell you, lad?' said his father, exasperated. 'Can't you see that we have to keep in the background? This kind of thing is bound to make people ask questions. How much did it cost you?'

'Oh, c'mon, Dad. Just tell them it was a birth-day present. And everyone knows you can afford it, anyway.'

Callum handed over what he hadn't spent on his car. He was like a child, McBain thought. Once his immediate need was gratified, he didn't see the point of holding onto the money. But when he wanted something, he'd come begging and expect to be given it, throwing tantrums if he didn't get his own way.

McBain riffled through the cash, which was still substantial and, he reminded himself with pleasure, tax-free. Perhaps Callum had been right. And he had to admit, it did make working for a living look like a fool's game. Something in that made him uneasy, it seemed to challenge everything he had built his life on, but he didn't want to think about it and so pushed it to the back of his mind and thought instead about the fortune growing in the safe he kept concealed in his office at home. That made him feel better.

Having done it once, the next time was easier and the one after that, easier still. The drops were only every few months, no more than four times a year. It was too good and too easy an opportunity to miss.

McBain turned his back on the soggy soil and mud of the building site and went back to his car. Sitting inside, he remained there for a while, the ignition key in his hand, thinking. There was no doubt that Callum had enjoyed being a playboy for a time and that McBain himself had welcomed cash injections into the business when owning a fishing fleet became a little less lucrative than it had once been. But he was no longer happy about their role as drugs couriers – there was no pretending any longer. Callum had a serious drug habit, and endless supplies of the stuff were never going to help him to kick it.

It must have been on that first drop in Glasgow

that Callum got his real taste for coke. No doubt he'd tried a few lines before then, but now he had it on tap and he must have snorted for Britain. He had always had a manic streak in him and a tendency to slump into misery, so it wasn't easy to tell at first just how much the drug was affecting him. But then Greg had gone with him a couple of times to help with the drop-off, and he'd come back with stories that had made McBain's heart sink.

'I'm not joking,' he'd said, his expression sombre. 'The kid's off his head on toot most of the time. He's racking up lines like you and me might eat Smarties, one every minute or so. He gets through grams of the stuff in an evening. And he's shagging his head off too.'

'He's just a lad having fun,' McBain said, aware of how weak it sounded. 'He's playing around with the girls.'

'No,' Greg replied. He shook his head. 'This man Karl he hangs around with – he's no good. He hands out the stuff to Callum like it's free. He gets the boy coked up to the eyeballs and sets him off, laughing at all the stuff he does. Makes him chat up girls and try and shag them then and there. The bouncer of the club where they hang out told me that Callum tried to make two girls have sex with him on a sofa in the VIP area one night. When they wouldn't he went berserk and beat them up, or tried to until he was yanked off them. Broke the nose of one poor girl.'

McBain went to Callum after this and asked him straight out about it. 'What's this I hear about what you're up to in Glasgow?'

Callum looked peeved. 'I knew that bastard Greg wouldnae keep his mouth shut,' he muttered.

'So it's true – the drugs and the girls?'

'It's not me!' Callum cried, suddenly furious. 'Stop picking on me! It's not me that does it, it's the coke.'

After that McBain's eyes were opened. He noticed how Callum began to swoop into depression and then get agitated as the next shipment was due. He obviously had a serious problem. McBain had to admit it to himself – his son was addicted to cocaine and while that was all right for all the people they shipped the drugs in for, there was no way it was going to happen to his Callum.

It was time to call a halt to their drugs involvement.

McBain started the engine and drove carefully down the slippery hill back to the road. He was worried, he couldn't pretend he wasn't. He and Callum were in it up to their necks, and he had no idea how easy it would be to extricate themselves now that they had started. He was sure there was a way out – it was just a question of finding it, and then of guiding his unpredictable son down the path he wanted him to go.

This house would help divert him, McBain thought. And I'll think up other ways to keep him entertained. He'll see it my way in the end.

Chapter Thirty-four

Mary tried to avoid mirrors these days.

It was not just because her dark hair had faded and was streaked with great ribbons of grey, or because her white skin had furrows and crevices etched into it. She didn't even mind seeing her skinny frame and the clothes that hung off her sharp-boned shoulders and hips. It was her eyes. She couldn't look herself in the eye. In them there was the haunted memory of the Mary Burns who had once lived in this self-same body – a girl of passion and spirit, capable of love and of standing up for herself.

She was gone now, of course. It had been a gradual process; she'd been worn down by years of scorn and contempt, first from her husband and then from her son. At first she'd tried to resist it, but after a while she had given up and concentrated on getting through each day. She had found refuge in two places. The first was sleep – she slept as much as she could and was always hungry for more. It was blessed oblivion and as often as she could, she crept upstairs and shut herself away in darkness to sleep for hours at a time.

The second was her daughter, her beloved Heather. From the moment she was born, Heather had provided the light in her life. She had given Mary hope that the future held something worth living for, and she had provided her with the strength to face each day. The little girl had been her delight, and the love that radiated from her smiles had, Mary truly believed, saved her life. Without it, she would easily have found a way to slip permanently into the easeful darkness of her slumbers.

The pregnancy had been a matter of delight and wonder to her, but also of great fear because it had come so soon after her afternoon with Hamish. When she had realised that she was expecting a baby, she'd sat down with her calendar and counted days, trying to work out if, possibly, it could be Hamish's child that she was expecting. At first she had thought it must be, and in her heart, she rejoiced. The two of them were parted for ever, she knew that. They had had their chance and they had lost it and were now irrevocably tied to other people. But if the child she was having was Hamish's, then something would exist that bound them together, something that was proof of the love they had once shared. And why would it not be Hamish's baby? After all, she had not been pregnant by her husband after three years of marriage and all those countless times when she'd had to endure his hateful lovemaking.

As she had sat there with her calendar, aware of the tiny life growing inside her, she had also remembered again what the doctor had said to her, that women get pregnant more easily with the men they find satisfaction with.

If that were true, then there was no question but the baby was Hamish's.

When Heather was born, she had been terrified that the baby would look like Hamish, but, apart from her blue eyes that were not so different from Mary's own, she was just a normal, bald, squashed-faced infant. Everyone had said cooingly how much she looked like McBain – 'she has his nose!' or 'that's her daddy's chin, and no mistake,' – but to Mary's eyes she looked only like a baby, even if she was a particularly darling one.

It was McBain's reaction to the pregnancy and the baby that puzzled her. She had come back from the doctor's with the news feeling lighter in herself. This was what he had wanted so badly, what he had taunted her with, and that now she was able to offer him the baby, perhaps he would soften towards her and show her the love he once had. But when she had told him, after dinner when they were together in the sitting room, his reaction had been nothing like what she had expected. He had stared for a long time at the floor, and then he had laughed – not a happy laugh but a strange, twisted, joyless sound that had chilled her to hear.

'Aren't you pleased?' she'd asked in a small voice. 'Isn't this what you wanted?'

He hadn't answered her for a long time but when he did, nothing about him had changed. 'Aye,' he said brusquely. 'Looks like you're a woman after all.'

His dismissive attitude did not change throughout her pregnancy, or after the birth. He looked at the little girl and then turned away, as though she held no interest for him whatsoever.

In her heart, Mary had always believed that the child was Hamish's daughter. But did McBain suspect anything? How on earth could he? No one but the two of them knew what had happened that afternoon, and she was certain that Hamish would never breathe a word to another living soul. Perhaps it was the fact that the baby was a girl that disgusted him – it was evident he thought little of women – but nothing she ever did could make him happy, even when she tottered towards him, her arms outstretched, asking for her dada.

When Heather was four years old, Mary was astonished to find herself pregnant again. She had believed that, for whatever reason, she and her husband would never have children together. She had no reason to query anything this time. McBain was most certainly the father and little Callum obligingly looked the image of his daddy right from the start. Perhaps, she thought, that was why he had adored his son so from the moment he had held him in his arms. A great division appeared in the family, with McBain and Callum on one side, and Mary and Heather on the other, the men against the women. Mary loved her son, of course – he was an unexpected gift – but right from the start she understood that this boy was her husband's property, not hers. More than that, Callum was nothing like Heather as a baby. He was irritable and irascible, where she had always been placid and eager to please. He was prone to long screaming fits for reasons Mary could not fathom, and as he grew older, almost had convulsions when his will was thwarted. When he was not throwing passionate tantrums or executing his latest bit of mischief, she sometimes found him sitting alone, staring into space, almost in a trance and completely unresponsive to her voice. He could stay that way for an hour at a time.

Her instinct told her that something was not right with Callum but when she tried to broach the subject with her husband, and with the doctor, no one seemed particularly concerned.

'You've had a daughter, Mary, and she's a little angel. Not all babies are, you know. You can't be surprised if boys are different,' said the doctor comfortingly. 'He's full of energy, that's all, and you know what lads are like – they're naughty and rough when little lassies sit quietly and play with dolls.'

Mary so wanted that to be true, but something told her that Callum was not just a normal, high-spirited boy. Sometimes she saw him almost possessed by a greater force, that took his little body out of his control and sent him haring about on a rampage of violence and destruction that nothing could stop. Anything that got in his way was a target and more often than not it was Heather, who came to her crying with bite marks and slap marks and bruises where Callum had attacked her. More than once Mary had had to prise him off his sister as though she were rescuing her daughter from a mad dog, with the little boy snarling and gnashing, his eyes wild, while Heather cowered in a corner, terrified. Mary herself was not immune – her arms and hands bore the scars of Callum's violent rages,

359

his bites and scratches and punches.

Like his father, she sometimes thought. She was covered in the marks McBain had left on her over the years. As the years went by, they were joined by the ones made by his son. As he grew up, Callum's strange, maniacal personality only became more pronounced.

Perhaps it would have helped Callum if his father had been stronger with him, but the boy was the only person in the world McBain softened for. The little lad could do nothing wrong in his eyes, and he was even tacitly encouraged when he flailed out at his mother and sister. But then he had seen the same contemptuous attitude from his father, so why would he be any different?

Heather must be kept safe, she thought. She was the one person who could be rescued from this almighty mess, and Mary decided that she would do whatever was necessary to set her free. But there was little she could do to protect her daughter. She understood that McBain saw her affection for Heather as a vital weakness, a way to hurt her, and as Callum grew up with the same streak of vicious bullying inside him, he too realised that Heather was an easy target if he wanted to cause his mother pain. As a result, Mary began to distance herself from the one person who brought her any joy in her life, in order to protect her. If McBain and Callum thought she didn't care much about Heather, then they had nothing to gain by victimising her, mocking her and trampling all over her, the way they did Mary.

It worked, but only up to a point. And had it really been worth it? She had lost the trust of her beloved daughter. She could never forget the day Heather had come to her crying when Callum had used his strong, hard little fists on her again and maliciously destroyed one of her favourite toys, and she had said harshly, 'How many times do I have to tell you not to provoke your brother, Heather?'

The look in the girl's eyes was not of anger but of shock at the betrayal, and a terrible realisation that there was no one to fight for her.

Heather has a chance, Mary told herself. I'm only doing this to help her get away from here. She has a future. She would need to be tough and independent to get there, and that's what I am helping her to become. It will be worth it in the end.

When Heather had gone to university, her relief had been great. And afterwards, when Heather stayed on and took a job in a media agency, she was even more delighted. Her daughter had gone. She had survived this terrible family and made a life for herself where she was free and independent – Mary only hoped that the damage done to her in her early years wasn't too great and that she wouldn't make mistakes in the partners she chose. In her heart she was sure Heather was tough and resilient and, somehow, endowed with a goodness and a self-confidence that would see her through.

And then, to her horror, Heather came back.

The house was always immaculate. When Mary

wasn't sleeping, she was cleaning and cooking and washing and ironing and tending to the men of the family. Sometimes she laughed when she pictured her young self, newly married, and remembered how she had not known how to do housework properly. Imagine – once she had had a maid and a cook and had never so much as dusted the top of a table. She'd learned her lesson well since then. As the years went by, Mc-Bain had become more exacting about what he expected, forcing her to clean and reclean until things were done to his satisfaction. Watching her work often excited him, and sometimes he would make her scrub a floor three or four times before roughly having sex with her on the newly washed surface – and then make her clean it again.

He didn't do so much of that these days. He didn't bother her nearly as much as he had in the past. Perhaps now that she had become so meek and submissive, allowing him to do whatever he wanted without demur, he was losing interest. He had broken her will so successfully that she held no further challenge for him. He might be finding his pleasure elsewhere – probably not with another woman, she thought. More likely through the computer in his study, where he spent long hours shut away. She didn't care. She was grateful for it. Let him look at pictures of girls suffering the kind of thing she had had to put up with over all these years, and leave her alone.

Now that the housework was done, she went to her sewing room, the only private space she had in the house. It was her little refuge and she had spent countless hours lying on the shabby old red sofa she kept in there.

She took a bottle of sleeping pills from her desk drawer and sat down on the sofa, looking at it. Shall I take some? she wondered. If I took three now, I could wake up in time to make the dinner, as long as I set the alarm...

She had an extra-loud alarm clock to wake her if she slept too long, and when she took the pills, she sometimes went straight to such a deep un-consciousness that the bell could ring for min-utes before it dragged her up and out of it.

'Mum? Are you there?'

The sound of her daughter's voice broke into her thoughts. 'In here, Heather.' She pushed the bottle under a cushion.

Heather came in, bright and cheerful as usual.

'Hello, sweetheart. You're not at work today?' Mary said, tilting her cheek up for a kiss.

'No. Rachel's getting some professional cleaners in to do the pub over. She says she does it once a year and the rates are good because all the cleaners are Chinese immigrants or something. Anyway, she doesn't need me, so...' Heather smiled as she sat down on the velvet footstool by the sofa. 'Free time for me. I'm not complaining.'

Mary studied her daughter, feeling the pleasure she always had when she looked on the pretty open face with the wide blue eyes, and the brown hair glinting with rich darkness. Nevertheless, she was uneasy. She sat up straight on the sofa and leaned forward towards her. 'Heather, I know there are many times over the years when I've let you down, but I need you to be honest with me now. I have to ask you what you're doing here.

Why you're here...'

'Mum, I told you—'

'You told me you're worried about me, that you want to be at home for a while, but if that's true, then you have to listen to me. I don't want you here, sweetheart, you know that. Not because I don't love having you around, but because I want you far away from everything that goes on here and as far as possible from your father and Callum. Their influence isn't healthy, you know that. You had a life in Edinburgh, a proper life away from here. Why did you leave it?'

'I needed some time out. I've already told you – my previous job came to a natural end and it seemed like a good opportunity to stand back and look at what I wanted out of life. And once Steve and I had broken up and given up our tenancy on the flat, it seemed like the right time to come home.'

'I'm sorry about your boyfriend—'

'Don't be,' replied Heather shortly. 'I wasn't. It was never really right – just one of those things you fall into, you know? We both knew it wasn't going to last the distance, even if he thought he wanted it to for a while.'

'Well ... that's good. I don't want you to be un-happy, darling. But that's why I don't think you should be here. It's not best for you.'

'It's not best for you, either. What do you do all day? Run around after those two like some kind of unpaid servant. And if you're not doing that, you're locked away in here all on your own. You never leave the house.' Heather put a hand up on her mother's arm. 'You're right, I'm worried about you.'

'We've been through this before. I don't want you to worry about me. I'm fine just the way I am – no, I mean it,' she said firmly, seeing her daughter's expression. 'I'm perfectly happy. Just let me deal with things the way I want to, that's all I ask.'

'Hmm.' Heather frowned and Mary could tell that she wasn't convinced.

'It's not right that you should still be here, sleeping in your old bedroom, living with your parents, working as a waitress in the local pub. You're a grown woman. You've been standing on your own two feet for years now. You don't need to come back here – so for God's sake, Heather, go back and carry on with your old life. Don't get tangled up with everything here. *Please.*' Mary hoped that her daughter would pick up on the earnestness in her voice, and guess that there were things she couldn't speak of but which she was trying to convey with her voice. Let her understand me! she thought. I can't involve her in the things I know are happening, but I must somehow get her away from here without making her suspicious. If only she wasn't so curious...

For a moment, they gazed at each other as if trying to work out how far they could take this conversation, but neither spoke.

Finally Mary whispered, 'Heather, I know what you're doing and I won't have it. I won't have you sacrifice your life through some misguided sense that I need looking after. I'll be fine.'

'Maybe there's more to it, Mum. Maybe I can't go.'

'What do you mean?' Mary was suddenly frightened that her daughter might somehow already be involved. Had she stumbled on something? Seen or heard something accidentally?

Heather stared at the carpet for a moment and then looked frankly at her mother. 'I don't know anything for sure, and I don't expect you'll tell me what's happening, though I'm certain you know. However, we both know that something bad is going on here, Mum. And we both know that Callum is out of control. Don't try and deny it. Perhaps it isn't as obvious to you as it is to me, but I've been away for ten years and I'm seeing him through fresh eyes. He was pretty frightful as a child but lots of children go through bad phases and come out the other side. Callum hasn't. He's worse. There's a light in his eye that frightens me, Mum. He's not normal, you must see that, and he needs help. He's not like anybody I've ever met, no matter how high-spirited they are, or whatever you want to call it. I'm worried that he has a psychiatric condition and I think he needs treatment. I honestly believe he's dangerous, Mum, and if by any chance he's dabbling in drugs, it can only exacerbate any problem he has. What do you think, Mum?' Heather stared at her as though trying to read her expression.

Mary shut her eyes. How much did Heather know? How much had she guessed at? You didn't have to live for very long in this house to sense the atmosphere and to realise that something was going on.

'He ... might be using drugs. I think it's when he goes away at weekends, to those parties of his.'

Heather nodded slowly. 'Mum, we've got to stop it.'

'No, Heather!' Panic rose in her and she grasped her daughter's hand. 'Don't get involved!'

'But Callum's sick...'

'He probably is – but it's too late now! The damage is done. Perhaps he could have been helped once, but not any more, it's all gone too far for that and your father will never admit it, he'd never allow it. If Callum had to go away from us for a while, perhaps be hospitalised or worse... No, your father would forbid it. I don't know how he'd live without Callum. That's why you have to leave us, and stay away from whatever is going on here. I mean it, Heather! Callum's capable of many things and I don't know how far he'd go if he ever thought he was being stopped from doing what he wants. Please, Heather – I'm begging you... The right thing for you is to walk away, right now, and not come back.'

'What about you?' Heather demanded. 'If he's capable of hurting me, he's certainly capable of hurting you. I've seen the way he treats you, the way they both treat you. They don't care if you live or die! Why should you sacrifice yourself for them?'

Tears sprang into Mary's eyes as she looked at her daughter and the indignation burning on her face.

'Because I'm Callum's mother,' she said at last in a quiet voice. 'I must look after him. I don't believe this is his fault. And I'm married to your father. But you've got hope, you've got a chance. If you want to make me happy, Heather, you'll leave. You don't realise how terrible it is for me that you're here – it makes everything ten times worse and so much harder to bear.'

She put every ounce of pleading into her voice and for a moment, it looked as though Heather might be swayed. Then her stubborn chin came up and she said, 'No, Mum. If you're here, I'm here. We'll leave together or we'll both see it through to the end.'

Chapter Thirty-five

Callum paced around his father's desk, running his hands through his short black hair until it fluffed up like a chick's.

He glanced up at McBain, his eyes bright with that strange force that so often came into them.

'Ah, come on, Dad,' he said, with the air of one who knows that he'll get his own way. 'What's the point in stopping now?'

'I'm not happy with this, you know that. Customs are patrolling this stretch of the coast more and more frequently. It might be that they've narrowed the focus down here, worked out this is the most likely area for the drop-offs. Or it might be that there's someone passing along some information. We can't possibly know. The point is that if we go on, we're bound to get caught. This whole thing has always made me uneasy, you know that, because we're just little cogs in a big wheel and we don't know who we're working with, or who for. It was madness to get involved in the first place.' McBain frowned. It sounded convincing. He didn't want Callum to know that the real reason he wanted out was to stop his son's drug addiction. 'The money was too good. I couldn't resist it. But now – everything is telling me it's time to get out.'

Callum stopped pacing and sighed heavily, frowning. 'But, Dad,' he said, in a wheedling tone, 'what'm I going to do without that money? I need it. I can't do without it now. How will I finish the house?'

'We'll find a way. It might take a bit longer, that's all.'

Callum's expression changed to defiant sulkiness. 'No. I want it now. It's just getting to the good bit. They've done all that boring stuff, now it's about to take shape. We can't stop now. Come on, Dad.'

McBain took a deep breath. It was unfamiliar territory, denying Callum something he wanted. But this was a serious business, and McBain had made up his mind. He could be as stubborn as his son when he wanted. 'You heard me, Callum. You're to go to this friend of yours and tell him that we're going to scale right down. Then, gradually, we'll work out how to get out altogether.'

'Are you crazy?' yelled Callum, suddenly furious. His whole body seemed to bend over and then rise up again, now shaking with rage. 'You want me to go and tell these guys that we don't want to be involved any more? Do you think it's that simple? You must be mad if you do. We're in it up to our necks, Dad, and we can't just walk away when we feel like it. It doesn't work that way!'

McBain felt a swirl of cold fear in the pit of his stomach. This was what he had been afraid of – that he would not be able to control this situation and that they'd get themselves mixed up in something bigger than they were. But Callum had always said it was relatively small-time; the chain ended with his mate Karl and no major criminal gangs were involved. He cursed himself for ever listening to his son in the first place but outwardly he remained completely calm. 'Don't get hysterical, Callum. This friend of yours must appreciate the realities of the situation. We've no interest in talking to anyone about this operation – why would we? We would only incriminate ourselves. Just explain to him that if we carry on we're likely to be busted, and that would take everyone down, and stop the importing immediately. Much better to shut it down now, before it's found out, and move it on somewhere else. It makes sense – anyone could see that.'

'Well, perhaps you'd like to be the one to explain it!' yelled Callum, his face red. 'You want me to go to Glasgow and tell them? Is that it? You might never see me again! You might hear about me floating in some loch somewhere with a bullet through my head. Do you no understand? These are big bad boys we're talking about. Bigger and badder'n you, Daddy.' He said the last word like a sneer.

Keep calm, McBain told himself. He's trying to frighten you, to get you to do what he wants. 'I'm sure they are. But nonetheless, I want you to talk

370

to them, and tell them, in the nicest possible way, that we want out.'

'Dad, come on, now. What if I do it all on my own, and you're not involved at all?' Callum was back to his wheedling. 'You don't have to know a thing and if we get caught, that's my lookout.'

McBain stood up, putting his fists on the desk in front of him. He set his face and brows in an expression he knew could reduce his workers to abject terror. 'What don't you understand, Callum? We're out of this game, and that is that. Now do as I say.'

Callum stared at him for a moment, as though unsure whether to lose his temper entirely or start crying and wailing. In the end, he did neither. 'Fine! OK! Have it your own fuckin' way,' he snarled, and stormed out of the room, slamming the door behind him like a flouncy teenager.

A few minutes later, McBain heard the sports car rev up and then zoom off down the driveway.

The nightclub was packed to the gills, a mass of bodies heaving in the darkness that was lit every few seconds by a flash of neon. The whole place shuddered to the bass that thumped as regularly as a heartbeat, and the dance music drowned out every other sound.

Callum fought his way through the crowd, jabbing and elbowing to get past. Eventually he got to the roped-off VIP area, where a bouncer, colossal and meaty in a tight white tee shirt that strained over his muscles, stood guard.

'Eh, Sean, how's it goin'?' Callum shouted. His

accent always got rougher and tougher when he was in Glasgow. He sniffed and wiped his nose. Even though he'd meant to keep straight before he was having his meeting with Karl, he hadn't been able to resist doing a line in the loos. There was something hypnotic about the nightclub, and he'd found himself doing exactly what he would normally do on a night out: he scored some coke, chopped himself a fat line, then followed that with a brandy and coke – his favourite drink at the moment. Now he was jigging in time to the beat and feeling wired. He'd have a smoke soon, maybe – bring himself down a bit. These evenings were all about balance, firing himself up with drugs to just the right tempo and maintaining it all night – a bit of coke or speed to give him a rush, a bit of weed to settle him down, some alcohol to cheer him up, some more coke to fight the come-down, and on it went.

The bouncer looked him over and then smiled at him. 'It's you, you crazy fucker. What're you up to tonight, eh, pal? No rough stuff in here, OK? Take all that to the Box.'

The Box was a rival nightclub, but seedier and shittier all round than this one. They didn't mind if you and your pals decided to play target practice with the optics or beat up a booth, as long as you paid for it afterwards.

'No way, pal! I'm cool tonight.' Callum grinned at him.

'Yeah?' The bouncer gave him a practised look that told him he knew exactly what Callum was on but that he was well within the confines of what he could safely manage. 'OK. How can I help you?'

'Is Karl around? I'm supposed to be seeing him.'

The bouncer cocked his head towards the room that lay beyond the red rope. 'Back there.' He stood aside to let Callum in.

'Thanks, mate.' He couldn't resist looking over his shoulder to check out if anyone was noticing him. Maybe some hot girl would see him go into the VIP and be ready to pounce when he came out, in the hopes they could both go back in and perhaps get some Cristal champagne or whatever that fancy shit was that the footballers drank.

He sauntered in and wandered about looking for Karl. It was quieter in here and instead of a huge mass of writhing bodies, there was a dance floor in the centre surrounded by red velvet booths, each with a large table and a crescent-shaped banquette around it. All were occupied by glamorous men and sexy women – almost every girl was under thirty, tanned, wearing a minute wispy dress and high-heeled sandals and lots of jewellery.

Callum grinned at one or two of them but he didn't get much response. Most were too interested in the men they were with: arrogant-looking blokes with sharp suits, white shirts and a big ice bucket of something expensive on the go.

Fuck 'em, he thought, with a mental shrug. All the whores will come running fast enough when they see the cash.

He found Karl in a booth nearest the bar, a frosted-glass construction backlit with icy pink neon.

'Hey, Karl.' Callum felt a flicker of nerves but the coke helped him ignore it.

'Callum, my man. How's it going?' Karl was a big white man with a bald head and small, mean-looking eyes.

'Yeah, good.' Callum slid into the booth and sat down next to Karl, who indicated his associates on the other side.

'Jerry. Mick. Loz. Want a drink?'

'Go on, yeah.'

Karl poured him a flute of fizzing champagne. It always made Callum a bit surprised that all these hard men drank such a girly drink. Offer them a glass of white wine and they'd run for the hills. Put some sparkle in it and they were happy as larks. It was probably just that it was the most expensive thing behind the bar, he thought. Just a show, like everything else.

'So what can I do for you, young man?' Karl frowned as Callum drained half his glass in one go. 'Been at the gak, have we?'

Callum grinned sheepishly. 'Just a little. To get the party started, you know.'

'Not very professional, though. A salesman sampling his own wares. Or maybe it's a perk of the trade, though, eh?'

'Actually, pal, that's what I wanted to talk to you about. The pickups, you know – the collection business. You see, my dad and me... Well, it's my dad really – he thinks that it's getting a little bit hot around our area. The customs are round all the time, we see boats patrolling nearly every day now. It's not making sense to keep taking the risk so we're thinking it's a good time to cool off

374

for a while, you know?'

That sounded pretty good, Callum thought, pleased. Another good thing about coke – it made him talk really well, much better than he could when he was straight.

Karl took out a cigarette and lit it. He puffed out a lungful of acrid smoke and said, 'You telling me that you're off the operation?'

'Well – yeah, I suppose so. Not for any reason except that it's in your interests as much as ours not to get caught.'

'Very generous, I'm sure.'

One of Karl's associates snickered.

'It's my old man, he's sure we're about to get busted.'

'I see.' Karl breathed out more smoke. 'It's quite unorthodox, if you must know. To suddenly decide that you're not interested any longer. It's the kind of thing that could offend me, actually. If I was the type to get offended, and luckily for you, I'm not.' He observed Callum for a while with no expression. Callum twisted in his seat a little, wishing he could have another line. He needed some confidence right now. Karl continued, 'You know what? Maybe this isn't such a bad idea after all. You're not the first to come to me with news that things are hotting up in your area. They're on the lookout for drugs, that's obvious. I reckon I agree with your old man. It's time to cool off for a while.'

'Oh,' said Callum, taken aback. 'Right.' Then he smiled. 'Cool.'

'But that doesn't mean it's all over between us, Callum. Far from it,' Karl said. 'You've got yourself in a bit deep now, mate. You can't just back out when you feel like it. And as it happens, I've got another job for you. One that I think will be right up your street, play to all your talents.'

'Oh?' said Callum, interested. 'What's that, then?'

'Good money, too. Better than the little trips you've been making. It's just a one-off this time, but if it goes well we'll be setting up a regular supply chain. I'd love you to be a part of it.'

'Oh, yeah, me too, pal.' Callum thought about money, how much he loved having it and spending it and getting more. 'But my old man – he's not keen. I don't think he'll agree to it.'

'Like I said, mate, I don't think you have a choice in the matter and your old man certainly doesn't. Now...' Karl smiled coldly. 'Listen very carefully and I'll tell you what you have to do.'

Chapter Thirty-six

'Your father thinks this is all right, aye?' asked Greg. He was at the helm of the largest of the McBain fishing trawlers, following a course that Callum had set earlier in the evening.

'Sure,' said Callum impatiently. He was looking at a map by the light of a torch. All the lights on the boat were off, in contravention of marine rules, and they were motoring along by the light of the moon which shone strongly in a clear sky, only occasionally covered by dark grey cloud.

'Shouldn't take much longer.' He looked up to where his friend Tom was keeping watch. 'Any sign, Tom?'

'No, nothing yet.'

'Dinnae forget there won't be any lights on.'

'No, I've not forgotten.' Tom continued scanning the horizon as best he could.

Greg was silent for a while and then he said, 'Are you gonna tell us what this is all about?'

'In good time, in good time,' Callum said. It was fun being in charge of his own operation. He'd taken a trawler out for the drugs drop many times, but it was always with the permission of his father. This time he was striking out on his own and he liked the way it felt. If this was successful, he would think about cutting his father out of it altogether and keeping all the profits for himself. Why not? He was taking the risk, wasn't he? He was doing his father a favour by not even telling him about it – that way he could always say truthfully that he had had no idea what was happening if it all went wrong. But it wouldn't go wrong. It was easy, easy, easy. And the money...

Callum spent a happy twenty minutes planning everything he would do when he got his hands on all the cash he'd been promised.

Tom whistled gently. The mother ship had been spotted. Callum went forward with his torch and flashed the agreed signal. There was no response from the other vessel, so he did it again.

'Come on,' he muttered. 'It has to be you. No lights, the right position ... give me a sign.'

'There she goes,' whispered Tom. A series of answering flashes came from the other ship.

'What do we do now?'

'We go as close as we can. Get alongside her.' Callum called to Greg. 'Get her alongside!'

'What are they going to do? Throw it across?' asked Tom. This ship was a big one, larger than their trawler by some margin. It wasn't like the pleasure craft they were used to, that came buzzing right up to the side and passed the packages up on a rope.

Callum giggled. 'Throw it! Nice one. No, pal. You can't throw this stuff.'

Greg switched off the engines as they neared the other craft and they drifted in towards her, Greg expertly manoeuvring her so that she bumped gently into the other, side to side.

'Should be all right like this for a while,' he called softly to Callum. 'But you'd better do whatever it is you have to do fast. We'll drift apart before too long.'

Callum rushed to the side and peered into the darkness. 'Hi there!' he called. 'This is Lucky Jim!'

'Lucky Jim, you've made contact with Pretty Woman. Cargo is here and ready for transfer. Are you prepared?' The disembodied voice floated over the deck towards them.

'Aye,' answered Callum, delighted. This was just what he'd hoped, it was like a movie. 'Tom,' he said urgently, 'open the storage hold.'

Tom looked surprised. 'How much are we taking? There's room for tonnes in there.' He was used to the several black holdalls containing hundreds of thousands of pounds' worth of cocaine. What were they going to get this time? Millions?

'Just do as I say.' Callum was too impatient to

explain himself. He was busy straining to see something on the other ship. Then, as the moon drifted out from behind a cloud, he saw dark shapes massing on the other side. 'Ah – here we are, me hearties.'

Yes, he thought, I could be a pirate captain, a pirate king. That would suit me very well.

The shapes moved closer and closer until they were standing silently at the side of the other ship.

'Move,' said a harsh voice. 'C'mon, get climbing. C'mon!'

The shapes were reluctant but they were obviously being prodded from behind. Suddenly one seemed to be standing on the deck rail and the next moment a man had landed on the trawler's deck. He looked up, stunned, and Callum saw an oriental face framed by dark hair. So it was Chinese, then.

Another landed, and then another.

'Out the way,' chided Callum, kicking one over so that he was not blocking the landing site for whoever was next. 'Move it.'

'What the hell is going on?' said Greg, astonished. 'Who are these people?'

'Visitors,' said Callum briefly. He pushed the men who had begun to stand up towards the stern. 'Come on, go there, go there.'

After about twenty had landed on board the trawler, there seemed to be no more and Callum approached the side. A shadowy figure stood on the other boat, its face invisible.

'Cargo safely transferred. Do you know what to do next?' it asked roughly.

'Aye,' Callum said, trying to hide his excitement. 'All instructions received and understood.'

'Good.'

Callum turned back to Greg. 'Let's get moving, pal. We need to get these in the hold and back to the warehouse.'

Tom did not ask any questions as they motored back to Kinlochvegan, but then he never did. Whatever Callum wanted was good enough for him. The sudden appearance of nearly two dozen Chinese, clearly bewildered, frightened and exhausted, did not faze him at all. As directed, he pushed them down the loading hatch into the hold which the trawlermen used for fish – it was cold, stinking and very unpleasant, but no doubt these blokes were used to that by now. They'd obviously come a long way in less than salubrious conditions. They looked accepting of their latest berth and too tired and hungry to care.

Greg, though, had a grim expression on his face and his mouth was set. 'I hope you know what you're doing, Callum,' he muttered.

'Of course I do.' Callum was swaggering about the boat, enjoying the role he'd just invented for himself. He was a gangmaster, a man of power who toyed with the lives of his inferiors ... yes, that was good, he liked that. Maybe he'd had enough of fish and drugs and would start directing the destinies of hundreds of people instead, smoothing their path from wherever they came from to a new life in the UK. He might even get the gun out of his father's safe in the study. It used to go with them when they picked up their drugs packages, just in case anyone turned nasty, but it had never been needed. Still, when he could persuade his father to let him hold it, Callum had enjoyed the smooth weight of it in his hands and the feeling of strength it gave him. He'd thought it would be cold but it was almost warm and so silky that he'd liked stroking it, putting his finger over the trigger and pretending to shoot.

He looked at his father's friend and grinned. 'Och, come on, Greggy, old pal! Why so down in the mouth, eh? Don't worry about it. No problem.'

'No problem.' Greg looked pale even in the darkness. 'Those boys are illegal immigrants, it's bloody plain as the nose on your face. We're trafficking, Callum. Human trafficking. I can't believe your dad is all right with this.'

Callum shrugged. 'He will be.'

He'd have to be, and that was that. It was too late now to go back.

They chuntered into the harbour as quietly as possible, the lights still out. When they had moored by the McBain business premises, the wretched Chinese, now freezing cold and smelling strongly of stale fish, were chivvied out of the hold and into the warehouse, where they stood huddled in a small group, waiting to be told what to do.

'All right, Callum,' said Greg as they stood together in the little office overlooking the processing plant. 'What happens next, eh? What's the next stage of the grand plan?'

'Cool down!' said Callum loftily. 'A truck is

arriving in a few hours to take them away, OK?'

'When? When is it coming?'

Callum consulted his watch. It was two a.m. already. 'I think it's coming between three and four.'

'It had better get here soon. The fishing boats start preparing to go out at four. I take it you don't particularly want any witnesses to this.'

'Oh, yes, Greg!' exclaimed Callum sarcastically. 'Yes please! Of course I don't, you fuckin' idiot. Now who the hell is the boss here? Eh? I'll tell you – it's me. I'm on top of this, all right, so just do me a favour and do as you're fuckin' well told, OK?'

Greg looked away for a moment and then took a deep breath. 'OK, boss. So what next?'

'Um...' Callum frowned. He hadn't really thought the logistics through, if he was honest. He'd not imagined the consignment he was receiving as people who might need somewhere to sit, some toilets to use, maybe some water to drink. 'Just make 'em sit on some boxes?' he suggested at last.

'Poor fuckers look cold. I'll see what I can do for them.'

'Yes.' Callum nodded. He wished he had that gun, so he could wave it about a bit. 'Yes, you look after them, Greg. I'll wait here until our contacts arrive.'

Greg went off and Callum sat down at the office desk, flicking through papers which had to do with the fish orders but, he thought, made him look impressive. He imagined the immigrants watching him through the glass window, sitting at his desk reading papers and organising things.

They would think, 'He must be an important man. Amazing for such a young one.'

While he sat there, Greg tried to make some arrangements for the score or so of Chinese men, finding them chairs and boxes to sit on and giving them some plastic sheeting to wrap around themselves, in the absence of blankets. They took it silently but gratefully, clearly chilled to the bone.

'Tom, let's make 'em some tea,' he said, sorry for them. He and Tom raided the workers' supply of mugs, tea bags and digestives and provided tea and biscuits for the Chinese, who fell ravenously on the food and drink.

'I hope that boy knows what he's doing,' he muttered to Tom. 'This looks like a nasty business to me. Drugs I can cope with. These poor fuckers... Christ, look at them.'

The minutes ticked by. It was past three a.m. and there was still no sign of the truck.

In the office, Callum was becoming more and more agitated. He opened the wrap of paper he'd brought back from his weekend and tapped out a pile of white powder onto the desk top. Then he rolled a note and used it to snort up the fat line he'd made. There. He ought to feel better now – stronger and more confident. Instead, he felt his heart pounding unnaturally hard as adrenalin coursed through him. Concentrate, he told himself, and glanced at the clock. It was nearly four a.m. Where was the truck, for Christ's sake?

Where the fuck were they? He ran through the arrangements in his head again. Was there anything he'd forgotten? Had he remembered everything rightly? He took out of his pocket the crumpled piece of paper where he'd written everything down and examined it, trying to read his own scrawl. Yes – he'd done everything, just as it said. But he must have taken the contact mobile down wrongly because when he rang it, there was no connection. Had he given them the right information? Yes, he was sure he had. So where on earth were they?

The problem was, it was not really Karl's operation. He was just a go-between for someone that Callum did not know. As the clock moved round towards four thirty, and after he'd taken another couple of lines to keep him going, he decided to ring Karl anyway and tell him that the collection contact was late and see what he could do. Perhaps he could reach them somehow, find out where they were.

Karl was not answering his mobile phone. Callum left a message asking him to call and then sat down nervously at the desk again.

Greg put his head round the door. 'Any news, lad? Only we're gonna have to do something with them soon, like, eh?'

'Yes, yes, I'm well aware of that, thanks very much. Piss off, yeah?' Callum waved him away.

He could see the cargo, hunched over as they sat on their chairs and boxes, wrapped in their plastic sheeting. In half an hour, the fishermen would start preparing the boats. A few hours after that the processing staff would get here, ready to begin work when the boats returned with the catch. How was he going to explain away twenty stinking Chinese, for fuck's sake?

One of them was watching him through the office window, and the sight of those dark eyes made his tension fire up into anger. Stupid bastards, he thought. I wouldn't be in this position if they hadn't decided to leave fuckin' chinky land or wherever it is they come from.

Greg came back. 'Look, Callum, we're gonna have to do something with these guys, and fast.'

Callum thought quickly. Where could he take them? There was nowhere he could think of, and even if he could, how would he get them there? People were going to be up and about very soon. Then he had a brainwave. 'Put 'em in one of the cold stores,' he ordered, pleased with his inspiration.

Greg blinked with surprise. 'But ... I might be stating the obvious but won't it be a bit ... cold? And what about when the staff go to use it later?'

Callum sighed heavily. Did he have to do all the work himself? He said slowly, 'Empty one out, transfer the contents to the other. Switch it off and put a notice on the outside saying "No entry – broken" or something like that. And we'll put them inside with their plastic sheets and something to drink and a bucket and they'll be fine until they're collected. Probably the most comfortable they've been the whole way.'

'All right,' replied Greg. Clearly he could see that this was just about their only option. 'Better leave Tom here to make sure no curious bastard decides to open the door. Cos he'd get a hell of a shock if he did.'

'Yeah, yeah, good idea.' Callum nodded. 'And we'll hear from our contact during the day, no mistake.'

Chapter Thirty-seven

Heather opened the door of the sewing room and looked inside. Her mother's huddled form lay on the sofa, a crocheted blanket draped over it. She was sound asleep. Heather pulled the door back to, and tiptoed down the corridor.

She didn't remember her mother sleeping this much when she was younger, but now it seemed to be a daily occurrence. Where some lonely, unhappy housewives turned to alcohol, it seemed that her mother had turned to sleep. It rang a bell in her memory – had she read somewhere that excessive sleeping was a sign of depression? It made sense – after all, it was hardly a sign of ecstatic happiness and a full engagement with life, was it?

The house was quiet. Her father had left that morning for work as usual. Surprisingly, he had been annoyed with Callum, who had come back from one of his little outings at around dawn and was still asleep. He had never been an early riser, and it looked as though nothing had changed.

Heather padded through to the kitchen, deciding to make herself a cup of coffee. This peace was welcome enough but, like everything in this house, it didn't feel quite right. It was uneasy and menacing, like the calm before a thunderstorm. It was only when she had left home and gone to live in Edinburgh that she had realised quite how unhappy her home was. The minute she had left, it was as though she was lighter and easier in herself. She was also exhausted after years of strained nerves, and of having to be alert as an animal constantly aware of predators circling. Perhaps that was another explanation of why her mother slept all the time.

Being back was not easy, but she could not resist the sense that she had to be here, that her mother needed her. Once she was back, the familiar blanket of oppression covered her, just as it had all the years she was growing up. The difference was that now she was stronger in herself, more resistant to the tactics of her father and brother. Now she was able to see them for what they were: nasty-minded, arrogant, selfish bullies who despised women and anyone they considered weaker than themselves.

It made her want to weep when she considered how her mother had sacrificed herself for these sorry excuses for men. Nevertheless, her mother would not be moved on the subject. She seemed to consider herself bound for life to them, like some feudal subject who had taken an oath of eternal fealty. Perhaps it was because of the state of Callum. Heather had been shocked when she'd seen him from her fresh, adult perspective. As a teenager, she had simply hated him for his cruelty, stupidity and monstrous selfishness. Now she looked at him and felt fearful, because to her it was obvious there was something abnormal about him. It wasn't simply eccentricity, she felt, or a tendency to aggrandise everything as though he was the main actor in some great drama. His mood swings, inhibitions and fierce rages seemed to indicate to her that he suffered from some kind of chemical imbalance in his brain and that, at the very least, he ought to see a doctor.

No one would listen, though. Callum was Callum to his parents – a mercurial child whose violent rages could be avoided simply by giving in to them and making sure he had everything he wanted.

If Callum had not been a nightmare to start with, she thought ruefully, then he certainly was now, chemical imbalance or not. He had been thoroughly spoiled by his parents – or, more specifically, by his doting father. And if there was ever an argument for saying no to a child, then Callum was it.

Heather wanted to feel some kind of bond to him, some kind of love for him. After all, he was her family, her only brother. But she couldn't. It was hard to relate to him as a human, let alone as a relative. He was so shut off from everyone else around him, it was as though he didn't feel anything for anyone, except himself. He had frozen emotionally somewhere around two years old, where nothing mattered except having his wants satisfied as quickly as possible.

That's why he's so dangerous, she thought. It's why he gives me the chills.

Her mobile rang, vibrating in her pocket

against her. She took it out and answered it. 'Hi?'

'Hello, Heather. It's Hamish here.'

'Hamish – hello.' She had forgotten that he had her mobile number. She had scribbled it down for him along with her email address.

'I wondered if you might be able to come over to the cottage this afternoon? I've got something I want to talk to you about.'

'Sure, what time?'

'Let's say four o'clock. All right?'

'Yes. See you then, Hamish.' She put the phone on the table and looked at it, thinking about the old man. She hadn't given him a thought in all the years she'd spent away from Kinlochvegan but now that she'd come back, she was strangely drawn to him. All the things about him she'd taken for granted when she was a child – his lone-liness, the mysterious disappearance of his son, the way he seemed so isolated, especially after his parents died – suddenly seemed very mysterious and odd. She knew that part of his attraction for her had always been the fact that her father was so set against him – it was a small rebellion of her own, one tiny bid for independence. But why did her father dislike him so much? It seemed to her that the lonely old fisherman who clearly found more than a little solace in the bottle was one of the few people who had ever been kind to her. Certainly he was a hundred times more pleasant to be with than her own father.

What if, she wondered idly, I could rescue my mother, make her leave Dad, and bring her and Hamish together. Maybe they would be able to comfort each other. After all, he needs a woman and she's desperate for a bit of kindness. They could spend a happy old age together – if she didn't mind the whisky and he didn't mind all the sleeping.

She smiled to herself at the thought.

Now, that would be nice.

Callum appeared just before she went out. She was pulling on her boots when he dragged himself into the kitchen, obviously in a terrible mood and with the stale breath and rough stubble of someone who'd just woken up.

'Morning, Callum,' she said brightly.

'Ah, fuck yerself,' he growled.

'As charming as ever. I'm going out now, so maybe I'll see you later.' She grinned at him. It was far more effective, she'd found, simply to let all his rudeness and lack of grace wash over her and leave her untouched. It irritated him that he couldn't bring her down as easily as he once had, and she'd learned in the years she'd been away that she was nothing like the worthless piece of rubbish he'd always told her she was.

'Have there been any calls for me?' he said roughly.

'Nope. Nothing. Looks like you still haven't made any friends. I'll be sure and let Arseholes Reunited know that you're looking for some, though.' She grinned at him again before letting herself out of the back door to set off down the hill towards the village.

Dad loves this house, she thought, looking back over her shoulder at it. But it's so charmless. Just like him.

The day had begun brightly but the weather was on the turn, she could tell. Big banks of fuzzy grey clouds were massing in the distance and although it was warm, there was the sense in the air that rain was not far away. The sea was turning the slate colour that presaged bad weather, as well, and she could see foaming white tops far out on the horizon. She shivered.

Once she'd got to the main street, she made her way to the pub and went in. Rachel was behind the bar.

'Am I on tonight, Rach?' she asked.

'Aye, if you like. But it's so quiet at the moment. I tell you, if this weather comes up like they say it will, I might give you some time off if you want it. We're always dead quiet when it's as wet as they say it's going to be.' Rachel polished down the bar with a cloth. 'Looking nice and clean, isn't it? They sent me some Eastern Europeans this time. They couldn't speak a word of English but they did get it lovely for me. Very keen on bleach they are, though. Every bathroom smells like a chemical factory.'

'Yeah, it's looking fine. See you later then,' Heather said, heading for the door. Rachel was sweet enough but she could talk for Scotland. Heather wanted to make her escape as quickly as possible before she got entangled in an hour-long discussion of the rights and wrongs of polishing balustrades, or whatever.

'See you later, pet,' Rachel answered absent-mindedly.

The arrangement they had was very informal. Heather would work whenever she was required.

She didn't need much money at the moment anyway, with no rent to pay. It was more to keep her occupied for a while than anything else, and to get her out of the house during the hours when her father and brother were most likely to be at home.

She climbed the steep hill path up to Lachlan Cottage and knocked at the door. Hamish answered and led her inside to his plain and bare sitting room. Once he'd furnished her with a cup of coffee, he sat down opposite her, a serious expression on his face.

'So, what's all this about, Hamish?'

He coughed and looked as though he didn't know where to begin. At last he said, 'Heather, I've not been entirely straight with you, ye know.'

'Haven't you? What about?'

'About ... about some of the goings-on in the village. Since you've come back, you've probably noticed that quite a lot has changed.'

'I should say so. Not least that monstrosity my brother is building. Someone should do us all a favour and blow it up. Who designed it? A five-year-old with a blunt crayon?'

'Aye, it's not pretty.' He paused. 'Actually, it's about your brother that I wanted to talk to you.'

'Callum? What's he done now? He's a bit old for breaking windows and running off, I hope.' She laughed and then saw Hamish's expression. 'What is it? You look serious.'

Suddenly the old man couldn't meet her eye.

'Come on – what is it?'

'Och, now that you're here, I'm not sure if this is the right thing to do...'

392

'You know you can tell me anything.' She leaned forward, pushing her brown hair back behind her ears, and said earnestly, 'Hamish, haven't we been friends for years, since I was just wee? And haven't we kept it a secret from everyone? You have to trust me by now. If there's something you know about Callum – well, you know you can tell me. You won't shock me. I've got no love for my brother, he's just as vicious a bully as my dad, and I can well believe him capable of just about anything. So come on, what is it you know?'

'Well, you know, lass...' Hamish spoke hesitantly. 'It's not that I don't trust you, not at all. You know I think just about as highly of you as I could. It's just that I don't want to talk about things and make a mistake about them. I don't want to tell you things that aren't right. Not just because I don't want you to have false impressions of your own family, but because... I don't want to put you in danger.'

'In danger!' she echoed. 'What are you talking about? Come on, Hamish, you have to tell me now.'

The old man still looked reluctant but at last he said, 'You know how I sit here on board the *Bella Maria* almost all the time. She's not in such a bonny condition any more, she's rusting. It's not good to take her out too often these days, she's not really up to it. Well, I suppose I've become a bit of a fixture, sitting out on deck when the weather's fair, with my wood and my nets. People have stopped noticing me, stopped seeing me. It's almost as though I'm not really there, d'ye

393

know what I mean? They've stopped thinking that I see and remember things, that I'm here all hours.'

Heather nodded. Hamish went on.

'Well, I've seen comings and goings. Not the usual comings and goings. I know when the best fishing times are and when the fleets go out and come in. And I know when the time isn't right for the fish, and when trawlers going out to sea probably aren't going for catching any fish. And...' He frowned again.

'And what?' prompted Heather.

'I've seen your brother go out and come back at the wrong times. He's taken command of one of the trawlers and off they've gone, towards the wrong place and at the wrong time for any kind of fishing. And anyway, fishing isn't making the money it once did. We've got quotas now, restrictions, health and safety, talk of various bans... Even with the processing that your father does on site, well ... it's hard to see how they're making as much money as they seem to. But Kinlochvegan is immune to the problems that are afflicting all the other small fishing villages, it seems. In fact, we're all doing better than ever. There's no cuts in wages, no cuts in the number of men employed – your dad still gives half the men in this village a living.'

Heather said quietly, 'What are you saying, Hamish?'

Hamish looked discomfited. He twisted the piece of twine he had been knotting, staring at it intently. 'I don't like making allegations,' he mumbled at last.

'You've not said anything yet,' she pointed out. 'I've no idea what you're talking about.'

'You've just come from the big city. You know what's going on there, don't you? In Edinburgh, in Glasgow, in all the big towns. I know we're remote here, shut off, but I still read my papers and I still listen to my radio and we're all aware of what's happening...'

'What do you mean?' she asked, puzzled.

'I mean drugs, lassie! I mean the modern scourge, the thing that's destroying so many young lives in the towns.'

'Oh, drugs,' she said, her face clearing. 'Well – I've seen a bit of it, I suppose. There was a fair amount at university – you know what students are like. But in my circles – well, the fellas I was with – maybe they smoked a bit of weed every now and then. A couple of my friends took tabs of acid but I've got a thing about pills so I never did it. Some people did Ecstasy and the rich kids dabbled in cocaine, or so I heard. I never saw any.'

Hamish looked relieved. 'I'm glad to hear you never got mixed up in any of that stuff, lass. But all it means is that you've been protected from the reality of what's happening. Have you no heard of heroin?'

Heather almost laughed. 'Aye, of course I've heard of heroin. But no one I know does it.'

'Then you're lucky. What you don't realise is how many people are only too happy to use anything they can to feed their habit. It's the scourge of Scotland, Heather. Our inner cities are desperate places, full of people addicted to that stuff.

Young women are turning to prostitution, young men are turning to crime, violent and otherwise, to find the money to buy the stuff that's killing them. Look at this...' He got up, opened the door of a dresser that stood against the wall and took out a box of cuttings. He passed it to Heather, who began to leaf through the articles. Each one was about the drugs menace and its effect on Scottish cities.

'Where do you think it's coming from?' asked Hamish quietly.

'Heroin? I don't know,' she said, half paying attention as she read.

'It's opium. It comes from Afghanistan principally. Other countries too, but Afghanistan is the main producer at the moment. And how do you think it gets here?' He answered his own question before she had time to reply. 'Sometimes through the airports – but that's a dangerous tactic. Not only does it mean someone concealing the drug somewhere on – or in – themselves, but it also means passing several checkpoints in places where they are most alert to it. So the safest and most convenient way is to take a blameless-looking boat – maybe a pleasure craft or a fishing trawler – out to sea, to a rendezvous, and pick up a stash of whatever it is you're in the market for and bring it back into the country. Perhaps into a quiet fishing village, where it never occurs to anyone that such a thing could be going on.'

Heather looked at him, her face grave. 'You think that's what Callum is up to.'

'Now, I've no proof, lassie...'

'Of course not. It's all completely hypothetical, I'm sure – but that's what you're saying, isn't it?'

'I've taken the *Bella Maria* out a few times and when your brother has taken out one of the trawlers I've sometimes gone after him, just for a few miles to see in what direction he's headed. Not so's he'd notice. And it's always been in the same direction, and at the same time. And I don't believe it has anything to do with fishing. Do you understand?'

'Aye.' She looked suddenly pale.

'Do you realise it's serious? You're not to tell anyone else, understand?'

'Yes, but...'

'If this turns out to be what I think it is, and if someone has to reveal it all, then that's going to be me, all right? Not you.'

'But...' She looked flummoxed. 'I know my brother is an idiot and a thug, but could he really be mixed up in something like this? And does my father know?'

'If your brother is dealing in drugs, then I would say that your father most certainly must know. He knows what he pays your brother and he'll know the price of that car and that house, and whether or not he could afford it.'

Heather considered all the ramifications. 'But what happens next? Where do they take the drugs?'

'I've no idea. They're probably just a small part of a bigger operation. I can't believe your father is a drugs baron, or that he'd want to be.'

'But why would he want to get mixed up in all this in the first place? It's so dangerous! And illegal. Not to say wicked.' She picked up one or two of the cuttings that showed young people in a desperate state through their addictions.

'It's the old story, Heather. Money. You know what the Good Book says: love of money is the root of all evil. I don't imagine your father or brother looks at pictures like these and feels responsible. No doubt they would say, well, if it wasn't me then it would just be someone else and no one is forced to buy drugs – they do it because they want to.' Hamish put a hand out and rested it on her arm. 'Remember what I said, Heather. I don't have any proof yet. This must stay deadly quiet until I do, do you understand?'

'So – are you actively trying to find out?' she asked slowly. 'Do you intend to bring them down, if what you suspect is true?'

Hamish looked sad. 'You know, lass, I don't know. I've no interest in destroying anyone–'

'Even after the way my father treats you?' she demanded, interrupting him. 'I know how he scorns you and treats you like a nothing, I've seen it for myself!'

'Hush, you don't know anything about it, Heather!'

To her surprise, Heather saw real anger sparking in the old man's eyes and instantly quietened down.

'You really don't,' said Hamish more gently, 'and you won't hear about it from me, do you understand? Things happened in the past, but the past is where they are. We must always look forward. I've had some hard times, Heather, and I need to think about what I'm going to do with the last years of my life. And you know what? If I can help some young people escape this awful fate, this drug addiction, then perhaps my life hasn't been wasted after all.'

'So you *do* intend to turn them in.'

He paused, as if trying to decide what to say to her. 'Heather, the reason I'm telling you this is simple. I'm going to try and follow the trawler next time it goes out on its own under Callum's command. It could be tonight, tomorrow, the night after, who knows ... but if habit is anything to go by, then they should be going out in the next week or so. I plan to keep watch and then to trail them at a distance. If I'm right, then they've moved into the kind of territory where men are capable of anything. If I'm found out and if, by any chance, I don't return–' Heather gasped, but Hamish continued '–then you'll know why. I had to tell you, just so one person would know what had happened. But you mustn't breathe a word to anyone, even if I don't come back. I could never forgive myself if I put you in danger.'

Heather looked stunned. Then she gathered her wits and said, 'All right.' She leaned over and took his weathered brown hand in hers. 'I shan't breathe a word. But Hamish – I'm on your side. If there's anything I can do to help you, you know that I will.'

'Thanks, lass. But if anything happens – even if it doesn't, come to that – you need to get away from here soon, do you understand? You're as dear to me as my own daughter. You know that, don't you? And if your father isn't proud of you ... well, I am. I mean that.'

'Thanks, Hamish.'

They smiled at each other in the gathering gloom.

Chapter Thirty-eight

Callum punched at the keys on his mobile phone until it brought up the number he was looking for. He pressed dial and waited impatiently until the ringing tone was answered.

'Callum? Any news?'

'No. How is it going down there?'

'All right,' said Greg, evidently deflated. 'Tom has kept the curious away today. I ordered some meals up from the pub at lunchtime but I couldn't ask for twenty, so the poor bastards have had to share their steak pudding and chips. I gave 'em another bucket too. Jeez, it's starting to smell in there, and even though we've turned the cold unit off, it's still pretty bloody cold. They don't look happy.'

'It doesn't matter how they feel,' Callum said impatiently. 'What about me? I'm fuckin' all over the place here. This truck has got to come tonight and that's that.'

'Nothing from your contact?'

'No. The number I've got hasn't been answered.'

'And this Karl fella?'

'No reply.' Callum began to feel panic stirring in his stomach. 'Jesus, Greg, what the fuck am I going to do if it doesn't come off?'

'Don't think about that now. I'm sure it will be fine,' Greg said, soothingly.

'Really?' asked Callum hopefully. He didn't like it when things went awry. He wanted someone to come in and sort it all out for him.

'Yeah. Look, I'm gonna order up some more food later for the poor shites, all right?'

'Whatever,' said Callum, and rang off.

He was getting increasingly edgy as the day wore on and evening approached. His mood wasn't helped by having that cow of a sister around the house. He had thought she'd gone for good and then she'd turned up unannounced a few weeks back, God only knew why.

All he could really think about, though, was the major problem he had brewing on his hands. It was fine for now – and his father was at the garage today, not at the processing plant. But how long could he keep a parcel of Chinese immigrants locked in an oversized fridge without anyone noticing? Sooner or later he was going to have to let them out, or someone was going to get curious and open the door. Then what?

'Ah, fuckin' shite!' he muttered to himself, pacing back and forth in the sitting room. 'Fuck 'em all. Christ, I need a line.' He sat down at the coffee table, took out his wrap with shaking hands and managed to cut himself a line, which he snorted up gratefully.

'Callum? What is it?' His mother was standing in the doorway, blinking slowly.

'Get out!' he snapped. He couldn't stand the sight of her, he really couldn't. Seeing her like

401

that, just woken up and a bit woozy, disgusted him.

'Is something wrong?'

'Nothing is wrong, for fuck's sake! Now pish off.'

His mother gazed at him for a second, then dropped her eyes to the floor and walked past him towards the kitchen. 'I'm getting supper ready,' she said as she went by.

'I don't know if I'll be in or not.' Then his mobile rang. He scrabbled it out of his pocket, panic making his hands clumsy, and saw to his relief that it was Karl calling him. 'Yeah, Karl, pal?'

'Callum? We're in trouble, mate.' Karl's voice was urgent and more serious than he'd ever heard it. The smooth wisecracks were gone.

'What?'

'Big trouble. The whole thing's collapsed. Turns out there was some kind of undercover journalist involved further down the line, doing an exposé for some news programme, and he's broken the story to the police. A whole shipment of people has been picked up. The entire chain has broken. Everyone's running for cover, no one knows exactly what this bloke found out and what he's passed on.'

'What d'ye mean?' Callum blinked, uncomprehending.

'For Christ's sake, Callum. Didn't you hear me? We're all in the fucking shite now... It's every man for himself now, OK?'

'But my contact... The truck...' stammered Callum.

'Get it into your thick head, mate. He's not fuckin' coming, yeah? I've told you it's all finished.'

'My money...'

Karl laughed. *'Your* money. What about my fuckin' money? I was expecting a lot from this job. Now just put your head down, keep quiet and hope to fuck that no one's written your name down anywhere, or kept your details, or blabbed into some secret camera, otherwise you're going to be bloody sorry.'

Blood rushed to Callum's face. 'Keep quiet!' he screamed. 'I've got twenty bastard Chinamen sitting in my warehouse. What the fuck am I going to do with them?'

'Sorry, mate. That's your problem. Don't call me on this number again. I'll reach you if I need to.' The phone went dead.

'Shite!' shouted Callum at the top of his voice. He pulled out his wrap again and began struggling to unfold it. If he ever needed a line, it was now.

'What is it?' Mary appeared in the doorway, her face frightened.

'Ah – nothing! Leave me alone, you stupid old bitch,' he yelled. He sat down suddenly on the sofa and put his head in his hands, trying to understand what had just happened. 'What am I gonna do?'

He sat like that for ten minutes, his thoughts chasing round and round his head, the fury and confusion building up in him until he thought he might burst. Then he shook out another line, hoovered it up and stood up. He had to get down to the warehouse, tell Greg. He would know what to do.

By the time Callum arrived at the warehouse, everyone had packed up and gone for the day. The gloom of evening was falling as he let himself in and the bad weather that had been due all day was setting in. A fierce wind was blowing up and the first flurries of sharp rain were drifting in from the sea.

'Hi Greg,' he said cheerfully. He'd been shaking with fear before, now he was bouncing with energy. He was feeling hyper, on top of the world, buoyed up by coke and by a certainty that he would be all right. 'How's it going?'

Greg looked decidedly worried as he came up to meet Callum. 'All right, I suppose. Under the circumstances.' He was obviously surprised by the younger man's good humour, but then pleased. 'Have you had good news then?'

'Oh aye,' Callum said carelessly. 'It's all in hand, all fine. They had a breakdown last night, that's all, and couldn't contact me. But it's all in order for tonight, so I'm going to hang around here and wait for them. Could be any time from midnight so why don't you go home and get some rest, OK, pal? Tom and I can handle it from here.'

'Oh, that's great,' said Greg, clearly relieved. 'I'll sleep easier once these folk are off our hands. Now listen, Callum – don't go doing this again, or I'm gonna have to get your old man involved, yeah? We've got out of it this time but next time we might not be so lucky, and I'm not gonna let this go on without him knowing about it. I'm sorry but that's the way it is.'

'Oh, yeah, sure, you're right. I've learned a lesson, pal, make no mistake. So – you head off and we'll be fine. By the time you get back, all of 'em will be gone.' He smiled happily at the other man and watched with satisfaction as he left the warehouse.

When Greg was gone, he called Tom to the office.

'We gotta get those poor blokes something else to eat,' said Tom as he came in. 'They're no in a good state in there.'

'Forget about that,' Callum said brusquely. 'The plan's changed, OK? We've got to unload our cargo as efficiently as possible and as soon as we can.'

'What do you mean?'

'There's been a cock-up. No one's coming to collect them. We have to get rid of them. It's unfortunate but that's the reality of where we are. Now, I've got a plan but you have to do as I say, all right? No questions, just do exactly as I say. Can I trust you, Tom?'

The tall young man gazed back at him, his strange grey eyes unreadable. 'Sure, pal. Course you can depend on me.'

'Good. Then let's have a quick toot beforehand, to get our heads straight. Then we can do what we've got to do.'

Tom did exactly as Callum ordered. Together the two of them hauled over one of the high-performance hoses used to sluice down the processing plant after each shift. Tom opened the door of the cold store, revealing the sight of the

405

wretched men inside, shivering, hungry and miserable.

They looked up hopefully as the door opened. Callum stared in at them, loathing the very sight of them and the pathetic pleading in their eyes. They were disgusting: filthy, revolting scum sitting in their own shit and thinking the world owed them a living. Well, they were about to get a wake-up call. Callum would put them right on that.

He directed the hose into the store and shouted to Tom to turn it on. A second later, a fierce jet of icy water shot out of it. The Chinese yelled and jabbered in their strange-sounding language as it hit them, drenching them all to the skin in moments. The stream of water was so strong that it dazed and bewildered them as it soaked them, and they barely had time to register what was happening before Callum had shut off the flow.

He laughed at the sight of them floundering around, sopping wet. Then he slammed the door of the cold store shut and went to the control panel at the side. Switching it back on, he selected the thermostat and turned the temperature down as far as it would go, to minus forty degrees.

There, he thought, satisfied. That should do it.

Back in the office, he and Tom sat down. He was impressed with Tom, who didn't appear to have any of Greg's bleeding-heart issues with the whole thing. After all, gangmasters and their henchmen couldn't afford to be sentimental about the lives of a few Chinese. They were in a sticky situation and they needed to get out of it, that was that.

'What's your plan?' asked Tom, leaning back and folding one long leg over the other.

Callum looked at his watch. 'How long do you think it will take?'

'What for?'

'For them to freeze to death, what do you think, you fuckin' idiot?'

Tom gasped and a look of horror passed over his face. 'Is that the plan?'

'Course.' Callum eyed him suspiciously. 'You're all right with that, aren't you?'

Tom tried to sound nonchalant. 'Yeah, of course. They'll freeze in a few hours. Probably less. They're pretty weak already and hypothermia sets in quicker than you'd think.'

'Good.'

'Then what are you going to do with them?'

'Do you remember my dad bought some small ship's containers? I'm gonna take one of those, load 'em into it, put it on the trawler, take it out to sea and dump it.' Callum grinned proudly. 'Problem solved. End of story. Fancy another snort?'

'OK,' said Tom, and watched as Callum chopped out yet more lines for the two of them. 'You've got to work out some logistics, though, haven't you? I mean, how're you gonna move the container? It's gonna take ages for you and me to move frozen bodies around, and then we've got to get the container on board and far enough out to sea to dump it. By the time we're ready to do that it will be broad daylight, and this is definitely a night operation. Besides that, have you looked outside? There's one hell of a storm coming. I don't think we'll be able to go out tonight.'

Callum's happy, coke-induced relaxation instantly disappeared and he snarled with rage. His plan had been a good one – trust the fucking weather to let him down and it was all right for Tom to sit there so calmly, picking holes in everything. He was going to be in just as much trouble if it all went wrong.

'Then what'm I gonna do? Huh?' Callum leapt to his feet, fired up with rage. 'What do you suggest?'

It suddenly occurred to him that having twenty dead Chinese in his cold store was a much, much worse situation than having twenty live ones. Should he haul them out, heat them up and just abandon them somewhere? No, there was no way it wouldn't all be traced back to him. Things must be tidied up completely so that no one ever found out what had happened. But how could he do that on his own? He knew he couldn't – he'd have to get some help.

Chapter Thirty-nine

There couldn't be anything worse than this.

For a moment, McBain thought over times in his life when he'd felt as terrible as he did now. Of course, his entire childhood had been a succession of awfulness, the endless beatings from his father and the things he had had to witness at home. And then there had been the day he'd made himself look a fool in front of Hamish Fraser, falling overboard and nearly drowning, the long humiliation he'd suffered at the other boy's hands. The day he'd made the discovery that had eventually led him to take his final revenge on Hamish.

All those things had angered him and made him burn with ambition and a desire for revenge. He'd always found a way to get even, and then to get ahead. His anger had fuelled his path through life.

But this ... this sickened him. He felt nausea crawling round his stomach and up the surface of his skin, making it clammy. Bitterness rose in his throat. The rage was there too, though, and this time directed at the only person in the world he loved.

'Callum, how could you be so stupid?' he choked. He could hardly breathe with the force of the emotion rushing through him. 'My God, I just can't believe it...'

Callum looked sheepish and then put on the beseeching expression that had worked so well for him in the past. 'I'm really sorry, Dad. I thought I was acting for the best, in our interests – I honestly did.'

'How can it be in our interests to get mixed up in illegal trafficking? Do you know what we're looking at if we get caught? The rest of our lives in jail!'

'We took that risk with the coke and heroin,' Callum pointed out. 'You didn't mind so much then.'

'I did mind! That's why I wanted out! But can't you see there's a difference between bringing in packets of Class A – and trafficking in people?'

'No,' Callum retorted sulkily. 'What's the difference? It's all just cargo.'

McBain turned incandescent with anger. He let out a furious roar and took a step towards Callum, who cowered back. Then he suddenly turned to Tom, who'd been standing quietly by the desk. 'I blame you for this!' he screamed, his face crimson with rage. 'Why didn't you stop him?' He lashed out with all his might and smashed a powerful blow onto Tom's jaw. Tom's head flew back and then his legs buckled, and he crashed to the floor, out cold.

Callum whimpered.

'Shut up!' growled McBain, rubbing his knuckles.

'Listen, Dad,' Callum said meekly. 'They're all dead and the operation is finished. All we have to do is lie low for a bit and hope we don't get pulled into the police investigation.'

'Ah shit! For Christ's sake!' McBain ran his hand through his hair and shook his head, unable to comprehend how Callum could not see the depth of the trouble they were in. 'Greg – what do you think?'

His trusted right-hand man sat in a corner, listening, his face impassive. Now he said, 'Let's make sure we have this right. The police are investigating a trafficking organisation and we've got twenty of its imports down at the warehouse, dead. This is serious stuff.'

'Thanks for that, Einstein!' sneered Callum.

Greg continued. 'Callum's right, we have to get rid of the bodies. But getting them out to sea is not so easy. It's a howling gale out there. Boss,' he turned to McBain, 'we'll have to get the cold store emptied no matter what. Health and safety could turn up at any time for a random inspection. At the very least, let's move the bodies into the sea container as Callum suggests and load it on board. The weather might calm down and we have to be ready to take advantage of it right away. Then we can clean up the warehouse and it'll be business as usual.'

Thank God Greg was keeping his head, thought McBain. He was still trying to come to terms with what he'd been told, and even though he was furious that Greg had let himself be talked into going out alone with Callum and not telling him, he would let that go for now. There were more important matters to deal with.

'Yes. That's our plan. Right. We go down to the warehouse, the four of us – when he wakes up.' He indicated Tom, still prone on the floor, though he was moving and groaning quietly. 'We load up the bodies and then we clean up and wait for our opportunity. Agreed?'

Greg and Callum nodded.

Outside the office, Heather heard them approach the door. She turned on her heel and ran lightly back down the corridor to her room, her nightdress fluttering palely about her in the darkness.

From the safety of her room she heard the men emerge and leave the house and a moment later, through the pattering of the rain beating down on the roof, she could hear the sound of an engine as a car pulled out of the driveway.

What was going on? She had been able to make out almost nothing of what had been said in her father's office – the sound of the weather had drowned out their voices, except for the occasional shout. She had heard her father roar in the way she was used to from her childhood and couldn't help shivering, grateful that for once it wasn't directed at her.

But who was he angry with? Surely not Callum? And if so, why?

She sat down on her bed and tried to gather her thoughts. Ever since Hamish had told her only yesterday what he suspected, she'd been working out how she felt about it. She'd always known about drugs, of course, and about how they destroyed lives, but she'd known in a removed, detached way. It was all very far from her own life. Her circle of friends preferred drinking and smoking to snorting and injecting, and anyone she knew who took cocaine or other stimulants did so very rarely. But she'd seen *Trainspotting* and she'd read reports and watched the news, like everyone else. She knew that there were people in the grip of terrible addictions, thieving and mugging to get the money to pay for them, mistreating and neglecting their children and dying in awful circumstances, and yet, somehow, she'd never really thought about where drugs came from and the fact that others were getting obscenely wealthy on the detritus of these lives. She'd never thought about the chain of supply and all the little links in it ... and here she was, sitting in a house where the heat and the water, where the sofa she sat on, where the very food she ate, might have been paid for by money made from dealing in drugs, from sending great packets of narcotics out onto the streets, to be cut up with God knew what and sold to the poor and the desperate and the broken, making them still more poor and desperate and broken.

And what about the people in the countries it had come from, poor bloody souls? In Hamish's clippings she'd read about the innocent people, including children, being murdered in the cocaine-producing countries in the course of battles between the drug barons. She'd read how agriculture was dying and people were starving, because of the land turned over to growing the raw materials for narcotics. It was a tragedy everywhere you looked, except for the vile people who profited from all this human misery. Maybe for them, too.

She felt sickened. And she knew that Callum was capable of it. The fact that her father was mixed up in it frightened her even more. No matter how much she'd hated him throughout her life and how much she despised him for his cruelty and violence, she'd thought he was too smart to get mixed up in something like this.

Whatever she could do to stop it, she had to do. She knew that. She went to the wardrobe and began dressing as quickly as she could.

'There is no way you're coming with me,' Hamish said brusquely.

'Come on, Hamish, don't be stupid, you can't

413

go on your own.' Heather rubbed at her hair with the towel Hamish had given her. She was soaked through from the weather outside: rain was bucketing down and a fierce wind howled.

'I can, and I will. Listen, what good can you do? It only needs one of us to see what they're doing. It'd be worse for you than for me if they caught us, and I can look after myself. Besides which, I've told you before, if something happens to me, you're the only one who knows the circumstances. So wait for me.' He pulled on his dark waxed waterproof coat that fell almost to his feet, the one he wore on the *Bella Maria* when the weather turned bad. Once he had his hat on, he would be almost invisible in the wet darkness outside.

Heather was torn. She wanted very badly to go with him, but she could see that he wasn't going to allow it. She was also not well equipped to be outside. Her coat was designed for withstanding Edinburgh squalls during quick dashes between shops and offices, not the storm outside.

'What are you going to do?' she asked, watching him make his last preparations. He was changing the batteries in his torch now.

'I'm gonna find out where they are – probably at the docks if they're planning an expedition – though in this weather, that would be pure madness. I cannae believe anyone is going out on a sea in this state. Then I'm gonna stay well back and watch what happens.'

'What if it's nothing?'

He turned to look at her, his blue eyes strong in the weathered and lined old face. 'Do you think it's nothing, Heather? Do you think that those men going out to work in the middle of the night when it's blowing a hurricane is normal?'

'No,' she answered quietly. She knew in her heart that Hamish was right, and that she'd known he was right from the minute he'd started explaining his suspicions. 'Shall I stay here?'

'No – go home. It'll look suspicious if anyone sees you here alone. If your father or Callum goes home, you ought to be there as normal. Just stay alert and watch for a message from me.'

'OK.'

'Right. I'm ready.' He grinned at her. 'I feel quite invigorated by all this. What do you think? Am I too old to be James Bond?'

'Oh, Hamish...' She laughed. 'Just a little bit. You be careful, you hear? What have you got to protect yourself?'

'My native wit, darlin', and not much else. But don't worry about me. I'll be fine, you'll see.'

Heather suddenly scrabbled in her pocket and took out a mobile phone. 'Here, take this. It's my phone. Use it if you need to get in touch with me.' She started pressing keys. 'I'm going to programme my number into it and show you how to call me.'

'How can I call you if I've got your phone?'

'I've got another one – a work one they forgot to take off me when I left. I keep meaning to send it back to them but we can use it now. I'll put it on to charge when I get back. Now, if you want to call me, this is what you do...' She showed him how to call up her number quickly. 'And if I'm calling, you'll see it's from me. Look – the name

415

Heather comes up on the display. And this is how you turn it on and off. I would show you how to text but I don't think we've quite got time for that.'

'Very nifty. I've not used one of these wee things before. It seems straightforward enough, though.' He grinned at her again.

'Take care, Hamish. OK?'

'I'll do my best, lass, I promise.'

Chapter Forty

The village was sound asleep, locked away behind doors and windows shut tight against the elements. They were all used to such conditions – no one could live on the west coast of Scotland for long without learning about the power of the weather and how often it was exercised.

In a way, it's a help, thought Hamish, bending his head against the driving rain and striding down the hill. No one is going to be looking out of their windows tonight. Even Mrs Brodie wouldn't see anything from behind the curtains with all this going on.

He felt strangely excited in a way that he had not experienced for years; he hadn't been joking when he'd told Heather how invigorated he was. The years immediately after Louise and Robbie had left were mostly a blur. He remembered feeling great pain, unlike anything he'd suffered before that, but not much else. It had taken decades for him to begin to recover and even now, he hadn't really healed.

Well, he'd been lying down for too long. It was time to do something at last. If he could be a part of closing down some part of the evil trade in drugs, then it would be worthwhile, no matter what happened as a result. There wasn't much else to live for, if he was honest. If he was going to get anything good out of his existence, besides Robbie, then perhaps this could be it.

From the road the warehouse looked deserted, but as he skirted it he noticed that one lone light flickered through a window at the back. Approaching it through the darkness, he saw that it was in an office and that two men were inside. He couldn't make out any more; the window was too high in the wall for him to look through, there was nothing to stand on and he wasn't confident that he wouldn't be noticed if he got close enough to look through it.

He'd have to find another way.

He soon spotted a likely place. The metal fire escape at the side of the warehouse on the dockside climbed up the building to the top, where he guessed there must be a high balcony for access to the roof space and any machinery. The rain was pounding onto it, making a noise like a hundred tuneless xylophones. He ran over to it and climbed up. At the top was a locked door with a glass panel, but this was useless as a means of looking down into the warehouse. All he could see were the metal roof joists, lighting, and some cogs and winches for lifting machinery.

Hamish scanned the area. The warehouse roof

had long glass panels in it every few yards to let in natural light. Perhaps this would be the way he could get sight of what was happening, but getting onto the roof in this weather would be a perilous business. Water was streaming down it, running down the ridged metal and sliding down the glass illuminated by the light below. But it was his only chance.

He climbed up onto the fire-escape rail and grabbed hold of the edge of the roof. There was very little to cling onto, but he didn't have to go very far before he'd be able to look through the nearest glass pane. He scrabbled for something to hold and realised that if he used the metal ridges of the roof itself, he could get just enough purchase to haul himself up. They were not easy to grip, as they were smooth and now, with the rain, wet, but he only needed to go a little way...

Damn it, he was going to try.

Clenching his teeth with the effort, he gripped two of the slender ridges as far up the roof as he could stretch, and pulled. Thank God for a lifetime hauling nets, he thought. His arms were strong and supported him for long enough for him to get his knee up and onto the roof. Carefully, moving one hand only a fraction at a time, he inched his way up the slope towards the nearest panel. It took long minutes and once or twice he felt his grip slipping and panicked as his fingers fluttered for a stronger hold.

'Shit!' he shouted, as he rubbed one hand against his sleeve, trying to dry it and make it less slippery.

Then he was in position, stretched out along

418

the wet roof and gazing into the warehouse below. He rubbed at the glass but it was covered in rainwater again almost immediately, so he took off his rain hat and used it as a dam so that the water ran around it, leaving a dry patch for him to look through. The skylights were glazed with toughened glass inlaid with a wire mesh for strength, so his view was even more obscured.

The warehouse was not huge and he was only about thirty feet above the floor. He thanked God that his eyesight had always been good, as he could now see something of what was going on below. A ship's container had been moved into the centre of the warehouse where it stood on a large trolley, and a man was painting it white. The door to the container stood open, a ramp coming down from the interior. It was a smaller variety of container – Hamish had seen vast things, big enough to hold entire buildings inside them, but this was compact and would fit neatly onto the deck of a vessel smaller than the great steamers he used to travel on.

Two other men were moving about on the warehouse floor and he recognised them as Callum McBain and Greg McDonald. So McBain himself must be in the office alone now. Callum and Greg appeared to be unloading something from one of those big walk-in freezers they stored the fish in. If it was a fish, it was a damn big one, thought Hamish. He watched as the two of them took the long unwieldy thing between them and staggered towards the container. A moment later they'd disappeared inside, only to reappear without their load and go back to the cold store.

He had expected to see packages of drugs, if he saw anything at all, and he was puzzled by the strange stiff thing they'd been carrying.

What was it? Hamish squinted as they came out of the cold store with another of their burdens. It was long and black, and he thought for an instant it was a dolphin and then a slender young whale – or perhaps a seal. Then they rolled it slightly and the head fell back and Hamish yelped. The weather drowned his cry easily.

Oh my God, he thought, stunned. Men! They're loading up dead men!

He began to breathe fast, horrified, but he forced himself to watch as Callum and Greg collected more and more of the corpses. It was obvious they'd frozen to death. The faces were blue and the dark hair they all had was frosted on the ends. Some were curled up tight into a foetal position, others seemed to be rolled up in some kind of plastic sheeting.

Poor bastards! he thought. Poor fuckin' bastards. They must have died in there. There's no way they could have got that frozen anywhere else, bar Siberia. Oh, shit – what are they mixed up in here?

The bodies looked foreign to him, all with dark hair and wearing similar dark, simple clothing in no way suitable for the Scottish climate.

How does this fit into drugs? he wondered. Are these people addicts who didn't pay for their fixes? Couriers who died in transit or once they'd arrived in the country? Henchmen who double-crossed the barons?

It all sounded ludicrously far-fetched, but here

he was, watching men he knew carting dead bodies about as though they were nothing but butchers' carcasses.

He watched and counted as fifteen bodies were loaded into the container. Meanwhile, the third man was now painting something on the side. Hamish cocked his head and read 'Field & Company'. Just some made-up name, no doubt, to cover their tracks.

With the loading complete, Callum and Greg stood about talking while the other man finished his painting. McBain came out of the office to join them. From his vantage point, Hamish saw three heads close together as the men below carried on their discussions.

McBain, he thought. Are you really capable of this? What kind of man are you?

He thought back to the boy he'd known, the one who had once been his friend. Of course there had always been something awry inside him – he'd always had that anger, that propensity for cruelty, the greediness and selfishness of someone who had to look out for himself to survive. And he'd had that stupid pride, that forced him to do things that could only hurt him in the long run.

Then, later in life, he'd become a violent, dreadful man, a bully who hurt women, who had beaten Mary and slapped his daughter around. He was despicable.

But a killer? A murderer? And not just of one, but of many. He'd seen fifteen bodies, but there could be dozens more already in the darkness of the container. And the men stood below, so calm and unmoved by the sight, like old footage of the

Nazis presiding serenely over death camps. That was a step further along the path to true evil.

He would never have believed McBain capable of it. But he had seen it with his own eyes.

He was on the *Bella Maria* when they loaded the container onto one of the McBain fishing trawlers. Guessing that matters in the warehouse were coming to a close when they shut up the container, he had let himself slide very slowly down the metal-ridged roof until one foot was safely on the handrail of the fire escape. After that, it was simple enough to ease himself down.

The rain had let up a bit, he noticed, as he jogged through the darkness towards his mooring. There was still a fierce wind but the torrent had stopped by the time he got on board the *Bella Maria*. He huddled into the shadows and watched as the men worked together in the dim light of a few lamps on board the trawler, slowly wheeling the container down to the vessel, attaching it to the dockside crane and eventually winching it up into the air. The wind made it swing alarmingly and, for a moment, Hamish worried for the safety of those inside, until he remembered that the passengers were long past caring now.

Despite the strong sway, the men managed to manoeuvre the container down onto the trawler's deck. Then the line was detached and the first part of the operation was complete.

Are they planning to go out in this? Hamish wondered as he watched them conferring, four silent silhouettes moving about on board the trawler. Yes, the rain had eased off, and the wind seemed to be dropping, but the conditions were still dreadful. They'd be taking a terrible risk going out to sea. Where were they taking the container?

He waited for almost half an hour, observing them. Should I call the police? he wondered. But just as he was deciding whether or not this was a good idea, he heard the engine of the trawler start up and then it was heading out of the harbour, riding the swells as it went.

Hamish thought for a moment, then started up the *Bella Maria*'s engine and, with almost no lights, motored after them.

The swell was fierce a few miles out. It was years since Hamish had been on a sea like this and then it had been on a huge ship of about ten thousand tonnes. No sensible fisherman would be out in these conditions, especially not in these little craft. Hamish just hoped that they weren't going too far out.

Despite his years of experience and the way he knew the *Bella Maria* back to front, he was nervous standing at the wheel, trying to keep her on course, far enough away from the other vessel not to be noticed but close enough to trail her. The trawler had a mast light that flashed at regular intervals as she climbed the waves and sank into the troughs behind, and he took this as a guide as the little fishing boat used all its might to negotiate the stormy sea. Water lashed the deck and Hamish could barely see out of the window to steer.

Fear was not a familiar sensation to him, but he knew he was frightened now as he felt the little boat straining under the force of the storm. This had been reckless and foolhardy, he knew that. There was a real chance that he could drown out here, go to the bottom with the *Bella Maria*, and, despite all the misery he had endured over the years, he didn't want that. Something told him that he wanted to live, that there were still things to do and places to go. There was unfinished business he needed to deal with before he died, he knew that suddenly and clearly.

I'm calling Heather, he thought. I have to tell her where I am, get her on alert in case I have to abandon ship and need the coastguard.

Pulling the mobile phone out of his pocket, he tried to dial her number but there was no tone at all. He looked again, his hand moving up and down in front of his face with the motion of the sea. No signal.

He'd just have to rely on his shipboard radio and hope he could send out a distress signal in time if things turned nasty.

Then, to his astonishment, the light on the trawler appeared to be getting closer and closer instead of further away.

'Shit!' he said aloud. 'They've only bloody turned round, the fuckin' madmen! What the hell are they doing leading me on this wild goose chase?'

He would have to rely on them passing the *Bella Maria* and not seeing her in this weather. His lights were now all off, he would probably get away with it. All he had to do was keep her afloat until the trawler had passed, turn her round and head for home. And pray with all his heart that he made it back from this fool's errand.

Chapter Forty-one

'This is the stupidest thing I've ever done in my life!' yelled McBain, his voice weak against the power of the storm. The rain was starting up again, just as Greg had predicted. He was furious but felt so impotent, one tiny man on a tiny boat out on the immense sea, at the mercy of nature.

'I told you it was risky,' yelled back Greg.

'Why do I let myself be talked into things by that boy?'

Callum was below decks, keeping well out of the way, no doubt snorting up some more of his little helper. He'd insisted they could do it – that the seas were not so rough that they couldn't somehow get far enough out and then manage to drop the container overboard. But it became apparent that as they got further out, the sea was becoming rougher and more dangerous. The storm was blowing itself up again, the rain returned and the mighty squalls increased in violence. There was no way they could go any further out.

'We'll have to drop it here!' yelled Greg as the trawler pitched horribly.

'It's not far enough!' McBain shouted back. 'It's too close to shore.'

'We don't have any choice!'

As it was, winching the container over the sea was a perilous, foolhardy thing to do. Altering the ship's balance in such conditions was madness, but they had to do it. Fighting the wind and the mountainous waves, they managed to swing the container out over the side and release it. It dropped like a stone, swallowed at once by the hungry water beneath.

'Now let's turn the fuck around and get out of here!' yelled McBain. He heard a strange keening sound and looked round to see Callum, his face upturned to the wind and rain, howling into the great fury of the storm. Was he crying? wondered his father. Had the events of the last twenty-four hours finally caught up with his emotions?

Then he saw that Callum was laughing with excitement. Callum turned and saw McBain watching him. 'Yeee – hah!' he crowed like a cowboy. 'We did it! Straight down to Davy fuckin' Jones's locker. Did you see that, Dad? Didn't she go beautifully? I told you we could do it.'

It was a white-knuckle ride back into harbour and it was with great relief that McBain saw the familiar Kinlochvegan docks. Day was supposed to be breaking soon but the storm clouds meant that it was still as dark as night. Long experience of the black winter dawns, though, meant that they were able to find their way easily to the mooring spot once they'd negotiated the sea itself.

'Thank the blessed Lord,' said McBain as they came alongside. Callum had come up once more and now leapt ashore to help tie the trawler up.

'Aye,' said Greg with feeling. 'We've been lucky.'

'So far,' said McBain. 'But we're not out of the

woods yet. We've dropped that container far too close to shore. There's every possibility it's going to wash up somewhere or get discovered in the shallow water. What happens if they trace it back to us?' He couldn't bring himself to mention the ghastly contents.

'Dunno, boss,' said Greg. 'But it's done now. No point in worrying about it until it happens. Let's get home and get dry first, anyway.'

Tom came into the cabin, his hair plastered against his scalp. 'Did you see it?' he asked breathlessly. He was talking awkwardly through a swollen jaw, the legacy of McBain's punch.

'See what?' said McBain sharply. 'Police?'

'No – the little fishing boat that's been coming back into port behind us all the way!'

'What?'

'Her lights are off, but I saw her as we went by.' Tom's curious grey-white eyes seemed to flicker with excitement. 'She was quite close but not close enough for me to make her out. The rain's as thick as a blanket, I couldn't even make out her colour.'

McBain was pale. 'Where is she now?' he said, trying to see something out of the cabin window.

'She's out there,' said Tom. 'She's almost back into harbour, look, you can see her now, rocking in on the swell.'

McBain squinted and stared out. Sure enough, he could make out the shape of a small fishing boat, buffeted by the waves but still pressing forward, heading out of the open sea and into safety.

'Who the hell is crazy enough to be out?' he muttered.

'Crazy as us?' asked Greg.

'What's happening, Dad?' Callum came in, shaking the water off his shoulders. 'I've made her fast. Shouldn't we get inside?'

'Look,' said McBain grimly, pointing. 'We've been followed.'

Hamish made the *Bella Maria* fast, tying her expertly to her mooring despite the force of the wind that seemed to want to blow him down the jetty and up the hill home. When she was secure, he patted her side.

'Thank you, lassie,' he said with a broad smile. 'You brought me back home safe and sound. I knew I could trust you.'

Now, he thought, I'd better get home and call Heather and let her know I'm all right.

He turned to see two men standing behind him. 'Hello, Hamish,' said one, his voice muffled by the wind. The other stared at him silently, his hands thrust deep in his pockets.

Hamish stared back at him for a moment. 'Morning. What can I do for you?'

'I think you know very well. You'd better come with us.'

'What if I don't want to?' The rain began to splatter down again, increasing in a few moments to a vicious downpour.

'To be honest, pal, you don't have a choice.'

It was then he saw that Callum McBain was holding a gun, and it was pointed at his chest.

From where he was sitting Hamish couldn't see what was going on, but he could hear. Greg

McDonald was supposed to be guarding him – not that he could go anywhere, tied up like this – but the man was obviously exhausted and his head was nodding and his eyes dropping as he slipped in and out of sleep.

Fools don't realise that their office is made out of plywood, he thought scornfully. When the plant is working they probably can't be heard, but when it's quiet, it's as clear as a bell.

'We don't know what he's seen,' McBain was saying, his voice tense.

'We can take a pretty good guess,' Callum replied. To Hamish, he sounded overwrought and keyed up to an alarming extent. 'Why would he be following us if he didn't know?'

'How could he know?'

'Fuck knows! Don't ask me! But only a maniac would be out there if he didn't have to be. It's obvious he was following us, so he must know we're up to something we don't want anyone else to clock onto.'

'Perhaps he thinks it's the drugs.'

'Oh, the drugs. He just thinks it's a consignment of cocaine and heroin we were dumping? That's all right then,' said Callum with heavy sarcasm. 'That's *so* much better. Don't you see it makes no difference? Whether it's ... what it was, or whether it's drugs, it's still not going to be fuckin' funny if we get found out. So either way, we have to get rid of him.'

'We could have sorted this out some other way, Callum. If you hadn't gone rushing over with the gun...'

'Dad, wake up. There is no other way, can't you

429

see that?'

'Well, he knows for sure we're involved in something illegal now.'

'Och, he knew anyway! He must have been tailing us for ages. Stupid old man, why'd he want to poke his nose into this? Look, it's obvious what we have to do.'

There was a pause. Hamish strained to hear what was going on. Greg McDonald made a sudden movement, woke up and stared at Hamish for a moment, and then sank immediately back into sleep.

'I told you, Dad. We have to get rid of him.'

McBain groaned. 'Och, Callum ... what are you talking about?'

He's talking about killing me, thought Hamish, strangely calm.

'I'll do it,' said Callum in an eerily light voice. 'I've already done a batch of 'em. One more isn't going to make any difference.'

There was another long silence.

'No,' said McBain at last. 'There has to be another way.'

'There is no other way! Can't you see?'

McBain exploded. 'For Christ's sake, Callum, what planet are you on? We can't just go around killing people. Fraser lives in the village, people know him. If he disappears, questions are going to be asked!'

'Who's going to care, Dad? I mean, really? Some old man who sits on his boat all day with his bits of string and his bits of wood? He's got no family, he's got no friends, he's nothing! We'd probably be doing him a favour.'

No, thought Hamish. That's not right. I know that's not right.

'Think about it. He's got that shabby old boat – God knows how it got through that sea out there. We knock him out, put him in his boat, take 'em out to sea, scuttle her and let it all go down. It'll look like an accident that was bound to happen.'

There was another long silence before McBain said, 'We can't do it now. It's too late. People will be getting up soon. And we can't risk going out again in this weather – the storm's blowing up again.'

'Fine. We'll do it tomorrow.'

'And where are we going to keep him until then?'

Callum thought for a moment. 'Put him in the cold store again?'

'Too risky. Too many people have access to it.'

'But it's the perfect way to kill him, Dad, think about it!' Callum sounded excited again. 'He'll die of hypothermia, no marks on him, nothing for forensics to find if he gets discovered before the water and the fish have had him.'

'All right, all right! Let me think!' After a moment, McBain said, 'If we have to do it, then we'll do it that way. But where are we going to keep him in the meantime?'

'I know the perfect place,' answered Callum.

Callum appeared in front of him a moment later, his eyes glinting with excitement.

'All right, old man. You're coming with me.' He yanked Hamish to his feet and started to untie the ropes around his ankles. 'I'm not fuckin' carrying you, though. You can walk.'

Hamish said nothing. There was an air of unreality about the whole thing, as though they were play-acting. Had he really heard McBain and his son plan how to kill him? This was absurd. These things didn't really happen.

And yet here he was, being pulled around by this hotheaded young man at gunpoint.

'Now,' said Callum, standing up. He was obviously enjoying his role. 'Let's make sure you've not got anything you shouldn't.'

He patted Hamish up and down as though looking for a weapon. Then he put his hands in his pockets, pulling out what he found there. From one pocket he took the penknife Hamish used for whittling. 'Oh dear, oh dear,' Callum said happily, clearly pleased to have found something that could be classed as a weapon, no matter how small and blunt it was. 'I'd better remove this, I think. And,' he pulled out Hamish's mobile phone, 'this too. Don't want you making any calls for help.'

Callum pulled him along towards the warehouse door. 'Tom!' he called.

The other young man appeared. 'Yeah?'

'Come on, we're taking this one away for storage.'

'OK, boss.' Tom opened the warehouse door.

Callum looked down at the gun he was holding in his hand, and grinned. 'Let's get going,' he said, and pushed Hamish roughly into the storm outside.

Chapter Forty-two

Shall I call or not?

Heather sat on her bed, staring at her mobile phone, Hamish's number on the display, and debated whether to call it. What if he wanted to speak to her but had forgotten how to work her phone? But what if he was somewhere where it would alert other people to his presence if the phone went off?

Shit, she should have showed him how to put it on silent.

Looking anxiously at the clock, she saw that he'd been gone for hours. Day was breaking outside. Why hadn't she heard from him? What could be happening?

I'm going to call, she decided, and pressed the dial key. A moment later she heard her own voice. 'Hi, it's Heather. Leave me a message. Thanks.' The phone must be off.

She couldn't bear this waiting. Thoughts were running round and round her brain, all about what Hamish could possibly be up to and what he might have found out about her father and brother's activities.

If they are dealing drugs, she thought, they deserve everything they get. I won't be sorry to see them caught.

For a moment she envisaged a future without them, with just her mother and herself, building a new life free from their oppressive presence.

What can I do? she wondered. I must be able to do something to help... She thought about it, jiggling the phone in her hand with nerves.

Of course! Why didn't I think of it before?

She got up, opened her bedroom door and went quietly down the corridor.

I should have done this earlier, she thought, cross with herself. I've wasted time. They could be back any minute. I can't bank on much time at all.

She was in her father's office, a place she knew only as somewhere she'd spent some of the most terrified moments of her childhood. It was here he had summoned her when she had infringed one of his many rules or angered him in some way, and it was here he had often whacked her as her punishment. The room was full of his presence, and she shivered as she felt it. It went against everything she had learned in her youth to start touching his things and going through private drawers and cupboards – but that was what she was determined to do.

What am I looking for? she asked herself. Anything that seems to shed a light on what he and Callum are up to. I'm sure he's not going to have a file conveniently marked 'Drug Smuggling' – but you never know, there might be something, some kind of clue...

She went round his desk and sat down on his chair. The desk top was very neat. Her father was passionate about keeping everything just so – it was another way that he had oppressed everyone, not least his wife, whose responsibility it was to keep the house pristine. She hardly dared to touch anything in case he noticed it was out of place.

The drawers were open but inside were only the usual office bits and bobs – pens, pencils, notepads and anything else McBain might need. The bottom drawer was locked. She looked about and her gaze dropped on the filing cabinet, something she had seen many times but never really taken in. She went to it and tried the top drawer. Locked, of course.

She tutted with annoyance. This was a quick road to nothing. Her father wasn't going to leave his private documentation open to anyone to look at, particularly when he didn't trust the people he lived with.

A memory floated into her head. She had come into the room summoned by an angry bellow by her father. Frightened and apprehensive, she'd crept quietly in to face whatever she had done wrong. Her father had been standing at the filing cabinet as she entered and he turned towards her, his face red with anger. He'd been turning a key in the lock at the top of the cabinet and then ... she remembered how he had swung away from her, picked up the china elephant on the windowsill and put the key underneath it somehow, and then swung back. It had been such an automatic movement for him, one he'd done so many times that he hadn't noticed that he'd done it in front of her.

Jumping up, Heather went to the windowsill and picked the elephant up. There was nothing underneath it – the windowsill was bare. Then she turned it over and, stuck into a small wodge of sticky tack, was the key to the filing cabinet.

She smiled to herself. Her father had hidden it, but not that well. He obviously didn't really expect anyone to come snooping in his office. If he did, he'd have done a better job than this.

She took the key, unlocked the cabinet and began flicking through the files. In the top drawer was home administration: insurance documents, bills, files on the family cars, receipts for goods and so on. The next two drawers were devoted to aspects of the businesses her father ran. She tried to look through some of the files but was soon discouraged. It all looked very ordinary, and there was so much of it. Anything could be hidden among all this run-of-the-mill stuff and her chances of stumbling on something, and even recognising it if she did, were minimal.

This was a waste of time. She pulled open the bottom drawer and began to look through its contents.

This was more interesting. These files related to the family. There was a slim one for herself and she peeked inside, seeing her old school reports and other bits and pieces. She wanted to stop and look for longer, but she didn't dare to waste time going over her own past. The file for Callum was much bigger and she saw that her father had preserved lots of his son's baby scrawls, pictures and letters, along with a thick file of photographs and a lock of soft dark baby hair in an envelope.

She felt stabbed with sadness. Her own file was so small in comparison, and her father had clearly seen no value in keepsakes of her childhood. What had she done to make her father think so little of her? Whatever it was, it must have been when she was very young. It looked as though he had never loved her.

Her eye was caught by another file at the back of the cabinet. FRASER it said in scrawled letters. She picked it up and opened it. A letter on the top fell out, headed with a London address. She quickly scanned the first lines.

Dear McBain

Thank you for coming to see Robbie and me last week. It was nice to see you and to hear how things are going in Kinlochvegan. I appreciate the gift you gave us. I've now been able to buy Robbie a new school uniform and he looks very good in it...

Heather turned to the back. It was signed *Louise*.

She gasped, her heart pounding. That was Hamish's wife and son – Louise and Robbie. She and Hamish had talked about Robbie many times and Hamish must have mentioned his wife's name at some point.

What the hell was this? Why was her father in touch with Hamish's wife? She flicked through some more of the file's contents and saw receipts, tickets, solicitor's letters, photographs, postcards, more letters...

She had to read it. She would risk taking it out of the office so that she could concentrate on it and return it another time, and gamble that her father would not miss it in the meantime.

Having decided, she closed the cabinet and

locked it, stuck the key under the elephant again, took up the file and left the office as she had found it, in darkness.

Part Five

Chapter Forty-three

'What do you know about why my parents split up?' asked Robbie, his voice quavering with emotion.

'What does your mother say? Have you ever asked her?' Heather suddenly didn't seem able to meet his eye.

'She can't say anything now – she's dead. And yes, I did ask her a few times but she never told me anything. Not a thing. When I got your letter, it was the first time I'd even heard of Kinloch-vegan.'

'I'm sorry about your mother,' Heather said, looking solemn.

'Thanks.'

'I'll come clean now and tell you what I know. It might change your whole attitude to all this – it might mean you don't even want to help me. But if we do find Hamish, and he's alive, then you ought to know this before you see him.' Heather came over and sat next to him. She took his hand in hers. Robbie was frightened. Was even worse news coming?

She said slowly, 'I think my father paid your mother to leave your dad. It's possible that he even paid her to marry him in the first place.'

'*What?*' Robbie felt as though he couldn't take any more surprises like this. 'Why? Why do you think that? It sounds like the maddest thing I've

441

ever heard.'

'I know it's a shock, but I'm not just saying this out of the blue. You see, I did some snooping in my father's office and I found a whole file there, devoted to you and your mother. It had your address in it – that's how I knew where to write to you – but not just that. It had lots of information on your mother in it – and some photographs – she was very pretty, wasn't she? – and information on your grandparents, too, and you, from the time you were about three years old. And there were receipts – receipts for money, some of them quite sizeable. My father even paid off the outstanding mortgage on your mother's house. It's all there, it's all in the file. Why would he do that?'

'I don't know,' Robbie said, frowning. He tried to take it all in.

'He's hated your father for years, and I think he had his revenge on him by paying his wife to go away. If my theory is right, he may even have found Louise and paid her to pretend to fall in love with your dad and have you – and then make her leave.'

Robbie laughed. 'Your imagination's running riot, Heather.'

'You don't know what Dad's capable of,' she protested.

'No, but it isn't right, I'm sure it's not.'

'Then why would he support you both like that?' Heather was gazing at him anxiously.

That's really why she brought me here, thought Robbie. She wants some answers for her own life, about why she doesn't love her father. She's willing, maybe rightly, to believe anything of him now. But I can't believe this story. He said at last, 'It doesn't ring true to me because of the photo album.'

'What album?'

'The one I found upstairs. It's got pictures of my parents in it and if what you say is true, then my mother could never have really loved my father, and I believe that she did. The pictures ... the way she looks at Hamish ... she adored him, it's obvious. The photos of the family together... me and my mum and dad. They're not faked, Heather, I promise you. She was happy.'

'Show me,' she said simply.

They went upstairs and sat on the bed in the main bedroom, looking at the pictures in the album. There was Louise again, gazing up at Hamish with her luminous eyes, her love clear to see. And there was Hamish, fresh-faced, sparkling with youth and possibilities.

'Look at him!' breathed Heather, staring at a photo. 'He's not much like that now.'

'What does he look like?'

'Old. White-haired and wrinkled. But still, there's something about him, a trace of this young man... What's this?' Heather picked up the photograph that Robbie had slipped back into the cover of the album. It had come loose and fallen out.

'Oh, that. I've no idea. Some woman – but there's no name.' He took it from her and looked at it again. 'She's pretty, isn't she? I don't suppose she looks much the same, either.'

'She doesn't,' said Heather in a strange high

voice. 'She's beautiful in this picture. It must have been taken before all her spirit and independence were beaten out of her.'

'Do you know who it is?' asked Robbie.

'Of course I do. She's my mother.'

Before Robbie could begin to absorb this, there was a knock at the door. They both jumped and looked at each other nervously.

'You'd better answer it,' Heather said urgently. 'Don't act suspiciously. And whoever it is, you don't know who I am, OK?'

'OK.'

Robbie went downstairs and opened the front door. A short, stocky man with black hair streaked with grey stood on the doorstep. He looked in his late fifties: his rather fat face made it hard to tell his age more precisely. He was smiling broadly at Robbie.

'Ah, Mr Fraser, hello,' he said in a jolly voice. 'I heard that you were paying us a visit and I thought I'd come by and offer you a warm Kinlochvegan welcome. My name is McBain.'

'How do you do?' Robbie said politely. So this is McBain, he thought grimly, feeling a shudder crawl down his spine though he didn't show it. This is the man who's made Heather miserable all her life and may have killed my father. Then he felt suddenly sick. The one who paid my mother for years. The one who has a file on my family in his study.

His impulse was to grab the man by the shoulders and shake him and shout, 'Tell me everything, you bastard! Right from the beginning and right to the end. What the hell is going on here? I want some answers!'

But instead he kept his expression as neutral as he could and said, 'If you're after my father, I'm afraid he isn't here.'

The other man looked nonplussed for a moment, as though he was not sure what to say. 'Oh – isn't he? Hamish not there? No ... no, of course he's not. And now I come to think of it, we haven't seen him about for a few days. He's usually on his boat down in the harbour, amusing himself on board, or going out with the fleet for the fishing. So – where is he?'

You tell me, mate. But he said, 'I don't know. It's all a bit mysterious.'

'I'm sure he'll turn up,' said McBain cheerfully. 'And in the meantime, I wondered if you would like to come for dinner at our house? We'd love to have you over. I have a daughter and a son around your age, and they'd be delighted to meet you. So would my wife.'

He's not my father, thought Robbie. *I'm sure of it. I would feel something if he were, I know I would.* 'That's very kind of you. Yes ... yes. I'd be happy to.'

'Excellent. Come over at eight o'clock. You see that house on the hill – the white one above the warehouse? That's us. Just follow the road up from the village. Do you have a car?'

'Yes. It's in the pub car park.'

'Well, you may find a car easier. The walk can be a little steep if you're not used to it. Up to you.'

'I'm sure I can manage it,' Robbie said lightly. 'Thanks for the invitation. I'll see you tonight.'

When McBain had gone, Heather crept down the stairs and joined him in the sitting room.

'That's very strange,' she said. 'He must have found out pretty quickly that you had arrived here. No doubt everyone in the pub was rushing to tell him. But why would Dad ask you to our house for dinner?'

'He wants to interrogate me, I suppose,' Robbie answered. He felt chilled by his encounter with the other man, though he couldn't think why – he had been perfectly friendly, after all. 'It'll be easier in the setting of a dinner party. Lots of polite conversation and interesting small talk. He must think it's quite a coincidence, me turning up like this just when my father has disappeared. He's bound to be trying to work out why it's happened. I don't know whether that means he's guilty of something or not.' A thought occurred to him. 'There isn't any way he could trace this to you, is there?'

'I don't think so. I put the file about you back exactly where I found it. There's no copy of the letter I sent you, or any evidence that I sent anything at all.'

'I wish I could see that file,' Robbie said.

'Maybe you can. We might be able to work out a way.'

'Let's not take any unnecessary risks. So you'll be at this supper tonight?'

'Just try keeping me away.' Heather grinned and her face transformed. She had been looking worried and frightened, Robbie realised. Now she seemed pretty again, her blue eyes dancing. 'I can't wait to see my father and Callum trying to be nice to you.'Then she was serious. 'But you've also got to do some questioning of your own, as well as you can without being suspicious. We need to find out what we can about where Hamish might be, or what they've done to him if he's ... if it's all gone wrong.'

'We don't really have a plan, do we?'

'No.' She shook her head. 'I'm afraid I'm a hopeless amateur at all this. I was hoping you might be able to come up with some ideas.'

'Do I look like the police? I'm at a loss as well. I guess we'll just have to play it by ear.' Robbie grinned back at her.

'Och, you've not disappointed me,' she said softly. 'I'm glad we've finally got to meet. I guess I won't be wondering about the mysterious Robbie Fraser any more.'

'I guess not,' he said slowly.

'I'd better go. Now, give me your mobile number and I'll give you mine. If there's any news at all, I'll text you or leave a message and you do the same, OK?' When they'd swapped their respective numbers, she smiled at him. 'I'll see you tonight then, Robbie Fraser.'

'OK. See you later.'

After Heather had left, Robbie stared into space for a very long time. Then he made himself a cup of tea and stoked the fire, still thinking over everything that had happened.

He was gazing into the flames when he suddenly put down the poker and said, 'Screw all this – I've got to do something. What if Hamish

447

is still alive somewhere? I've got to do something to find him, I can't just sit around.'

Quickly he put on his coat and let himself out of the front door of Lachlan Cottage, locking it behind him with a spare key he found on the hook just inside the door. He strode down the hill. The path was still wet from the torrents of rain that had fallen the night before, although the river that had flooded down when Robbie was climbing up in the dark seemed to have dried up.

In the daylight, the village looked quite different. His imagination had painted it as some eerie, almost horror-movie-esque place, with creaking signs swinging in the wind, broken-down houses and deserted streets, but now, with the storm over, the sun shining out of a clear blue sky, it seemed like a rather comforting place. The houses were neat and mostly cheerful-looking, the ones that weren't in shades of slate painted white or in candy colours. They lined the hillside above the harbour in neat yet slightly higgledy-piggledy terraces. The pub was in the main street, and he was glad to see his car still parked where he had left it. There were also shops and normal-looking people walking up and down, going about their business.

The idea that his father might have been murdered suddenly seemed ridiculous, and the notion that the friendly man who had called on him today was some sort of ruthless killer laughable. Except...

Robbie strode down the main street towards the docks, breathing in the tangy salt air.

Except that he believed Heather. And there had been a coldness in that man McBain's eyes that he

448

had noticed almost immediately. And the crux of the matter was – where was his father? Why had he disappeared? No, there was something very suspicious going on and if he could get to the bottom of it, so much the better. He just wished that Heather had been frank about what she suspected was happening – she was holding information back, he could tell that much. He could make some guesses – getting involved in some sort of contraband was the most likely option – but it would help if she just came out with it and told him.

I'll ask her later, he decided. I'll tell her that if we're going to help each other, we'll need to be completely honest.

He recognised the *Bella Maria* immediately, even though she was far from being the shining little vessel in the photograph album. Her sides were weathered and in need of a fresh coat of paint, and she looked dried out and battered.

So that's my father's boat, he thought as he looked down at her from the dock. He was on that boat just a few days ago.

It still astonished him to think that all the time he had been growing up, lonely and questioning, his father had been right here, alive and well, sailing out on this little boat to go fishing.

Best not to think about it, he told himself, as something knotted hard in his chest at the thought. But he couldn't shut out the knowledge of what Heather had told him – what if he never found out the answers?

No, he thought determinedly. I'll make that man tell me if I have to beat it out of him.

Chapter Forty-four

He rang the doorbell, trying to quell the nerves in his stomach. Everything relied on his acting perfectly normally, as though he suspected nothing.

McBain appeared. 'Ah, Robbie – may I call you Robbie? – please come in.'

He followed the older man down the hall and into a sitting room. The house was modern and spacious, but it had a dated feel about it. The decor hadn't been touched in years, that was obvious, and while everything was neat and clean, it felt like it needed a good shake-up to bring it into the present.

'Cannae get you a drink?' enquired McBain pleasantly. 'A beer?'

'Thanks, that would be nice.' I mustn't drink too much, Robbie reminded himself. I have to keep my wits about me.

When McBain went to get the drink Robbie looked quickly about him, but the whole place looked like a normal family home, as blameless and innocent as it could be. There was no sense of nefarious goings-on.

A bottle or two of wine on a Saturday night is probably as exciting as it gets, he thought. It feels a universe away from the world of Class A drugs here. He sat down on the sofa.

On the *Bella Maria* that afternoon, he had

found very little of interest. She was messy inside and there was a feeling of disruption, as though the boat had been given a huge jolt lately and it had made everything on board slide out of place. It seemed that Hamish had spent a lot of time there – there were many intricately carved pieces of driftwood and a heap of raw, unwhittled wood on the floor that had perhaps been in a basket and somehow fallen out.

What had caught Robbie's eye, though, were two newspaper articles cut out and stuck to the wall. One was about the degradation of the Scottish inner cities and the plight of the drug addicts. The other was an investigative piece about how the trade in illicit substances was carried out – methods of importation, transportation and gang involvement.

I thought so. Heather wouldn't say but it had to be drugs, he thought. Well, well. What were you trying to do, Dad? Save the world?

It seemed that his father might be a bit of a crusader. He liked that, and was pleased to have another insight into his father's character. He'd come up to the McBain house even more determined to find out what was going on and where his father might be.

McBain came back into the room with a glass of beer for him, which Robbie took politely.

He longed to ask McBain straight out what had happened in the past, but he couldn't do that without causing trouble for Heather. Unless there was another way... He was thinking fast about how he could possibly broach the subject when McBain said, 'Ah, you must meet my wife, Mary.'

451

A woman came into the room. When she saw Robbie, she stopped and gasped, her hands flying to her mouth. Her legs almost appeared to buckle under her for an instant but she recovered herself and instead looked at her husband, her questioning eyes wide with surprise.

McBain seemed to find this amusing. A smile played about his lips. 'Mary – this is Robbie Fraser, Hamish's son. He has a real look of Hamish when he was young, doesn't he?'

Mary had turned deathly pale but she managed a shaky smile and nodded. 'Oh yes, he does. Welcome, Robbie. What brings you here?'

'Oh, lots of things,' he said. 'Scotland's a beautiful place, isn't it?'

He looked curiously at Mary McBain. Heather was right, there was little left in this woman of the beautiful girl in the photograph hidden in Hamish's album. Why had his father kept her picture? Had they been sweethearts once? What had happened between them? The obvious shock she'd had seeing Robbie was not one of nostalgic pleasure, but rather one of fright and something like sadness.

'Beautiful,' she said in a small voice, still looking at her husband.

A young man swaggered into the room. He was very like McBain, with broad, powerful shoulders on a small frame, and a mass of dark hair over black brows. 'Who's this?' he asked carelessly, glancing at Robbie.

He knows very well who I am, thought Robbie. And he doesn't like it.

'My son, Callum,' explained McBain. 'He

452

works with me in the family business. It has two arms, a fishing business and a mechanical business...' He talked on for a while about the McBain enterprise. Callum flung himself into an armchair and sat hunched, his heavy brows in a constant frown, his knees jiggling and hands twisting with pent-up energy.

Robbie listened politely, his mind half somewhere else. Then came the moment he'd been anticipating. Heather walked in.

She's good, he thought. She gave away nothing in her voice or her face about their prior meeting. Instead she was polite but uninterested, as though she'd been coerced into a family meal with a stranger she had no desire to meet. After a quick hello, she ignored him almost completely. He hoped he was doing as good a job. He tried not to look at her, though he was intensely aware of her presence.

McBain talked on, holding court easily as if he was used to dominating proceedings. Then dinner was served and they all went through to the dining room and took their places.

A family meal, thought Robbie. Not something I'm used to. It was strange to see a father and mother and their grown-up children sitting down to eat together. He thought about the undercurrents of fear and violence beneath the placid facade, and the way Heather had said so passionately how much she hated her father and brother.

Maybe he'd had a lucky escape, not having a family.

Mary sat quietly at one end of the table, hardly looking up from her food. She seemed to be trying to control herself, or keep a lid on her emotions but what those emotions were, Robbie couldn't guess. Heather sat opposite him, so now she had to look at him but she said very little. McBain continued to dominate the conversation until, in one of his pauses, Callum broke in. His voice was rough and edged with hostility.

'So why are you here?' he said abruptly. 'Why have you come here? You've no shown any interest in this part of the world before, have you?'

Fuck it, thought Robbie. I'm going to say what I've got to say. 'I'm looking for my father,' he said loudly. 'My mother died recently and she left me a very illuminating letter. You see, for years she told me nothing about where I'd come from or where my father was. I didn't even know if he was dead or alive. I'd never heard of Kinlochvegan. I've no idea why she didn't want me to know about Hamish until after her death, but that was the way it was. Instead, she told me I had a guardian, someone who looked after me from afar and paid for a lot of my upbringing. When my mother died, it turned out she was quite comfortably off even though we'd had very little money all my life. She wasn't rich or anything, but she owned her house and the mortgage had been paid off by this guardian, so she had some security.'

'How fascinating,' said McBain smoothly. 'And you've no idea who this guardian was?'

Robbie stared him straight in the eye. 'Oh no. I've got a very good idea. My mother was very informative on the subject.'

'Well, well...' The expression in McBain's eyes

changed to one of flinty hardness. 'And now you're looking for your father.'

'It seems my timing is rather bad. You see, apparently he disappeared only two or three days ago. How's that for bad luck? I don't see him for thirty years, and then we miss each other by three days. So I'm going to stay here and look for him.'

'That's very laudable,' McBain remarked. His voice was utterly composed. 'Like I said before, I was only thinking myself I'd not seen Hamish for a while. But he lives alone, you see, and it's not unusual not to see him for a while, especially when the weather's bad. His boat's in the harbour, isn't it? Well, maybe he's taken a trip to Inverness or something like that. His brother lives in Fort William, I believe. He could have gone to stay there.'

An uncle, Robbie thought. Now I have an uncle as well. He filed the information away to think about later.

'So,' he said carefully, 'you don't think there's a possibility he might be dead?'

'Dead!' McBain raised his eyebrow as Callum shifted in his seat. 'Well, that's a terrible thing to consider, Robbie, terrible. I didn't like to speak of it, but as you've raised it... Well, I suppose we must think of the worst. This is a dangerous place in many ways – the sea, the cliffs, the great stretches of uninhabited land. I suppose it is possible that Hamish could have gone for a walk and been stranded somewhere and not been able to get any help. And this storm... Bad things happen in weather like that.'

'I suppose my father would have thought he

could do just about anything.'

'Oh yes, Robbie, he's like that, he surely is. And you know, I recall now that one of his favourite walks was up to the point to look out over the sea. If he'd been caught in bad weather... It's a slim chance, mind you, and of course I pray that misfortune hasn't overtaken my old friend but... well, it's no secret that Hamish liked a dram or two as well, and you know how drink can give you courage.' McBain looked suitably saddened by the idea of his old friend falling drunkenly off a cliff in a storm. 'And we might never know what had happened.'

'I hadn't thought of that,' Robbie said. Anger was swirling inside him at the man's hypocrisy. He hadn't given a damn for Hamish, Heather had told him that. And this old quarrel between them ... and now he was trying to look sorry at the thought that Hamish might be dead. It made him sick.

Mary got up to clear the plates of their first course. Robbie watched her and a few moments later excused himself, asking for the toilet.

'It's down the hall, past the kitchen. Third on the left,' said McBain.

He left the dining room and went into the dark corridor. A shaft of light showed him where the kitchen was and he went towards it. Looking in, he saw Mary bent over the dishwasher putting the dirty plates inside it.

'Mrs McBain?' he said softly.

Mary jumped and turned round. As she saw him, her face softened and she came towards him, and the next moment he was wrapped in

456

her embrace.

'Oh, little Robbie,' she murmured. 'He would have been so happy to see you. Poor wee lad – you've lost your mother too. I'm sorry. I'm so sorry.'

She was a thin, bony woman but nonetheless her hug was soft and warm and the hand that stroked his hair for a moment was gentle. Something in him seemed to collapse at this first gesture of affection he had had for so long. His mother hadn't been able to touch him in her last months, she hadn't had the strength, and it was two years since he and Sinead had broken up. No one had touched him with compassion like this for such a long time.

He tried to control himself. He couldn't break down here in McBain's kitchen in between courses. Mary let him go and stood back to look at him.

'You're so like him,' she said with a smile.

'What happened between you? I found your picture in Hamish's album. What was the reason my mother left?'

Her blue eyes became fearful and she was clearly tense. 'Don't ask me, I can't tell you. You're in danger. I believe your father is dead. I think the best thing you can do is go back home. I know it's terrible to take in but it's for the best if you go. Things here are... It's not right here. That's all I can say.'

'If my father's been murdered, then I'm not going to rest until I've brought whoever did it to justice,' Robbie said firmly. He felt surprised at himself. He hadn't known that he wanted to do that, but now he had said it, he'd never been more sure of anything in his life.

'You don't know ... you've no idea how dangerous it is! Don't get involved, please, I beg you. Let Hamish go and get on with your own life. You didn't know him, don't sacrifice yourself for him. He would never have wanted that.' She spoke quietly and urgently, her expression pleading.

'I can't do that. I need to find out the truth about the past.'

'Oh God, you don't know what they're capable of...'

'And I've promised to help Heather. I'm not leaving her here virtually alone.'

Now Mary's eyes were terrified. 'Heather! Listen to me, Robbie, stay away from Heather–'

Callum walked into the kitchen. 'What are you two jabbering about?' he asked brusquely.

'Nothing,' said Mary lightly, but looking guilty. She went back to the dishwasher. 'Just this and that. Robbie's thinking of going back to England.'

'Are you?' Callum turned his dark gaze onto Robbie.

'Well...'

'I think it's a good idea,' said the young man. 'Your father's dead more likely 'n not. You just leave your number and we'll call you if they ever find him. We can deal with everything here for you. If they don't find him for a few years, I suppose his things will go to you, won't they?'

Robbie heard the old woman gasp quietly at her son's callousness. 'Thanks, Callum. I'll bear your kind offer in mind.'

They went back to the dining room together.

Chapter Forty-five

McBain's thoughts were in a whirl.

'We have to do it tonight, Dad,' Callum was saying urgently. 'We can't wait any longer. The old man's on his last legs anyway.'

'What? Do what?'

Callum sighed heavily. 'For Christ's sake, Dad, keep focused, can't you? Listen, we have to kill Fraser tonight and dump his body. This kid is not going anywhere till he's found his dad, so let's give him something to find.'

McBain sat down at his desk and put his head in his hands. This was all getting too much for him. 'Where are we going to dump him, Callum? We can't take his boat out now. It's too obvious that he hasn't been near it for days. Greg says Robbie spent about an hour on it this afternoon, looking over it.'

'Forget the boat. It was a shite idea anyway. Look, all we have to do is get rid of Fraser and we're home and dry. He's the only one who knows anything about all this. I say that we freeze him like I did with those others and then we toss him off the point and let the sea take him wherever it wants. He'll wash up in a few days and it will look like an accident.'

'Except that a post-mortem might show that he died about four days after he disappeared...'

Callum scoffed. 'Not after he's been in the

water, Dad! You know what that does to a body.'

'Maybe. But they'll certainly know he hasn't drowned if he's dead before he goes in the sea. He won't have any water in his lungs.'

Callum scowled. 'Och, that's true. I hadn't thought of that.' Then his face cleared. 'So we just drown him then. Or freeze him till he's unconscious and then dump him so he drowns on his own.'

'Oh God,' groaned McBain. He stood up, anger coursing through him. 'What the hell are we talking about? How has it come to this, that we're talking about the best way to murder a man!' He looked at his hands as though he could hardly believe what they might be capable of. 'I can't do it. We can't do it!'

'Don't be stupid, Dad. Can't you see we don't have a choice? What are you going to do – let him go?' Callum employed his sarcastic voice, the one McBain hated. 'Oh, sorry, Hamish. We didn't mean to keep you prisoner for the best part of a week after you witnessed us dumping bodies at sea! Off you go home, pal, oh, and would you mind awfully not mentioning to anyone what's happened? Thanks so much!' He laughed sardonically. 'Get real, Dad. Unless you want to see your whole life collapse around you, Fraser has to die.' He looked at his father, who seemed to be breaking under the strain of what he was contemplating. 'You know what, Dad, you surprise me. I thought you hated that man. I didn't think you would care less if he had to be got rid of.'

'Nor did I, son,' he replied. But, thought McBain miserably, it doesn't work like that. The

460

desire to crush Hamish had forced him on through life. Did it include wanting to crush the life out of him? Something in him cowered at this final, irrevocable, dreadful step. He knew that if Hamish died, something important inside himself would die too. 'But I can't do it.'

'Don't worry about that,' Callum said carelessly. 'Greg and I will see to it. You don't have to do anything. But it has to be tonight, yeah?'

McBain stared down for a long time before he said quietly, 'Aye then. Do it.'

When Callum had gone, he went to his filing cabinet and removed the file about Robbie and Louise. Flicking through it, he recalled the years during which he had provided for Hamish's wife. He didn't give her riches, just enough to supplement her wage as a music teacher. He had visited her several times over the years, though always at night or when Robbie was at school, so that the boy wouldn't see him. Louise had been adamant about that.

'He mustn't ever think you're his father,' she'd said.

So he'd only ever seen the boy asleep in bed, when she'd let him peep through the door at him. The sight of the child had filled him with triumph. This, he thought, is my revenge. The fact that I can see this boy and Hamish cannot. That's my real victory.

One night, he and Louise had got drunk and ended up in bed together, but it had been a miserable experience. Almost throughout she had been weeping silently and when it ended, he having managed to achieve the damp squib of a climax, she had only rolled away and cried into her pillow until they both fell asleep. He'd gone before dawn.

What does Robbie know? wondered McBain. Did Louise really tell him everything? The agreement was that he would never know, that she would never tell, and he had no reason to think she would have gone back on it. If she was going to weaken, he thought, it would have been much earlier. Or did she have a deathbed desire to tell Robbie the truth?

'Ah, what does it matter anyway?' he said out loud. 'It's her word against mine. I can always tell him a good story about why it all happened.'

But he had a bad feeling about tonight. It was the night Hamish would die. Tonight was the night Robbie Fraser had come to him, with accusations in his eyes, wanting to know how he had come to lose his father all those years ago, wanting to know why his mother had become a bitter and broken woman, locked into a life of inescapable despair.

He tried to draw on the dark strength that had always sustained him in the past. All he had to do was remember and stir up the fury that constantly bubbled inside him, ready to boil up when he needed to force himself onward.

But tonight it was not working the way it always had. Tonight his fury turned inward and began to be directed, for the first time in his life, at himself.

Before Robbie had left, Heather had managed to snatch a word with him in the hall.

'Callum's in a strange mood,' she'd said in a low voice. 'I think something's up tonight. We'd better tail him if we can.'

'OK,' he'd replied quietly. 'I won't go home.'

'I'll text you if I can. Don't forget to put your phone on silent.'

That was all they had been able to manage to say to each other. It had been strange to watch him all evening, pretending that she didn't know him. The dinner had been dreadful, of course, like any family dinner in her house always was, with all the tension that inevitably accompanied it. Sitting across from Robbie, she had watched him covertly, enjoying the sight of familiar expressions pass over his face, reminding her of his father. Now that she observed him, having seen those pictures in the album, he had an unmistakable look of the young Hamish about him, in the brown wavy hair and the shape of his blue eyes.

The thing that was really occupying her thoughts, though, was the extraordinary reaction of her mother to the Fraser boy. She had never seen her in the grip of emotion like it, even though she had done her best to keep it hidden. No doubt McBain and Callum barely noticed, but Heather had seen clearly how shaken her mother was, and during the second course her hand had trembled as it lifted her fork.

Why?

Now that Robbie had gone the house was quiet, though she knew that Callum and her father were in the office. After a short time she heard Callum come out, walk down the hall, stop to put on his coat and then leave the house. Taking up her mobile she quickly texted Robbie: *Callum has gone out. Shall I follow?* The answer came back almost at once. *No. I'm on him. Stay away.*

She chafed at the restriction. It reminded her of the night Hamish had vanished. But her father was still here, so perhaps the mission Callum was on was just to go to the pub.

She was restless. I'll see if Mum's awake, she decided. Her mother was usually sound asleep as soon as dinner was finished and cleared away, but she felt that tonight might be different.

Her mother was not in bed as Heather had expected. Instead she was in her sewing room, lying on the sofa and staring up unseeingly at the ceiling.

'Mum?' Heather crept in and sat on the sofa next to her. 'Are you all right?'

Her mother shook her head slightly and looked at Heather with a smile. 'Hello, my darling. How are you?'

'I'm fine. But you're not, are you? Is it to do with Robbie Fraser?'

Her mother made an unconvincing attempt at a light laugh. 'Why would you think that, dear?'

'Come on, Mum. I saw the way he affected you.'

Mary sat up suddenly and pulled her blanket tightly about her. 'Heather, I'll be honest with you. The sight of that boy shook me very much. You see, many years ago his father and I felt something for each other, though it came to nothing in the end and I married your father...'

'I thought so. There's a photo of you in Hamish's album.'

'You've seen it?' Mary looked shocked. 'Heather,

464

how mixed up are you with Robbie Fraser?'

'I met him for the first time this morning.'

'How? What is it binding you together?'

Heather looked away, unsure how much to reveal. Each step led on to the next, and it was hard to tell one thing without having to tell another. Did her mother know that McBain had supported Robbie and Louise over the years? Should she know, or would it simply add more hurt and despair to a life that was already full of pain?

'He's here because of me,' Heather said at last. 'But I can't say more than that.'

Mary groaned and fell back against her cushions.

'What's wrong?'

'Oh, Heather... I've got something to tell you. You must listen very carefully. And please, try to forgive me if you can...'

Chapter Forty-six

Callum McBain came out of the family house and stopped in the dim light that came from the hallway within. He put his hand in his coat pocket and pulled out something smooth and dark.

A gun? thought Robbie, squinting through the darkness, trying to see more clearly.

Callum replaced whatever it was in his pocket and then walked over to a sports car. He hesitated for a moment and then evidently changed his mind. He went instead to a four-by-four that

465

was standing nearest the entrance to the drive, climbed aboard and started the engine.

Shit! I should have brought the car! How far is he going? I'll just have to follow as best I can on foot, thought Robbie. He crouched down and dashed out from his hiding place as the four-by-four pulled out of the driveway and began to bump down the road. The road was only used as a way to get to the house, and had never been properly metalled. Even with the strength of the car Callum was driving, he had to slow down to negotiate some of the bigger potholes and ridges of semi-solid mud. This gave Robbie more time to tail him than there would have been on a normal road, though he had to go slowly himself, with the danger of slipping and sliding on the barely dry surface.

At a fork in the road, Callum surprised Robbie by taking the left-hand route, rather than the way that led down to the village. This road went round and up, curving further up the hillside into the darkness. Where was he going?

As the hill became steeper, Robbie fell back. The car's steady strength kept it climbing while Robbie began to feel the strain of running uphill through difficult terrain in shoes not designed for much more than an amble round a shopping mall.

Shit, I'm going to lose him, he thought, furious. His heart was pounding with the exertion and his lungs were hot in his chest. But he had no choice. He had to keep going.

The car disappeared round a bend in the road. Robbie wanted to take a short cut, avoiding the curve, but it was almost pitch black up here and he simply couldn't see well enough to find his way. He'd have to stick to the road and hope that Callum wasn't going too far away.

He'd been climbing for about twenty minutes when he saw a dark shape rising up to meet him. In the cold starlight he could just about see that the four-by-four was now parked by what looked like a building site, though it was hard to make out exactly what it was in this darkness. He could also hear the murmur of voices floating up to meet him. Cautiously, he approached, following the sound. As he got close, the sounds resolved into words.

'God, you stink, old man!' he heard Callum say.

His stomach flipped nervously.

'Where are you taking me?' came a weak voice.

'None of your business. Now let's get going.'

'I can't walk,' was the reply.

'I've untied your legs – what more do you want?'

'I'm too weak. I've no eaten for a day and a half. Gimme some water, Callum ... please?'

Callum thought for a moment. 'There's no point,' he said roughly.

'C'mon ... a dying man is allowed a last request, isn't he? Ye wouldn't let me die without givin' me the small mercy of a bit of water, would ye?'

There was another pause and then Callum said, 'Ah, all right. I've got a bottle in the car. Wait here.'

Robbie dropped to the ground and lay still as Callum crunched past him along a path of gravel that had been laid no doubt to help the workmen on the site. Adrenalin was coursing through him and a wild excitement filled him, making his ears roar. He knew absolutely that he had just heard the voice of his father, for the first time in his memory.

He's alive! Robbie hadn't realised until then that he had begun to accept that his father was dead and that he would never see him again. Perhaps, in a way, that was easier to contemplate than his father living and their having a chance to meet.

What shall I do? He fought with himself, trying to keep calm and restrain the impulse to jump up and rush over. Callum had a gun, he was sure of that. And he'd sensed at dinner tonight a madness in the younger man that had put him on edge, making every sense alert. If danger were coming from any direction, it was this one.

Callum was illuminated as he opened the car door and the interior light came on. He had a strange hungry look on his face, as though he couldn't wait for whatever he was about to do. He found what he wanted, shut the door and crunched back to where he had come from.

'Here you are.'

Robbie heard the old man drinking gratefully. 'Now walk.'

'I'll do my best, Callum, but I'm no strong.'

'Come *on*,' said Callum brusquely as he hauled the man to his feet. 'We've got to get a move on. Ah, shit, it's no good. I'll have to take you in the car. You'll take fuckin' hours to get down the hill. I'll put some sheeting in first.'

So he doesn't leave any evidence in it, thought Robbie, chilled. It was obvious that Callum intended to kill Hamish. But when and how? He wanted to get down the hill first – where were they going? The not knowing was agonising – how could he guess when to act? If he revealed himself at the wrong time, it was likely that he and his father would both be killed – the worst possible outcome.

How did I get here? wondered Robbie, suddenly feeling removed from himself. He saw himself lying face down in the mud on a cold Scottish hillside in the middle of the night, while a homicidal maniac pointed a gun at his father. Could this really be happening? I want it to be over!

Then he realised that there was more movement. Callum went back to his car with a piece of sheeting he must have found on the site, and then returned to the building. He emerged a few moments later, now half dragging a hunched figure that stumbled along next to him, clearly weak and hampered by being tied up around his arms.

His father. That pathetic silhouette stumbling to his death. Hamish Fraser, his father.

'You stink of pish!' grumbled Callum.

'You didnae give me much option, boy. I've been tied up there for days. What did you expect?'

'Disgusting,' said Callum, ignoring the question. 'I'm gonna have to clean my car after this, that's for sure.'

He bundled the old man into the back seat of the four-by-four, climbed into the driver's seat, started the engine and reversed round until he was facing the way he had come. He switched on the headlights which he had left off on the journey up. Then the car set off, bumping back down the path towards the village.

Panic gave Robbie a speed that overcame his tiredness from the journey up. He ran as fast he could, cutting away from the road and over the hillside, trying to keep track of the headlights as he went. Occasionally he tripped and fell, rolling over into swathes of heather, or tumbling over a hillock. Once he stumbled into a patch of gorse but while he was aware of the scratches he received, they didn't hurt. Adrenalin was forcing him onward, helping him to ignore the breathlessness and shooting pain in his side.

Don't let him kill him before I get there! he prayed. Please, oh please. Let him be alive.

To his despair, as he got further down the hillside, he realised he had lost sight of the pinprick headlights that gave away Callum's position. He looked frantically for the car, scanning the area, trying to trace the road through the village. Then, just as he was on the brink of sobbing with frustration and despair, he saw a light come on almost immediately below him. It came from a warehouse-style building that stood a little way over the harbour.

That's where they must be. He set off again with fresh determination. He should be there in just a few minutes.

When he reached the side of the warehouse, he

had to take a few moments to get his breath back. His panting sounded so loud, it would give him away if he wasn't careful.

Calm, be calm, he told himself. Just then, his mobile twitched in his pocket. He took it out and saw it was a text from Heather. *Are you OK?*

He replied quickly. *Hamish alive. At warehouse. Call police.* He pushed 'Send'. The little outgoing envelope appeared on the screen, turning and turning to show that sending was in progress. Then the screen suddenly flickered off.

Shit! What was wrong with it? He tried to switch it back on again. It was dead. The battery had run completely down. He cursed himself for not charging it up earlier – he hadn't done it since he'd left London. It was a miracle it hadn't died before now. Had Heather got the message? Would she be able to call the police? He'd have to assume that she didn't get it – and he didn't know how far away the nearest police station was, anyway. It might be miles. He had to act right now if he was going to save his father.

I'll have to take on Callum alone, he realised, fear crawling over his skin. Can I do it? I've got to, or my dad will die. I can't have come this far just to lose him again now.

He skirted the building until he came to a door where the four-by-four was parked. They were inside, that was certain. The only thing to do was try and slip in after them.

Pushing the door, he found it was unlocked. When it was far enough ajar, he put his head carefully round it, trying to locate Callum as quickly as he could. He soon pinpointed him – he was standing on the far left of the warehouse by an open door that seemed to lead into a storage unit of some kind. There was no sign of Hamish.

Gathering up his courage, Robbie darted into the warehouse and pressed himself against the shadows by the wall on the other side to where Callum was. Then he edged along, trying to see what was going on around the processing machinery that stood between them. Callum's voice floated over in the stillness, echoing in the empty building.

'Hey, do you know the humane way to kill a lobster, old man? You put it in the freezer until it goes to sleep – then you can kill it with a sharp knife or drop it into boiling water and it'll never know what happened. Well, that's what I'm going to do, you see? It's a brilliant idea, I don't know why people haven't done it before now. Everything slows right down and gradually the cold takes over and you pass out and eventually you die. Nice and clean, no mess, no bullets, no pain. See what I'm like, Hamish? I'm a kind guy at heart.' Callum reached over and grabbed something, Robbie couldn't see clearly what it was. 'The only thing is, I need to speed the process up a bit, so it's going to be a bit less comfortable for you. Sorry about that – really, I mean it.'

There was a hissing noise that grew louder and louder, accompanied by a splattering of water.

He's turned a hose on him! Robbie realised, horrified. That must be a freezing unit. He's going to shut him in there, covered in cold water!

It wasn't difficult to see that an old man already weakened by three days of imprisonment inside a cold wet building site, with no food, was not going to be able to withstand the cold for very long. If the temperature dropped quickly and his clothes were icy to begin with, he might have as little as ten minutes... Robbie had even heard that in the North Sea, hypothermia and a slide into unconsciousness was possible after three minutes.

There was no sound from inside the refrigeration unit.

Fury rushed through Robbie, crushing his fear. What kind of a man could do such a thing? His head buzzed with hatred and anger. What should he do now?

Callum turned off the hose and slammed shut the door to the cold store, then twiddled with the thermostat, taking the temperature down to its lowest. Then, humming to himself, he checked his watch and ambled towards the back of the warehouse, where Robbie could see there was an office. No doubt he was going to pass the time there while Hamish sank into unconsciousness in the bitter cold.

He was a madman, a cold and callous psychopath. It was the only explanation.

Robbie thought fast. He had a window of a few minutes to get across the warehouse unseen, open the door of the unit, get Hamish out – weak as he was, that would be difficult – and out of the door. All without Callum noticing a thing. It was virtually impossible. And once he got him outside, what then? They wouldn't have a hope of getting very far before Callum clocked that Hamish was gone. They didn't even have a car.

No, that was a stupid plan. He had to get the time he needed to free Hamish. He had to deal with Callum. Could he? Did he have the strength? He'd never been in a proper fight before, just the odd drunken ruckus when he was younger. What a time to find out if he was up to it...

Chapter Forty-seven

Heather's phone beeped. She picked it up and read the text from Robbie.

Hamish alive. At warehouse. Call police.

Elation rushed through her, along with a sense of huge relief. Hamish was alive, fantastic news. And Callum and her father were not guilty of murder, after all. She hadn't realised how desperately she had hated the idea that they were killers until now. It had been horrible and unreal, but perhaps there had just been some terrible misunderstanding that was now being cleared up.

She looked at her mother, who was still lying on her sofa. 'Mum! It's Hamish! He's OK!'

Her mother half sat up. 'Really?' She shut her eyes and fell back. 'Oh, thank you, thank you. Oh...'

Heather put down her phone and took hold of her mother's hand. 'Are you all right?'

'I'm ... I've never talked about these things before. It's deeply upsetting for me. I have to look at things I've shut away from myself for many years. I've coped only by not thinking about them, by ignoring them. Telling you about them has drained me more than I could have guessed it would.'

'But, Mum, I'm so glad you did. Do you think I'm angry with you? I'm not – I'm happy. At last I know why Dad – the man I thought was my dad – hated me so much all those years. Because he must have known at some level that I wasn't his daughter and that Hamish was my real father.'

'But I don't know how he found out,' Mary said weakly, frowning. 'Hamish and I were only together once, and he had no way of knowing.

'He must have guessed intuitively.' Heather smiled at her. 'I'm so pleased that Hamish and I had those hours together through my childhood – we already have a bond, you see. He's been more of a father to me than that man has, and now I know for sure that he's my real dad. And I've got a brother too... I'm delighted.' She stood up. 'But now I have to call the police. Robbie's told me to send them to the warehouse.'

Suddenly the door burst open and her father stood there, his eyes burning with fury.

'There you are, you little bitch!' he snarled, advancing into the room towards Heather. 'It was you, wasn't it?'

Panic tightened in Heather's chest and she backed away. 'What are you talking about?' she said, trying to sound brave, but her reaction, as it had been since childhood, in the face of her father's fury was to shake and feel tears sting her eyes, much as she wanted to keep her composure.

'You know what I'm talking about,' he said, his voice low and vicious. 'You were in my study. You went through my files. You nosed around there, didn't you? What have you been telling your mother? Telling her all the little secrets you dug up?'

'I don't know what you mean,' she said stoutly.

Mary pushed herself up on the sofa. 'Mc-Bain...' she said weakly.

He turned towards her. 'Shut up! You shut up, you whore. You lost the right to say anything to me years ago, when you foisted this little bastard on me.'

'Leave her alone!' cried Heather.

'With pleasure,' sneered McBain. 'She's no use to anyone now, anyway, just a dried-up old crone no one wants. I only put up with her because she keeps the house clean and cooks for me. Besides, I like watching her pining away, being endlessly punished for her sins.'

'Her mistakes, you mean. Her mistake was marrying you.'

'That's probably right,' he said, with a nasty smile. 'But she did, you see. She did marry me, from her own free will. And everything that's happened since then is a result of her behaviour, her dirty, filthy behaviour. And you ... like mother, like daughter! You even gave yourselves away in just the same way.' McBain held up a small yellowed piece of twine that sagged between his fingers.

'What's that?' asked Heather.

A small moan escaped from Mary.

'Yes – you know what it is, don't you, Mary? Tell Heather. Go on.'

'It's...' Mary licked her dry lips. 'It's one of

Hamish's knots of twine. He always made them. The order the knots went in meant different things – sometimes it meant good luck, sometimes it was supposed to bring the fish, or fair weather. It's a little token.'

'That's right.' McBain turned back to Heather. 'I just found this on the floor of my office. It must have fallen out from a file, a private file I kept in my cabinet. And I think that the same person who dropped it there, read the file and contacted Robbie Fraser. That person is a scummy little bitch traitor, just like her mother.'

Mary gasped. 'You mean...'

'That's right.' McBain's hand was shaking, the little piece of twine gripped between his fingers. 'I found this nearly thirty years ago. It was in a bed in this very house. The cover was neat and tidy, but underneath it the sheets were rumpled and damp and in one of the wrinkles was this, a sign of who had been there. And a month or two later, my wife told me the glad news that she was expecting a baby.' He laughed, a nasty, rasping sound. 'I was supposed to be happy about this, happy that she'd let that bastard Fraser in our house, let him push himself inside her and put his child into her body.'

Mary turned away, burying her face in a cushion. A muffled sob escaped her.

'Yes,' he said to her, his voice almost breaking. 'I always knew. I always knew that you loved him best, that you'd let yourself enjoy him the way you never enjoyed me. I revolted you, I knew that. You hated me touching you. You were a woman of ice in bed with me, when I'd expected a woman of fire and passion. The only way to make you react to me was to–'

'Stop!' cried Mary, turning back to him, holding up a hand. 'Not in front of the girl! Please, not in front of her! Don't say it!'

Heather closed her eyes and put her hands over her ears. She could no longer hold back her tears.

'The only way was to force you to notice me!' McBain walked towards the woman on the sofa. 'I had to make you say something, even if it was a shriek of pain. And after you had had your way with Hamish – after you'd rolled together in our bed, in our home – well, you had to be punished. And so did he.'

'You did it, didn't you?' Heather said in a shaking voice. 'You made Louise leave him and take Robbie with her. You did it.'

'Yes, I did.' He spoke with a quiet triumph. 'It was the most thorough act of revenge I could think of. He took so much from me. I could never enjoy a minute of your childhood, Heather, because I knew what you really were. My wife didn't love me. My daughter was not my own. Why should Hamish enjoy what I couldn't have, what he'd stolen from me? I watched that boy of his growing up and I hated the way he was able to love his son. I saw how Louise worshipped the ground he walked on – just like every woman he met. Why should he have all that, and I have nothing?'

'But you had so much!' whispered Mary.

'Money, aye. My business ... but no one knew about the way my wife loathed me putting my fingers on her skin, or the fact that the child I

478

clothed and fed wasn't my own. One day I couldn't take it any more. I wasn't going to let Fraser get away with it, I was going to destroy his life the way he'd destroyed mine. I'd seen him on the beach that day, playing with his son. They were laughing together – Robbie was giggling – and then Hamish gave him a hug that I'd never be able to give my own child. That night, when Hamish was out fishing, I went to Louise and I told her everything. Very carefully, I killed her love for her husband and turned it into implacable hatred. She loved him so much, you see, and she was such a desperate little thing. Life had to be perfect for her, or she couldn't stand it. Once I explained to her that her husband really loved someone else and always had, and that my daughter, younger than her own boy, was his child, her world collapsed and it was beyond repair. She wanted to go – she said she couldn't bear to be with Hamish for a second longer – and I said that if she went and took Robbie with her and never came back, I'd make sure she was looked after. I'd give her money and help her. And she left the same day. I watched her go – she took the little boy, he was crying, and left the cottage with just a suitcase. Hamish was shouting and begging to know where she was going, but she wouldn't say a word to him. Then she put herself and the child on the bus to Inverness and she was gone and never came back. To know that Hamish was feeling just one tenth of the pain he made me feel was worth it, believe me.' He turned back to his wife. 'So you see? You destroyed my life and Louise's life. That's what

479

your whoredom did.'

'No!' shouted Heather. 'That's what *you* did. You're the one who did all the destroying around here! You've ruined Mum's life, my life, Hamish's life and Robbie's life. But you know what – you've ruined your own worst of all!'

McBain snarled at her, stepped forward and whacked her hard across the face. The pain swept over her head and down her body as she stumbled backwards. He advanced towards her, his fist clenched and drawn back for a punch, but she scrambled away over a pile of sewing.

'Leave her alone!' screamed Mary, leaping up. She ran to her husband and grabbed at his shoulders, trying to hold back his arms. He spun round and let his fist fly at her instead. It hit her cheekbone with a crunch and her head flew back as she shrieked.

'Stop it! Stop it!' cried Heather. 'I'm calling the police!' She held her mobile phone. 'Keep away from her.'

McBain paused at the mention of the police. 'Put the phone down, Heather.'

'No,' she said. She looked over at her mother, who was clutching at the side of her face. 'I think you've broken her cheekbone. I'm calling an ambulance.'

'You're not calling anyone!' McBain advanced on her again. 'This is private business.'

'You can't order me around. You're not even my father.'

'That's why I want you out of my house, tonight. I never want to see you again.'

'Fine with me. But Mum's coming with me.'

'No. No way. She stays here.'

'You go, Heather,' urged her mother, speaking stiffly through the pain in her face. 'Go. I'll be fine.'

'Piss off, you little bastard,' said McBain. 'If I see you this side of eternity, it'll be too soon.'

Heather looked at him for a moment and then at her mother. She understood the pleading in her mother's eyes and she knew what she would do. 'All right,' she said. 'My pleasure. I'll go right now.'

Chapter Forty-eight

Robbie crept up towards the office. He had to move fast. The temperature in the refrigeration unit would be dropping by the second.

As he got closer, he could hear Callum mumbling to himself, a series of disjointed words and half-sentences. There were some tapping sounds and then a long sniff. So that was how it was – Callum liked a bit of charlie. Quite a lot, from the sound of him. Well, that gave Robbie an advantage. He was lucid, while Callum was high.

What am I going to do? Robbie wondered. Whack him over the head with something? He's got a gun. Whatever I do, I'll have to do it fast. He started to look around for a weapon.

'Hey, it's the old man's mobile,' he heard Callum say to himself. He cautiously put his head round the door, keeping low. Callum was

481

turning the mobile over in his hand. 'I'll have to get rid of it,' he muttered. 'Put it back in his pocket maybe. That'd be easiest. Why does he have a mobile anyway? Who's he got to call?' Callum pressed the on button, and the phone chirruped as it came to life. Then it beeped several times in quick succession. 'Three missed calls,' Callum read. 'Who's been ringing you, Hamish, eh? Let's find out.' There was a pause and then he said slowly, 'Heather. Well, well. Why would she be ringing you? Maybe I'd better go and wake you up and find out.' Then he laughed. 'Who'm I trying to kid? It makes sense. There had to be someone giving you information. So now I know. Poor Heather! She's got no fuckin' idea what kind of trouble she's got herself in.'

Shit! thought Robbie. I've got to do something. He saw a broom leaning up against the far wall and scuttled towards it. He'd just reached for it when he heard the sound of a gun cocking and a voice saying, 'Well, hello! Our dinner guest has dropped by.'

He looked round to see Callum lolling against the doorway, a gun in his hand that he was pointing almost lazily straight at Robbie's chest.

'Robbie,' he said casually, 'it feels like we only just said goodnight. You know, in some circles it's not considered polite to spy on your hosts.'

'It's not exactly done in court circles to murder old men and plan violence against your sister.'

'Oh really? I thought that was the kind of thing they got up to all the time. Makes no difference. We do things the way we want to in Scotland, so you English bastards can fuck off.'

482

'I take it murder is illegal in Scotland.' Robbie was desperate to seem calm. I'll try and keep him talking, he thought, while I work out what to do next.

Callum shrugged. 'Aye. But who've I murdered, eh?'

'What about Hamish? He's freezing to death in that fridge over there.'

'Oh. You saw that, did you?' Callum made an exasperated face. 'Ah, shite. Why'd you have to go and be so nosy? I'm gonna have to think about what to do with you now. Although,' his face cleared, 'maybe I could put you two in together. Ah, that'd be quite sweet, wouldn't it? Father and son, united in their final hours. Just time for a tearful reconciliation before...' Callum made a slashing gesture across his throat. 'Whoops!'

'Listen, Callum, don't do anything stupid,' Robbie said urgently.

Callum laughed. 'I don't think so. No, sorry, pal. You've made it very easy for me. No one knows you're here. You told us at dinner, no one knows you're even in Kinlochvegan except for the locals, and they'll just think you've fucked off back to where you came from.'

'Heather knows. She knows where I am and what I'm doing.'

'Yeah, well, don't worry, she'll get what's coming to her all in good time. I know how to handle her and so does my dad.'

'You can't just kill everyone who gets in your way, Callum!' Robbie said desperately. 'You're going to get caught sooner or later. Let's be sensible about this.' He felt like he was saying all the lines that the guys in the movies said just before they had their heads blown off.

'I can't kill everyone, you're right. But the great thing is, I can kill you and be pretty sure I'm gonna get away with it. Think of yourself as target practice, if you like!' Callum grinned, and Robbie noticed how white and even his teeth were. He was quite a good-looking man, if you liked that intense, dramatic look.

Move, he told himself. Move.

In an instant he made his decision and launched himself at Callum's legs, rolling against them as hard as he could. Callum immediately fired the gun but he had already lost his balance and released the shot as his arm flew upward. The bullet whistled harmlessly up towards the roof.

Callum fell back against the doorway, groaning with pain as the door frame caught him between the shoulder blades. Robbie scrambled to his feet and darted away. He found a metal staircase on the other side of the office and started up it, two steps at a time, his feet ringing out on the metal, aware of his vulnerable back and expecting to feel the thud of a bullet in his spine at any moment. He flew up faster than he would ever have imagined he could climb a flight of stairs and reached the metal balcony at the top. It appeared to skirt the entire warehouse and he dashed along it for a few feet, staying close to the wall. Below, Callum had found his feet and was pointing the gun upward into the gloom towards Robbie.

'You can't get away!' he called. 'You might as well give in, you know!' He swung the gun around into the darkness in the roof. Robbie pressed himself back into the shadows. 'All right, if you won't come down, I guess I'll have to come up.' He went to the staircase and started to climb, his steps resounding dully on the metal.

Robbie looked about for a means of escape. The only thing to do was to keep moving, but eventually, surely, Callum would get him. Shit.

With no other option, he carried on edging round in the darkness as Callum reached the top of the staircase and squinted into the darkness.

He laughed suddenly. 'I can see you!' he yelled and fired off a shot in Robbie's direction. Robbie ducked and heard it ricochet off a metal strut a few feet to his right. Callum had missed by quite a way. Perhaps he was bluffing and couldn't really see where Robbie was at all.

Staying low, Robbie scuttled along the balcony. Below him was the plant machinery, some kind of processing facility, he guessed. At the far end of the warehouse opposite the cold stores were three great vats reaching up almost to the balcony. What was in them? he wondered. Was there any way he could jump down onto them and use them to get down to ground level? He wasn't sure he'd be able to make it back round to the staircase and if he did, he'd be a clear, easy target as he went down it.

'It's like a rat in a drainpipe!' bellowed Callum, as he gained on Robbie. He was thudding round the metal walkway after him, able to move much faster without the necessity of keeping himself as concealed as possible. He let another bullet fly and again it whistled harmlessly past.

485

Perhaps he'll run out of ammunition, thought Robbie. Shit, I know nothing about guns! The closest he'd come to shooting anything was on his PlayStation.

He was above the vats now. He looked down. They were half full of water and immersed in each one was a trawler engine. This must be some system of cleaning them. Could he jump down? No – it would be stupid. The engines almost filled the diameter of the vats and if he missed and fell in, landing on them would be a nasty business.

His only hope was to make it back to the staircase and get down it before Callum could take a shot. Or... He looked upward. Callum was striding along towards him from the far end of the balcony. He knew that the part he was standing in was in shadow and that the other man was unlikely to be able to see him. He spun round, grabbed a steel strut attached to the wall and pulled himself upward into the framework of metal joists that criss-crossed the roof of the warehouse. Christ, he hoped this worked or there was no doubt about it, he was a dead man.

Callum slowed down as he approached, wary as he realised that he had seen Robbie disappear into this area but not emerge. He stopped when he was above the vats and, as Robbie had, he looked down into them. From Robbie's viewpoint, he could see the top of Callum's head and the shaft of the gun as it moved about. His heart was pounding and his hands were so slippery with sweat that he feared at any minute he'd slip and fall before he was ready.

Callum glanced warily about and then, as Robbie prepared himself, he began to lift his head to look up into the roof.

I must get the right moment! thought Robbie in panic, and readied himself to leap down.

Just then there was the noise of the warehouse door slamming. Callum reacted at once, gazing down onto the floor below, his gun at the ready. Robbie squinted and tried to make out who it was. If it was one of Callum's cohorts, then it was as good as over. He couldn't deal with two of them.

Then, to his horror, he saw Heather walking carefully down the middle of the warehouse floor. She was looking about her, alert. 'Robbie!' she called softly. 'Are you here?'

Robbie saw the black barrel of the gun clearly as Callum aimed it at Heather's head as she walked obliviously towards him.

'Heather, duck!' Robbie yelled at the top of his voice and then jumped.

Heather gasped and threw herself behind some plant machinery as Callum spun round to find Robbie just as he landed on top of him.

This is it, Robbie thought clearly and then the rest was a blur as he and Callum were locked into a desperate wrestling match. Robbie's advantage of surprise was gone almost immediately and it was obvious that Callum was much stronger than he was, with the advantage of his fisherman's muscles. Robbie went for the gun but Callum had it clenched tight in his fist and was trying to manoeuvre it towards Robbie's head. They rolled and twisted together, their faces clenched in desperation and pain as each used all his force on the other. They slid towards the edge of the balcony and Robbie found himself with his head, shoulder and chest protruding out over one of the seawater-filled vats, his wrists held tight by Callum, whose bared teeth were only inches away from his face.

With all his strength and some extra that came from somewhere he didn't know existed, Robbie heaved himself over, taking the other man with him. Grasping the wrist of the hand Callum held the gun in, Robbie smashed it against the sharp edge of the balcony. Callum growled in pain but Robbie continued pounding until the gun flew from Callum's grasp. It somersaulted through the air and landed on the long slim casing of a fluorescent light that was suspended from the roof and hung down almost on a level with the balcony but a few feet away. The gun skittered along the light and came to a halt, balanced precariously on the edge over the vat below.

'Argh! Fuck!' shouted Callum, rolling forward to see where his weapon had landed. As he moved he pulled Robbie with him, and their combined weight began to take them too far over the edge of the balcony floor.

Robbie struggled with him, trying to get a purchase on something to stop them both sliding forward, but Callum seemed unable to recognise the danger they were in as he strained over, reaching out towards the gun although there was no hope he would be able to get it from this position.

'Leave it, Callum!' shouted Robbie. 'You're

taking us both down!'

But Callum merely grunted as he stretched out his arm, his fingertips trembling with the effort to reach the gun that lay only tantalising inches away.

'Callum, stop!' They were almost at the point of no return.

Robbie suddenly wrenched one arm free of Callum, kicked away with his feet and felt himself begin to topple over the side. As he went, he threw his free arm up and over the lower railing on the metal balustrade that edged the balcony, and a second later he was swinging over the vat, hanging from the railing that was caught in the crook of his elbow. As if in slow motion, he saw Callum, now without the extra anchor of Robbie's weight, fly forward and over the edge of the balcony with a shout. He fell head first, turning in the air as he went so that he landed in the vat on his back.

Robbie stared down. Callum was utterly still, his eyes and mouth open wide with surprise. The dark water had a darker cloud spreading out within it. A great piece of the trawler engine jutted out of Callum's chest like a fin where he had been impaled upon it.

Chapter Forty-nine

Robbie swung himself back and pulled himself up onto the balcony floor, where he lay staring upward. Shock began to grip his body, making him shake. He heard Heather race down the warehouse and come up the stairs to him.

She knelt down next to him. 'Robbie – are you OK?'

'Callum?' Robbie said in a strained voice.

Heather looked over the edge into the vat and then back at him, her eyes wide and her face pale. She shook her head. 'There was nothing you could do,' she whispered, seeing Robbie's expression. Then she frowned and said, 'Where's Hamish?'

'Oh fuck.' Robbie rolled over and got up on his feet. 'C'mon – he's in the freezer. Christ, I hope we're in time.'

They ran down to the cold store and wrenched the door open. An icy blast of air came out to meet them. Hamish was lying on the floor, tightly wrapped up into a foetal position and not moving.

'Hamish!' cried Heather, and they rushed over to him. He was ice-cold to the touch and his lips were rimmed in blue. His eyes were shut and his hair was stiff with frost.

'We're too late!' Robbie said, agonised. 'He must be dead.'

Heather was checking for a pulse. 'No, no, he's

490

not dead. There's something flickering in there. Everything's slowed right down but we must get him out of here, get him warm. Come on, I've got the car outside. We'll take him back to Lachlan Cottage. I called the police on the way down here – they're coming as soon as they can but they've got a way to go. I'll phone and let them know where we are and get an ambulance sent too. We'll keep him warm till they get here.'

Together they managed to carry Hamish out of the cold store and through the warehouse, though it hurt to hold him, his clothes and body were so chilled. Once they were in the car, with Hamish safely in the back, Heather fired up the engine and they roared away, heading for Lachlan Cottage.

'I don't understand why Callum didn't kill me,' Robbie said, a strange elation filling him as he realised that he was still alive after the death struggle. 'He had a gun, he shot at me several times but he always missed.'

Heather laughed grimly. 'You know what, Robbie? I doubt the idiot had ever fired a gun before in his life.'

Back at the cottage, they did all they could to warm Hamish up, stripping the wet clothes off his unconscious body and wrapping him in blankets. They put him in front of the fire and Heather filled hot-water bottles which she wrapped in pillowcases and put on top of the blankets. The frost in his hair melted and the blue around his lips began to diminish.

'What am I going to tell them?' Robbie whispered as they sat together next to Hamish's sleeping body. 'I've killed a man.'

'You did not kill him,' Heather said firmly. 'It was an accident. But you'd have had every right to kill him – he was trying to murder you.'

'Oh Heather...' He gazed into her blue eyes. A strange thrill went over him as he looked into her face. Was it only this morning they had met? They'd been through a lifetime together since then. He leaned towards her, putting his hand out to stroke her face. 'Heather,' he said huskily, suddenly full of desire to kiss her.

She put her hand up and stopped him. 'No, Robbie.'

He pulled away, embarrassed. 'Of course you wouldn't want to kiss me,' he mumbled. 'I've killed your brother – or, at least, he's dead because of me.'

'No.'

'No?' Robbie was confused. Callum was most certainly dead.

'No, you haven't killed my brother. Callum wasn't my brother. And the reason you can't kiss me is that my brother is ... *you*.'

'What?' Robbie could hardly take in what she had just said.

Heather nodded. 'Hamish is my father. That's why McBain hates me. My mother told me everything.' Suddenly her face changed and her hands flew to her mouth. 'Oh God, I forgot! I've left my mother alone with him!' She quickly told Robbie what had happened, and how her father had thrown her out in a fit of rage and that Mary's infidelity was at last out in the open between them.

'What if he kills her?' Her eyes were frightened. 'Oh God, I've got to help her. I've got to go there now.'

'I'll go,' Robbie said, determined. 'If you go, it'll make things worse. Listen – stay here with Hamish. When the police get here, send them up to the house first, OK?'

'I don't want you to go,' Heather whispered.

'We can't leave your mother alone with him.' She nodded. 'Be careful.'

'I will.'

Robbie took Heather's car, racing through the village as quickly as he could and up the hill to the McBain house. He pushed open the front door. All was in silence.

He padded quietly along the hall and into the sitting room. It took a moment for his eyes to adjust to the gloom, then he made out the figure of McBain sitting in the armchair by the fire staring out into the darkness.

Robbie stood there, uncertain of what to do or what to say. He was about to ask where Mary was when McBain spoke.

'Robbie Fraser. So you've come back. What have you got to tell me, eh? What's happened?' The voice was eerily calm.

'I've come to make sure Mary's all right. Where is she?'

'Asleep.' McBain laughed hollowly at Robbie's expression. 'Oh don't worry, I haven't killed her. She really is asleep. She's taken some pills or something, for the pain in her cheek, she said.'

'Where is she? I want to check on her.'

'Down the hall – but first, tell me about Hamish. Is he dead? Has Callum killed him?'

The calm manner in which they were discussing these things was bizarre, Robbie thought. There was a resignation and a serenity about McBain that was curious to witness.

'No. Hamish is alive. The ambulance is on its way to him. I think he'll pull through if they get to him in time.'

'Ah.' McBain let out a huge sigh. 'Then it really is all over. Everything I've achieved in my life is finished. Callum will go to jail and very likely I'll go with him...'

Robbie said softly, 'Callum is dead. I'm sorry.'

The old man sat in silence for a moment. 'He was marked for it, that boy. Right from the start, I always knew that he was set for some violent end, that he'd die young. Maybe that was why I loved him so much – I always felt our time would be short. My only son.' He looked up at Robbie and smiled. 'Well – it won't be long now. Was it quick?'

Robbie nodded.

'Good. I wouldn't want him to suffer.'

The telephone rang suddenly and Robbie went and picked it up. 'Yes?'

'Robbie, is that you? What's happening?' Heather's voice sounded tight and strained.

'It's all quiet here.'

'How's Mum? Is she OK?'

'Your father says she's asleep. I'm just going to check on her now. Have the police arrived?'

'I think I can hear them now. Call me back when you've made sure Mum's OK.'

494

'Will do.' He put the phone down. 'Where's Mary's room exactly?'

'Her sewing room – it's third on the left. She'll be fine, Robbie. Will you no join me in a drink?' McBain held up a bottle of whisky and a glass that he'd clearly been swigging from. Now that Robbie thought of it, the old man's voice was slurring and his eyelids drooping. He'd been drowning his sorrows, it seemed.

Robbie ignored him and went along the hall until he came to Mary's sewing room. Mary was huddled on the sofa. He went in.

'Mary, Mary, wake up!' He shook her. She groaned and shifted but stayed firmly asleep. He saw that two white pill bottles sat on the table beside the sofa, both empty. 'Christ, how many have you taken? Mary! Mary!'

He tried to rouse her but she would not wake, her head lolling over to one side, showing a massive bruise spreading up over her jaw. He pulled her down onto the floor and put her in the recovery position so that if she was sick she would not choke. Then he went back to the sitting room where McBain was still in the armchair, slumped a little to one side.

'Where's Heather's mobile number?' he asked urgently.

'It's programmed into the phone,' McBain said slowly. 'Number three, I think.'

Robbie was trying to work out how the speed dial function operated when the phone rang suddenly under his hand. He answered it.

'Heather, thank God it's you,' he said with relief. 'Listen, I think your mum's taken an over-

495

dose of sleeping pills.'

'What?' Panic filled her voice.

'Where are the police?'

'There's an officer here. The others have gone to the warehouse.'

'OK. When the ambulance crew have finished with Dad, send them here as soon as you can – and send the police officer up with them. I've put her in the recovery position.'

'Oh no!' wailed Heather.

'Don't lose it now,' he said firmly. 'I'm sure we've got to her in time.'

'Yes... I'll see you in a minute,' she said. 'I'm coming up now. Robbie – you won't let her die, will you?'

'I'll do whatever I can.'

Heather rang off.

McBain was watching him, the glass of whisky tight in his hand. His eyes glinted as though they were full of tears.

'D'you know what she said to me, Robbie?' he said, his voice slurring. 'She said – she said that we'd had a chance, that she had loved me once, way back when she agreed to marry me. She said that over the years I had killed that love, but that she would never leave me. She said she was mine for ever and I was hers. Can you imagine that? After everything I've done to her. It was me who stopped her and Hamish from being together. It was me that punished her daughter for the mother's sins, never telling her why. If you could have seen Heather as a girl, and the torment I put them both through. But I felt it was only fair, that it was to equal my own. Ah, Robbie! I've done wrong by you too. It was me that made sure your mother left here and never came back. It was me that took your dad from you. It was me that killed Callum, too, sure as anything.'

'Did you really make my mother leave here?'

'Oh yes. One thing I've always known is how to hurt people, how to break their hearts. I even took a pleasure in it. Louise had such happy eyes – a soft grey like rainclouds – until I told her what her husband and my wife had been up to together. She'd have gone even if I hadn't offered her the money, but I felt sorry for her. And if she took the money then I could afford to impose a few conditions to make sure my revenge was complete. No contact with Hamish. No return visits. No letters from him to you or vice versa.'

Robbie sank onto the sofa, his head dropping down. 'Do you know what you took away from me?' he said, his voice cracking.

'Not really, no. My father was a bastard. He died a few years back and I didn't give a damn for him. That's what fathers have always been like to me.'

'But you tried with Callum...'

'Look what I did to Callum! I failed him. Now he's dead, my poor, poor boy.' McBain whimpered and his shoulders shook.

Robbie was untouched by his grief. Instead he stared at his hands, and the two of them sat in silence until it seemed from the heavy breathing coming from McBain that he had fallen into a deep, whisky-fuelled sleep.

There was a noise in the doorway and Robbie looked up. Heather was standing there, panting slightly. She had clearly run all the way from Lachlan Cottage.

'Dad?' she said softly. He didn't reply and she said more loudly, 'Dad!'

He stirred.

She went over to him and shook him. 'Dad, look at me.'

McBain opened his eyes and squinted up into the gloom. 'Ah, wee Heather.'

'Where's Mum?'

'She's out cold, Heather,' Robbie said, his voice as gentle as he could make it. 'There's nothing we can do until the ambulance gets here. How's my dad?'

'Hamish is much better. In fact, he regained consciousness not long after you left. That's why I need to talk to Mum and Dad.'

'You'd better not call me that, lass,' McBain said, his speech increasingly slurred. 'I'm no your daddy.'

'Yes. Yes you are.'

McBain stared at her.

'Hamish just told me something very interesting, you see. When I tried to tell him that he was my natural father, he wasn't having any of it. He told me that after Robbie was born he had a severe attack of mumps, and when he and Louise tried to have another baby with no success, they were both tested and it turned out that he couldn't have any more children. Don't you see? He's always known I wasn't his. He never knew that Mary thought I was his child.' Heather's eyes filled with tears. 'So ... all along ... I really was your daughter.'

McBain groaned, a terrible and pitiful sound.

'No – it can't be true.'

'It is,' Heather said simply. 'Hamish is absolutely sure.'

McBain moaned again and slumped forward in the chair.

Robbie put his hand on Heather's arm. 'Are you OK?'

'Yes ... yes. I'll be fine.' She smiled a crooked smile at Robbie, one that showed how near she was to breaking down. 'I knew it was too good to be true. I always dreamed that Hamish was really my father. I suppose it was inevitable that it would be just a dream.'

There was the sound of a siren as the ambulance pulled up outside. Robbie rushed to the door and opened it. Two paramedics ran in, followed by a police officer.

'Where's the casualty?' shouted one.

'Follow me,' said Heather and they all raced down the hall to the sewing room. The paramedics were instantly busy, preparing an adrenalin injection and turning Mary over. The police officer began to scribble into a notebook and say, 'Right, I'll be needing some details here...'

'What's her name? Mary, Mary!' shouted one of the paramedics. 'What have you taken, love?'

'There are the bottles,' said Robbie, indicating the little white containers.

The paramedic picked one up. 'Oh dear, this is strong stuff. If she took both of these, we're in trouble, I'm afraid.' He crouched down next to Mary again. 'Mary! Wake up! Stay with us. We have to get her in as soon as possible.'

Mary groaned and her eyelids flickered.

'Mum, Mum,' cried Heather desperately. 'Mum, wake up.'

Mary's eyes opened and she looked groggily about her. 'Heather? Is that you? What's happening?'

'Mum? Oh, thank God, you're awake. How many pills did you take, Mum? We need to know.'

'Pills?'

'Your sleeping pills – how many did you take?'

'I ... I took two pills, as usual. I needed to sleep...'

The paramedics looked at each other and then at Mary. 'You've not taken an overdose, darlin'?'

'No ... no ... just two pills. What's going on?' She looked confused and shaken.

'But the bottles are empty, Mum,' Heather said, picking one up and showing it to her. 'Two empty bottles! If you didn't take them, who did?'

There was a silence as Heather and Robbie stared at each other, realisation dawning in their eyes.

'Oh my God,' Heather said. 'Dad.'

Chapter Fifty

'Robbie! Robbie, are you there?'

Robbie clambered up from below onto the deck of the *Bella Maria*. Heather was standing on the dock, one arm shading her eyes from the summer sun. It was a beautiful day in Kinloch-vegn, with the bluest of skies, a fresh breeze and delicious warm sunshine. Heather wore a white summer dress that showed her bare brown shoulders.

'Here I am,' he said with a smile. 'What's up?'

'I've had a call from the police.'

'Oh yes?' Robbie felt apprehensive. Despite the fact that Callum's death had been accepted as accidental, with himself and Heather as witnesses, the police investigation into what had gone on in the McBain family's past was long and complex and he felt sure that he would be involved again at some point.

'Come with me, and I'll tell you all about it,' she said.

He climbed onto the jetty. She came up to him, smiling, her blue eyes warm, her hair ruffled by the breeze. He wrapped his arms round her and dropped a kiss onto one bare shoulder. The feeling of her body against his set him tingling with the unquenchable desire he'd had for her since their first night together.

They held hands and began to walk along the jetty.

'It seems they've made a discovery,' Heather said, leaning her head against him as they walked. 'Police divers went to the spot where Hamish said he thought Dad's trawler must have made a drop. They've found a sea container with twenty bodies inside it – illegal Chinese immigrants, just as Hamish said.'

Robbie whistled. 'Oh my God. So it was true. They were involved in people trafficking.'

'The police seem to think this operation had only just begun. Their source on the inside broke it all open before they got going properly – they think that Callum must have been left in the lurch with the consignment of immigrants, panicked and decided the best thing to do was get rid of them. He always did live in a fantasy world.'

'But to be able to kill twenty people...'

Heather nodded. 'It's unimaginable, isn't it? Well, Callum was off his head. He was unstable to start with, but his drug use made him virtually psychotic. And I expect Dad only went along with the drugs because Callum wanted to.'

'Yes. You're probably right. But we won't ever know now. He's taken that secret with him.'

McBain had been slipping into unconsciousness when the ambulance crew went to him that night six months ago, and by the time they reached the hospital he had slid into a coma. He lay for a week in intensive care until the doctors confirmed that the condition was irreversible, that he was brain-dead. Mary sat by his bed every day and, when she and Heather had agreed that the life support should be turned off, she held her husband's hand as he slid away from her for ever.

Now the police investigation into the McBains' activities was going to be still more time-consuming and difficult, even with Greg McDonald and Tom Brodie in custody. While that was happening, the businesses and all their assets were frozen. To Mary and Heather's astonishment, they'd discovered that the house was in Mary's name, perhaps as a tax dodge. She had sold it immediately and bought a cottage a little way out of the village, where she had just settled in.

'I think we should go and tell Mum,' Heather said. 'She ought to know.'

They walked together along the main street of the village, heading out towards Mary's little house. The summer weather had brought out the tourists and the walkers. It was half-term, so there were children everywhere. Occasionally one would say, 'Hi there, miss!' to Heather as she walked past.

'They seem to like you,' Robbie said, smiling at her.

'Yes – they're a good bunch. I like it there. The headmistress said I should think seriously about retraining. There aren't many avenues for expansion as a classroom assistant, but if I were a qualified teacher...'

'Does that mean leaving here?' Robbie asked, panicked.

'No, no. I could do a course part-time, some of it over the Internet – you know the kind of thing.'

'Oh good.' He squeezed her softly to him. 'I can't be doing with you going away anywhere.'

Every day he woke up, breathed in the fresh air and couldn't believe he had spent so many miserable years in London. Why would anyone do that, when there was this? The gorgeous scenery and the magical sea that held him spellbound. And there was Heather.

He sometimes tried to pinpoint exactly when he had fallen in love with her. It could have been when he opened the door of Lachlan Cottage for her that first day and she sashayed past him to light the fire. Or perhaps it was when he saw her walk into the warehouse and realised that Callum had a gun pointed at her head. Or when she sat up with him late at night when it was all over, weeping for all the terrible things that had happened, the mistakes and misunderstandings that had led to years of misery. He had held her tight while she cried, mourning her father and the wasted years they could never get back, and the future that was now lost to them.

Or was it the night when she'd taken him Scottish dancing and he'd made her laugh as he managed to get himself twisted up in knots trying to follow everyone else and work out what the hell was going on? That was the night he had finally kissed her, a dizzy and delicious experience that had lit a passion for her that he couldn't imagine ever fading away. They'd wanted to go home together but Heather had said, 'We can't go back to my place – my mother is there. And your father is at your place! We're like a couple of teenagers with nowhere to be alone.'

So they'd had to wait, going on long walks so they could lie down in the heather and kiss for long hours, slowly and carefully exploring each other but holding back until they could have the night they'd planned.

When they finally spent the night together, on a weekend away in a tiny hotel up the coast, Robbie realised that, at last, he knew what it meant to feel alive.

'I think I'm in love with you,' he said wonderingly as they lay in bed.

'Are you now, Robbie Fraser?' She grinned happily at him.

'Do you think you might ... you know...'

'Might what?' She stroked the curve of his jaw with her forefinger.

'Might be able to – feel the same?'

'You know what? If you're very, very nice to me, I just might.'

Mary's cottage was painted a pale blue and she'd already made it look picture-book pretty, with hanging baskets of flowers trailing deep purple, pink and red blossoms. She was in the garden as they approached, weeding a flower bed. When she saw them coming, she stood up and waved.

'Hello! I was just about to stop and make some tea. Would you like some?'

In her sitting room, they drank tea from delicate china cups as Heather told her mother what the police had discovered. Mary was pale as she finished.

'That's too terrible, Heather, too terrible. Those poor, poor people – each one with a family, with a life he'd left behind, no doubt hoping that he'd get a job here and send money back to whoever was waiting for him at home. I always knew Callum was capable of cruelty but this... I'm glad he died before we knew about this, before I had to face how to be his mother after that.'

'There was always something wrong with him, Mum, wasn't there?'

'Always. He was never able to empathise with anyone else. He never understood that other people felt pain just like he did. And I sometimes think his emotions were stunted so that he just didn't feel things like love and fear and wonderment. He was my son and I loved him – but I always knew something wasn't right.' Mary got up and walked over to the window. 'I feel I failed him.'

'Mum.' Heather went to her, hugging her. 'There was nothing you could have done – there really wasn't.'

After a moment's silence, Mary turned back. 'Well. I just wish this ghastly investigation could be over so we can get on with our lives. Robbie, what are your plans now? Are you going back to London?'

'Never!' he said so emphatically that the two women laughed. He smiled back. 'I've got everything I want right here. I'm going back next month but only to oversee the sale of my mother's place and sort out a few things. I've got mountains of stuff to get rid of. Some of it I'll bring up here but the rest I'll just sell or give away. I feel like I've carried too much with me all my life, now I want to travel light for a while. Live the way my dad lives – very simply with nothing he doesn't need to weigh him down. He's going to show me how to fish. I've got some money to invest. We might go into business together.'

Over the last few months he and Hamish had been living together in Lachlan Cottage, fishing together in the daytimes and spending evenings, when they weren't at Mary's cottage, talking over their pasts, Robbie telling endless stories of his childhood, and Hamish asking for them over and over again, as if to make up for the fact that he hadn't been there to see for himself.

'I wanted you back so badly,' Hamish had said. 'But your mother would only communicate with me through her lawyers and sent all my letters back unopened.'

'Did you never think of challenging her through the courts? So you could see me?'

Hamish had blinked. 'I never did. I was unfaithful, you see. She was right about that. I never thought they'd be on my side. Losing you was my punishment.'

That was the difference between them, Robbie thought. There was the older generation, thinking they should suffer for their mistakes and denying themselves what was there for the taking – Mary and Hamish, staying apart even though they loved each other, because they'd made promises to other people and couldn't break them. While Robbie and Heather seized every moment of happiness, even now, Mary and Hamish were gentle and old-fashioned. Robbie could see that his father was wooing the woman he had loved from boyhood, slowly and simply. He called on her every day, did jobs for her in the house and garden, brought her pretty bunches of flowers or the best of his day's catch. They went to church together and on walks and, gradually, they were forming a new relationship that acknowledged the past and all that had gone between them, but that looked forward to the future as well.

'So,' Mary said now, 'will you carry on living at Lachlan Cottage?'

'That depends,' Robbie said.

'On what?'

'On you.'

A faint blush crept along Mary's face. 'I... Well, I...'

'Don't listen to him, Mum,' Heather said, batting Robbie's knee lightly. 'He's teasing you. Where is Hamish?'

'In the garden. I called him in for tea – ah, here he comes now.'

Hamish bent his head to come through the low doorway, then looked up at them all and smiled. 'Hello there. Have I missed the tea?'

'No, no, I'll pour you some,' said Heather, while Mary fussed about getting him a cushion and making sure he was comfortable.

Robbie grinned over at him. It was hard to believe that this was the father he had dreamed about for all those years, sitting in front of him now, with soil under his fingernails from digging the garden, his white hair ruffled up by the wind. Even now, six months on, he had to pinch himself. There was so much they still had to catch up on. Thank God they'd been given the time to do it.

'Do you think your dad and my mum will get married?' Heather asked as they walked back into the village after tea.

'I don't know. It would be nice though, wouldn't it? After all this time. It feels like it was meant to be.'

'I hope they do,' declared Heather. 'She deserves some happiness in her life.'

'And what about us?' Robbie said.

Heather widened her eyes. 'Was that a proposal, Mr Fraser?'

'Oh – well, no...'

She laughed. 'Don't worry, I don't know if I'm

the marrying type. But I like being happy and you make me happy, Robbie, did you know that? Very, very happy.'

'I like being happy too.' They stopped together on the path and looked out across the magnificent blue-green sea, the misty sky and the great coast curving away on either side of them. Robbie put his arm round her shoulders and she slid hers round his waist. He kissed the top of her head. 'So I think I'll stay and be happy here with you.'

'And with your dad,' Heather reminded him.

'Yes. And with him. That's why it wouldn't be right to go, even if you wanted to come with me. I feel like my past and my future are here.'

The reunion with Hamish had been strangely quiet. He had been by his father's hospital bed, arriving unannounced while the old man was asleep. They had said he would make a full recovery, though he needed rest and convalescence for a while. The experience of being abandoned without food or water in the foundations of Callum McBain's house had weakened his system, and the prolonged exposure to sub-zero temperatures had caused total collapse.

'I'll stay as long as I'm needed,' Robbie said. 'I'll look after him.'

It was amazing just to sit by his bedside and look at him, this father whom he had thought he would never see, who he thought had betrayed him and his mother. Sometimes the wretched waste of years made him twist up inside. At other times, he was simply grateful for what he had.

When Hamish opened his eyes, the first thing he saw was Robbie sitting by the bed. He had stared for a long time and then a sigh escaped him. 'You're Robbie, aren't you? My boy.'

'Yes, Dad. It's me.'

He'd shut his eyes and said, 'You look like Louise.'

'Heather found me,' Robbie half-whispered. 'She sent for me. She brought me here. She saved your life.'

'Heather. She's a good girl.' Hamish opened his eyes and looked at him again. 'My boy. At last, you've come home.'

Robbie grasped his hand. 'Yes, Dad. I've come home.'

The publishers hope that this book has given you enjoyable reading. Large Print Books are especially designed to be as easy to see and hold as possible. If you wish a complete list of our books please ask at your local library or write directly to:

Magna Large Print Books
Magna House, Long Preston,
Skipton, North Yorkshire.
BD23 4ND

This Large Print Book for the partially sighted, who cannot read normal print, is published under the auspices of

THE ULVERSCROFT FOUNDATION